CLIVIL!US
JOURNALS

Jenny Triffett (4338.209.1 - 4338.216.2)
© 2025 Nathan Cowdrey. All rights reserved.
First Edition, 15 January 2025
ISBN 978-1-326-70591-6
Imprint: Lulu.com

Step into Clivilius, where creation meets infinity, and the essence of reality is yours to redefine. Here, existence weaves into a narrative where every decision has consequences, every action has an impact, and every moment counts. In this realm, inhabitants are not mere spectators but pivotal characters in an evolving drama where the lines between worlds blur.

Guardians traverse the realms of Clivilius and Earth, their journeys igniting events that challenge the balance between these interconnected universes. The quest for resources and the enigma of unexplained disappearances on Earth mirror the deeper conflicts and intricacies that define Clivilius—a world where reality responds to the collective will and individual choices of its Clivilians, revealing a complex interplay of creation, control, and consequence.

In the grand tapestry of Clivilius, the struggle for harmony and the dance of dichotomies play out across a cosmic stage. Here, every soul's journey contributes to the narrative, where the lines between utopia and dystopia, creator and observer, become increasingly fluid. Clivilius is not just a realm to be explored but a reality to be shaped.

Open your eyes. Expand your mind. Experience your new reality. Welcome to Clivilius, where the journey of discovery is not just about seeing a new world but about seeing your world anew.

Also in the Clivilius Series:

Karl Jenkins (4338.209.1 - 4338.214.1)

Plunged into Tasmania's most chilling cases, Senior Detective Karl Jenkins confronts a string of disappearances that entangle with his clandestine affair with Detective Sarah Lahey. As a dangerous obsession emerges, every step toward the truth draws Karl perilously close to a precipice threatening their lives and careers. "Karl Jenkins" is a riveting tale of suspense, where past haunts bear a perilous future.

Sarah Lahey (4338.209.1 - 4338.214.2)

In the grip of Tasmania's eerie disappearances, Detective Sarah Lahey's quest for answers becomes a personal crucible. As her investigation draws her deeper into the shadows, her tangled relationship with fellow detective Karl Jenkins blurs the lines between ally and liability. Together, they face a darkening path that tests their bond and the very heart of their resolve. "Sarah Lahey" weaves a tale of relentless pursuit and suspense, where the quest for truth risks more than just a partnership—it tempts a treacherous fate.

Luke Smith (4338.204.1 - 4338.209.2)

Luke Smith's world transforms with the discovery of a cryptic device, thrusting him into the guardianship of destiny itself. His charismatic charm and unpredictable decisions now carry weight beyond imagination, balancing on the razor's edge between salvation and destruction. Embracing his role as a Guardian, Luke faces the paradox of power: the very force that defends also threatens to annihilate. As shadows gather and the fabric of reality strains, Luke must navigate the consequences of his actions, unaware that a looming challenge will test the very core of his resolve.

Paul Smith (4338.204.1 - 4338.209.3)

In a harsh, new world, Paul Smith grapples with the remnants of a hostile marriage and the future of his two young children. Cast into the heart of an arid wasteland, his survival pushes him to the brink, challenging his every belief. Amidst the desolation, Paul faces a pivotal choice that will dictate where his true allegiance lies. In this tale of resilience and resolve, Paul's journey is a harrowing exploration of loyalty, family, and the boundless optimism required to forge hope in the bleakest of landscapes.

Gladys Cramer (4338.204.1 - 4338.214.3)

In a world frayed by tragedies, Gladys Cramer seeks solace in wine, her steadfast refuge amid life's turmoil. Tethered to a man ensnared by duty and love, she stands at a pivotal crossroads, her choices poised to weave the threads of her fate. Each glass of wine deepens her reflection on the decisions looming ahead and the silent vows brimming with untold consequences. Amidst tragedy and secrets, with wine as her guiding light yet potential harbinger of misstep, Gladys's journey veers onto a path set for an inevitable collision.

4338.209.1 - 4338.216.2

JENNY TRIFFETT

CLIVIL!US
JOURNALS

"Sometimes the fight isn't about winning. Sometimes it's just about keeping the pieces together long enough to see the next sunrise."

- Jenny Triffett

4338.209

(28 July 2018)

A WHISPER IN THE MIST

4338.209.1

The Tasmanian winter had wrapped its icy fingers around Hobart, seeping through the cracks of our weatherboard home with an insidious persistence that seemed to mirror the growing unease in my mind. Outside, a heavy mist clung to the slopes of Mount Wellington, its looming presence a constant reminder of nature's dominance over our lives. I stood at the kitchen window, my breath fogging the glass as I gazed out at the grey morning, the chill seeping into my bones despite the warmth of our home.

The date on the calendar caught my eye: 28th July, 2018. Another day, another chance for the universe to test my resolve. At thirty-two years old, I had a life that looked perfect on paper but felt increasingly like a beautifully crafted illusion, a house of cards waiting for the slightest breeze to topple it all.

My reflection stared back at me from the window – honey-blonde hair framing a face that still turned heads, blue eyes that sparkled with intelligence and a hint of mischief. I'd always known I was attractive, not out of vanity, but as a simple fact of life. It was a tool, a weapon, and sometimes, a curse. In the ghostly reflection, I could see the slight furrow between my brows, a tiny betrayal of the thoughts that had been gnawing at me lately.

The aroma of freshly brewed coffee filled the kitchen, a small comfort against the chill that seemed to permeate everything these days. I wrapped my hands around the steaming mug, savouring its warmth as I contemplated the day ahead. The rich, bitter scent wafted up, momentarily drowning out the musty smell of old wood and the faint trace of last night's dinner that still lingered in the air.

Sammy would be up soon, his innocent chatter a welcome distraction from the thoughts that had been plaguing me. I could already imagine his excited footsteps pattering down the hallway, his high-pitched voice calling out, "Mummy, Mummy!" The thought brought a genuine smile to my face, a warmth that spread through my chest, momentarily chasing away the chill of uncertainty.

My mind drifted back to the previous night, to the hushed phone call that had pulled Nial from our bed at an ungodly hour. His whispered words, too low for me to make out, had sent a shiver down my spine that had nothing to do with the cold. It wasn't the first such call, and I knew with a sinking certainty that it wouldn't be the last.

I closed my eyes, trying to recall every detail. The sudden vibration of Nial's phone on the bedside table, the blue glow illuminating his face as he squinted at the screen. The way he had slipped out of bed, his movements careful and measured, as if trying not to disturb a sleeping predator. I had feigned sleep, my heart racing as I strained to catch even a fragment of his conversation.

"Yes, I understand," he had murmured, his voice barely above a whisper. "No, that won't be necessary. I'll handle it personally."

Handle what? The question echoed in my mind, a persistent itch I couldn't scratch. Nial's fencing business, *Triffett Fencing Solutions*, had always been demanding, but recently, it seemed to dominate his every waking moment. Late-night calls with disgruntled contractors, last-minute adjustments to complex client agreements, and a troubling fixation on securing high-stakes commercial projects had become the norm. Yet there was something different now—

something darker. His carefully chosen words and guarded demeanour felt less like the stresses of running a small business and more like the weight of secrets threatening to spill into our lives.

The sound of running water from the ensuite upstairs pulled me from my reverie. Nial was up, going through his morning routine as if nothing was amiss. I took a deep breath, inhaling the comforting scent of coffee, steeling myself for the performance that had become our daily life. With practiced ease, I slipped into the role of the loving, supportive wife – a part I had played for so long that sometimes I forgot where the act ended and the real Jenny began.

Setting the cup down on the counter, I glanced at the clock. Time was moving faster than I realised. Barefoot, I made my way up the stairs, each step creaking softly beneath me. The cold of the wooden floorboards sent a faint shiver up my legs, the chill seeping into my skin like a reminder of the world beyond our fragile façade.

As I reached the bedroom, the sound of Nial humming reached my ears—an old tune we used to dance to during our university days. I hesitated just outside the door, the familiar melody tugging at my heart. It was a bittersweet echo of simpler times, moments untouched by the tensions that now defined our lives. Pushing the door open slightly, I peered in, catching a glimpse of Nial through the crack in the ensuite door, his reflection blurred by steam on the mirror. For a fleeting moment, I allowed myself to linger, torn between the love I still felt for him and the growing suspicion that had started to consume me.

Steam billowed out as I pushed the door open, enveloping me in a warm, moist embrace. Through the fog, I could make out Nial's silhouette, broad-shouldered and solid—a stark contrast to the uncertainty that seemed to hang in the air between us. He stood there, staring at his reflection in the foggy mirror, lost in thought. My mind flickered back to that phone call, the whispered words that had felt like cracks forming in the foundation of our life. The anxious tingle it left in my body was still there, an ever-present whisper of unease that refused to let go.

"Everything okay, honey?" I asked, my voice soft, carrying a concern that was only partly feigned. I stepped closer, the floor tiles cool beneath my feet, and reached out, my fingers finding his bare shoulder. The familiar contours of his muscles beneath my touch were grounding, a fleeting reminder of the man I thought I knew. His skin was warm and slightly damp from the shower, a stark contrast to the chill that seemed to linger in my chest.

Trying to dispel the tension, I pressed a little harder on his shoulder, a silent offer of support. It was a dance we'd perfected over the years—the gentle probe for information paired with the unspoken reassurance that said, "I'm here," without demanding answers I knew he wouldn't give. Yet, as I studied his reflection in the mirror, searching for any flicker of vulnerability, I couldn't ignore the widening chasm between us.

Was he keeping something from me? And if he was, was it to protect me—or himself? The questions churned in my mind, creating a hollow ache that settled in my gut.

"I think so, Jen," Nial replied after a moment, his voice steady but carrying an undertone of hesitation that only deepened my unease. He turned to face me, his eyes meeting mine. For a brief moment, I saw something in his expression —a shadow of guilt, or perhaps fear—but it vanished too quickly for me to grasp. Instead, he smiled, warm but distant, the kind of smile you give to reassure someone without letting them see the cracks beneath.

I forced a small, reassuring smile of my own, a mask I'd worn so often it felt like a second skin. "Well, okay then," I said, my voice a careful balance of affection and concern. But even as the words left my mouth, I couldn't shake the feeling that everything wasn't okay, that something was quietly unravelling beneath the surface.

I gave his shoulder one more squeeze, a gesture that was as much for me as it was for him, before gracefully sliding out of my bathrobe. As I stepped into the shower, the water cascading over me, I tried to focus on the here and now. Yet the questions lingered, insidious and persistent, each one a thread pulling at the edges of my composure.

The steam might have blurred the mirror, but it couldn't hide the truth: whatever was going on with Nial, it was only a matter of time before the cracks in our façade could no longer be ignored.

The warm water cascaded over me, its soothing touch encouraging a fragile sense of relaxation. My silky blonde hair became drenched, heavy with water, as my fingers combed through the strands. The slight anxiety that Nial's guarded demeanour had sparked began to dissolve, carried away in the steam and warmth enveloping me. I closed my eyes, tilting my face up to the spray, letting it wash over me, as if it could cleanse the tension that had woven itself into the fabric of my thoughts.

Yet even as the water worked its magic on my body, my mind refused to quiet. Memories surfaced unbidden, vivid and bittersweet. I found myself transported to the day Nial first kissed me, a smile tugging at my lips despite the ache in my chest. It had been our final year of college, a time when the world felt limitless, and every moment was laced with possibility. True to dramatic form, I had fallen ill the day before the opening night of our college play—a moment I'd waited for all year.

I could still feel the ache in my throat, the way my voice faltered during rehearsals. After a particularly exhausting dance routine, I had crumpled onto the stage, overwhelmed and defeated, tears streaming down my face under the unforgiving spotlight. Nial had been there, his applause the loudest in the empty theatre, his grin unwavering. I remembered him rushing to my side, his presence a beacon of reassurance.

And then, that kiss. It had been everything a first kiss ought to be—unexpected, tender, transformative. I had kissed boys before, but Nial's kiss had made the world fall away: the dazzling stage lights, the sequins of my costume, the distant hum of the theatre. All of it vanished in the warmth of his lips, the gentle pressure of his hand against my cheek, and the rapid thrum of my heart that seemed to sync with his.

The memory lingered for a moment before fading, leaving behind a hollow ache. Where had that Nial gone? The one who would rush to my side, who would sweep me off my feet with gestures that felt grand yet sincere? Now, it felt like we were actors reciting lines from a script that had long lost its meaning, going through the motions of a life we once dreamed of but had somehow drifted away from.

I reached for the shampoo, its lavender scent filling the steamy air as I lathered it into my hair. The familiar aroma helped ground me, anchoring me in the present and pulling me back from the edge of melancholy. I reminded myself of the good—the beautiful home we shared, our precious Sammy, the life we had built together. Surely, these were worth more than the vague suspicions and unanswered questions gnawing at me?

Just as I began to rinse the suds away, Nial's voice broke through the stillness. "I'm just heading out to get the details on a new potential job. Shouldn't be more than a few hours," he called out from the doorway, his tone carrying a mix of excitement and something else—an edge of urgency I couldn't quite place.

I jumped slightly at the intrusion, opening one eye as the water streamed down my face. "Okay, hun," I replied, my voice steady but tinged with a cautious undertone. I tried to catch a glimpse of him through the fogged glass, the familiar silhouette that I told myself I could still trust. Despite ten years of marriage, there was a part of me that clung to the belief that we were still the couple from that stage, the love story worth fighting for. Or maybe I just wanted to believe it, forcing the doubts back into the shadows where they wouldn't take root.

The door clicked shut, and the bathroom fell silent. I let out a breath I hadn't realised I was holding, the steam now feeling oppressive rather than comforting. As I turned my face back to the shower spray, the water drummed against my skin in rhythmic percussion, echoing the unease simmering beneath the surface. I tried to let the water wash away the conflicting emotions swirling inside me, but they clung stubbornly, refusing to be swept away. The questions I had been trying to bury rose again, persistent and unrelenting, as the shower's warmth did little to ease the growing chill within me.

Unexpectedly, a shiver of excitement ran through me, my left nipple hardening in response. I couldn't hold back a soft giggle at the playful thoughts that danced their way across the stage of my creative mind. Tonight, I thought to myself, Nial would play the role of the frog-prince. The way he would squat on the floor, his long, flaccid endowment dangling freely between his legs, and leap onto the bed where I would be waiting to give him the transformational kiss, was my favourite bedroom scene.

As the warm water cascaded over my head, I let out a soft, pleasurable moan, relishing the sensation of the steamy shower enveloping me. It was one of those small moments of bliss, a brief escape from the world outside. But this tiny slice of paradise was quickly interrupted by the unpleasant, soapy taste of shampoo that had inadvertently dribbled its way inside my mouth.

The sharp, chemical flavour instantly jolted me from my reverie. Spluttering in surprise, I hastily spat out a glob of the sudsy shampoo. My eyes narrowed in concentration, hoping against hope that it would follow the path of least resistance and find its way to the drain. I watched the foamy substance as it swirled briefly on the shower floor before being swept away by the stream of water, a miniature whirlpool of bubbles and regret.

"That's enough distraction for one shower," I murmured to myself, a hint of amusement in my tone despite the situation. With another quick spit, I ejected another mouthful of shampoo, watching it smear against the clear shower glass, distorting the view of my bathroom. The action was oddly satisfying, a physical manifestation of expelling the morning's minor nuisances.

Shaking my head slightly, I refocused on the task at hand. It was time to get myself ready, to shift gears from the fleeting calm of my morning shower to the day's plans. There was an important appointment ahead, one I hoped might bring some clarity to the questions that had been gnawing at me. The thought of it sent a ripple of unease through me, but I pushed it aside, forcing a smile. For Sammy's sake, I had to keep the day feeling ordinary, even as the undercurrent of uncertainty swirled just beneath the surface.

As I stepped out of the shower, wrapping a fluffy towel tightly around my body, I caught sight of myself in the fogged mirror. The steam had begun to clear, revealing a face I barely recognised. The carefree college girl who had once fallen in love with Nial seemed like a distant memory, replaced by a woman with eyes that held a hardness born of unanswered questions and growing suspicion.

I traced the line of my collarbone, pausing on the small, heart-shaped birthmark just below it—a feature Nial used to say was proof I was made for love. The memory of his words, once a source of joy, now felt almost mocking. Promises whispered in the glow of intimacy, promises of forever and unshakable devotion, felt as insubstantial as the last wisps of steam clinging to the edges of the mirror. My lips curved into a sad smile, though it was quickly chased away by a sigh that felt too heavy for the moment.

I began to dry myself off, the motions automatic, my thoughts already racing ahead to the day's plans. Sammy would need some extra encouragement this morning, his recent struggles casting a shadow over all of us. Thoughts of his wide, innocent eyes, now edged with exhaustion and confusion, haunted me as I dressed. I chose a pair of comfortable jeans and a soft, blue sweater, its familiar warmth and colour offering a shred of comfort in the face of so much uncertainty.

We had a good life, didn't we? A beautiful home, a sweet and curious child, and a business that, for all its challenges, kept us stable. So what if Nial's fencing contracts had grown more demanding, his clients more insistent? So what if the late-night phone calls and his frequent absences were fraying the edges of my patience? I was Jenny Triffett, and I could hold it all together. I smoothed the sweater over my stomach, as though its soft fabric could somehow hold the growing tension inside me at bay.

But as I applied my makeup, the familiar routine of foundation, blush, and mascara, the unease gnawing at my chest refused to be ignored. It wasn't just Nial's evasiveness that loomed large in my thoughts, though that was undeniable. It was Sammy—his pale face in the mornings, his nights filled with terrors he couldn't explain. It was the bruises that appeared without cause, the dark shadows under his eyes that spoke of restless nights and something more insidious.

And then there was the other tension, the stories on the news, the murmurs that seemed to ripple through Hobart like an undercurrent. Disappearances, inexplicable accidents, whispers of corruption woven into the very fabric of the city. I couldn't shake the image of the local businessman found dead in his car last week. The official report had labelled it a heart attack, but the rumours were harder to dismiss. Conversations overheard at school and the murmurs in supermarket queues hinted at something darker—debts unpaid, deals gone awry, and consequences that extended far beyond the financial.

As I set down the mascara, I stared harder at the woman in the mirror. My reflection held my gaze, the slight widening of my eyes a desperate search for strength, for answers, for any sign that I could hold onto the fragments of my crumbling reality.

Something was off. Not just with Nial, but with everything around us. The weight of it all pressed down on me, an oppressive force that threatened to crush the resolve I fought so hard to maintain. But I wouldn't let it. I couldn't. If Nial was tangled in something dangerous, if these shadows creeping closer to our family were real, then I would uncover the truth.

For Sammy. For us. Whatever storm was coming, I would face it head-on. Because the thought of losing what little we had left was far more terrifying than the fight I knew was ahead.

SAMMY

4338.209.2

The persistent Tasmanian drizzle tapped against the windows, a rhythmic backdrop to the quiet tension simmering within our weatherboard home. I stood in the hallway, my back pressed against the cool plaster, feeling the chill of the morning seep through my cashmere sweater. The house was alive with sound: the soft patter of rain, the hurried thud of small feet on polished floorboards, and Buffy's distant bark from the garden. It was a comforting symphony of domesticity, but today, it felt like a fragile mask, barely concealing the undercurrent of dread that lingered beneath.

"Come on, Sammy, get a wriggle on, mate," I called out, forcing my voice into a playful lilt. The cadence was second nature by now, a relic of my days on the stage at the Theatre Royal. It was the sort of tone that invited trust, that hinted at ease. But it was a performance, no less scripted than the roles I'd once inhabited. My eyes flicked to the digital clock on the oven, its green numbers cutting sharply through the dim kitchen light. *9:42 AM.* Each illuminated digit seemed to pulse with urgency, a reminder of how little time we had before we needed to leave.

I inhaled deeply, catching the faint scent of last night's pasta mingling with the fresh, earthy aroma of rain drifting through the slightly open kitchen window. It was a comforting combination, a sensory nod to family dinners and quiet nights that now felt like distant memories. Today, the same smells felt bittersweet, tainted by the creeping tension that had become an uninvited guest in our home.

"Go and find your shoes," I added, my voice warm but firm, "and then you can give Buffy a treat before we leave." I imagined Sammy scrambling to comply, his usual cheerful determination lighting up his little face. My mind briefly flickered to Dr. Carmichael, the disapproving tilt of his wire-rimmed glasses, the subtle tightening of his jaw when we arrived late. A shiver ran through me, unrelated to the morning's chill. His sterile office, with its incongruously cheerful animal posters and faint antiseptic smell, was a place I both dreaded and needed. It represented the thin line between hope and fear that I walked daily.

"Okay, Mummy!" Sammy's voice carried back to me, bright and buoyant, filling the house with a fleeting warmth. I watched as he disappeared into his bedroom, his dinosaur pyjama bottoms dragging slightly on the floorboards as his little legs worked furiously. A wistful sigh escaped my lips as I leaned against the wall, allowing myself a rare moment to simply feel the ache of time slipping away. Where had the years gone? In a matter of weeks, my baby boy would turn four. His freckled nose, the dimple on his cheek when he smiled, even the light in his eyes—they were all reflections of Nial, echoes of the man I had fallen in love with.

The man I thought I knew.

The thought stung, sharp and unwelcome. I shook my head, pushing it aside. This wasn't the time for musings that threatened to unsteady me. There was an appointment to keep, a son to wrangle, and the mask of normality to hold firmly in place.

I glanced at the hallway mirror, catching my reflection. The woman staring back was no longer the carefree actress who once graced the local stage. Dark circles framed her eyes, though the concealer expertly applied from years of practice masked them well. I straightened my sweater, smoothing the soft fibres as though they could lend me some strength, and pasted on a smile that didn't quite reach my eyes. It was a performance, but one I had become adept at delivering. After all, there was no audience more important than the little boy who depended on me to make the world feel safe, even as it threatened to crumble around us.

Entering Sammy's room, I felt the familiar tug at my heart, a bittersweet mix of love and longing. He was perched on the edge of his racing car bed, utterly absorbed in the task at hand. In one small hand, he gripped a brown sandal, while the other dangled precariously from his right foot, held on by just three tiny toes. It was such an endearing slice of toddler life, a moment so pure and uncomplicated that it almost made me forget the swirling chaos outside these walls.

His room was a sanctuary of childhood wonder, its walls painted with drifting clouds against a bright sky-blue backdrop. Along the skirting board, a cheerful parade of dinosaurs marched in their eternal formation. It was a world untouched by adult worries, a place where Sammy could be safe, and for a fleeting moment, so could I.

"Good effort," I praised, kneeling in front of him. The carpet felt soft under my knees, still marked with the indents of toy cars and tiny feet from the night before. Gently, I lifted his leg, adjusting the sandal so his foot slid in snugly. My fingers lingered for a moment on his warm ankle, feeling the steady pulse of life beneath his skin. It was such a small thing, yet it filled my chest with a fierce, protective love—and a creeping sadness. These little moments felt increasingly rare, slipping away faster than I could hold onto them.

Sammy beamed at me, his grin wide and uninhibited, revealing teeth conspicuously smeared with black. I paused, leaning in closer as my brow furrowed. "Did Daddy give you liquorice again?" I asked, my voice playfully stern, though my mind raced ahead. Nial knew about this appointment. He knew how important it was to keep Sammy's sugar intake under control. What once might have been a shared moment of amusement—the two of them sneaking treats—now felt like another small fracture in the trust between us.

Sammy's smile vanished instantly, replaced by a hasty shake of his head. It was the same innocent denial he'd practised before, the kind of fib that came with childhood. But today, it felt different. Heavier. As if even Sammy could sense the tension that had seeped into our home, the secrets that hung in the air like the persistent Tasmanian mist. His eyes, so like Nial's, darted away from mine, settling on a spot just beyond my shoulder.

"I think he did," I murmured softly, brushing my fingers through Sammy's curls. They were growing darker, taking on more of Nial's colouring with each passing day. The silky strands slipped through my fingers, a tactile reminder of how fast time was moving, how quickly he was growing. "We'd better brush those teeth before we leave."

With his characteristic energy, Sammy slid off the bed, his bare feet thudding softly on the floor. He was a whirlwind of motion, always one step ahead of me. I reached out instinctively to steady him, but he stumbled and caught himself, giggling at his near-fall. My heart jumped into my throat, but his laughter soothed me almost immediately.

"Sammy!" I called after him, my voice equal parts exasperation and affection. "Come and do your other sandal first."

"Not yet, Mummy!" he shouted back, his voice carrying from the hallway with a mix of defiance and excitement. I smiled despite myself, shaking my head. That stubborn streak —so undeniably his father's—was both a joy and a worry. I had once admired Nial's determination, his ability to forge ahead no matter the obstacles. But now, I couldn't help but wonder what else Sammy might inherit. Would he one day share his father's penchant for secrecy? For late-night phone calls and unexplained absences?

I turned toward the open bedroom door, lost in thought, only to be startled by Buffy, our Dalmatian, bounding into the room. Her black-and-white coat was a blur of motion as her tail wagged with enough force to rattle the nearby toy chest. She lunged toward me with her tongue lolling out, aiming directly for my face. My reflexes kicked in, and I pushed her head aside just in time to save my carefully applied makeup from her enthusiastic licks.

"Buffy, no licking faces!" I scolded, though my voice held more affection than reprimand. She flopped down onto the carpet with a playful huff, her tail still thumping against the floor. As I watched her settle, I couldn't help but think how simple her world was—just love, loyalty, and the joy of being near us. It was a stark contrast to the complexity of the life I was trying so hard to hold together.

The sudden clatter of toothbrushes hitting the bathroom floor sent Buffy scampering away, her nails clicking against the floorboards in a frantic rhythm. I closed my eyes for a moment, counting to three as I drew in deep, steadying breaths. It was an old technique, one that had helped calm my nerves before every stage performance, now repurposed to navigate the beautiful chaos of raising a toddler. Each breath felt like a lifeline, tethering me to calm before the next act in the unpredictable play of motherhood.

But as I opened my eyes, the fragile calm dissolved, replaced by the heavy weight of reality crashing over me like a wave. The appointment with Dr. Carmichael wasn't just a routine visit. It was a chance—a desperate hope—to understand what was happening to my son. The nightmares, the unexplained bruises, the moments when Sammy seemed to slip into a world I couldn't reach—they had been growing more frequent, each one a small fracture threatening the foundation of our family life.

I moved toward the bathroom, my pace quickening as Sammy's giggle echoed down the hall. Normally, that sound was a balm to my soul, a reminder of the unfiltered joy of childhood. But today, it sent a chill rippling through me. It was too sharp, too high, almost manic in its intensity. Rounding the corner, I found him on his step stool, toothbrush in hand, smearing a thick layer of minty toothpaste across the mirror.

The air in the room felt damp and cool, the minty scent clinging to the lingering condensation from a cold night. The scene should have been a snapshot of childhood innocence, but instead, it felt disorienting, like a frame just slightly out of focus. The familiar had taken on an edge of the surreal, unsettling and strange.

"Oh, Sammy," I sighed, reaching for a washcloth. As I began to wipe the smeared paste from the mirror, I caught sight of our reflection. There he was—my beautiful boy, all tousled hair and a grin as mischievous as it was charming. And then there was me, dark circles lurking under my eyes, barely hidden by a thin layer of concealer. Together, we looked like a mismatched pair in some offbeat comedy, the kind that made you laugh but left a hollow ache behind.

Behind us, the edge of the bathtub peeked into view, its rim still stained with the colourful rings from last night's bubble bath. It was a scene of domestic simplicity, almost idyllic, but the constant gnaw of worry turned it into something bittersweet.

"Mummy," Sammy said suddenly, his voice dropping into a seriousness that was far too heavy for his age. "Is the doctor going to make the bad dreams go away?"

The question stopped me cold, the washcloth frozen mid-air. How could I explain to my three-year-old that not all monsters could be banished by nightlights or brave teddy bears? That sometimes, the scariest things weren't the ones hiding under the bed but the ones lurking in plain sight, impossible to define or defeat.

"We're going to try, sweetheart," I said, forcing a smile I didn't feel. The words tasted bitter, the uncertainty clinging to them like the mist that lingered over Mount Wellington outside our window. "That's why it's so important that we're not late. Now, let's get those teeth brushed, shall we?"

As I guided his little hand, helping him brush properly, my mind drifted to the night before. Nial had come home late again, his clothes carrying the faint but unmistakable smell of cigarette smoke and something else I couldn't quite place. When I'd asked about his day, he'd given me that smile. Once, it had made my heart skip a beat. Now, it filled me with dread.

"Just work stuff, Jen," he'd said, pressing a kiss to my cheek. His lips had been cold, leaving an involuntary shiver in their wake. "Nothing for you to worry about."

But I did worry. I worried about the hushed phone calls, the way he slipped out of bed in the middle of the night, the absences that had no clear explanation. I worried about the way he sometimes looked at Sammy—an expression caught between love and something darker. Was it guilt? Fear? Whatever it was, it gnawed at me, a splinter lodged deep in my mind, impossible to ignore.

"All done, Mummy!" Sammy's voice jolted me back to the present. He grinned up at me, his teeth sparkling clean, the earlier liquorice stains now a distant memory.

"Well done, my little man," I said, ruffling his hair. The silky strands slipped between my fingers, a comfort I clung to. "Now, let's get that other sandal on and we'll be ready to go."

As Sammy darted off, a whirlwind of energy and excitement, I lingered for a moment in the bathroom. The toothpaste was gone, but the reflection in the mirror lingered—me, holding it all together for Sammy's sake while the cracks in our world threatened to widen.

Making my way back to Sammy's room, my gaze caught on a framed photo hanging on the hallway wall. It was from our wedding day—a snapshot of a time when the world seemed wide open and full of promise. Nial and I were beaming at the camera, my head thrown back in laughter at something he'd whispered in my ear, his arms wrapped securely around my waist. The setting sun painted the sky in hues of gold and amber, our silhouettes merging into one, as if we were two halves of a single, unbreakable whole.

I remembered how invincible I'd felt that day, certain that our love could conquer anything. But now, a decade later, that certainty felt like a distant memory. The woman in the photo seemed almost like a stranger—naïve, trusting, blissfully unaware of the storms that lay ahead. My fingers brushed against the frame, the cool glass a stark reminder of the barrier between that moment and the present. A silent prayer formed on my lips, though I wasn't sure who I was praying to anymore. *Please, let this appointment bring us answers. Let us find our way back to that happiness.*

"Mummy, look!" Sammy's excited shout shattered the silence, pulling me back to the here and now. I turned to see him proudly displaying his work—his other sandal was on, though backwards and barely hanging onto his little foot. The sight was so endearing, so purely Sammy, that I felt my throat tighten, tears welling unexpectedly in my eyes. The intensity of the love I felt for him in that moment was overwhelming, a physical ache that seemed to radiate from my chest.

"Oh, darling," I laughed, dropping to my knees beside him. The sound startled me—it had been so long since I'd heard my own laughter, unforced and real. Sammy grinned at me, his eyes crinkling at the corners in a way that made him look even more like his father. "You're getting to be such a big boy."

My fingers moved quickly, securing the strap of his sandal with practised ease. Each movement felt like a vow—an unspoken promise to protect him, to shield him from the shadows that loomed over our little family. Whatever it took, I would keep him safe.

"There we go," I said, standing up and taking his hand in mine. His small fingers curled around mine, warm and full of trust. That tiny gesture was both comforting and heartbreaking, a reminder of how much he depended on me.

"Ready for our big adventure?" I asked, my voice light, as though we were heading somewhere exciting rather than to another appointment.

He nodded enthusiastically, his earlier worries about the doctor seemingly forgotten. His resilience amazed me—the way he could bounce back, finding joy in the smallest things. I envied that about him, even as I feared the day he might lose it. The world had already taken so much from us; I couldn't bear the thought of it taking his light too.

Making our way to the front door, I slung my handbag over my shoulder, pausing for one last check to make sure I had everything. Keys, purse, Sammy's favourite toy car for the waiting room, and tucked into the hidden pocket, the burner phone I'd bought last week. The small, cheap device felt heavier than its actual weight, a constant reminder of how much our lives had shifted. It was a symbol of the lengths I was willing to go to protect my family, and the quiet desperation I now carried with me every day.

Outside, the rain had softened to a fine mist, the kind that clung to the skin and settled in the air like a cool shroud. The sharp scent of wet earth mingled with the crisp, slightly damp tang of eucalyptus, a smell so quintessentially Tasmanian. The air carried the chill of late winter, the kind that seeped into your bones, hinting at the promise of spring but not quite delivering its warmth yet.

I locked the door behind us, the click of the lock breaking the morning silence with a sense of finality that made my chest tighten. Our front garden, usually a riot of colour by late spring, looked subdued under the grey sky. The once-bright foliage of the hardy winter plants glistened with rain, their leaves drooping under its weight. Even Sammy's vibrant pink daisies, brave outliers in the winter gloom, seemed dulled, their cheerful faces bowed and soaked, waiting for a warmer season to thrive again.

As I bent to buckle Sammy into his car seat, a prickling sensation crept over the back of my neck. The feeling was so sudden and visceral that I froze, my hands hovering over the seatbelt buckle. It was the kind of instinctual warning that didn't come from logic but from something deeper—primal, ancient. My pulse quickened as I scanned the street, trying to appear casual.

My gaze landed on an unfamiliar car parked across the road. It was the kind of vehicle designed to blend in— nondescript and unremarkable. But the darkly tinted windows made my stomach knot. For a second, I thought I saw movement inside, a fleeting shadow that disappeared as quickly as it came. I told myself it was nothing, but my mind refused to let it go. In a world that no longer felt safe, even the mundane seemed loaded with danger.

"Mummy?" Sammy's small voice broke through my spiralling thoughts. "Are you okay?"

I turned back to him, forcing a bright smile that felt paper-thin, as if it might crumble under the weight of his innocent question. "Of course, sweetheart," I said lightly, adjusting the strap on his sandal to buy myself another moment. "Just checking we haven't forgotten anything."

Sliding into the driver's seat, my hands trembled slightly as I started the car. The low rumble of the engine seemed too loud, too intrusive against the morning's stillness. As we pulled away from the curb, I cast one last glance at our house in the rearview mirror. The pale blue weatherboards, the native garden, the porch where Nial and I had spent countless summer evenings watching Sammy chase butterflies—it all looked so normal. Yet it felt like a lie, a facade hiding a darker reality I was only beginning to grasp.

I couldn't shake the sense of foreboding that clung to me like the mist. My eyes flicked to the strange car again. It hadn't moved, its windows still inscrutable, but the unease it inspired remained, settling in my gut like a stone. This wasn't paranoia. It was something more.

For the briefest moment, I considered turning back. It would be so easy to retreat, to pull Sammy out of the car, lock the door, and wrap us both in the illusion of safety within those familiar walls. But I couldn't. Not if I wanted answers. Not if I wanted to save us.

"Ready for our adventure, Sammy?" I asked, injecting as much steadiness into my voice as I could muster.

"Ready, Mummy!" he chirped, his excitement unclouded, his world still simple and bright.

I tightened my grip on the steering wheel, feeling its cool beneath my fingers. My eyes flicked to the rearview mirror again as we drove away, watching the car grow smaller in the distance. It didn't follow, but I couldn't shake the feeling that this wasn't the last I'd see of it.

THE ROOM WITH NO ANSWERS

4338.209.3

The waiting room of Dr. Carmichael's office was a masterclass in forced cheerfulness, the kind designed to pacify uneasy children and distracted parents. Bright cartoon animals frolicked across the walls, their painted grins fixed in a cheerfulness so exaggerated it bordered on unsettling. They stood in stark contrast to the atmosphere of quiet tension that filled the room, thick and suffocating like a winter fog.

I sat stiffly in a hard plastic chair, the edge digging uncomfortably into the backs of my thighs. My fingers gripped the strap of my handbag, nails biting into the soft leather as my eyes fixed on Sammy. He was absorbed in the battered wooden train set in the corner, his little hands moving the cars in an endless loop around the warped tracks. The sight brought a fleeting sense of calm, though it was fragile at best.

The drive here had been uneventful, much to my relief. The strange car parked near our house hadn't followed us— or, at least, I hadn't seen it. Yet the memory of it lingered, a spectre at the edges of my thoughts. Now, as I sat in the waiting room, I found myself scanning every face, scrutinising every movement. Each time the door opened, my heart jumped. Was I expecting a threat? A clue? Or had my mind become so tangled with paranoia that I no longer knew what I was looking for?

A woman sat across from me, her face pale, her eyes red-rimmed and swollen. A crumpled tissue trembled in her hand as she dabbed at her nose. I wondered what had brought her here, what shadows haunted her family. Did she, too, sit awake at night, wrestling with fears she couldn't voice, watching helplessly as someone she loved slipped further away? The thought sent a shiver down my spine, and I quickly looked away, afraid of seeing too much of myself reflected in her grief.

The gentle hum of the heat pump filled the room, a low, monotonous drone broken only by the occasional sound of quiet sobs. In the far corner, a young boy clung to his mother, his face buried in her shoulder as she whispered soothing words and rubbed gentle circles on his back. The scene was painfully familiar, tugging at memories I'd tried to push aside—nights spent comforting Sammy, holding him close as he cried in fear of things I couldn't see, couldn't protect him from.

When I looked back toward Sammy, I realised he was staring at me. His blue eyes—so like Nial's—were fixed on mine, and I struggled to interpret the emotion there. Was it concern? Fear? Or something deeper, something I wasn't ready to name? Lately, he'd been doing this more often, those long, piercing stares that made me feel as though he could see right through me. It was unsettling, as though he were glimpsing things no child his age should be capable of understanding.

"You okay, sweetheart?" I asked, forcing a smile and injecting my voice with an air of lightness I didn't feel.

Sammy nodded, but slowly, his gaze unwavering. "The shadows are quiet here, Mummy," he whispered, his voice soft and hauntingly matter-of-fact.

The words sent a chill down my spine, my heart stuttering in my chest. I opened my mouth to respond, but no words came. What did he mean? Before I could even attempt to untangle the knot of fear and confusion tightening inside me, a nurse's voice cut through the thick air.

"Samuel Triffett?"

The sound snapped me back to reality, but the weight of Sammy's words stayed with me, heavy and unrelenting. The shadows might have been quiet here, but I couldn't shake the feeling that they were waiting, watching, just beyond the edges of the bright, painted walls.

I looked up to see a young woman standing at the doorway, a clipboard in one hand, her scrubs a riot of cheerful cartoon characters. The bright patterns were clearly meant to comfort, to project an air of friendliness, but here in this space heavy with worry, they felt jarringly out of place.

"That's us," I said, rising from my chair and extending my hand toward Sammy. "Come on, sweetheart. It's our turn to see Dr. Carmichael."

For a moment, I thought Sammy might resist. His little body stiffened, and his grip on the wooden train tightened. My heart began to race, bracing for the negotiation that often followed. But then he surprised me, as he so often did.

"Okay, Mummy," he said softly, slipping his hand into mine. His small fingers curled around mine, warm and trusting. It was moments like these that made everything—the fear, the sleepless nights, the constant uncertainty—worth enduring. Sammy was my anchor, my reason for every fight I had to take on.

"Will you stay with me?" he asked, his voice trembling slightly with vulnerability.

My chest tightened as I knelt to his level, looking into his wide blue eyes. "Of course, darling," I said firmly, my voice steady despite the storm inside me. "Every step of the way. Just like always."

We followed the nurse down a long corridor, the soles of her shoes squeaking faintly against the linoleum. The space was awash with contradictions—walls adorned with bright, whimsical paintings designed to calm young patients, but the sterile scent of antiseptic that lingered in the air betrayed the reality of what this place was for. The fluorescent lights overhead buzzed faintly, their cold glow casting sharp shadows that seemed to follow us as we walked.

The nurse, whose name tag read *Nicole*, glanced over her shoulder with a warm smile. "Dr. Carmichael is looking forward to seeing you both again," she said, her tone gentle, almost practised in its reassurance. "He's been reviewing Sammy's latest test results."

I nodded, not trusting my voice. The weight of those words—*latest test results*—settled heavily on my shoulders. The endless string of tests Sammy had endured over the past few months was a torment I wouldn't wish on anyone. Blood draws, neurological scans, psychological evaluations—they had drained both of us. And yet, they had brought us no closer to answers. Instead, they had only added more layers to the tangled web of uncertainty.

We reached Dr. Carmichael's office, the familiar door looming before us like a threshold into yet another round of questions without answers. Nicole knocked softly before pushing the door open, her voice cheerful as she announced, "Dr. Carmichael, the Triffetts are here."

The weight in my chest grew heavier as I stepped inside, Sammy's hand still clasped tightly in mine. Whatever awaited us in this room, I knew one thing for certain: I had to be strong, for him and for us both.

Dr. Carmichael's office felt like stepping into another world, a stark contrast to the cheerful sterility of the clinic outside. The dark wood bookshelves that lined the walls were crammed with weighty medical tomes, anatomical models, and curiosities that seemed pulled straight from a Victorian cabinet of wonders. A detailed model of a brain sat next to a brass microscope, and a jar on a high shelf contained something that looked unsettlingly like preserved eyeballs, their cloudy forms catching the light just enough to make me shiver. The space was imposing, intellectual, and faintly eerie, a reflection of the man who occupied it.

Behind a massive oak desk sat Dr. Carmichael, a figure whose appearance seemed at odds with the gravity of his domain. He looked younger than I'd expected for someone of his expertise—early forties, at most—with prematurely grey hair that stood out starkly against his darker complexion. Thick-rimmed glasses gave him an owlish look, his sharp eyes glinting behind the lenses as he stood to greet us.

"Jenny, Sammy, good to see you both again," he said warmly, his accent carrying an elusive hint of Eastern Europe—Russian, perhaps, though I'd never been quite sure. His voice had a calm authority, soothing yet precise, as though every word was carefully chosen. "Please, have a seat."

I guided Sammy toward one of the plush leather chairs that faced the desk. He climbed into it with a childlike ease, his legs dangling well above the floor, while I lowered myself into the chair beside him. My hand found its place on his shoulder, a silent gesture of reassurance that was as much for me as it was for him. The leather creaked beneath us, the sound unnaturally loud in the stillness of the room.

Dr. Carmichael settled into his chair, steepling his fingers as he studied us for a moment. His gaze was intense but not unkind, his expression giving nothing away. "Now then," he began, leaning back slightly. "I've been reviewing the results of Sammy's latest tests, and I have to say, they're quite... interesting."

A pit formed in my stomach at his words. *Interesting* was rarely a good thing in medical discussions, especially not with everything we'd been through. My voice sounded steadier than I felt when I asked, "Interesting how, Doctor?"

Dr. Carmichael leaned forward, the leather of his chair groaning softly as he rested his forearms on the desk. His eyes behind those thick glasses seemed to sharpen, and his tone grew more deliberate. "As we discussed in our last session, Sammy's nightmares have been increasing in frequency and intensity. And the episodes of sleepwalking and sleep talking—those have also become more frequent, correct?"

I nodded, flashes of the past week flooding my mind in vivid detail. Sammy standing at the foot of our bed, his eyes open but blank, murmuring strange, guttural words in a language I didn't recognise. The night I'd found him in the backyard, barefoot and shivering under the cold Tasmanian sky, staring up at the stars as though they were whispering to him. Each moment had left me shaken, unable to reconcile the sweet boy I knew with the one who seemed trapped in some unknowable dream. "Yes," I said, my voice quieter now. "It's... it's getting worse."

Dr. Carmichael nodded, his expression grave but focused. He turned his attention to Sammy, his tone softening as he addressed him directly. "Sammy, can you tell me about your recent dreams? Have you seen the shadows again?"

Sammy looked up at him, his little body shifting slightly in the large chair. For a moment, I thought he wouldn't answer, but then he nodded slowly. "Yes," he said in a small voice. "They're... hiding now. But I can still feel them. They whisper sometimes, but I don't know what they're saying."

The room seemed to grow colder, the weight of his words settling heavily in the air. My hand tightened instinctively on his shoulder, the warmth of his small body grounding me against the chill creeping into my chest.

Dr. Carmichael's brow furrowed, and he jotted something down in his notebook with a quick, practiced hand. "I see," he said quietly. His gaze flicked back to me, and I saw something in his expression I hadn't seen before. Concern? Curiosity? Or something deeper, something he wasn't yet ready to share?

"Has he mentioned this kind of whispering before?" he asked me, his voice carefully neutral.

I hesitated, thinking back to all the fragmented comments Sammy had made, the half-formed sentences about shadows and strange feelings that I hadn't wanted to believe were significant. "Not in detail," I admitted, my voice faltering slightly. "But he... he's mentioned hearing things. And the shadows—they're always there, in his dreams."

Dr. Carmichael nodded again, his fingers tapping rhythmically against the desk. Whatever he was thinking, he didn't share it right away. Instead, he turned his attention back to Sammy, offering him a small, reassuring smile. "Thank you for telling me, Sammy. You're very brave to share your dreams with me."

Sammy didn't say anything, but he leaned slightly into my side, his small hand gripping mine tightly. It was a quiet, wordless plea for reassurance, and I squeezed his hand back, trying to convey a strength I wasn't sure I had.

"They're always there," Sammy whispered, his voice so faint that I had to lean closer to hear. "In the corners, in the dark places. They watch. They wait."

The words sent a chill crawling up my spine, each syllable spoken with the kind of certainty that no child his age should possess. Dr. Carmichael leaned forward, his expression sharpening with interest. "And what are they waiting for, Sammy?" he asked gently.

Sammy's reaction was immediate and visceral. He shook his head violently, pressing his face into my side, his small body trembling against mine. I wrapped an arm around him, stroking his hair in the familiar rhythm that had comforted him through countless nights of terror. "It's okay, sweetheart," I murmured, my voice soft and soothing, even as my own nerves jangled with unease. "You don't have to talk about it if you don't want to."

Dr. Carmichael didn't push. Instead, he scribbled a note on his pad, his brow furrowing deeply. The motion was so measured, so deliberate, that it made my anxiety spike further. "Mrs. Triffett," he said, his voice calm but probing, "have you noticed any new behavioural changes since our last meeting?"

I hesitated, my thoughts racing. How much could I tell him? How much could I admit without sounding like I was losing my grip on reality? Sammy's behaviours had become so unsettling that I'd started questioning my own perceptions, but this was why we were here, wasn't it? To understand what was happening.

"He's become... even more withdrawn," I said finally, my words cautious, each one carefully selected. "He spends hours in his room, talking to himself." I paused, the weight of the next admission pressing heavily on my chest. "Or... not to himself. It's like he's having conversations with someone I can't see."

Dr. Carmichael's eyes narrowed slightly, but his tone remained even. "Can you elaborate on that?"

I swallowed hard, steeling myself. "The other day, I was passing by his room, and I heard him say, 'The stars are aligning. The gateway will open soon.'" The words, so strange, still echoed in my mind. "When I went in to check on him, he was sitting in the middle of this... this pattern he'd made with his toys. It wasn't random. It was intricate, almost like a mandala." I faltered, feeling exposed as I added, "When I asked him about it, he just looked at me blankly, as if he didn't remember saying or doing anything."

Dr. Carmichael's expression shifted subtly, his posture stiffening ever so slightly. A flash of something—concern? Alarm?—crossed his face before he carefully masked it. Whatever it was, it sent a fresh jolt of unease through me.

"Mrs. Triffett," he said slowly, his voice unusually measured, "has Sammy experienced any new physical symptoms? Any changes to the nosebleeds or bruises we discussed last time?"

The air seemed to grow colder, pressing down on me. My breath hitched as his question dredged up the images I'd been trying to ignore. The bruises—deep, dark, and inexplicable—had been getting worse. They appeared in places no normal childhood tumble could explain, on his arms, his back, even the soles of his feet. But it wasn't just the bruises.

"The bruises are... different now," I admitted, my voice barely above a whisper. "They're not just random marks anymore. They... they form patterns. Shapes. Like the ones he makes with his toys."

Dr. Carmichael's expression darkened, his eyes flicking toward his notepad as though confirming something private and troubling. His pen hovered for a moment before he nodded to himself, a gesture that sent my anxiety spiralling. Without a word, he turned to his computer and began typing rapidly. The click-clack of the keyboard filled the silence, each keystroke unnaturally loud, a mechanical punctuation to the tension saturating the room.

I clutched Sammy closer, my free hand gripping the arm of my chair as though it could anchor me to some semblance of stability. The silence stretched on, oppressive, as I tried to decipher the meaning behind Dr. Carmichael's sudden intensity. When he finally turned back to us, his expression was carefully controlled, but his eyes betrayed a weight of knowledge that made my stomach twist.

"I'd like to run a new series of tests," Dr. Carmichael said, his tone carefully measured, as though trying to cushion the weight of his words. "Some will repeat what we've done before to confirm our findings, but there are a few additional ones I'd like to explore. I've also been in contact with a colleague, Dr. Elena Petrov. She specialises in... unusual paediatric cases."

"Unusual cases?" I repeated, the words catching in my throat as a wave of dizziness rolled over me. "What exactly does that mean, Dr. Carmichael? What do you think is happening to my son?"

Dr. Carmichael removed his glasses and pinched the bridge of his nose, a weary gesture that made him look older, more burdened. For a moment, the confident veneer he wore so well cracked, revealing the toll this case was taking on him too. When he spoke, his voice was soft, almost reluctant.

"Mrs. Triffett... Jenny," he began, his tone shifting to something more personal. "I want you to understand that what's happening with Sammy is... highly unusual. The combination of his symptoms—the nightmares, the behavioural changes, the physical marks—they don't align with any standard diagnosis I've encountered."

My chest tightened, and I could feel my pulse thrumming in my ears. "Are you saying..." I hesitated, the words too terrifying to fully voice. "Are you saying you don't know what's wrong with him?"

"I'm saying we're dealing with something... unique," Dr. Carmichael replied carefully. His eyes held mine, his calm demeanour a fragile barrier against the chaos his words threatened to unleash. "Something that may require a more specialised approach."

Beside me, Sammy stirred. He had been unnervingly quiet throughout the conversation, his small body unnaturally still. Now, he sat up straight, his posture rigid and his gaze locked on Dr. Carmichael with an intensity that sent a chill crawling up my spine.

"The stars are falling," Sammy said suddenly, his voice shifting, deeper and far older than his years. The timbre of it was wrong, unsettling, as though something ancient and unknowable was speaking through him. "The shadows are growing."

The temperature in the room seemed to drop, and I felt every hair on my body stand on end. My hand instinctively tightened on Sammy's shoulder, though whether to comfort him or ground myself, I wasn't sure.

Dr. Carmichael's brows lifted slightly, his otherwise controlled expression betraying a flicker of surprise. He didn't speak immediately, and the silence that followed was deafening, broken only by the relentless ticking of the wall clock. Each second stretched into eternity, the sound amplifying the unnatural stillness in the room.

Finally, Dr. Carmichael cleared his throat, his voice just a fraction less steady. "Yes, well," he said, his tone regaining some semblance of composure, "I think we should proceed with those additional tests as soon as possible. And I strongly recommend bringing in Dr. Petrov for a consultation, assuming you're agreeable."

"Yes," I said quickly, the word tumbling out before he'd even finished. "Of course. When can she see us?"

Dr. Carmichael turned to his computer, the clatter of his keyboard a jarring interruption to the eerie quiet. "She can fly in early next week—Tuesday, to be precise," he said, his voice regaining its professional steadiness. "I'll arrange for the tests to coincide with her arrival. We'll need the weekend to coordinate the necessary resources and equipment."

Relief and frustration warred within me. Relief that action was being taken, that someone as skilled as Dr. Petrov would soon join the effort to help Sammy. But the thought of waiting, of enduring three more days of the unpredictable changes in my son, made the frustration almost unbearable. Every day felt like a gamble, a precarious game where the stakes were my little boy's well-being.

"Tuesday," I murmured, half to myself, nodding as I tried to steady my swirling thoughts. It felt both unbearably far and uncomfortably close, a deadline that seemed to carry the weight of the unknown.

I glanced at Sammy, who had slumped back into his seat, his expression calm once more, his small frame suddenly looking fragile against the backdrop of the oversized leather chair. The words he'd spoken replayed in my mind, their ominous weight settling heavily on my chest. *The stars are falling. The shadows are growing.*

Whatever this was—whatever was happening to Sammy—I wasn't sure how much longer I could hold on.

"What kind of tests are we talking about, Doctor?" I asked, trying to keep my voice steady, though the effort felt Herculean.

"We'll need to do some more comprehensive blood work, another MRI, and a few specialised neurological tests that Dr. Petrov has already recommended," he explained, his tone clinical but edged with caution. "It's quite an extensive battery, but it should give us a clearer picture of what's going on."

I nodded, the words barely registering. This morning, my concerns had revolved around nightmares and bruises. Now, I was discussing neurological tests and international specialists. It felt as though I had stepped into another world, one where the rules of my familiar life no longer applied.

"In the meantime," Dr. Carmichael continued, his voice drawing me back, "I'd like you to keep a detailed log of Sammy's behaviour. Note any unusual statements, sleep disturbances, or physical changes. The more information we have, the better equipped we'll be to help him."

"Of course," I said, though my mind was already racing, replaying every strange occurrence over the past weeks. The unexplained bruises, the bizarre patterns he formed with his toys, the chilling words he muttered in his sleep. How would I even begin to catalogue it all? "Is there anything else we should be doing?"

Dr. Carmichael paused, his hesitation almost imperceptible but enough to make my stomach clench. When he finally spoke, his words were slow and deliberate. "Try to keep Sammy's routine as normal as possible. But... be vigilant. If anything drastic changes, or if you feel at all unsafe, bring him to the emergency room immediately. I'll ensure they're aware of his case."

The weight of his words hung in the air, the unspoken implication chilling. *Unsafe.* What did he think might happen? My grip on Sammy's shoulder tightened instinctively, as though I could shield him from whatever unnamed danger lurked in the shadows.

"Mummy?" Sammy's voice cut through my spiralling thoughts. I looked down to find him gazing up at me, his blue eyes wide and tired, filled with a vulnerability that broke my heart. In that moment, he looked like my little boy again—innocent, unburdened. Not the strange, otherworldly child who spoke of falling stars and creeping shadows. "Can we go home now?"

I forced a smile, though it felt brittle on my face. "Of course, darling. We're all done here for today."

As I stood and helped Sammy to his feet, Dr. Carmichael reached out, placing a gentle hand on my arm. "Mrs. Triffett," he said softly, his eyes meeting mine with unwavering seriousness. "I know this is overwhelming. But please remember, you're not alone in this. We're going to figure out what's happening to Sammy. I promise you that."

I nodded, though I couldn't quite trust my voice enough to reply. His words were meant to be reassuring, but they only amplified the gravity of the situation. Whatever we were dealing with wasn't just strange—it was unprecedented.

As we left the office and stepped into the waiting room, the familiar sight of the cartoon animals on the walls should have brought some comfort. But now, their exaggerated grins seemed sinister, their cheerful eyes leering as though they knew more than they let on. The hum of the heat pump and the murmur of other patients barely registered as I gripped Sammy's hand tightly, pulling him closer to me.

The walk to the car felt like wading through a dream—slow, surreal, and thick with the weight of uncertainty. As the doors of the clinic closed behind us, I glanced at the sky. The fine drizzle had returned, blurring the edges of the world and wrapping everything in a haze. It felt fitting. My once-clear life was now shrouded in shadows, with no path forward, only the relentless hope that somewhere in the mist lay answers.

As I buckled Sammy into his car seat, I caught myself studying his face intently, searching for... what? Some flicker of the little boy I knew so well? Or perhaps some clue to the strange, unknowable force that seemed to be entwining itself with his very being. His features were so familiar, yet I couldn't shake the feeling that I was looking at someone—something—else entirely.

"Ready to go home, sweetheart?" I asked, my voice trembling slightly, though I tried to mask it with forced cheerfulness.

Sammy nodded, his eyelids already drooping with the exhaustion that seemed to cling to him like a second skin. In sleep, he looked so small, so fragile. How could this be the same child who spoke of shadows and falling stars, whose words sent chills through my very soul?

Sliding into the driver's seat, I realised my hands were trembling. I gripped the steering wheel tightly, willing them to steady. *We have a plan now,* I reminded myself, repeating the thought like a mantra. *Tests, specialists, answers. We'll figure this out. We have to.*

But as I pulled out of the carpark, that fragile thread of reassurance frayed against the weight of my unease. The low-hanging clouds over Hobart seemed to press down on the city, smothering it in a bleak, grey light that turned even familiar streets into something oppressive. The drizzle on the windscreen blurred the world beyond, casting everything in a shifting haze that felt almost otherworldly.

The farther I drove, the heavier the atmosphere seemed to grow. It wasn't just the weather—there was something else, something intangible that settled into the car with us. A sense of inevitability, as though we weren't driving away from the clinic but towards something dark and unknown.

I glanced in the rearview mirror. Sammy's head lolled slightly to the side, his chest rising and falling in the steady rhythm of sleep. His little face was peaceful now, the furrow of worry gone, replaced by the innocence of dreams. My heart ached at the sight, an overwhelming mix of love and dread.

"It's going to be okay," I whispered, the words so quiet they were almost swallowed by the rain tapping on the roof. I wasn't sure if I was trying to reassure Sammy or myself. "Mummy's here. I won't let anything happen to you. I promise."

The promise hung in the air, unacknowledged but binding. Yet even as I said it, doubt crept in. Because for the first time, I wasn't sure if it was a promise I could keep.

AN ORDINARY AFTERNOON

4338.209.4

Guiding our black 4WD into the driveway, I couldn't shake the heaviness that seemed to hang in the air, mirroring the oppressive cloud cover blanketing Hobart. The wintry sun barely managed to pierce through the grey, its weak rays doing little to warm the world or my spirits. The muted light transformed our weatherboard house, once a place of comfort and familiarity, into something shadowy and unwelcoming. Even the cheerful trim around the windows seemed dulled, the whole scene steeped in a quiet foreboding.

When I turned off the engine, silence descended, thick and unsettling. Only the soft ticking of the cooling motor and Sammy's gentle, rhythmic breathing from the back seat punctuated the stillness. For a moment, I didn't move, my hands still gripping the steering wheel as though it were an anchor. My knuckles were white with tension, the ache in my fingers unnoticed amid the storm in my mind.

The events of the morning replayed in an endless loop. Dr. Carmichael's calm yet probing questions. Sammy's unsettling whispers. The promise of more tests, more waiting, more unknowns. Each memory seemed to pile onto the growing knot of anxiety in my stomach, its weight threatening to crush me.

My gaze drifted instinctively to where Nial's ute should have been parked, the empty space glaring at me like a missing puzzle piece. The sight of the vacant driveway struck a discordant note, amplifying the unease that had been steadily building since we left Dr. Carmichael's office. Where was he? Nial had mentioned that he'd only be gone a couple of hours. He should have been home by now.

With trembling fingers, I reached for my mobile, the harsh blue glow of the screen cutting through the dim interior of the car. Scrolling through my notifications, I found no missed calls, no messages—nothing to explain his absence. "Hmm," I murmured aloud, though the sound carried little conviction. The worry was rising again, creeping into my voice despite my best efforts to keep it at bay.

The questions I'd tried to suppress all day surged to the forefront of my mind. Where is Nial? Why hasn't he called to check-in about Sammy? My thoughts flitted back to the strange car I'd seen earlier outside our house. To Dr. Carmichael's furrowed brow and Sammy's cryptic murmurs. It all felt connected, though I couldn't piece together how. Was I overthinking it, letting my fears twist every detail into something sinister? Or was there really something darker at play, lurking just beneath the surface of our lives?

I closed my eyes, trying to centre myself with a deep breath. The familiar scent of the leather seats mixed with the piney aroma of the air freshener dangling from the rearview mirror. Nial had picked it, saying it reminded him of camping trips from his youth, the kind of carefree moments that felt like we hadn't known in far too long. The smell was a small but tangible comfort, a fragile tether to the normal life I was so desperate to cling to.

"Mummy." Sammy's voice from the backseat broke through my spiralling thoughts. His tone was soft, but it carried a weight that startled me. Glancing into the rearview mirror, I met his eyes, wide and blue like Nial's. For a fleeting moment, I thought I saw something in them—fear, perhaps, or an understanding far beyond his years. It was unnerving, but before I could dwell on it, the flicker disappeared, replaced by the impatient wiggle of a child eager to escape the confines of his car seat.

"Coming, mate," I replied, my voice bright and cheerful, the kind of forced enthusiasm that had become second nature. My theatre training had taught me to deliver convincing performances, and this was no different. Sammy had been through enough for one day; he didn't need to see the cracks forming in his mother.

Unbuckling my seatbelt and reaching for the door handle, I steeled myself against the tide of worry threatening to pull me under. Whatever this was, whatever was happening to my family, I couldn't let it break me. Not yet. Sammy needed me to be strong. And for him, I would find a way to keep going, no matter how dark the road ahead seemed.

As soon as his little feet hit the ground, Sammy darted towards the front door, a blur of energy that seemed out of step with the oppressive stillness around us. I followed quickly, catching up just in time to steady him as he wobbled on the last of the three steps leading up to the front porch. The wood creaked beneath our combined weight, a sound I'd always found comforting in its familiarity. But today, it felt different—less a gentle protest from our old home, more a groan of unease, as if the house itself could sense the tension that had settled over us.

With a determined shove from Sammy, the door unlocked with a click that seemed unnaturally loud, the sound reverberating in the quiet of the street. I hesitated, glancing over my shoulder, half-expecting to see a neighbour peering out from behind their curtains, their curiosity piqued by the jarring sound. But the street remained eerily empty, the other houses standing silent and still, their windows darkened under the heavy winter sky.

Sammy yanked on my arm, breaking my moment of unease as he rushed inside, his excitement unbridled and oblivious to the undercurrent of wrongness I couldn't shake. "Sammy! To your bedroom. It's nap time!" I called after him, my voice carrying down the hallway with a firm but gentle tone.

Instead of obeying, he tore past the open office door, his little feet thudding against the floorboards as he headed straight for the kitchen. It wasn't his disobedience that stopped me in my tracks, though—it was the sight of the open office door.

My heart stuttered as I stared at it, the wrongness of it slamming into me like a physical blow. Nial was meticulous about his office. He never left it unlocked, let alone ajar. The thought sent a chill coursing through me, and I called out, my voice betraying a flicker of hope. "Nial? Are you home?"

Silence. The house gave no reply, no creak of floorboards or sound of familiar footsteps to fill the void.

From the corner of my eye, I saw Buffy emerge from the office, her tail wagging lazily as she trailed Sammy down the hallway. Her presence was both comforting and unsettling. If Nial was home, why hadn't he greeted us? And if he wasn't, why was the office door open?

Clutching at the fragile mask of normality, I pushed aside the unease gnawing at my thoughts and turned back toward the car to retrieve the groceries. The weight of the bags seemed heavier than usual, or perhaps it was the weight of everything else—the unanswered questions, the growing sense of dread—that made them feel so burdensome.

As I reached into the backseat, an eerie tingle prickled up my neck, the sensation crawling over my skin and leaving the fine blonde hairs on my arms standing on end. I paused, glancing around the front yard, the mundane scene suddenly charged with tension.

The neatly trimmed lawn and native garden beds stretched out before me, a testament to Nial's pride in maintaining our home. Every detail was so typically him—carefully tended, painstakingly orderly. He'd poured so much of himself into creating this space, a beautiful sanctuary for our family.

The thought of him brought a pang of longing and worry, sharp enough to make me catch my breath. *Where are you, Nial?* I thought, the question looping endlessly in my mind as I balanced the heavy bags in my arms. It wasn't just the mystery of his absence that weighed on me—it was the silence, the gaping void where his presence should have been. Something wasn't right. I felt it in my bones.

Buffy's bark rang out, sharp and gruff, shattering the oppressive silence that had wrapped itself around the house.

My head snapped up, my eyes immediately darting to where she stood on the top step, her body rigid, ears pricked forward. She was staring intently at the bushes by the side fence, her tail motionless—a rare and unnerving sight for a dog usually so animated. "What is it, Buffy?" I called out, trying to keep my voice steady, though a thread of fear wove its way through my tone.

She barked again, the sound echoing into the quiet street and sending a shiver cascading down my spine. For a moment, she stood rooted to the spot, her focus unbroken. Then, just as suddenly, she cocked her head, gave me a strange, almost questioning look, and trotted back inside as though nothing had happened.

I lingered, my gaze following hers to the side fence. Through the sparse bushes, I could see the weathered wooden palings, their surfaces dappled with rainwater. Nothing appeared out of the ordinary—no movement, no shapes lurking in the shadows. And yet, the uneasy sensation remained, like an itch I couldn't reach.

"Get a grip, Jenny," I muttered under my breath, forcing myself to turn away. The groceries weren't going to unpack themselves. Reaching back into the car, I grabbed the last bag, my fingers fumbling slightly as I hauled it out.

Before heading inside, I hesitated, giving the front yard and street one last sweep with my eyes. The neighbourhood remained as still and quiet as before, the other houses standing in resolute silence. I locked the car door with an exaggerated click, double-checking it—something I'd never done until recently. The front door got the same treatment, my fingers brushing over the cool metal of the latch, ensuring it was secure.

The act of locking up, once so automatic, now felt like a ritual. A defence against the creeping unease that seemed to be seeping into every corner of my life.

Inside, the warmth of the house should have been a comfort, but it only heightened the sense of stillness. Buffy had settled in the corner of the living room, her head resting on her paws, but her eyes remained open, tracking my movements as I carried the bags to the kitchen. Her unusual quietness added another layer to the unease gnawing at my mind.

On my way back from the front hall, I passed Nial's office. The door was slightly ajar, just enough to invite a peek inside. My steps faltered, and I found myself pausing, curiosity overriding the sense of unease that had been my constant companion all day.

Nial was meticulous about keeping his office closed, and the sight of the door ajar unsettled me. Slowly, I stepped closer and peeked inside. His desk was there, decorated with the usual assortment of invoices, blueprints, and scribbled notes.

Something caught my eye—a sheet of paper near the edge of the desk. Unlike the others, this one seemed deliberately placed, as though it had been consulted recently. I moved closer, my gaze narrowing as I took in the list scrawled across the page. Names and addresses, some violently crossed out with heavy, angry lines. My stomach twisted as one name leapt out at me: *Dr. Carmichael.*

I felt the air leave my lungs in a sharp rush. My mind scrambled to make sense of it. Why would Nial have a list of names? Why would Dr. Carmichael, of all people, be on it? And what could it possibly mean that his name—along with several others—had been crossed out?

My hand trembled as I reached for the paper, my fingers hovering just above its surface. The questions swirled faster, pulling me into a vortex of speculation and fear.

The creak of a floorboard snapped me out of my spiralling thoughts. The sound echoed through the house, sharp and sudden, like a warning shot. My heart jolted into overdrive as I whipped my head toward the hallway, my breath catching in my throat.

"Nial?" I called out, though my voice was barely above a whisper. Silence answered.

Clutching the paper tightly in my hand, I stepped back from the desk, my pulse thundering in my ears. Every instinct screamed for me to retreat, to put distance between myself and the unsettling clues on Nial's desk. I carefully laid the paper back where I'd found it, my hand shaking as I smoothed it down.

With deliberate calm, I pushed the office door shut, the creak of the hinges grating against the silence. The click of the latch felt unnaturally loud, reverberating through the still hallway. I gave the door a gentle nudge to ensure it stayed closed, as though sealing it away might also contain the disquiet it had unleashed.

I stood there for a moment, my hand still resting on the doorknob, listening intently to the house. The usual creaks and groans of the old weatherboard home sounded louder, more pronounced, each one carrying a weight that set my nerves on edge.

Every instinct told me something was wrong, that Sammy and I weren't alone. But the silence stretched on, unbroken, and I forced myself to move, my feet heavy as I carried the groceries towards the kitchen. Each step felt like an effort, as though the weight of the house itself was pressing down on me, urging me to stop, to listen.

But there was nothing—just the house and the questions it refused to answer.

Continuing down the hallway, I called out softly, "I'll be there in just a minute," my voice carrying the gentle reassurance of a mother's promise. Yet, beneath the calmness, there was an undercurrent of tension I couldn't entirely hide. As I passed by Sammy's door, I stole a glance inside, my heart softening at the sight of him perched on his bed, his small fingers delicately turning the pages of his favourite picture book.

In the kitchen, I hefted the last grocery bag onto the bench with an exaggerated groan, a theatrical flourish that was as instinctive as it was unnecessary. The performance was for no one but myself, an attempt to impose some levity on the oppressive weight of the day. The theatre had always been in my blood, my flair for the dramatic spilling into moments as mundane as unpacking groceries.

I began unpacking the bags on autopilot, my hands moving mechanically as my thoughts spiralled back to the list I'd found in Nial's office. The names, the violent strokes crossing some of them out, the inclusion of *Dr. Carmichael*. The implications loomed large in my mind, each possibility darker than the last. Was it tied to his work? Or did it point to something far more insidious? The questions churned endlessly, each one more unsettling than the last, making it hard to focus on the simple task in front of me.

The sharp crash from outside jolted me like a slap, yanking me out of my racing thoughts. I froze mid-motion, a tin of beans clutched tightly in my hands. My heart thundered in my chest as I strained to identify the sound. Had the wind knocked over the bins? Or was it something more? Something sinister?

The silence that followed was deafening, every creak of the old house amplified as I stood there, listening intently. No more sounds came, no footsteps, no voices, just the heavy stillness pressing against my eardrums. Swallowing hard, I tried to push away the surge of paranoia clawing at the edges of my rationality.

Abandoning the groceries mid-task, I made my way back to Sammy's room. His sanctuary. "We're late today, so you can just have a short nap," I told him gently, reaching for the book in his hands. He resisted for only a moment before surrendering it with a small pout, allowing me to coax him under the blanket.

His room felt like a cocoon of safety, the soft glow of the nightlight casting warm, comforting shadows on the walls. The hand-painted clouds on the ceiling seemed to drift lazily, a soothing backdrop to the innocence of childhood that still lingered here. But as I tucked him in, smoothing the blanket over his small frame, the weight of an ominous thought pressed heavily on my chest: that innocence was under siege. The shadows I feared weren't confined to his nightmares—they were real, encroaching on our lives, and I didn't know how to stop them.

As I turned off his light, a flicker in the hallway caught the corner of my eye. I froze, the sensation sharp and immediate, like cold water down my back. My arms prickled with goosebumps, my body's instinctive response to a threat I couldn't see. My heart quickened, the steady rhythm becoming a thunderous drumbeat that echoed in my ears.

I glanced down at Sammy, relief flooding me when I saw his eyelids softly closed, his breathing even and peaceful. Whatever had sent a shiver through me hadn't touched him, hadn't invaded this moment of quiet.

Leaning down, I brushed a strand of hair from his forehead and pressed a soft kiss against his warm skin. "Sleep well, Sammy," I whispered, my voice barely audible over the pounding in my chest. The words felt more like a plea than a wish, a prayer sent to no one in particular that I could shield him from the encroaching darkness, from whatever was coming for us.

As I stood, the hallway beyond his door loomed, its shadows deeper, more oppressive than they should have been. I forced myself to leave the room, closing the door partway behind me, and stepped back into the uneasy silence of the house.

The sensation of unease clung to me as I stepped back into the hallway. The house felt subtly, inexplicably different—like a stage just before the curtain rises, the atmosphere charged with anticipation. It was as if the walls themselves were holding their breath, waiting for something I couldn't yet see. Every creak of the floorboards beneath my feet seemed amplified, each shadow cast by the dim hallway light stretching a fraction too long.

Then, a loud thud echoed from the kitchen, shattering the fragile stillness. My heart leapt into my throat, its frantic pounding reverberating through my chest. I glanced back at Sammy's room, my eyes lingering on the soft rise and fall of his tiny chest. His breathing remained steady, undisturbed by the noise that had sent my own thoughts spiralling into panic.

Should I wake him? Grab him and run? The questions raced through my mind, each one colliding with the next. *But where would we go? And what if I'm overreacting?*

I tiptoed across the floor, my movements slow and deliberate, my ears straining for the faintest sound. The hallway stretched before me, empty and unassuming, its silence almost mocking. I longed for Nial's steadying presence, the way his arms could ground me even in the worst moments. But he wasn't here. He hadn't been here all day, and whatever was waiting in that kitchen, I had to face it alone.

A sudden rustling sound from the kitchen made me freeze, my pulse quickening. My hand shot out instinctively, grasping the nearest object within reach—a small photo frame on the side unit. The sharp metallic edges of the frame offered a paltry sense of protection, but it was better than nothing.

Glancing down at the photo within, my breath hitched. It was from last summer: Nial, Sammy, and me, all beaming at the camera with sunburnt noses and carefree smiles. The sight of it sent a pang of longing through my chest, a sharp ache for the life we'd had before shadows began creeping into our world.

Clutching the frame tightly, I edged toward the kitchen, every step deliberate and measured. The hallway seemed to stretch endlessly, the distance to the kitchen door yawning wider with each step. My grip tightened on the frame, the edges digging into my palm as adrenaline coursed through me, sharpening every detail.

As I rounded the corner, I burst through the kitchen doorway with a sharp turn, the photo frame raised defensively, ready for anything. The scene that greeted me wasn't the danger I had feared, but neither was it the relief I'd hoped for.

"Buffy! Get out of it!" My voice was a hushed shriek, more exasperated than angry, but still mindful of Sammy sleeping nearby.

Our Dalmatian stood in the middle of the kitchen, her paws braced against a tipped-over grocery bag, happily lapping up milk from a carton she had managed to puncture. The sticky white liquid pooled across the linoleum, glinting faintly in the afternoon light. Buffy's tail wagged furiously, her delight at the forbidden treat unspoiled by my scolding.

Relief coursed through me, washing away the tension that had coiled in my chest like a spring. I set the photo frame down on the counter with a trembling hand, my heart beginning to slow from its frenzied rhythm.

"Go nap with Sammy," I said, nudging her gently with my foot towards the kitchen door. Buffy complied with a mix of guilt and excitement, her tail wagging as she trotted out. But as she passed, my gaze caught on her coat, speckled with tiny leaves and twigs.

I frowned. Her white fur was usually spotless, thanks to her obsessive grooming and my frequent brushing. *Had she been in the bushes by the fence? Was that what she'd been barking at earlier?*

The thought prickled at the edges of my mind as I grabbed a cloth and crouched to clean up the spilled milk. The task was mundane, grounding, but it did little to settle the unease that had taken root. The oddities of the day piled up like the scattered groceries on the floor: the thud, the open office door, the strange car I'd seen earlier, and now Buffy's dishevelled state.

As I wiped up the mess, I tried to shake the nagging thoughts that clung to me like the milk's sticky residue. Surely, this was just a chaotic day compounded by my fraying nerves. But deep down, I knew better. The small incidents—the spilled milk, Buffy's bark, the rustling outside—felt like the tremors that precede an earthquake.

The calm before the storm wasn't supposed to feel like this. It wasn't supposed to feel like the storm had already arrived, despite it creeping ever closer, just out of sight.

"Finally," I murmured under my breath, a sigh escaping my lips as though it had been waiting all day for release. The sound hung in the air for a moment, a fragile bubble of calm in a house that seemed to hold its breath alongside me. With Buffy now stretched out beside Sammy's bed, her quiet presence offering an unspoken assurance, and the kitchen restored to its usual order, I could steal a precious moment for myself.

I sank into my favourite recliner, the worn leather moulding to my frame like an old friend. It was my sanctuary, the one spot in the house where I could let my guard down, even if only for a little while. The soft creak of the chair as I settled into its embrace was familiar and comforting—though this afternoon, it seemed louder, sharper, like an intrusion into the house's unnatural quiet.

Reaching for the book on the small coffee table beside me, I let my fingers trail over the familiar grooves of its worn cover. *The Silence of the Lambs* by Thomas Harris. The title glinted faintly in the dim light, its promise of suspense and psychological intrigue drawing me in even as I acknowledged the irony. Here I was, seeking solace in a story of fear and danger while my own life seemed poised on the precipice of something just as harrowing.

As I picked it up, a small piece of paper fluttered loose, landing softly on the armrest. My makeshift bookmark—a chemist receipt. I picked it up, the neat, clinical text staring back at me: *Triffett, Samuel - Prescription #4721*.

My chest tightened as I read it, the weight of the last week pressing down on me anew. The date on the receipt—just seven days ago—felt like a cruel joke. How had time moved so quickly and yet dragged so unbearably slow? The medication it referenced sat on the shelf in the bathroom, the one thing that seemed to stand between Sammy and the horrors waiting in his sleep.

A fresh wave of anxiety rippled through me as I folded the receipt carefully and slid it back between the pages. How had our lives unravelled so quickly? The cheerful boy who used to giggle uncontrollably during bedtime stories now woke screaming in the night, his small body trembling with fears he couldn't articulate. And Nial—where was he now? His absence loomed larger with each passing hour, and the questions I'd been trying to bury surged to the surface, sharper and more insistent than ever.

I shook my head, pushing the thoughts aside. For now, I needed to escape. The book in my hands offered the promise of another world, one where the chaos and darkness were contained within its pages, not spilling over into every corner of my reality.

Gently, I opened the book to where I'd left off, the spine protesting softly as it stretched. The sound immediately reminded me of the floorboards in Nial's office, and my heart gave an involuntary jolt. My gaze flicked toward the hallway, half-expecting to see a shadow slipping silently past the doorway. But there was nothing—just the dim, empty stretch of wood-panelled walls and the faint hum of the house.

I took a deep breath, willing myself to relax. "Chapter Nine," I read aloud, my voice a quiet tether pulling me into the story. It was a habit of mine, a small ritual that helped me transition from the whirlwind of my daily life into the imagined worlds I loved. The familiar words flowed like a balm, each sentence peeling away a layer of tension as I let myself be drawn into the tale.

As I began to read, the world around me melted away, dissolving into a soft blur at the edges of my awareness. The lingering tension of the day—Nial's prolonged absence, the gnawing unease that had followed me like a shadow—faded into a dull hum. Even the comforting warmth of my living room seemed to retreat, leaving me untethered, free to drift into the story that unfolded in my hands.

No longer just Jenny, the overburdened mother, worried wife, and cleaner of spilt milk, I became an adventurer, a silent witness to the determined pursuit of Clarice Starling as she unravelled the dark threads of her investigation. The words flowed effortlessly, each one painting vivid images in my mind. The gritty details of Clarice's world came alive, her bravery cutting through the oppressive danger like a beacon.

Her unwavering resolve resonated with me in a way it never had before. Clarice wasn't just a character anymore; she was a reflection, her journey a distorted mirror of my own turmoil. Like her, I felt the weight of something sinister lurking at the edges of my reality, intangible but undeniably present. Her dogged pursuit of answers felt achingly familiar.

A shiver coursed through me as I read on, the parallels unsettling. The sense of being out of her depth yet pressing forward, guided by instinct and necessity. The knowledge that something was deeply wrong, even if she couldn't yet define it. And the gut-wrenching certainty that time was running out. It all hit too close to home.

The warmth of the room did little to banish the chill that ran down my spine. I paused, lifting my gaze from the book and taking in the stillness around me. The house was unnervingly quiet, the kind of silence that amplifies every creak and tick, making even the faintest sound a jarring intrusion.

The clock on the mantelpiece caught my attention, its soft ticking cutting through the silence. Each measured beat seemed louder now, echoing in the room as if marking time for something unseen. The steady rhythm was hypnotic, a quiet reminder of the minutes slipping away.

I returned my focus to the book, but my eyes struggled to stay open, the lines on the page beginning to blur. The story's grip on me faltered as fatigue crept in, its weight heavy and insistent. I blinked hard, trying to banish the haze that blurred the words into an illegible jumble of black ink.

"Just a few more pages," I murmured, my voice soft and hoarse from the day's strain. But even as I spoke, a yawn overtook me, pulling my jaw wide as my grip on the book slackened. My hands, once so firmly holding onto the pages, began to falter.

The recliner's embrace was too inviting, its leather cushions moulding around me like a cocoon. The clock's ticking, rhythmic and soothing, became a lullaby. I felt myself sinking deeper, the tension in my shoulders loosening, the storm of thoughts quieting to a distant murmur.

The day's worries—Sammy's worsening condition, Nial's baffling absence, the oddities that had marked the hours—drifted to the back of my mind, replaced by the heavy pull of exhaustion.

My last thought before surrendering to the weight of sleep was of Sammy, safe and peaceful in his room, with Buffy faithfully keeping watch. I clung to that image as if it were a talisman, a reassurance against the unease that had haunted me.

"Just a quick nap," I whispered to myself, my words slurred as my eyelids fell shut. The book slipped from my hands, resting against my chest as I sank fully into the recliner. "Just five minutes…"

The ticking of the clock continued, steady and unyielding, as I drifted off, the house falling into a silence that felt too deep to be natural.

INTRUSION

4338.209.5

The peaceful embrace of sleep shattered like glass, splintering into a thousand jagged shards. My eyes flew open, heart racing, as *The Silence of the Lambs* tumbled from my lap with a loud thud that echoed unnaturally through the silent house. For an instant, I was frozen, caught between the fading edges of my dreams and the unsettling reality waiting in the twilight.

Blinking rapidly, I scanned the room, struggling to reorient myself. The late afternoon light that had once bathed the living room in warmth had disappeared, replaced by the dusky gloom of encroaching evening. Long shadows stretched across the Tasmanian Oak floor, their shapes warped and unfamiliar, as though the room itself had shifted subtly while I slept.

I rubbed my eyes, trying to banish the fog of sleep that clung to me like a heavy veil. A dull ache in my neck demanded attention, and I tilted my head to the side, wincing as a crackling release of tension broke the silence. The sound felt deafening in the oppressive stillness, each creak of my joints amplified tenfold. I found myself holding my breath, straining to hear anything else—the comforting background noises of our home. Sammy's laughter, Buffy's playful barks, Nial's familiar footfalls—all were conspicuously absent, leaving only an eerie void.

"Oh dear, I must have dozed longer than I meant to," I murmured, my voice raspy and disoriented. The sound of it startled me, as if it didn't belong in the thick quiet of the house.

I reached up to knead the tight knot that had formed in my shoulder, wincing as my fingers pressed against the tender muscle. My gaze drifted toward the curtains, the last remnants of daylight filtering weakly through the fabric. Everything seemed muted, dulled, as if the house itself were holding its breath.

Finally, my eyes locked onto the clock on the far wall, its faint ticking cutting through the silence like a metronome of unease. The hands stood resolute: 5:15. My chest tightened as the realisation struck.

"Crap!" The word burst from my lips in a panicked exclamation, loud enough to seem almost inappropriate in the quiet room. My mind raced to catch up, spinning through the implications of lost time. "It's quarter past five—I've completely forgotten to put the chicken in the oven!"

I bolted upright, the sudden movement sending a rush of blood to my head. For a moment, I stood there, caught between action and inaction, my heart pounding with a mix of urgency and frustration. The thought of dinner derailed felt absurdly mundane against the backdrop of the unease that had plagued me all day, but it was something tangible to focus on, a momentary distraction from the growing shadows in my mind.

"Maybe I can convince Sammy and Nial to finish off the frozen lasagne instead," I muttered, forcing my voice to sound light as I tried to salvage the situation.

I bent down to pick up the fallen book, my fingers tracing the well-worn cover. Its familiar texture should have been comforting, a reminder of countless evenings spent lost in stories. But tonight, it felt foreign, at odds with the air of unease that clung to the room like mist. I placed it back on the side table, the act more deliberate than it needed to be, as though giving it back its place could restore some semblance of order.

I reached for my smartphone, the smooth, cool surface a jarring contrast to the worn leather of the book. My fingers unlocked it out of habit, the glow of the screen casting pale, unnatural light across the dim living room.

I squinted, my eyes adjusting to the brightness as I scanned the screen. My stomach churned, the absence of notifications glaring back at me with an almost accusatory silence. No missed calls. No messages. Nothing.

A pit formed in my stomach as I stared at the screen. "Hmm," I murmured, my voice barely above a whisper. The note of worry in it betrayed me. "Still no message from Nial."

I stared at his name in my contacts list, the icon beside it unchanging, unmoving—a stubborn reminder that he was out there somewhere, unreachable. The thought tightened the knot in my chest, dread threading through it. Where was he? Why hadn't he called?

Setting the phone down, I forced myself to breathe deeply, exhaling slowly as I tried to shake the unease. The house had grown colder, or perhaps it was just the weight of unanswered questions settling heavily over me. One thing was certain: the clock's steady ticking wasn't the only thing counting down.

The unease that had been quietly simmering throughout the day now boiled over, impossible to ignore. It felt as if the house itself was conspiring to magnify my growing dread. Each step down the hallway toward Nial's office felt heavier than the last, the floorboards groaning underfoot as if lamenting my approach. The familiar family photos lining the walls—moments frozen in happier times—no longer offered comfort. Instead, they felt like a collection of accusatory stares, their frozen smiles twisting into something foreign in the dim light.

"Nial?" I called, the name catching slightly in my throat, my voice quivering in the unnatural stillness. The only response was the echo of my own words, swallowed quickly by the house's oppressive silence.

As I neared the office, my breath hitched. The door stood ajar. I was certain I'd closed it earlier, nudging it firmly until I heard the reassuring click. Yet here it was, open just enough to reveal a sliver of shadowed interior. My pulse quickened as I frowned, confusion giving way to unease.

"Are you home?" I asked, though the emptiness of the house made the question feel absurd. Still, I hoped for an answer, some sound to ground me. Nothing came.

Reaching for the doorknob, my hand trembled, the cool metal sending a jolt through my palm. My grip tightened as I hesitated, steeling myself before easing the door open. The familiar squeak of the hinges seemed louder than ever, grating against the fragile quiet.

"Nial?" I ventured again, stepping into the room, my voice barely audible above the pounding in my chest.

The fading light from the window spilled across the room, elongating shadows and twisting the space into something unnerving. The air was heavy, cold, and it carried an unsettling stillness that prickled at my skin. Nial's desk, usually so organised and indicative of his meticulous nature, was almost bare, its emptiness stark and wrong.

It hit me like a blow: his laptop was missing.

The sight of the cleared desk turned my unease into a sickly dread. I lingered in the doorway, unable to move, as if the room itself were holding me in place. My eyes swept over the space, but there was nothing out of place save for the desk's unnatural vacancy. The absence of his things made the room feel unfamiliar, hollowed out, a shell of what it had been just this morning.

Why would Nial clear his desk? And if he had, why hadn't he mentioned anything?

I crossed the room hesitantly, my steps muted against the rug. The faint trace of Nial's cologne hung in the air, an almost mocking reminder of his presence—or absence. It was as though he had been here, tangible and real, only moments ago, and yet now felt impossibly far away.

The window overlooking the driveway caught my eye, and I turned toward it instinctively. The empty space where Nial's ute should have been was glaring, its absence magnified by the growing shadows of the evening. The encroaching darkness outside pressed against the glass, its weight mirroring the one growing in my chest.

My hands brushed over the desk, fingers trailing across the barren surface as if it might offer some explanation. It didn't.

I pulled my phone from my pocket, the smooth device cool against my shaking fingers. Dialling Nial's number felt both necessary and futile, the familiar motions grounding me even as I prepared for disappointment.

The ringing began, each tone stretching out interminably in the heavy silence. The soft glow of the screen illuminated the desk, casting faint, jagged shadows that danced across the walls like spectres.

"Hi. This is Nial Triffett. I'm busy at the moment, but if you—"

The voicemail cut through the stillness, its sterile cheeriness a cruel contrast to the fear clawing at me. I ended the call sharply, my thumb pressing the screen with unnecessary force.

It hadn't even rung properly.

My breath caught as the reality of that small detail hit me like a punch to the gut. The phone hadn't connected. Nial's number wasn't reachable.

Something was wrong. Terribly wrong.

A chill spread through my body, starting in my chest and radiating outward until my fingers felt numb. I dropped my hand to my side, gripping the phone tightly as if it could somehow anchor me. My gaze drifted back to the window, the darkness outside a reflection of the encroaching panic within.

"Nial, where are you?" I whispered, my voice trembling with the weight of unspoken fears.

The office felt colder now, emptier, the walls seeming to press closer around me. Every logical explanation I tried to summon crumbled beneath the relentless weight of my instincts. This wasn't just a misunderstanding or a case of bad timing. Something was very, very wrong.

I staggered back from the desk, my legs threatening to buckle beneath me. The room, once so familiar, now felt stifling, its silence heavy and suffocating. Each breath came shallow and strained, the air thick with an unnamed dread. Reaching the doorway, I clung to the frame as though it might hold me upright, my fingers pressing hard into the wood as if crossing the threshold could provide some kind of escape. But the unease followed, a shadow clinging to me, refusing to be left behind.

"Sammy," I called out, the sound of my own voice cracking in the stillness, reverberating through the hallway. Each syllable carried my growing fear, trembling at the edges. "Sammy. Time for you to wake up now."

No response.

The silence that answered was too deep, too absolute. My pulse quickened, my heart hammering against my ribs as if trying to escape. I stepped away from the office and into the hallway, my pace quickening with each step.

The hallway stretched before me, impossibly long, as though it had become a corridor in some surreal nightmare. The familiar family photos lining the walls—their smiling faces and frozen moments of joy—felt alien under the dimming light, their eyes following me with silent accusations. My own face stared back from the glass, distorted and pale.

"Sam—" My voice faltered as I reached Sammy's door, the words catching in my throat. Something was wrong. I could feel it in my bones. My hand hovered over the doorknob, trembling, before I pushed it open.

The sight inside hit me like a physical blow.

Sammy's bed was empty. The blankets were tangled in a chaotic heap at the foot of the mattress, as if he had left in a hurry. A single sock lay abandoned on the floor, a small, innocent detail that made my stomach lurch.

Time froze.

The air seemed to leave the room, every sound vanishing into a deafening void. My son, my sweet, precious Sammy, wasn't there. The stillness was unbearable, like a held breath that refused to release.

"Sammy!" I screamed, the sound tearing from my throat, raw and jagged. I spun around, clutching the doorframe for support as my knees threatened to give way. My mind raced, fragments of thoughts crashing into one another, impossible to organise. Where was he? How could this be happening?

I stumbled into the hallway, the familiar path now fraught with terror. My legs felt like lead, sluggish and uncooperative, but I forced them forward. A few desperate strides later, my foot caught on the uneven floorboards, sending me careening into the wall.

Pain exploded in my knees as they slammed into the wood. The sharp sting jolted me, pulling a gasp from my lips. For a fleeting moment, the physical pain was almost grounding, an anchor in the sea of panic threatening to drag me under.

Propped against the wall, I raised my head, my gaze darting wildly down the hallway. There, through the open laundry door, I saw it: the back door.

It was ajar, standing barely open, hinting at the deepening twilight outside.

A gust of cool evening air swept in, brushing against my skin and carrying with it the scent of damp eucalyptus and freshly disturbed earth. The faint laughter of kookaburras drifted from the distance, a cruel contrast to the chaos within me—a reminder that the world outside continued, oblivious to my nightmare.

"Sammy!" I screamed again, the name ripping through the house, raw with desperation. It echoed back at me, bouncing off the walls in mockery. My voice didn't sound like my own, filled with a panic so consuming it felt like a living thing, clawing at my throat.

I pushed myself upright, my knees shaking, my breaths coming in sharp, shallow gasps. The open door loomed before me, a silent taunt, daring me to step into the unknown. My mind raced with possibilities, each one more horrifying than the last. Where had he gone? Or worse—who had taken him?

Terror clawed at my chest, cold and relentless, as I stumbled forward. The normal world outside—the dusk, the birdsong, the scent of rain on the wind—felt like an insult, its tranquillity mocking the storm raging inside me.

"Sammy!" I called again, my voice cracking under the weight of my fear. The silence that followed was unbearable, the emptiness of it consuming me whole.

Ignoring the throbbing ache in my bruised knees, I bolted into the backyard, my heart pounding as though it might burst from my chest. The evening air hit me like a wall of ice, sharp and biting, raising goosebumps along my arms despite my jumper. Overhead, the sky had shifted into a bruised tapestry of purples and oranges, the last remnants of daylight sinking below the horizon and leaving the world cloaked in shadows.

"Sammy!" I called, my voice breaking with desperation. My eyes darted across the yard, sweeping over every familiar landmark now rendered strange and menacing in the encroaching dark. The towering gum tree, its gnarled branches reaching skyward, looked skeletal and forbidding. The rusted swing set creaked faintly in the evening breeze, its once-cheerful red paint peeling away to reveal the raw metal beneath. Even the vegetable patch, its once-tidy rows overrun with weeds, seemed alien, every shadow a potential hiding place.

"Where are you?" My voice cracked under the weight of my panic, tears threatening to blur my vision.

Then, from the edge of the sandpit, a small figure turned toward me, illuminated faintly by the dusky light. "I'm here, Mummy," Sammy's calm, sing-song voice carried across the yard, slicing through my fear like a blade.

My knees nearly gave way as relief crashed over me, leaving me weak and shaky. I staggered forward, my breath coming in shallow, unsteady gasps. *He's safe.* The words echoed in my mind like a mantra, soothing but incomplete. There was no reprieve yet, no true comfort. Too many questions loomed, their answers tantalisingly out of reach.

Sammy sat in the sandpit, his hands busy scooping and patting the grains into a castle, his focus entirely on his creation. The innocence of the scene struck me like a blow, so at odds with the storm raging inside me. The fine grains of sand clung to his clothes and curly hair, a quiet testament to how long he must have been sitting out here while I dozed inside.

I reached him with unsteady steps, dropping to my knees in the sand beside him. The grit pressed into my jeans, the chill of the ground soaking through the fabric, but I barely noticed. My hands found his small shoulders, gripping them firmly as I turned him to face me. His bright blue eyes, so much like Nial's, blinked up at me, wide and untroubled.

"Sammy," I said, my voice low and tight, laced with an urgency I couldn't suppress. "How did you get outside? Did you open the door?"

He stared at me blankly for a moment, his little face a picture of innocent confusion. Then he shook his head vigorously, his curls bouncing with the motion. "Uh-uh," he said, the sound soft but resolute.

The pit in my stomach deepened. I struggled to keep my voice calm, even as my grip on his shoulders tightened. "Are you sure? Sammy, you have to tell me the truth. Did you open the door?"

His expression didn't change, and he shook his head again, slower this time, as if sensing the weight of my question. "It was open," he whispered, his voice barely audible but cutting through the cool evening air like a knife.

The world around me seemed to tilt. The faint rustle of leaves and the distant call of kookaburras melted into a muffled hum, the enormity of his words crashing down like a wave. If Sammy hadn't opened the door, and I knew I hadn't either, then...

The conclusion was inescapable and horrifying. Someone else had opened it.

My gaze darted toward the back door, its edges now lost in shadow. The thought of an intruder—a stranger moving through the intimate spaces of our home, unseen, unnoticed—was almost too much to bear. Every fibre of my being screamed to gather Sammy in my arms, to run inside and lock every door, every window. But my limbs felt paralysed, rooted to the spot by a mixture of fear and disbelief.

I turned my attention back to Sammy, his small, delicate features bathed in the fading light. He continued to play with the sand, unbothered, his little fingers carefully shaping the corners of his castle. It was as if he were untouched by the same darkness that now gripped me so tightly.

"Are you sure, darling?" I asked again, my voice trembling. He nodded without hesitation, his focus still on the sandpit, as though the answer were so obvious it didn't warrant further discussion.

I swallowed hard, pulling him closer until his warmth pressed against me, a faint shield against the icy dread curling around my heart.

"Mummy. Did I do bad?" Sammy's words quivered, laden with a worry far too heavy for his young shoulders. His small face crumpled as he looked up at me, the tension radiating from me unmistakable despite my attempts to mask it.

My chest tightened, the fragility of this moment nearly breaking me. Emotion glistened behind my eyes as I pulled him into my arms, holding him close. His warmth was a balm, a fleeting respite from the storm raging inside me. "No, Sammy," I whispered, my voice trembling but resolute. "You did nothing wrong." My fingers combed gently through his curls, the familiar scent of his shampoo grounding me in the here and now.

The wind picked up, rustling the leaves of the old gum tree, its usually comforting whispers now laden with a strange foreboding. It sounded almost alive, the breeze twisting through its branches as if carrying secrets it couldn't quite articulate. I shivered involuntarily and held Sammy tighter, trying to shield him from the invisible menace pressing in on us.

"Did you see Daddy inside?" I asked, my words muffled as I pressed my lips to his soft hair.

Sammy shook his head against my chest, the motion small and silent but heavy with meaning. My heart sank further, the ache inside me spreading like ice. With one arm still wrapped protectively around my son, I fumbled in my pocket for my phone. My fingers felt clumsy as I dialled Nial's number, the screen's glow a harsh contrast against the dimming twilight.

The call went straight to voicemail again.

"Hi. This is Nial Triffett. I'm busy at the moment, but if you —"

I ended the call abruptly, the cheery tone of his recorded message striking me like a slap. It was a cruel echo of the man who should have been here, whose absence now felt like a gaping void.

As the screen dimmed, a flicker of movement at the far edge of the yard caught my attention. My head snapped up, my pulse spiking. My eyes scanned the darkening landscape, the trees standing like silent sentinels in the encroaching gloom. Was that a shadow moving between the trunks? Or had my mind conjured it, a phantom birthed from my growing paranoia?

"Mummy?" Sammy's small voice pulled me back, grounding me in his presence.

"Yes, sweetheart?" I murmured, pulling back just enough to meet his eyes. I searched his face, desperate for reassurance, for something to anchor me. His expression was innocent but shadowed with something deeper, something that didn't belong on the face of a child.

"Why did the man take Buffy away?"

Sammy's words struck like a thunderclap, tearing through the fragile remnants of calm I had been desperately clinging to. My breath caught, my grip tightening on his small shoulders as though I could anchor us both against the storm of fear swelling around us.

I pulled him closer, my eyes scanning the yard with frantic urgency. The gum trees loomed tall and menacing, their shadows stretching out like grasping fingers in the fading light. The rustle of leaves and the faint hum of distant traffic felt suddenly oppressive, as though the world itself conspired to keep me on edge.

Could Sammy be right? Could someone have taken Buffy?

The thought coiled tightly in my chest, squeezing the air from my lungs. I gently nudged Sammy back, needing to see his face, to search his wide blue eyes for answers. Those eyes, so much like Nial's, gazed back at me with a blend of innocence and something darker – a shadow that no child so young should carry.

"What man?" I asked, my voice trembling despite my efforts to keep it steady. My heart was racing, each beat loud and jarring, but I forced myself to focus on Sammy. I needed answers, but more than that, I needed to protect him, to shield him from the growing darkness that seemed intent on consuming our lives.

Sammy's bottom lip quivered, his small shoulders lifting in a shrug that conveyed both uncertainty and fear. "The man with the funny colours," he said at last, his words barely audible over the whisper of the wind through the gum leaves.

The funny colours?

The phrase was innocent enough, yet it sent a chill down my spine. My thoughts raced, piecing together fragments of an increasingly nightmarish puzzle. A stranger had been here, taken our dog, and now this – Nial's ransacked office, his missing laptop, the open back door. Everything felt connected, threads weaving into a picture I couldn't yet see, but whose outline was already too terrifying to contemplate.

"What do you mean by funny colours, sweetheart?" I asked softly, smoothing his hair with a trembling hand. My voice was calm, soothing even, but inside I was unravelling. I clung to Sammy's words like a lifeline, desperate for anything that might make sense of the impossible.

Sammy furrowed his brow, his face scrunching in concentration. Under different circumstances, the expression might have been adorable, but now it only heightened the tension clawing at my chest. "Like... like the rainbow, Mummy," he said after a moment. "They came from his hands, just like Spiderman."

A shiver ran down my spine, icy and relentless, as his words sank in. *Colours from his hands? Like Spiderman?* My rational mind recoiled, struggling to process what he was saying. *Was he describing some kind of light? A trick of his imagination, perhaps? Or – and this thought was the most unsettling of all – had Sammy seen something beyond my ability to comprehend?*

"Sammy," I said gently, my voice betraying the tight coil of dread building inside me. "Can you tell me more? What happened after the colours came from his hands?"

His eyes lit up, a mix of fear and excitement swirling in their depths. "It was so pretty, Mummy!" he exclaimed, his voice tinged with awe. "The colours made a big circle, like a door. And then..." His voice faltered, his brow knitting tightly as he struggled to find the words.

"And then what, sweetheart?" I prompted, my heart pounding so fiercely it felt as though it might burst from my chest.

"Then the man and Buffy went through the circle," Sammy whispered. His voice had dropped to a near-silent tremor. "And then they were gone."

Gone.

The word echoed in my mind, stark and final. My knees threatened to buckle beneath me as I knelt there, staring into Sammy's earnest face. A circle of light? A door? People disappearing into thin air? It was impossible. Unreal. Yet every fibre of my being told me Sammy was telling the truth.

The gravity of what he'd witnessed – what *we* might now be caught in – settled over me like a leaden cloak. This wasn't just a break-in or a missing dog. It wasn't even about Nial anymore, at least not in the way I'd thought.

This was something else.

Something otherworldly.

A chill rippled down my spine as my thoughts raced back to Sammy's nightmares—the ones that had robbed us both of sleep for months. His frightened whispers, the chilling descriptions of shadows lurking in corners, the voices he said came from the dark—all of it seemed to converge in this moment. *Could it all be connected?*

Dr Carmichael's face resurfaced in my mind, his brow furrowed, his words careful and measured. "Unprecedented," he'd said. "Unconventional approaches." Had he known more than he let on? Had he suspected that Sammy's nightmares were more than the usual terrors of childhood? The thought turned my stomach, my breath catching as I struggled to make sense of it all.

"Mummy," Sammy's small, uncertain voice broke through the storm of my thoughts. "The colours were like in my dreams. But not scary this time. Pretty."

My heart ached at the contrast in his words—so innocent, yet so laden with implications that I couldn't comprehend. Sammy's dreams, the ones that had stolen our peace and driven us to seek help, were no longer just figments of his imagination. They were spilling over into our waking world, intertwining with events that defied logic or reason.

How was I supposed to protect him from something I couldn't name, couldn't understand? How could I fight against shadows and colours, against a force that seemed to slip through the cracks of reality itself?

"Sammy, sweetie," I said, forcing a steady calm into my voice, though inside I was trembling. "We're going to go inside now, okay? It's getting cold out here."

He nodded, his trust in me absolute, even as I faltered under its weight. I scooped him into my arms, his small body pressing against mine. His warmth should have been a comfort, but instead, it only magnified the cold dread settling in my chest. He felt heavier than usual, though I knew it wasn't him. It was the crushing weight of my fears, of the unknowable threat that loomed ever closer.

As I turned toward the house, movement at the edge of the yard snagged my attention. My heart stuttered, my breath catching as my eyes locked onto a shadow—darker than the fading light of dusk—slipping between the trees at the property's edge. It was too fluid, too deliberate to be the wind.

My arms tightened protectively around Sammy.

"What is it, Mummy?" he asked, his voice small but laced with curiosity and concern.

I forced a smile, praying it didn't betray the fear coiling in my stomach. "Nothing, darling. Just the wind in the trees," I lied, my voice calm but brittle.

Even as the words left my mouth, I knew they were hollow. It wasn't the wind. Something—or someone—was out there, watching. The weight of its gaze pressed against me, intangible but undeniable, setting every nerve on edge.

I moved toward the house with measured steps, fighting the overwhelming urge to run. Every instinct screamed at me to flee, but I couldn't risk panicking Sammy—or drawing the attention of whatever was out there.

The back door loomed ahead, still yawning wide open, an unguarded portal that now felt like an accusation. How had I let this happen? How had I failed to notice the danger creeping into the very heart of our home?

Crossing the threshold, I kicked the door shut with more force than I intended. I twisted the deadbolt firmly into place, the sharp click momentarily satisfying.

But it wasn't enough.

I stood there, staring at the locked door, my hand still gripping the cold metal. The familiar contours of our home, the place that had always been our sanctuary, now felt violated and exposed. The danger wasn't just out there—it had already been here. It had crossed the line between the world outside and the one I thought I could control.

And I had no idea how to stop it.

UNEXPECTED VISITOR

4338.209.6

The darkness pressed heavily against the living room window as I stood there, my reflection faintly visible in the glass. Outside, the winter night had taken full hold, its deep shadows swallowing the landscape. The dim glow of a streetlamp down the road barely illuminated the edges of the scene, casting long, wavering shadows that seemed to stretch endlessly into the early night. I closed my eyes for a moment, the chill of the glass against my fingertips grounding me in the oppressive stillness. The absence of light mirrored the hollowness in my chest—a stark reminder of the normality that had once defined my life, now lost to the encroaching uncertainty of the dark.

The faint chill of the winter evening seeped through the weatherboards, nipping at my skin despite the supposed sanctuary of the house. I wrapped my arms around myself, a futile attempt to chase away the cold that was more internal than external. Every creak of the house, every distant rustle of wind, seemed magnified, feeding the unease that coiled tighter with each passing second.

And then it came—the sound of tyres crunching on gravel.

My breath caught, the soft hum of an engine outside slicing through the quiet like a blade. I froze, heart lurching painfully in my chest as hope surged, bright and immediate, only to clash against the darker possibilities lurking in the shadows of my mind.

"That was quick," I murmured, my voice thin and unsteady. Relief flickered through me, though it felt fragile, like it might shatter under the weight of my fears.

The flu outbreak had exposed Hobart's fragile infrastructure, highlighting cracks that were evident even in calmer times. Ambulance "ramping"—a problem that plagued the city regardless of emergencies—had become a nightly feature on the news, with harrowing stories of frantic families waiting hours for care in overcrowded hospitals. The strain rippled through every corner of the city's emergency services, with police often called in to assist stretched paramedics or handle the fallout of overcrowded facilities. Resources were stretched thin, and tensions ran high. Yet, despite the chaos, I clung to a sliver of hope that someone—anyone—might still take Nial's disappearance seriously. The thought that, even amidst this localised crisis, the police might prioritise finding him offered a small, flickering beacon in the looming darkness.

Adrenaline surged as I hurried toward the door. Reaching for the doorknob, my gaze briefly caught my reflection in the hallway mirror. The woman staring back at me was a stranger. My skin was pale, my cheeks hollowed by worry. My once-bright eyes were dulled, haunted by too many unanswered questions.

I drew in a deep breath, straightening my posture. There was no room for weakness now, not with Sammy depending on me, not with the unknown waiting just beyond this door. I gripped the doorknob firmly, the metal cold against my skin.

This was it.

I turned the knob, the motion smooth but heavy with anticipation, and pulled the door open.

The verandah creaked beneath my feet, its familiar groan taking on an almost accusatory tone in the cool evening air. The sky had deepened into a dusky grey, a canvas that seemed to mirror my growing sense of unease. And then, there she was—Rowena.

The driver's side door swung open, and my breath caught as the sleek black stiletto emerged, its glossy surface catching the faint glow of the porch light. The leg that followed was elegantly wrapped in leather trousers that clung like a second skin, the kind of outfit that would turn heads at Salamanca on a Saturday night. But here, in the quiet suburbs, it was so out of place it felt like a statement. A warning, even.

As her second stiletto touched the uneven gravel, Rowena's footing wavered. Her perfectly manicured hand gripped the car door for support, her red nails gleaming like blood against the black paint. "Shit," she muttered, the expletive slicing through the evening air with an unapologetic sharpness.

The car door slammed shut, the sound reverberating down the empty street. I flinched, glancing instinctively towards the neighbouring houses, half-expecting curtains to twitch or porch lights to flicker on. But the street remained quiet, the houses blind to the small drama unfolding on my driveway.

"Jenny. Darling," Rowena called out, her tone dripping with that particular mix of affection and condescension that only she could manage. She strode towards me with the confidence of a runway model, her Prada purse swinging from her wrist like a prop. Even in the dim light, her blonde hair gleamed, styled with a precision that bordered on military discipline. Her makeup was immaculate, the kind of effort that screamed she was ready for an audience, regardless of the stage.

I forced a smile, though it felt brittle, as though it might crack under the weight of everything I was holding back. "Hey, Mum," I said, the words stiff and awkward. I hadn't called her 'Mum' in years—it had always been Rowena, a name she insisted on, as if the title of 'Mum' diminished her somehow. Tonight, though, the word slipped out, an unintentional crack in my armour.

Rowena's sharp eyes swept over me, her critical gaze missing nothing. The faint furrow of her brow told me all I needed to know. I was too pale, my clothes too casual, my hair too undone. I braced myself for the inevitable commentary.

"You really must do something about that driveway," she said, gesturing with a dismissive wave at the gravel. "I nearly broke my ankle just now. Honestly, Jenny, it's like you're inviting the postman to sue."

I bit the inside of my cheek, willing myself to stay calm. "It's on Nial's to-do list," I replied, the words coming out sharper than I intended. Just saying his name made my chest tighten, the unresolved questions and growing fears rushing back in a flood. *Where was he? Why hadn't he called?*

Rowena arched a perfectly sculpted eyebrow, her expression hovering between curiosity and disdain. "Well, he ought to prioritise it," she said airily, as if my husband's hypothetical neglect of the driveway were the greatest crisis we were facing. "A proper driveway is the hallmark of a respectable home."

She stepped onto the verandah, her stilettos clicking against the wood. Her gaze shifted to the front of the house, lingering on the faded paint of the weatherboards, the chipped edges of the porch railings. I could practically hear her mental checklist forming, each imperfection another mark against my competence as a wife, a mother, a homeowner.

"It's a lovely little house, darling," she said, her tone suggesting the exact opposite. "But it could be so much more with a little effort. You've always had a tendency to let things slide, haven't you?"

I swallowed hard, my nails digging into the palm of my hand as I fought to keep my composure. "We've been busy, Rowena," I said, my voice tight. "Nial's been working nonstop, and Sammy's been... unwell."

Her expression softened, but only slightly. "Yes, I heard about poor Sammy," she said, her voice laced with a theatrical sympathy that set my teeth on edge. "It must be exhausting for you, juggling everything. You've always taken on so much, Jenny."

The words, meant to be comforting, felt like a subtle dig. I exhaled slowly, the tension in my shoulders mounting. "I'm managing," I said simply, unwilling to give her more ammunition.

Rowena reached out, her hand brushing lightly against my cheek. The gesture was almost tender, but it carried an undercurrent of something else—pity, perhaps, or control. "Well," she said, her tone brightening, "it's a good thing I'm here. You always did need a bit of guidance."

The effort it took to suppress an eye roll was Herculean, but the real battle was keeping the torrent of emotions inside me from spilling out entirely. Rowena had always had a way of disarming me, peeling back my defences with her sharp gaze and even sharper tongue. Tonight, with my already fragile composure, I felt as transparent as glass.

Her eyes narrowed, their usual glint of judgement replaced with something far more piercing—concern. Rowena's concern was a double-edged sword; when wielded, it cut through the walls I'd carefully built around myself. "Why is your lower lip trembling?" she asked, her tone direct, demanding an answer. There was no room for evasion in her voice.

I opened my mouth, but the words refused to come. How could I explain everything? The fear gnawing at me, the questions swirling like a storm, the dread that felt like a living thing coiled in my chest? My voice failed me, leaving only silence to speak for my turmoil.

"Tell me. Is it Sammy? Is he hurt?" Rowena pressed, her concern now tinged with an urgency that only a grandmother's love could summon. For all her faults, her love for Sammy had always been genuine, fierce, and unwavering.

A single tear betrayed me, escaping before I could blink it away, its warmth burning against my cheek. Rowena's sharp eyes caught it instantly, her expression shifting into something even more determined.

"I saw that," she said, her voice sharp but charged with unmistakable concern. Before I could stop her, she swept past me, her heels clicking decisively against the floor. "Sammy! Sammy, my child. Where are you?" Her voice rang through the house, breaking the heavy silence with its commanding presence.

I rubbed my temple, feeling the dull throb of a headache beginning to bloom. The events of the day had been enough to stretch me to breaking point—Nial's unexplained absence, the strange events surrounding Sammy, the gnawing sense that we were teetering on the brink of something I couldn't quite name. And now, Rowena, in all her well-meaning but overwhelming glory, had arrived to upend what little balance I had left.

"Why now?" I muttered under my breath, trying to steady myself. I'd already told her we'd visit next weekend, and I couldn't fathom why she had ignored that entirely. Taking a deep breath, I followed her into the house, the click of her heels echoing ahead of me like a countdown to the inevitable barrage of questions and unsolicited advice.

"Sammy's fine, Rowena," I called out, trying to temper the urgency in her voice. My own voice sounded thin and strained, even to my ears. "He's playing with his play-dough in the dining room." The words fell heavily, weighed down by everything I wasn't saying. I moved toward the sound of her clicking heels, each step feeling like a trek toward an ambush.

Moments later, Rowena's perfectly painted face appeared in the dining room doorway, her expression triumphant. "I know," she said, her wide grin both dazzling and exasperating. "I found him." Her voice carried a note of satisfaction, as though her ability to locate her grandson was a monumental achievement.

Steeling myself, I stepped into the dining room. Sammy sat at the table, engrossed in shaping a blob of green play-dough. His small hands worked the dough with focus, oblivious to the tension in the room. Rowena, on the other hand, immediately turned her laser-sharp attention to me. Her eyes, so much like my own, zeroed in on my face, her expression shifting from delight to something more calculating.

"So," she began, her voice a mixture of concern and curiosity, "what is your problem, dear?" The question wasn't cruel, but it was uncomfortably direct, cutting through my attempts to mask my unease.

I hesitated, the weight of her scrutiny pressing down on me. How could I even begin to answer that question? Where would I start? Everything felt like a problem—Nial's absence, Sammy's strange behaviour, the ominous shadow of something bigger lurking just out of sight. But Rowena's gaze demanded a response, and I knew I wouldn't escape her interrogation unscathed.

I took a deep breath, willing myself to remain calm, but the words came out sharper than I intended. "Nial has gone missing," I said, the weight of the admission pressing heavily on my chest. Hearing it spoken aloud made it feel disturbingly real, like pulling a secret from the shadows into the stark, unrelenting light. The room seemed to chill, the air thick with unspoken questions and the creeping unease that had been building all day.

"Missing?" Rowena echoed, her voice tinged with incredulity as her perfectly arched eyebrows shot up. "What on earth do you mean, 'missing'?"

I swallowed hard, trying to organise the jumble of fears and half-formed thoughts swirling in my head. "He went to work this morning, and I haven't heard from him since. His phone goes straight to voicemail." The words spilled out in a rush, a torrent of anxiety and dread I could no longer contain. Saying it made it real, but it also left me feeling exposed, vulnerable.

Rowena's response came swiftly, her tone brisk, almost dismissive. "Well, that's hardly unusual, is it? He's a busy man with clients to manage. You've always said he gets caught up in his work."

Her words landed like a slap, stinging and unwelcome. Dismissing my fears with a casual wave of her manicured hand, she seemed oblivious to the weight of the situation. I opened my mouth to argue but hesitated, considering her point. Yes, it wasn't out of character for Nial to miss calls when working. But this wasn't the same. Today was a Saturday. Today was Sammy's doctor's appointment. I couldn't shake the images in my mind: the missing laptop, the missing dog, Sammy's story about the strange man. It all pointed to something far more disturbing than a mere client meeting.

"This time feels different," I said, my voice rising involuntarily, the strain cracking through my usual composure. I drew a steadying breath, forcing myself to continue. "There are... other things. There are things missing from his office. Buffy is gone. Sammy said—" I cut myself off, unsure how much to reveal, even to her.

Rowena's sharp gaze fixed on me, her lips pressing into a thin line. "Different?" she pressed, her voice low but insistent. "How, Jenny? You're not making any sense."

I hesitated, the enormity of what I wanted to say catching in my throat. How could I explain what I couldn't yet fully understand myself? The fragments of truth I'd pieced together felt fragile, like they would shatter under the weight of her scepticism. "I—I don't know how to explain it. It's just... a feeling. Something's wrong."

"Feelings," Rowena scoffed, mimicking my uncertainty with exaggerated disdain. "Umm, I don't know. Something's wrong." She rolled her eyes dramatically, her impatience bristling. "Jenny, if you want me to take this seriously, you're going to have to do better than that."

I clenched my fists at my sides, frustration bubbling to the surface. "I'm telling you, Rowena, something isn't right! He's taken things from his office, and Buffy is missing." My pulse thundered in my ears as I met her unyielding stare.

Her reaction was instantaneous. "I knew it!" she declared, her voice triumphant. She jabbed a finger into the air as if she'd solved a puzzle no one else could see. "I always knew that man was no good for you!"

"Rowena, stop it!" I snapped, my voice trembling with anger and a flicker of guilt. The fierce protectiveness I felt for Nial rose up unbidden, even as doubts nibbled at the edges of my thoughts. "You love Nial," I added, my voice softening as I tried to appeal to her better nature. "Remember?"

Rowena's sharp features softened momentarily, her expression shifting to something more thoughtful. But then her jaw tightened, her eyes hardening. "Even people you love can do terrible things," she said firmly, her voice heavy with conviction. The chill in her tone sent a shiver down my spine, and I found myself wondering what past wounds she was referencing, what ghosts from her own life might be influencing her reaction.

Before I could respond, she turned towards the kitchen. "Enough of this," she said, waving a hand as if to dismiss the topic entirely. "I'll make us a pot of tea."

I let out a shaky sigh, recognising the futility of arguing with her when she was in this mood. Her presence was as much a storm as a solace, and I needed to conserve my energy for what lay ahead. At least tea would offer a brief moment of reprieve, however fleeting.

Lost in the whirlpool of my thoughts, I stared out the dining room window, my eyes unfocused on the dimming world outside. The winter twilight had deepened, blanketing the garden in murky shadows that twisted and shifted with every passing moment. Was that a figure at the edge of the property, slipping between the trees? Or just the capricious play of fading light and my overactive imagination? My chest tightened with the weight of unanswered questions. What if Nial was in trouble? What if he had left us? What if…?

The sharp, shrill whistle of the kettle shattered the loop of my spiralling thoughts, dragging me back to the here and now. The sound, though jarring, was almost comforting in its routine, a rare thread of normality in a day that felt like it had spun wildly out of control.

"Do sit down, would you," Rowena's voice broke through next, firm but laced with an undercurrent of concern. Her tone carried the unique mix of authority and care that only she could muster. The soft clink of a saucer meeting the benchtop punctuated her words. I turned towards her, watching her flit about the kitchen with an ease born of countless hours spent playing hostess. Despite her impeccable outfit and manicured nails, she moved with the precision of someone accustomed to orchestrating perfection, even amid disarray.

My gaze dropped to my phone, still clenched tightly in my hand, its screen blank and accusing. No calls. No texts. No updates. I let out a shaky sigh, the faint huff of my breath fogging the screen momentarily. *Am I just being paranoid?* The thought twisted uncomfortably in my mind, but I couldn't shake the growing certainty that something was deeply, irreparably wrong. Resigned, I placed the phone face down on the table and sank into one of the padded dining chairs.

Rowena approached with a porcelain teacup balanced gracefully in her hands. She placed it before me, the soft chime of ceramic on wood reverberating in the room. "Thank you," I murmured, my voice subdued, offering her a faint smile that felt as hollow as the reassurance I kept trying to give myself. As she stirred a dash of milk into her own cup, the swirling patterns reminded me of my own unsettled emotions – a chaotic blend of fear, doubt, and frustration.

"You know," Rowena began, her tone measured but probing, "you could have told me if things weren't going well between you and Nial."

The words hit me like a slap, their bluntness drawing my attention away from the tea in front of me. I blinked, startled, before fixing her with a sharp look. "We *are* doing fine," I replied quickly, too quickly, the defensiveness in my voice betraying me. Even as I said it, though, a part of me wondered if she was right. *Were we really fine? Had I been blind to something festering beneath the surface?*

Rowena tilted her head, her skeptical gaze boring into me. "Then why is he gone?" she pressed, her question as precise as a needle puncturing my thinly stretched composure.

Heat rose in my cheeks, my frustration bubbling dangerously close to the surface. "I… uhh…" I stammered, floundering for a response that could make sense of the thoughts swirling in my mind. How could I explain the inexplicable? The strange events of the day? Sammy's cryptic words about a man with "funny colours"? The empty office, the missing dog? It all sounded too bizarre, too detached from reality to share, even with my mother.

As I struggled to find the words, a sharp knock at the front door cut through the tension, echoing loudly through the house. The sound jolted me upright, my heart leaping into my throat. Relief and dread collided in an instant – could it be Nial? Or the police, finally responding to my frantic call?

"I'll get it," I blurted, grateful for the interruption. The chair scraped noisily against the floor as I pushed it back and rose to my feet. Without waiting for Rowena to respond, I strode quickly from the room, eager to escape her pointed gaze and the suffocating conversation.

The hallway felt longer than usual, each step carrying the weight of expectation and fear. As I reached the door, I hesitated, my fingers hovering over the doorknob. The knocking had been firm but not frantic – a good sign, surely? Swallowing hard, I squared my shoulders and turned the knob, bracing myself for whatever – or whoever – awaited on the other side.

OFFICIAL DISBELIEF

4338.209.7

As the door swung open, the crisp Tasmanian air swept in, bringing with it the unmistakable scent of impending rain, sharp and clean, but laced with something discordant – cigarette smoke and a cloying hint of perfume. The combination was jarring, out of place in the familiar stillness of our suburban street, and it immediately set my nerves on edge.

The porch light flickered uncertainly, casting its pale glow over the figure standing before me. I blinked, momentarily caught off guard by the sight. It wasn't the burly, seasoned detective I had imagined but a young policewoman, her appearance stark against the backdrop of the dimly lit street. Her uniform was impeccable, every crease and button in place, and her posture rigid, exuding an air of authority. Yet, it was her eyes that struck me the most – piercing and devoid of warmth, scanning me with an intensity that felt almost intrusive.

"Mrs Triffett?" she asked, her voice clipped and businesslike, each syllable carefully measured. There was no softness to her tone, no hint of reassurance. It was as if she had already decided that this was a routine call, one that didn't merit much of her attention.

"Ahh... yes, that's me," I replied, my voice faltering slightly. Caught off guard by her brusqueness, I instinctively straightened my posture, smoothing my sweater as though preparing for a school inspection rather than speaking to an officer.

"You called about your husband, Nial Triffett?" she continued, her expression remaining serious, almost severe. Her eyes seemed to pierce through me, assessing, questioning. *Did she think I was overreacting? That I was wasting police time? Or worse, that I was hiding something?*

"Yes," I answered quickly, the knot of anxiety in my stomach tightening. Relief that someone had come battled with a gnawing unease at the detached tone in her voice. As she spoke, doubts crept into my mind. Had I been too hasty in calling the police? What if they didn't take me seriously? Or worse, what if they suspected *me*?

"And you believe he's missing?" The words, though straightforward, felt weighted, as though she were already questioning my judgment. I nodded, swallowing hard against the lump in my throat, but before I could elaborate, I caught sight of the second officer stepping out of the car.

He was younger, his movements less assured than his colleague's, but what struck me most was the clinging scent of his cologne – overpowering and cheap. It was a scent I instinctively disliked, one that seemed to carry stories of late nights and ill-advised choices. He said nothing, his presence more a shadow than a tangible part of the interaction.

"Please, come in," I offered, stepping aside and gesturing towards the hallway. My voice wavered slightly, the forced hospitality masking my apprehension. The officers stepped inside, their boots heavy on the polished floorboards, each step reverberating through the quiet house and amplifying the tension in the air.

As we entered the dining room, Rowena looked up sharply from her tea, her reaction immediate and almost theatrical. Her eyes widened in surprise, but there was a gleam there – a mix of curiosity and barely contained excitement. I knew that look all too well. This was not just a police visit to her; it was *entertainment*, a new chapter in the ongoing saga of her daughter's life.

"Oh," she exclaimed, the single syllable loaded with unspoken questions. Her expression was that of a socialite stumbling into an unexpected bit of drama at a dinner party. I shot her a warning glance, silently willing her to hold her tongue. The last thing I needed was for her to turn this fraught situation into a spectacle.

"Mother!" I hissed under my breath, the edge in my voice unmistakable. Her reaction was as maddeningly predictable as it was infuriating – a serene smile that barely concealed her delight at being involved in something so intriguingly out of the ordinary.

"Watch Sammy for me, would you?" I asked, the words a polite veneer over my simmering frustration. My tone was calm, but inside, I was a knot of frayed nerves, each one pulled tighter by her presence.

Rowena tilted her head, her lips curving into a dramatic pout. "Please," she prompted sweetly, her voice dripping with saccharine expectation. Even now, in the midst of uncertainty, she couldn't resist asserting her authority, making me dance to her tune.

I sighed, feeling the weight of the day pressing down on me. "Please, Rowena," I added through gritted teeth, the concession stinging more than it should have.

Her smile broadened, the satisfaction of her small victory clear in her expression. "Of course," she replied airily, her tone magnanimous as though she were granting me a great favour. She rose gracefully, teacup in hand, and sauntered towards the dining room door, pausing briefly to glance over her shoulder. "You've got this under control, dear. Do let me know if you need help explaining things."

Her parting comment was delivered with a casualness that belied its barbed nature, and I clenched my fists at my sides, biting back a retort. At least she was leaving us be, for now.

My teeth clenched, but I forced myself to keep walking, leading the officers away from her persistent needling. The last thing I wanted was for her to overshadow this already stressful moment with her relentless commentary. "This way, please," I said evenly, gesturing for them to follow me into the relative sanctuary of the living room. Behind us, I could hear Rowena bustling about in the kitchen, her tone entirely too upbeat for the situation at hand.

"I'll put the kettle on and make some tea. What would you like? Peppermint? Chamomile?" Her overly cheerful voice carried through the house, her obliviousness to the gravity of the moment grating on my frayed nerves.

"Rowena!" The word shot out of me before I could stop it, sharp and unfiltered. My frustration bled into every syllable. "This isn't a social visit! Nial is missing. They're not here for tea!" My outburst hung in the air, startling even me. I rarely snapped at Rowena – not because she didn't deserve it, but because it never made a difference.

There was a beat of silence before she responded, her tone a mix of injured pride and forced magnanimity. "Well, I'm only trying to help, Jenny. Someone around here has to keep things civilised."

I inhaled deeply, willing myself to let it go. There was no point in escalating the tension. "Please, have a seat," I said to the officers, gesturing toward the sofa and armchair. I moved to close the white, wooden French doors behind us, a small but significant gesture of control. It was a temporary reprieve from Rowena's unsolicited commentary, a fragile bubble of privacy in a house that felt anything but private.

Turning back to the officers, I felt a rush of embarrassment, the flush creeping up my neck and warming my cheeks. "I'm so sorry about my mother," I said, my voice quieter now, more measured. "She really can't help herself." The apology felt inadequate, a meagre attempt to explain the complexities of a lifetime of managing Rowena's larger-than-life personality.

The younger officer, who had been shifting uncomfortably since we entered the room, let out a soft chuckle. "It's okay, ma'am," he said, his tone light, the hint of a smile softening his features. "I've seen worse." His attempt to ease the tension was almost endearing, a brief moment of humanity amidst the heavy atmosphere.

But the female officer was less forgiving. She cleared her throat, the sound precise and sharp, cutting through the moment like a scalpel. Her expression remained professional, her eyes flicking briefly to her partner as if to remind him of their purpose.

The young man's smile faltered under her gaze, and he quickly composed himself, nodding in silent acknowledgment. The room settled into an uneasy stillness, the momentary levity replaced by the weight of the reason for their visit.

I lowered myself onto the edge of the armchair, my hands clasped tightly in my lap as I prepared to recount the details of Nial's disappearance. My stomach churned, a mix of fear and hope tangling together. I wanted answers, but the thought of what those answers might reveal filled me with dread.

"Mrs. Triffett," Langley began, her voice firm but kind, though the formal address grated against my already fraying nerves. There was a flicker of understanding in her expression, a softening that hinted at empathy beneath her professional exterior.

"Jenny," I interrupted, my voice firm despite the turmoil within. "Please, call me Jenny." Somehow, the formality of

"Mrs. Triffett" felt too detached, as though it referred to a woman untouched by worries. I needed this to feel personal, grounded – not another procedural case on a growing list.

The officer paused, then offered a small, almost apologetic smile. "Of course, Jenny," she said, her tone gentler now. "Thank you. I'm Officer Langley, and this is Officer Cribthorpe. Why don't you start by telling us about your husband?"

The weight of her request pressed down on me as I perched on the edge of the sofa, my hands clasped tightly in my lap to stop them from trembling. The room, already too warm from the heat pump humming on the far wall, seemed to shrink around me. Each breath felt heavier, my lungs working harder to pull in the salty Hobart air mingled with faint traces of my mother's floral perfume and the unfamiliar tang of leather from the officers' gear.

"Well... umm..." My voice wavered, faltered. The enormity of everything I needed to say loomed before me like a tidal wave, threatening to swallow me whole. How could I convey the growing sense of dread, the gut-wrenching fear that had been my constant companion all day?

Langley leaned forward slightly, her hand brushing against mine in a gesture that startled me with its warmth. It wasn't just physical warmth – it carried a subtle assurance, a reminder that I wasn't alone in this, that someone was listening. "It's okay, Jenny," she said, her voice soft yet steady. "Take your time."

I nodded, drawing a deep, shaky breath, my fingers curling tighter around each other. "Nial left this morning," I began, my voice quiet but gaining strength with each word. "He was supposed to meet someone about a potential job. He said it might be with a past client, but... I haven't seen or heard from him since." Saying it aloud gave the events a terrible finality, as though speaking the words cemented them as truth.

Langley's pen moved across her notebook with quick precision, the scratch of ink against paper a strangely grounding sound. Across from her, Cribthorpe's sharp gaze flitted over the room, lingering on the scattered toys under the coffee table, the family photos on the mantelpiece, the fine layer of dust clinging to the edges of the windowpane. I could almost see him piecing together a story from these details, though I doubted it would be the one I was trying to tell.

"Do you know where he went? Or who this person might have been?" Langley asked, her question direct but not unkind.

I shook my head slowly, shame and frustration pooling in my chest. "No," I admitted, my voice tinged with guilt. "He didn't say. He seemed... distracted after the phone call. Agitated, even." The memory of his expression – tight-lipped and preoccupied – flashed in my mind, filling me with regret that I hadn't pressed him for details.

Cribthorpe's posture straightened, his interest sharpening at my words. "You mentioned a phone call," he interjected, his tone probing. "Can you tell us more about that?"

I closed my eyes for a moment, willing my thoughts to focus. The phone call. The memory was there, shrouded in the haze of everything that had followed. "He took the call in the bedroom," I said slowly, piecing together fragments. "It wasn't long – a few minutes, maybe. I didn't hear much, just the tone of his voice. He sounded... tense. Almost annoyed. But I didn't ask him about it." My stomach twisted as I spoke, the admission of my complacency weighing heavily. "He didn't offer anything, and I didn't think to push."

Langley was about to speak when I cut in, a sudden recollection flooding my mind. "But," I said, pausing to gather my thoughts. The officers leaned in slightly, their attention sharpening, like hunters sensing movement in the underbrush. "Right after hanging up, I saw him staring at himself in the bathroom mirror. He looked... concerned, like he was unsure whether he should meet this person."

Langley's brow furrowed, and she threw a glance at Cribthorpe. It was subtle, but I caught it – a silent exchange, weighted with caution. I recognised that look from years of mediating student disputes. Be careful. There's more to this. Don't jump to conclusions.

"No!" The word burst from me, more forceful than I'd intended, but I needed to cut off the direction I knew their thoughts were heading. "I know what you're thinking," I said firmly, my voice edged with indignation and fear. "And that's not what's happening." My gaze flicked between the two of them, daring them to challenge me. The implication of their unspoken suspicions – that Nial might have chosen to leave rather than being taken – hung in the air like an unwelcome guest.

Langley adjusted her position slightly, crossing one leg over the other as she returned her focus to me. "And when was this phone call?" she asked, her tone measured but her eyes keen, scrutinising every detail of my response.

"Early this morning," I answered, wiping my clammy palms on my slacks. The room felt smaller, the air thicker, as if the weight of their expectations was physically pressing down on me. My pulse quickened as doubt crept in. *Were they already dismissing me as paranoid? Or worse, as someone with something to hide?*

"Have you tried calling him?" Cribthorpe's question was gentler, his tone laced with what I almost dared to interpret as sympathy.

"Yes," I replied, my voice trembling slightly. "Several times. But it just goes straight to voicemail." The memory of Nial's voicemail message – his cheerful voice, the familiar cadence – now felt like a cruel taunt.

"It sounds to me like he really doesn't want to be disturbed," Cribthorpe offered, the remark seeming both practical and dismissive. But his eyes betrayed him. There was a flicker of something – doubt? Curiosity? – that suggested he wasn't entirely convinced by his own words.

Langley cut him off before I could respond, her focus shifting to a more direct approach. "How are things in the bedroom? How's your intimacy? Anything that might raise concerns?" she asked, her tone unflinching, her gaze piercing.

The question landed like a slap, the intrusion into such a private area of my life both startling and humiliating. Cribthorpe's cheeks flushed a faint pink, and he shifted awkwardly on the couch, clearly as uncomfortable with the line of questioning as I was. Langley, however, was unmoved, her expression unreadable, her posture steady.

"Umm. No," I said, my voice faltering as I twirled a strand of hair around my finger, a nervous habit I hadn't indulged in for years. The room seemed to grow warmer, the air thicker, as if the walls themselves were leaning in to listen.

Cribthorpe seemed equally uncomfortable, shifting awkwardly on the couch and leaning back into it. His discomfort was almost palpable, a stark contrast to Langley's unflinching demeanour.

"We actually had sex this morning," I added, the words feeling foreign and too intimate for the situation. I forced a practiced smile, one I'd used countless times in theatre productions when masking true emotions. "And then he showered, and it was right after that he received the phone call."

Cribthorpe straightened abruptly, his posture changing as his hands settled into his lap. I resisted the urge to roll my eyes at the obviousness of his discomfort. Some men were so easily redirected, and though I hated playing into that, it felt necessary to shift the conversation back to where it belonged – to the fact that Nial was missing and something terrible might have happened to him.

Langley's pen hovered over her notebook for a moment before she resumed writing, her eyes narrowing slightly as she studied me. The silence in the room thickened, broken only by the faint clatter of dishes from the kitchen where Rowena was likely listening in, no doubt cataloguing every detail for future commentary.

"Jenny," Langley said finally, her voice softer now, almost reflective. "You've given us a lot to think about. Let's continue with the timeline. After the phone call, did you notice anything else unusual about Nial's behaviour?"

I exhaled slowly, feeling the tension shift ever so slightly. For the first time since this conversation began, it felt like they were truly listening – like they were beginning to see the pieces of the puzzle I was trying to assemble.

Unexpectedly, my phone vibrated loudly on the coffee table, its sharp buzz breaking through the tense quiet. Nial's name flashed across the screen, and a jolt of adrenaline surged through me. "Oh!" I gasped, snatching the phone as if it might vanish at any moment. My hands trembled as I unlocked the screen, hope battling fiercely with a suffocating fear.

I read the text silently, each word landing like a physical blow. "Oh," I whispered again, this time softer, the sound escaping involuntarily. My fingers loosened their grip, and the phone nearly slipped from my numb hands. It felt as though the ground beneath me had shifted, leaving me unsteady, reeling.

"Is Nial okay?" Langley's voice cut through the haze, sharp yet tinged with concern. Her gaze locked onto mine, piercing and unrelenting.

"I... I don't know," I stammered, my voice cracking under the weight of emotion. A lump in my throat made speaking almost impossible, and tears threatened to spill over. With a shaking hand, I passed the phone to Langley, who accepted it with a quiet nod. Her expression was inscrutable as she studied the screen, her brow furrowing ever so slightly.

Langley read the message aloud, her tone measured and professional, yet the words felt like a verdict being handed down. "'I'll be home late. Don't wait up for me. Nial.'" The message was simple, almost mundane, but in the context of everything that had happened, it carried an ominous weight.

Cribthorpe let out a low, uncomfortable sigh, the sound breaking the stillness like a crack in fragile glass. His gaze darted nervously between Langley and me, his unease palpable. The text seemed to reinforce their initial suspicions – that Nial had left of his own accord. Yet to me, it felt wrong, like a piece of a puzzle forced into the wrong place. The tone, the timing – everything about it felt off.

Langley handed the phone back to me, her expression unreadable as she rose to her feet with a sudden decisiveness. Her movements were brisk, almost mechanical, as though she'd already reached a conclusion. "I think we're done here," she said flatly, her words striking me like a slap.

"Done?" I repeated, disbelief colouring my voice. The finality of her tone made my chest tighten. How could we possibly be done? Nothing had been resolved. Nial was still out there, and Buffy was gone. My family was unravelling before my eyes, and now the people who were supposed to help were walking away. "But... but..." I stammered, struggling to find the words, my desperation growing with each passing second.

Langley turned to face me, her expression softening just a fraction as she raised an eyebrow. "But what, Jenny?" she prompted, though her tone made it clear she thought the matter closed.

"What about Buffy... the dog?" I blurted out, my voice trembling as I clung to this one remaining thread of hope. My mind scrambled for some way to make them understand the gravity of the situation. It wasn't just about a missing dog – it was another sign that something was terribly, terribly wrong.

Langley tilted her head, her lips pressing into a thin line. "Nial must have her," she said dismissively, as though the idea were obvious, as though it didn't matter.

The casualness of her response sent a surge of anger coursing through me. My frustration bubbled over, my voice rising with a mix of disbelief and desperation. "That's preposterous!" I snapped, my words spilling out before I could stop them. "Nial would never take Buffy without saying a word! It's completely out of character for him!"

Langley's face remained impassive, but there was a flicker of something in her eyes – doubt, perhaps, or irritation. Cribthorpe shifted uncomfortably, his hands fidgeting in front of him as if searching for something to anchor himself.

"He wouldn't," I continued, my voice trembling with emotion. "You don't understand. He loves that dog. He loves us. Something's wrong. I know it. I can feel it."

Langley's gaze lingered on me for a long moment, her expression unreadable. Finally, she inclined her head slightly, a small, almost imperceptible gesture. "We'll make a note of it," she said, her tone lacking the reassurance I so desperately needed.

As they moved towards the door, a heavy sense of defeat settled over me. My pleas had fallen on deaf ears, and the fragile hope I had clung to was slipping through my fingers like sand.

Langley paused at the front door, turning back to face me. Her expression was stern, her jaw set with the kind of resolve that suggested she had dealt with countless crises before. Yet in her eyes, there was a flicker of something else – doubt, perhaps, or a reluctant acknowledgment that this case might not fit neatly into the boxes she was accustomed to ticking.

"Jenny," she said firmly, the use of my first name landing somewhere between a gesture of compassion and an assertion of authority. "I think you had better contact your family lawyer."

Her words hit me like a physical blow, my breath hitching as the implications sank in. Contacting a lawyer meant we were crossing a line – moving from confusion and worry into something far more serious. It felt like a door closing on the hope that this was all just a misunderstanding. A sob escaped before I could suppress it, raw and jagged in the stillness of the hallway.

Langley's face softened slightly, her professional veneer cracking just enough to reveal the human beneath. She placed a hand on my shoulder, the gesture fleeting but sincere. "I'm sorry," she said, her voice gentler now, as if speaking to a wounded animal. "There really isn't anything more we can do right now."

"Please," I whispered, my voice barely audible as the tears spilled freely down my cheeks. They burned hot against my cold skin, each one carrying with it a piece of the fear and helplessness that had been building all day. "I *know* something's not right."

The moment hung heavy in the air, thick with unspoken truths and the weight of uncertainty. Cribthorpe shifted, stepping forward hesitantly, his youthful face betraying a mix of discomfort and genuine empathy. "Try to be a little patient," he said, his tone softer, almost apologetic. "Wait and see if he comes home later tonight."

His words, though well-meaning, felt like a knife twisting in my gut. Patience? How could I be patient when every instinct screamed that Nial was in danger? Still, I clung to his suggestion like a lifeline, desperate for any semblance of guidance.

"If he isn't home by tomorrow afternoon and you still can't reach him," Cribthorpe continued, glancing cautiously at Langley as he spoke, "come to the station. We might be able to trace the call he received or find out who he went to meet."

"Cribthorpe!" Langley snapped, her voice cutting through the air like a whip. She turned to him, her glare sharp and unyielding. The unspoken reprimand was clear: **Stick to procedure. Don't promise what we can't deliver.**

Cribthorpe straightened, his cheeks flushing slightly under his superior's glare. Yet despite her scolding, there was no regret in his eyes – only a quiet resolve that mirrored my own. In that moment, I felt a flicker of gratitude towards him, his small act of kindness a balm against the cold indifference of protocol.

I reached out impulsively, my trembling hands finding his. "Thank you," I murmured, my voice thick with emotion. The gesture surprised both of us, but I held his gaze, willing him to understand just how much his words meant to me. "Thank you."

He nodded, a faint, almost imperceptible smile touching his lips before he stepped back. Langley, her face remaining unreadable, turned briskly and opened the door, motioning for Cribthorpe to follow.

I stood in the doorway as they made their way to the patrol car, the cold Tasmanian air biting at my forlorn face. The streetlights cast pale halos across the front yard, their glow failing to reach the yawning shadows that seemed to creep closer with each passing moment. I watched as the car's taillights disappeared around the corner, taking with them not just the officers but what little sense of security their presence had provided.

When I finally closed the door, the sound of it latching shut echoed through the house, a hollow, lonely sound. The walls seemed to press in around me, the familiar space now feeling oppressive. Shadows stretched long and dark across the floor, shifting with each flicker of the overhead light.

The house was quiet, too quiet, every creak of the floorboards amplified in the silence. Each sound seemed imbued with sinister intent, a reminder that the threat I feared most was still lurking somewhere out there – unseen, unknown, and terrifyingly real.

The house seemed to hold its breath as I re-entered the living room. The room, once a sanctuary of love and laughter, now felt like a stranger. Shadows stretched ominously across the walls, their shapes flickering with the uncertain light from the floor lamp. What had once been warm and inviting was now unnervingly cold, as though the house itself had absorbed my fear.

Suddenly, the French doors burst open with a ferocity that sent my heart into my throat. I gasped, my hand flying to my chest as Rowena swept into the room, her entrance as dramatic as ever. Her hair, usually an immaculate frame around her face, was slightly dishevelled, and her eyes burned with an urgency that was entirely out of character.

"Oh, Mother!" The words tumbled out, my voice cracking under the weight of my mounting emotions. My tenuous grip on composure snapped like a fraying thread, and the shield of stoicism I'd been hiding behind crumbled to dust. All the fear, the uncertainty, and the suffocating dread I'd been holding back came rushing to the surface in an overwhelming flood.

My knees gave way, and the world tilted as I collapsed under the weight of it all. But before I could hit the floor, Rowena's arms were around me, pulling me close. It wasn't the brisk, no-nonsense embrace I might have expected, but something softer, more tender. Her hold, firm yet comforting, caught me off guard, and for a moment, I felt like a child again, clinging to her for safety in a storm I couldn't navigate alone.

"There, there," she murmured, her voice a soothing balm against the jagged edges of my grief. She stroked my hair with a gentle hand, the gesture stirring memories of scraped knees and tearful nights long ago. Back then, it had always felt fleeting, a moment of softness quickly replaced by criticism or distance. But now, her touch was unwavering, her presence solid in a way I hadn't experienced before.

"Nial will come home," she said with quiet conviction. "It'll all be alright." Her tone was firm, as though sheer will alone could bend the universe to her will. But her reassurances floated around me like smoke, impossible to grasp. My heart was too heavy, weighed down by the shadows of fear and doubt that had wrapped themselves tightly around it.

I buried my face in her shoulder, the scent of her Chanel No. 5 filling my senses. It was a fragrance steeped in memories—of childhood mornings watching her dress for the day, of evenings marked by sharp criticisms that came with a kiss on the forehead. Now, it was grounding, a strange tether to familiarity in a world spinning out of control.

"What if—" I tried to voice my darkest fear, but the words stuck in my throat, too painful to utter aloud.

"No 'what ifs'," Rowena interrupted, her voice firm and unyielding. She pulled back just enough to cup my face, her hands warm and steady against my tear-streaked skin. Her gaze, usually sharp with judgment, was soft yet resolute. "Don't go down that road, Jenny. Not now. Nial needs you to believe he'll come back. Sammy needs you to hold it together."

Her words, spoken with a rare depth of understanding, cut through the haze of my despair. For a moment, the roles between us shifted, the mother who so often expected strength from me now offering her own in return. Her determination was like a beacon, and I clung to it, desperate to borrow some of the confidence I couldn't muster on my own.

I clutched at her blouse, the fabric soft under my trembling fingers, and let myself lean into her. My sobs, muffled against her shoulder, came in waves, each one releasing a fraction of the weight that had been pressing down on me. In her embrace, I allowed myself to be vulnerable, to stop being the strong one, the pillar holding everything together. Just for a moment, I let myself be the daughter seeking solace from her mother.

Through my tears, I glimpsed something in Rowena I hadn't seen in years—maybe ever. A fierce, unshakable love, free of the usual barbs or expectations. For the first time in a long time, I felt the safety of her presence, a sanctuary in her arms that I hadn't realised I needed.

And though her words couldn't banish the gnawing fear in my chest, they planted the smallest seed of hope. Maybe she was right. Maybe I just needed to hold on a little longer. For Nial. For Sammy. For the family I was so desperate to keep whole.

4338.210

(29 July 2018)

THE WEIGHT OF ABSENCE

4338.210.1

I awoke with a start, my chest heaving as if I'd surfaced too quickly from the depths of a restless sleep. My heart raced, its frantic rhythm amplified by the suffocating silence of the early morning. "Sammy," I whispered, the name escaping my lips like a prayer, tinged with panic. The remnants of a nightmare I couldn't quite recall clung to my consciousness, their shadows threatening to pull me under again. A cold, irrational fear gripped me, the thought that Sammy, like Nial, might have vanished into the same inexplicable void.

For a few agonising seconds, I lay motionless, my breath caught in my throat as I strained to hear any sign of him. Then, through the haze of my dread, I felt it—a small, warm body curled tightly beside me. Relief crashed over me, so profound it left me trembling. Sammy was there, his back pressed against mine, his soft breathing steady and rhythmic. In sleep, he was a picture of innocence, his tiny frame unbothered by the chaos that had upended our world.

I rolled over carefully, afraid to disturb him, and wrapped my arm around his small form. The contact grounded me, his warmth a reassurance that, amidst the turmoil, I still had this. Still had him. I kissed the top of his head, the gesture instinctive, my lips brushing against the soft curls that smelled faintly of sandalwood. The scent was soothing, a balm against the jagged edges of my fear.

Sandalwood. The memory of Sammy's peculiar fondness for it rose unbidden, drawing a bittersweet smile to my lips. I could still picture the day he'd discovered it, his little finger pointing to the bottle on the supermarket shelf as if it held the secrets of the universe. "It's my favourite smell in the whole world!" he'd declared with conviction, long before he'd ever even taken a whiff. That bottle had come home with us, becoming a cornerstone of our bath-time rituals. Even now, the scent brought with it a fleeting sense of normality, a connection to the simpler times before Nial's disappearance had cast its long shadow over our lives.

But the comfort was fleeting. Sammy's peaceful slumber was a stark contrast to the pain etched into our days and nights. I thought of last evening, of the quiet ache in Sammy's voice as he asked why Daddy wasn't there to tuck him in. Nial's bedtime stories, his voice a soothing cadence of adventure and reassurance, were a fixture in Sammy's world. His absence had left a gaping hole, one I could never quite fill, no matter how many stories I read or kisses I gave.

A fresh wave of grief and worry welled up, tightening my throat. My hand instinctively reached for my phone on the bedside table, its cold surface a jarring contrast to the warmth of Sammy beside me. I tapped the screen, the harsh blue light slicing through the darkness and momentarily blinding me. Squinting against the glow, I scrolled through my notifications. My heart sank. No missed calls. No messages. Nothing. The silence from Nial was deafening, a void that seemed to echo with the worst possibilities.

With a heavy heart, I dialled his number again, the motion as automatic as breathing. The ringing on the other end felt endless, each tone a taunt, a cruel reminder of the distance between us. Then, as expected, his voicemail clicked on, the cheerful message cutting through the quiet.

"Hey, it's Nial. Sorry I missed your call. Leave a message and I'll get back to you as soon as I can. Cheers!"

The sound of his voice hit me like a punch to the gut, the casual warmth of it so achingly familiar yet completely out of sync with the situation. My throat tightened, and I had to swallow hard to keep from breaking down.

"Where are you, Nial?" I whispered into the void, my voice trembling with the weight of the question. It hung there, unanswered, mocking me. His voicemail, once a mundane part of daily life, now felt like a cruel relic of a man who seemed further away with each passing hour.

I ended the call, my hand falling limply to my side, the phone resting against the bedspread like a forgotten artefact. The darkness of the room pressed in around me, and I stared into it, feeling the tears pricking at the corners of my eyes. How had everything unravelled so quickly? Where had Nial gone, and why wasn't he coming back? The questions looped endlessly in my mind, their answers as elusive as the man himself.

Beside me, Sammy stirred slightly, his small hand brushing against mine in his sleep. I gripped it gently, holding on as if he were my lifeline in a storm I couldn't navigate. For his sake, I had to stay strong. But in the stillness of the night, with Nial's absence looming over me, it felt like an impossible task.

Lying in the semi-darkness, the first feeble light of dawn beginning to seep through the curtains, I felt trapped within the walls of my own mind. The questions spun endlessly, relentless and unyielding, each one pulling me deeper into a maze of doubt and self-recrimination. Had there been signs I'd overlooked? Moments I'd dismissed as trivial that were now screaming for attention?

I closed my eyes, conjuring Nial's face with painful clarity —his familiar features, the way his mouth twitched into that lopsided smile, the steady warmth in his eyes. But yesterday morning, as he stood in front of the bathroom mirror, there had been none of that warmth. His reflection had seemed distant, almost like a man looking at a stranger. At the time, I'd barely noticed, distracted by the bustle of the morning routine. But now, that image loomed large in my memory, impossible to ignore. What had he been thinking? What had weighed so heavily on his mind?

The chill of self-doubt crept in. *Was Nial unhappy?* The question struck a chord of fear deep within me, a fear that grew louder with each unanswered call and empty moment. I searched frantically through the archives of our marriage, replaying conversations, fleeting glances, unspoken words. Had I missed something? Had my busy schedule—work commitments, late nights rehearsing for the school musical, countless hours at the community theatre—built an invisible wall between us?

I thought of our date nights, the quiet evenings watching TV after Sammy had gone to bed, the family trips to the beach where Nial and Sammy would build sandcastles while Buffy raced through the waves. They weren't grand gestures, but they were *ours*. A patchwork of moments that formed the life we'd built together. *We were happy. Weren't we?*

No. This wasn't about unhappiness. It couldn't be. Nial adored Sammy; anyone could see that. He wasn't the kind of man who would just walk away, not from his son, not from the bond they shared. And if there was one thing I was sure of, it was that Nial wasn't having an affair. He wasn't capable of that kind of betrayal—not the Nial I knew, the Nial who'd built our life brick by brick with care and devotion.

And Buffy. The thought of her absence gnawed at me, another piece of this fractured puzzle that refused to fit. If Nial had left willingly, he wouldn't have taken her. He knew how much she meant to Sammy, how inseparable they were. Buffy had been more than a pet; she was a guardian, a sister, a constant presence in Sammy's life from the moment we brought him home from the hospital. I could still see her, tail wagging softly as she nuzzled the bundle of blankets in my arms, her gentle instincts immediately attuned to the tiny life we'd introduced to her world.

But Sammy's words from last night sent fresh chills coursing through me. "The man with the funny colours took Buffy." Who was he talking about? His voice had been calm, almost matter-of-fact, as if it were the most natural thing in the world. My mind twisted itself in knots trying to reconcile the innocence of Sammy's description with the dark implications.

Who was this man?

I replayed the fragments of the previous day in my mind like a movie stuck on repeat. The ordinary moments—Nial's kiss on my forehead before getting out of bed, the brief, distracted exchange about his day ahead, the humdrum rhythm of getting Sammy ready—all seemed so unremarkable at the time. Yet now they felt laden with unseen significance, their ordinariness masking something ominous.

Had Nial been trying to tell me something in those moments? A coded message in his lingering look? An unspoken plea in the way his hands had rested on my shoulders? The more I thought about it, the more convinced I became that I had missed something vital. A clue. A warning.

The questions gnawed at me, relentless in their persistence. Each one opened a darker doorway in my mind, filled with possibilities I didn't want to confront. *Was Nial in danger? Had he stumbled into something he couldn't handle? And what about Sammy and me? Were we safe?* My stomach twisted at the thought, the protective instinct within me flaring to life.

I glanced over at Sammy, his small frame rising and falling in the rhythm of peaceful sleep. I stroked his hair gently, my fingers brushing against the soft curls. The innocence of his slumber was a sharp contrast to the disturbance in my mind, a fragile reminder of what I was fighting for. I needed answers—for him, for us.

Quietly, I eased out of bed, careful not to disturb Sammy. His small body shifted slightly as I tucked the blanket snugly around him, his hands clutching the edges instinctively, seeking warmth and comfort. He murmured softly in his sleep, the sound so innocent, so achingly unaware of the storm brewing around us. In that moment, I envied him—envied his ability to escape into dreams, to remain untouched by the fears that pressed down on me like a suffocating weight. If only I could shield him forever, cocoon him in this bubble of innocence.

With a sigh, I reached for my pink-framed glasses and slipped them on, the blurred edges of the world snapping into clarity. The sight of my bathrobe, draped neatly over the chair, brought a bittersweet pang to my chest. Its hibiscus pink fabric, still as soft as the day Nial had given it to me, felt like a relic from another life—a time when my biggest worry was planning our next anniversary dinner. I wrapped it around myself tightly, as if its embrace could stand in for Nial's arms, could offer the reassurance I so desperately needed.

At the mirror, I paused, taking in the reflection that greeted me. The woman staring back was unrecognisable. Her eyes, swollen and rimmed with red, betrayed a night spent wrestling with fears too monstrous to name. Dark shadows hung beneath them, matching the pallor of her skin. Her blonde hair, usually neat and glossy, was a dishevelled tangle, strands sticking out like they, too, were rebelling against this new, fractured reality.

I traced my reflection's shoulder lightly with trembling fingers, as though trying to offer comfort to the woman I saw there. But it felt hollow, meaningless. "Oh, Nial," I whispered, the words cracking in the stillness. "Where are you? What's happened to you?" My voice sounded foreign to my own ears—thin and fragile, a shadow of its usual strength.

Steeling myself, I turned away and made my way downstairs. Each step on the staircase creaked loudly in the pre-dawn stillness, the sound echoing through the house like a lament. I felt like an intruder in my own home, as though this place no longer recognised me without Nial and Buffy to complete its rhythm. Their absence was tangible, a haunting void that seemed to reverberate from the walls, infusing the air with an unnatural stillness.

In the kitchen, I leaned heavily against the bench, letting its cool surface steady me. My gaze drifted to the backyard, drawn instinctively to the familiar scene outside. The garden was shrouded in a grey haze, the early morning light weak and diffused. It was usually a source of pride, a testament to the life Nial and I had built together. But now it looked tired, neglected, as though it, too, felt the weight of his absence. The rosemary bush he'd loved to prune, the cheerful daisies Sammy had insisted we plant—they all seemed to droop in the absence of his touch, their vibrancy dulled.

My eyes fell on Buffy's chew toy near the back door, its once-bright colours faded from hours of play. The sight of it lying abandoned stabbed at my heart. She should have been here, wagging her tail, her ears perked at the sound of breakfast preparations. Instead, the toy was a cruel reminder of her absence, of the stranger Sammy had described, of the questions I still couldn't answer.

Anger surged through me, a flash of heat in the coldness of my fear. *Who had taken her?* The thought of someone leading Buffy away, of her trusting eyes looking back at me for reassurance I hadn't been there to give, filled me with equal parts rage and guilt. Buffy was a protector, a loyal companion, and I had failed her.

Tears welled up again, unbidden, as I clenched my fists on the countertop. I was drowning in questions, each one heavier than the last. Where was Buffy? Where was Nial? And who—*or what*—was responsible for tearing my family apart?

I pulled my phone from my robe pocket, my fingers hesitating over the keypad as doubt gnawed at me. Who could I call? Who might hold even the smallest piece of the puzzle that could lead me to Nial? Names swirled in my mind, each dismissed almost as quickly as it surfaced—until one lingered. Ken. He was Nial's closest friend, his confidant. If anyone might have some insight, it would be him. Or at the very least, he might have seen or spoken to Nial recently.

With a deep breath, I dialled the Chalker's number. The phone rang, each tone stretching endlessly in the early morning silence. Just as I began to lose hope, a soft click and a voice, thick with sleep, came through.

"Hello?" Marie's voice was groggy, the sound of bedsheets rustling faintly in the background.

"Marie, hi. It's Jenny Triffett," I said, my tone carefully measured, though the tension in my voice betrayed me. I winced internally at how abrupt I sounded.

There was a pause, then a neutral, "Oh, right. What can I do for you?" Her tone was unreadable, offering neither warmth nor suspicion. I imagined her sitting up in bed, perhaps nudging Ken awake, her mind battling to comprehend why I might be calling so early.

"I'm sorry to disturb you so early," I said quickly, the apology spilling out in a rush. "I was hoping I could speak to Ken for a moment. It's... it's important."

The pause that followed felt agonising, stretching long enough for doubt to creep in. *Was she waking him? Or was she trying to decide whether to involve him at all?*

"Why?" she asked bluntly, her tone sharper now, catching me off guard. It was a fair question, but the directness of it threw me.

I fumbled for words, my composure slipping. "I just wanted to check if he might have seen Nial yesterday," I explained, fighting to keep my voice steady. "Nial didn't come home last night, and I'm... I'm worried."

Another pause, longer this time. I held my breath, straining to hear anything—footsteps, murmurs, anything that might indicate what was happening on the other end of the line.

"Ken!" I finally heard Marie call out, her voice slightly muffled. "Did you see Nial yesterday?"

I listened intently, straining to catch Ken's response. My heart was pounding so loudly I was afraid I might miss his words. *Please,* I thought desperately, *please let him know something.*

The sound of my heartbeat thundered in my ears as I waited for a reply. My imagination filled the silence with every possible response. When Marie returned to the phone, her voice was clearer but devoid of any new hope. "Ken says he hasn't spoken to Nial since early last week."

"Oh." The single word escaped me, heavy with disappointment. I clutched the phone tighter, the answer landing like a stone in my chest. Another dead end.

Marie's tone softened, a note of concern creeping in now that the sleepiness had left her voice. "Is everything alright?"

For a moment, the temptation to pour everything out to her was overwhelming. To confess my fears, my suspicions, the strange events of the past day. But something held me back. A deep-seated instinct warned against sharing too much too soon. Until I understood more, I needed to keep this within our family.

"Yes, everything's fine," I lied, the words tasting bitter. "Thank you, Marie. Sorry to bother you."

"Alright, Jenny," she said, the concern lingering but unvoiced. I ended the call before she could probe further.

I stood there, staring at the now-dark screen, a heavy sigh escaping my lips. "Shit," I muttered under my breath, frustration boiling over. How had I missed asking Marie to let me know if Nial reached out? It was a rookie mistake, born of stress and exhaustion. I cursed myself silently, knowing that every detail, every connection, could be crucial.

The first rays of the sun began to peek through the kitchen window, casting soft golden light over the room. It should have been comforting, a symbol of a new day, but to me, it felt like a cruel reminder that Nial was still out there—somewhere—and I was no closer to finding him.

I inhaled deeply, the air cool and crisp, trying to push away the fear clawing at my chest. No more waiting, I decided. No more hoping that someone else might provide answers. If there were secrets to uncover, truths to face, I would find them myself.

The shrill whistle of the kettle jolted me from my thoughts, its sound cutting through the silence like a challenge. Without realising it, I had moved on autopilot, setting water to boil. I reached for my favourite mug, the one Sammy and Nial had given me for Mother's Day last year, the words *Best Mum Ever* etched in cheerful script across its surface. It was another reminder of what was at stake, of the life I was fighting to preserve.

As I poured the steaming water over a teabag, the rich aroma rising to meet me, my mind began to race with possibilities. *Who else could I call? What other avenues could I explore?*

❖

The kitchen was bathed in the soft, golden light of early morning, but its warmth did nothing to dispel the chill that had settled deep in my bones. My hands trembled slightly as I gazed at the silent phone resting on the benchtop. Its sleek surface reflected the weak sunlight, a stark contrast to the darkness that seemed to be closing in around me.

Four phone calls. Four dead ends. Each had been a desperate attempt to trace Nial, to find some clue that might explain his absence. But all I'd gotten were echoes of confusion, polite concern, and the same haunting refrain: *No information*. The weight of those unanswered calls pressed down on my chest, leaving me breathless with frustration and dread. And now, there was only one more call to make. A call I dreaded as much as I needed it.

I bit my lip hard, the metallic tang of blood sharp against my tongue. The sting grounded me, pulling me back from the edge of spiralling into panic. "It's for Sammy," I whispered, a quiet mantra to fortify myself. The thought of him, sleeping peacefully upstairs, unaware of the turmoil swirling around us, gave me the courage to press forward. For him, I would do anything. Even this.

My fingers hovered over the keypad, hesitant, before I finally dialled the number. Each ring that followed felt louder than the last, reverberating in the unnaturally still kitchen, amplifying my unease. Just as I was about to hang up, convinced this call would join the others in futility, there was a click.

"Good morning, dear," Rowena's voice chimed brightly through the receiver, its exaggerated cheeriness almost painful to hear. The incongruity of her tone grated against the raw edges of my emotions. Before I could say a word, she continued, her next question cutting straight to the heart of my fears. "Is Nial home yet?"

The lump in my throat swelled, threatening to choke me. Her words were like a hammer, shattering the fragile barrier I'd built to keep my worst thoughts at bay. How could I explain that not only was Nial still gone, but that every attempt to find him had led to nothing? That I was no closer to understanding why he had vanished or if he was even safe?

Silence stretched between us, heavy and oppressive. I could almost hear the faint tick of Rowena's mind, turning over possibilities, formulating opinions, crafting judgments about my marriage, about Nial, about me.

"Jenny? Are you there?" Her voice broke through my spiralling thoughts, sharp with concern and just a hint of impatience.

"Umm... yeah," I croaked, barely able to get the word out. Clearing my throat, I fought to steady my voice, to summon the strength I so desperately needed. "I'm here, Rowena."

"Well?" she pressed, her tone insistent. I could picture her perfectly: seated upright in her favourite armchair, one eyebrow arched, the corners of her mouth tugged down in expectation. Rowena, ever the embodiment of poised judgment, waiting for an explanation that met her standards.

I swallowed hard, gathering my courage. I knew once I spoke, there would be no turning back. No pretending everything was fine, that Nial's absence was just a minor inconvenience. "I wondered if you could look after Sammy for me," I said at last, keeping my tone as even as I could. "Just for a short while."

There was a pause. Long enough for me to regret making the call, long enough for me to imagine every possible scenario that would end with her refusal—or worse, her endless questions. But when she finally spoke again, her voice was unexpectedly warm, a softness creeping in that caught me off guard.

"Of course, dear," she said simply, and the genuine affection in her tone sent a flood of emotion surging through me. "You know I'm happy to have the little darling anytime."

Tears pricked at the corners of my eyes, hot and unbidden. Rowena's love for Sammy had always been fierce, unwavering, and in this moment, I was profoundly grateful for it.

"I know," I managed, the words barely audible past the tightness in my throat. I couldn't trust myself to say more, afraid my composure would shatter entirely.

"I'll be there within the hour," I added, ending the call abruptly before she could ask any more questions. I couldn't bear to explain, to put into words the fear and uncertainty that were eating away at me.

The silence that followed was deafening. I set the phone down on the benchtop with a trembling hand, staring at it as if it might come to life and deliver the answers I so desperately needed. But it remained still, its blank screen offering no comfort, no resolution.

My shoulders slumped as the tears I had held back during the call finally spilled over. They slid down my cheeks in hot, relentless streams, each one carrying a fraction of my pent-up fear and anguish. For a moment, I allowed myself to crumble, to let the weight of the situation press down on me completely.

But only for a moment.

"Mummy," Sammy's tiny voice broke through the haze of my thoughts like a gentle tug at my heart. I turned sharply toward the kitchen doorway, startled by his sudden presence. His blonde curls were a tangled mess, and his blue eyes—so like Nial's—blinked sleepily, still adjusting to the morning light.

"Where's—" he began, but I couldn't let him finish. I couldn't bear to hear him ask about Nial again. The question was a dagger that twisted with every repetition, cutting deeper into wounds that were still too raw.

"Come here, love," I said quickly, forcing a brightness into my tone that I didn't feel. I turned to him, plastering a smile onto my face, the kind that mothers perfect when they need to shield their children from the dramas of the adult world. For Sammy, I had to be strong. I had to be his anchor.

He shuffled toward me, his small feet padding softly against the kitchen floor, and I bent down to scoop him into my arms. He felt so light, so fragile, as though he might drift away if I loosened my hold even a fraction. His pyjamas were warm against my skin, carrying the comforting scent of sleep and sandalwood—a smell that always reminded me of innocence and safety. As I brushed a stray curl from his forehead and wiped the remnants of sleep from his eyes, I made a silent vow: no matter what happened, I would protect him.

"I've got an exciting day planned for you," I said, injecting my voice with as much cheer as I could muster. The lie tasted bitter, like a betrayal of the trust in his wide, unguarded eyes. But what else could I do? He needed to believe that everything was okay, even if I didn't.

"Really?" His eyes lit up, the corners crinkling in delight as a smile stretched across his face. That simple, unguarded joy pierced my heart. He was too young to know the weight of worry, too young to bear the burden of uncertainty.

"Yep," I said, the word feeling heavy despite its light delivery. Mothers lie when they have to, don't they? Shielding their children from life's harsher truths, keeping the shadows at bay for just a little longer. I could live with the guilt if it meant preserving his innocence.

"What is it? What are we doing?" he asked, his body squirming with curiosity and anticipation.

I forced another smile, steeling myself for what I had to say. "You get to spend the morning with Grandma Rowena," I said brightly, trying to make it sound like an adventure rather than the desperate necessity it was. "She's so excited to see you."

Sammy's cheer was immediate and infectious. "Yay! Grandma Rowena is funny!" he exclaimed, bouncing slightly in my arms. His laughter bubbled out, unburdened and pure, cutting through the heavy atmosphere like sunlight breaking through storm clouds.

I couldn't help but smile back, this time genuinely. Rowena might be overbearing and dramatic, but her love for Sammy was undeniable, and their bond was a blessing. She would keep him occupied, safe, and blissfully unaware of the storm brewing beneath the surface of our lives.

"Let's get some breakfast in you first," I said, gently setting him down at the kitchen table. His small legs swung freely beneath the chair, and he rested his elbows on the table, his chin cupped in his hands as he watched me with wide-eyed expectancy.

"Toast?" I asked, already reaching for the bread in the bin.

"Yes!" he exclaimed, his enthusiasm uncontainable.

"Vegemite?" I teased, drawing out the question as though it wasn't already part of our sacred morning routine.

"Yay!" he cheered, clapping his hands together. The ritual was comforting, familiar—a lifeline that tethered me to a sense of normality. For a moment, I let myself focus on the task of making breakfast: the scrape of the knife spreading Vegemite across the toast, the warm scent wafting up as it crisped in the toaster.

As I placed the plate in front of Sammy, his face lit up like I'd just given him the world. "Thank you, Mummy!" he said, his gratitude as pure as his joy. He bit into the toast with gusto, his legs swinging as he chewed.

I watched him, my heart both aching and swelling at once. His innocence was a fragile thing, something I needed to protect at all costs. Whatever had happened to Nial, whatever the coming hours and days held, I would face it all for Sammy.

As Sammy ate, his legs swinging rhythmically under the table, I cradled my mug, its warmth failing to chase away the chill that had taken root deep inside me. The bitter liquid slid down my throat, doing little to clear the fog of dread clouding my mind. My eyes rested on Sammy, his face soft with innocence, oblivious to the storm swirling around him.

I studied him intently, searching for traces of Nial in his features. The way his nose scrunched slightly when he concentrated on something, the way his eyes crinkled with every bite of Vegemite toast—it was all Nial. Sammy was his father's mirror in so many ways, a living embodiment of the man I loved, the man who had vanished as if he had been plucked from existence. The thought tightened my chest, fear and longing battling within me.

"Mummy, why are you looking at me like that?" Sammy's voice broke through my wandering thoughts, his words full of the simple curiosity only a child could muster. His gaze met mine, clear and questioning, and I realised I'd been staring, my worries no doubt etched plainly across my face.

I forced a smile, reaching out to ruffle his soft curls, the movement an anchor pulling me back to the present. "Just thinking about how much I love you, sweetheart," I said, my voice catching slightly on the words. It wasn't a lie, but it wasn't the whole truth either.

Sammy grinned, crumbs dusting the corners of his mouth. "I love you too, Mummy," he said, as though it was the most obvious thing in the world. His simple, matter-of-fact response brought a lump to my throat, a painful reminder of the purity of his love and the weight of my responsibility to protect him.

As he finished the last bite of his toast, I rose from the table, gathering his things with a kind of mechanical precision. Each item I placed in his small backpack felt like a piece of normality slipping through my fingers. His favourite toy truck, a spare change of clothes, a few snacks for the day—each object a tangible connection to the life we had shared before this nightmare began. Packing them felt like preparing for a journey into the unknown, a world where nothing was certain anymore.

"Are you ready for your adventure with Grandma?" I asked, crouching down to help him into his coat. The word *adventure* stuck in my throat, its cheerful connotations clashing violently with the grim reality we were facing.

Sammy nodded enthusiastically, his boundless energy a stark contrast to the heaviness weighing me down. As I zipped up his coat, I let my hands linger, brushing a stray lock of hair from his forehead, memorising the details of his face. The soft curve of his cheeks, the unguarded trust in his wide eyes, the slight pout of his lips as he waited impatiently for me to finish—each feature was etched into my heart, a treasure I couldn't bear to lose.

"I love you, Sammy," I said, pulling him into a fierce hug. The words carried the full weight of my emotions, a plea, a promise, a prayer wrapped into one. My arms tightened around him, holding him close as if I could shield him from the rest of the world around us.

"I love you too, Mummy," he replied, his little arms wrapping around my neck. His voice was soft, filled with the kind of unconditional love that only a child could give. It was pure, uncomplicated, and it nearly undid me.

I buried my face in his hair, the familiar scent of sandalwood and sleep grounding me, giving me a flicker of strength. My tears hovered just behind my eyes, threatening to spill over, but I blinked them back. Sammy couldn't see my fear—not now, not when he needed me to be his rock.

"You're my brave little adventurer," I whispered, forcing another smile as I pulled back to meet his gaze. He beamed at me, his trust unwavering, and I vowed silently to be the mother he deserved.

The winter air nipped at my skin as Sammy and I ascended the stone path to Rowena's front door, the gravel crunching under our feet in the stillness of the morning. The imposing Victorian house loomed ahead, its grandiose architecture a relic of my childhood, its familiar contours both comforting and oppressive. Every step felt heavier, as if the air itself resisted our progress, weighed down by the unknowns that had invaded my life since yesterday morning.

I tightened my grip on Sammy's hand, his small fingers a lifeline in this sea of uncertainty. He bounced along beside me, blissfully unaware of the turmoil gnawing at my insides. His laughter bubbled up as we neared the front steps, his excitement to see Rowena and her pampered cat, Mr. Darcy, momentarily lifting the heaviness that clung to me. I envied his innocence, the simplicity of his world where Grandmas were magical and mornings held only promise.

Before I could knock, the heavy door creaked open, its sound oddly foreboding despite the warm light spilling from within. Rowena stood framed in the doorway, her appearance as polished as ever. Her pearl earrings gleamed, her tailored blazer was immaculate, and not a strand of her silver-blonde hair was out of place. She was the picture of composed elegance, a stark contrast to my rumpled exhaustion.

"Sammy! My darling prince!" Rowena's face lit up with a rare warmth, her arms opening wide as she crouched to greet him. Her joy was infectious, and Sammy let out a squeal of delight, rushing forward to wrap his arms around her neck. Their embrace was a snapshot of unguarded affection, a reminder of the familial bonds that sometimes felt tenuous but were undeniably strong.

"Grandma!" Sammy's voice rang with excitement as he buried his face in her shoulder. For a moment, the weight in my chest eased. Seeing them like this, their bond so genuine and unreserved, brought a fleeting sense of normality. But as Rowena rose, her eyes met mine, and I saw the flicker of something else—concern, curiosity, and the unspoken questions I knew she was burning to ask.

Her gaze swept over me, taking in the tired shadows under my eyes. A faint smirk tugged at the corner of her mouth, a reminder that she missed little and judged even less quietly.

Sammy darted past us into the house, undoubtedly in search of Mr. Darcy, leaving Rowena and me alone on the threshold. I handed her the small backpack I'd packed, the weight of it oddly symbolic of the burden I was placing on her. It was filled with all the essentials—Sammy's favourite snacks, his well-loved teddy bear, and the unspoken trust that she would keep him safe while I tried to make sense of this nightmare.

"I've packed him some fruit, his water bottle, and Teddy's in there too," I said, my voice betraying the strain of holding it together. Gratitude and urgency tangled in my words, masking the deeper conversation we weren't yet having.

Rowena accepted the bag with a quiet nod, but her silence was pointed, her eyes narrowing slightly as she studied me. I could almost hear the wheels turning in her mind, the silent inventory of my failures and flaws she was likely tallying alongside her speculations about Nial. The tension in her expression was subtle but unmistakable, a mix of concern and a barely contained desire to pry.

"You'll call me if you need anything, won't you?" I asked, my voice barely above a whisper. I felt exposed under her gaze, like a child seeking reassurance from a parent.

"Of course," Rowena replied smoothly, her tone too polished to betray whatever she was truly thinking. She reached out, placing a hand lightly on my arm. "You'll sort this out, Jenny. You always do."

Her words were meant to comfort, but they landed with a weight I wasn't sure I could bear. Sort this out? How could I, when I didn't even know where to begin?

"I'll try not to be too long," I said, the words tumbling out in a rush. "I'm going to the police station in town to demand they open a missing person report immediately." My voice was steady, but the tremor in my hands betrayed the fear gripping me.

"That's my girl," Rowena responded with a small, knowing smile, the kind that held equal parts pride and critique. "Always demanding." Her words, though meant to encourage, carried the faintest edge, a reminder of the countless times my assertiveness had clashed with her decorum.

I chose not to rise to the bait. This wasn't the moment for one of our well-worn exchanges. The stakes were too high, the urgency too real. My focus needed to be on Nial and nothing else.

"Jenny..." Rowena's tone softened unexpectedly, her voice taking on an almost hesitant quality. "Are you sure that's the best course of action?" For once, there was no judgement, only concern, and it caught me off guard.

"Yes," I replied firmly, a certainty underlined by desperation. The word came out stronger than I felt, but I clung to that resolve like a lifeline. "I've called everyone I can think of—his work partner, some of his clients. No one has spoken to Nial in over forty-eight hours."

The weight of that statement hung in the air between us. Forty-eight hours. Each passing minute was another slip further into the unknown, another step further from answers. The unspoken truth loomed large: every hour mattered in cases like this, and we had already lost too many.

"Well, you'd better get going then," Rowena said after a brief pause, her voice firm with resolve. For all her critiques and carefully veiled barbs, there was something steady in her demeanour now, a quiet solidarity that I hadn't expected but deeply appreciated.

"Thank you," I murmured, managing a small, brittle smile. It wasn't easy to muster, but it felt important—to show her, and myself, that I was holding it together. "Call me immediately if anything happens," I instructed, my tone clipped but pleading. "Anything at all—if you hear from Nial, if something happens with Sammy, anything." My voice wavered slightly on the last word, betraying the tightrope of fear I was walking.

"I will," Rowena assured me, her gaze steady. For once, her usual air of superiority was absent, replaced with a sincerity I hadn't seen in years.

I turned towards the car, my steps brisk but deliberate across the damp grass. Leaving Sammy behind felt like an act of betrayal, but I knew I had no choice. He was safer here, with Rowena. And I had to focus on finding Nial. The thought spurred me on, even as the pit in my stomach grew heavier with each step.

"Do be careful, won't you?" Rowena's voice called after me, her concern cutting through the chill morning air.

I paused, glancing back at her. Her expression—usually so composed, so impervious—was tinged with something softer.

For a fleeting moment, it felt like we understood each other. I nodded silently, not trusting my voice to stay steady, and turned back towards the car.

As I slid into the driver's seat, the familiar scent of the car hit me like a gut punch. It was a blend of leather, Sammy's lingering snacks, and the faint trace of Nial's aftershave—so distinctly *us* that it made the empty passenger seat feel even more glaring. My throat tightened, and I gripped the steering wheel, willing the tears to stay at bay. There was no time for breaking down. Not now.

THE POLICE STATION

4338.210.2

The drive to the Hobart Police Station passed in a blur, the Brooker Highway stretching out before me like a path to answers—or more questions. My mind raced with every kilometre, replaying the last time I saw Nial, the phone call that unsettled him, Sammy's cryptic mention of a man and the colours. I clung to each fragment, searching for something I'd missed, something that could piece together this fractured picture.

When I arrived, I parked around the corner, needing a moment to gather myself before stepping inside. The weight of what I was about to do hit me hard. Reporting Nial as missing wasn't just a step; it was a plunge into the unknown. It would mean admitting, to the world and myself, that something was truly wrong.

Before stepping out, I pulled my phone from my bag and dialled Nial's number one last time. Each ring felt like a taunt, and when his voicemail picked up, the cheerful familiarity of his voice was a cruel twist of the knife.

"Hey, it's Nial. Sorry I missed your call. Leave a message and I'll get back to you as soon as I can. Cheers!"

The casual tone was unbearable, mocking the terror that had taken hold of my life. I mouthed the words along with the recording, the rhythm etched into my mind after countless desperate calls.

As the beep sounded, I couldn't find the words. What could I say that I hadn't already said a hundred times? That I was scared? That I needed him to come home? That Sammy missed him? The weight of it all silenced me.

In frustration, I tossed the phone onto the passenger seat. The clatter echoed in the quiet car, a sound as jarring as the turmoil within me.

I gripped the steering wheel, taking a shaky breath and letting the cool air of the Tasmanian morning fill my lungs. This was it. No more waiting, no more guessing. I had to push forward, had to make the police listen. For Sammy, for Nial, and for the life we'd built together, I couldn't stop now.

The alternative was unthinkable.

The automatic doors of the Hobart Police Station glided open before me, their quiet hiss heralding my entry into a realm of grim realities. The bustling noise of the street behind me was immediately replaced by an almost oppressive quiet, broken only by the hum of fluorescent lights and the soft burble of the fountain feature in the centre of the lobby. Its cascading water, flowing over smooth, polished stones, seemed indifferent to the weight of the world carried by those who crossed this threshold.

I paused just inside, the warm air conditioning brushing against my skin, its artificial heat adding to the tight knot in my stomach. My shoes scuffed softly on the tiled floor as I took a hesitant step forward, my gaze scanning the reception area. The room smelled faintly of disinfectant, a sterile undertone that did little to ease the raw emotions roiling inside me.

Ahead, the reception desk gleamed under the harsh lighting, a bright and impersonal barrier between the public and the inner workings of law enforcement. I gripped my handbag tightly, as though the physical contact could steady me. My breathing quickened as the enormity of what I was about to do settled over me. Reporting Nial missing would make it official, a public acknowledgment of the private nightmare I was living.

Then I saw her: Linda. My sister-in-law, her familiar face a lifeline amidst the unfamiliar surroundings. Relief surged through me, though it was quickly tempered by the knowledge of what I had to say. Linda was seated behind the desk, her head bent as she typed something into the computer. Her auburn hair was pinned back neatly, her posture the perfect picture of professionalism.

"Linda," I called softly as I approached, my voice barely carrying over the subdued murmur of the station.

Her head snapped up, and for a brief moment, confusion flickered in her eyes before recognition dawned. "Jenny?" she said, her voice tinged with surprise. Her expression shifted rapidly from detached professionalism to concern, her brows knitting together. "What are you doing here?"

I hesitated, feeling the weight of the words I was about to speak. My throat felt dry, and I had to swallow hard before I could reply. "I need to report a missing person," I said, my voice firm though it trembled at the edges.

Linda's face paled, her professionalism cracking under the personal nature of my statement. "Shit," she murmured, leaning forward as her eyes searched mine. "Sammy?" The single word was laced with alarm, and I felt a stab of guilt for the ambiguity that had caused her fear.

Quickly, I shook my head. "No," I said, my voice tinged with regret for the worry I had unintentionally caused. Relief flooded her features, but it was fleeting, replaced almost immediately by confusion. "It's Nial," I added, and the name felt heavy on my tongue, as if saying it out loud made his absence more real.

Linda's concern deepened, her gaze sharpening as she took in the strain on my face, the desperation I was barely holding at bay. "Oh, Jenny, I'm so sorry," she said, her tone softening as her fingers moved automatically to the keyboard in front of her. "What happened?"

Her simple question seemed to unravel me. I drew in a shaky breath, struggling to find the words to explain what had brought me here. "I... I don't really know," I admitted, the tremor in my voice betraying the tightly coiled fear in my chest. I tried to arrange the past two days into something coherent, something that would make sense, but the events were a tangled web of confusion and dread.

"He got a phone call yesterday morning," I began haltingly, my hands clutching at the edge of the counter as though it could steady me. "It was about work, I think. He seemed... off. Concerned, maybe. Then he left, and I haven't heard from him since." The words spilled out in a rush, their inadequacy hitting me like a physical blow. How could I convey the gnawing sense of wrongness, the instinct that told me this was far more than a missed call or an unplanned trip?

Linda's expression remained serious as she absorbed my words, her fingers poised above the keyboard. "Has he ever done anything like this before?" she asked, her tone gentle but probing.

"No," I replied quickly, shaking my head. "Never." I met her eyes, willing her to understand, to believe me. "Linda, this isn't like him. He would never just... leave without telling me. Without saying something."

Linda's brow furrowed as she processed my words. She hesitated before speaking, her voice low but steady. "Have you checked with the hospital?"

The question hit me like a jolt. "Oh," I murmured, the guilt washing over me. It hadn't even crossed my mind. How could I have overlooked something so basic, so obvious? "No," I admitted softly, my cheeks warming with embarrassment. "But I'm sure they would've contacted me if he'd been admitted. And..." I hesitated, the memory of the text message cutting through my doubts like a cold blade. "He sent me a text message yesterday afternoon."

Linda raised an eyebrow, her hands pausing mid-type over the keyboard. "He texted you?" she asked, her tone sharp with curiosity, but there was something else there too—a hint of doubt that set my nerves on edge.

"Yes," I confirmed, the words faltering in my throat. "But... I don't think it was him. I don't know how to explain it, but it didn't feel right. It didn't sound like him."

Linda leaned back in her chair, her professional mask slipping into place. "Jenny," she began, the use of my first name feeling like a lifeline, though her tone was laced with caution. "Are you sure you're not jumping to conclusions here? If he sent you a message, that means he's okay. Maybe he just needed some space."

"No," I said, shaking my head firmly. "You don't understand. Nial wouldn't do this. He wouldn't just disappear without telling me where he was going. And he certainly wouldn't leave Sammy like this." My voice cracked, the weight of my fear and frustration bleeding through.

Linda exhaled, her lips pressed into a tight line. "Jenny, I want to help you, I really do," she said, her voice softening slightly. "But if he sent you a text, that's considered a form of contact. Officially, he's not missing."

Her words were like a slap in the face. "What do you mean he's not missing?" I demanded, my voice louder than I'd intended. Heads turned in the lobby, curious gazes brushing against me like needles. "I haven't seen or spoken to my husband in over twenty-four hours, and you're telling me that a single text message is enough to dismiss my concerns?"

"Jenny, please," Linda said, her voice a mixture of sympathy and exasperation. "I don't make the rules. If there's evidence of contact, we can't classify him as missing. Not yet."

I clenched the edge of the counter, my knuckles turning white. "Linda," I said, my voice trembling. "This isn't like Nial. You know him. He would never do this. And then there's the dog—Buffy's gone too. Sammy says a man took her. Doesn't that mean anything to you?"

Linda's brow furrowed again, her fingers fidgeting slightly. For a moment, I thought I saw a flicker of understanding in her eyes, but then her professional demeanour snapped back into place. "I'm sorry, Mrs Triffett," she said firmly, her tone final. "There's nothing more I can do right now. If you don't hear from him or see him within forty-eight hours, come back, and we'll reevaluate the situation."

The formal tone, the shift from personal to professional, felt like a betrayal. "So that's it?" I asked, my voice shaking. "I just... wait? Hope that he decides to come back?"

Linda looked away, avoiding my gaze. "I'm sorry," she repeated, her voice barely above a whisper.

Linda's averted gaze was like a door slamming shut, and her whispered apology felt like a betrayal. My voice cracked as I pressed on, a desperate plea spilling from my lips. "But that just isn't like Nial," I said, the words trembling under the weight of my despair. "He would never leave, not like this. Not without saying goodbye to little Sammy."

The mention of Sammy stabbed through me, fresh and sharp. How could I explain this to him? How could I tell our son that the man who had been his everything – his storyteller, his protector, his hero – was now a gaping absence? That his dad, the man who had fought imaginary monsters at his bedside, had become one in his absence, a shadow looming over our fracturing world?

"Mrs Triffett, you know there's nothing I can do," Linda said, her voice laced with weary resignation. "The system just doesn't have the resources—"

"To hell with your system!" I shouted, my hand slamming down onto the counter with a force that startled even me. The sound ricocheted through the lobby, a loud, defiant crack against the oppressive quiet. Heads turned – officers, civilians, passers-by – all their gazes converging on the scene I had created. I didn't care. Let them look. Let them see my desperation, my rage, my refusal to be dismissed.

"You *know* me, Linda," I said, my voice thick with tears and anger, shaking with the effort to keep myself together. "You *know* my husband! You were at our house just last week for dinner. You know Nial would never abandon his family. Not like this!" My words spilled out, raw and untamed, a storm of anger and fear aimed directly at the one person I thought should care.

Linda's expression was a perfect mask of professionalism, but her eyes betrayed her. There was conflict there, a flicker of recognition, of guilt. Her lips parted as if to speak, but she hesitated. The hesitation was enough to crack my resolve. Before she could say anything, another voice sliced through the thick tension, authoritative but not unkind.

"Mrs Triffett, was it?"

I spun around, startled to realise someone had approached without me noticing. The man standing behind me was tall and solidly built, with dark hair neatly combed and a measured expression that seemed to take in everything at once. His eyes met mine with a mixture of curiosity and caution, as though he were assessing whether I might explode again.

"Yes," I said, trying to compose myself. My voice wavered slightly. "Do I know you?"

"No," he replied, extending a hand. "I'm Detective Karl Jenkins." His tone was calm but firm, and there was a flicker of something in his expression – perhaps understanding. "Why don't you come with me? You can tell me what's been going on," he suggested, his hand gesturing towards a corridor that led away from the reception area.

For a moment, I hesitated, glancing back at Linda. She still wasn't looking at me, her fingers fidgeting with her keyboard in a way that betrayed her discomfort. Whatever sympathy she might have felt was buried under the weight of bureaucracy, a wall I couldn't break through.

I turned back to Detective Jenkins, searching his face for any sign that this wasn't just another dead end. I saw no pity there, only calm patience. It wasn't much, but it was enough.

"Alright," I said, my voice quieter now. I felt a pang of finality as I stepped away from the counter, leaving Linda and the impenetrable machinery of the system behind me. Her gaze burned into my back as I walked away, but I didn't turn around. Something had shifted – whatever trust or connection we once had now felt fractured, irreparable.

Detective Jenkins led the way, swiping his security card across a panel beside a door. The soft beep and the metallic click of the lock disengaging seemed unnaturally loud in the charged silence between us. "After you, ma'am," he said, gesturing politely for me to enter first.

I stepped over the threshold, feeling as though I was leaving one world and entering another. The familiar bustle and noise of the station's public face faded behind me, replaced by a maze of beige corridors that seemed to stretch endlessly in every direction. Each turn blurred into the next, the monotony broken only by notice boards pinned with wanted posters and safety announcements. The fluorescent lights overhead hummed faintly, their harsh glare stripping away any semblance of comfort or warmth.

As we walked, my mind wandered to the stories these walls must hold. How many people had passed through here before me, desperate for help, for answers, for closure? How many had left with their hopes dashed, their pleas unanswered? Would I be one of them?

Finally, Detective Jenkins stopped in front of an open door at the end of a narrow hallway. He cast a quick glance inside, his sharp eyes scanning the space before he motioned me forward. "This way, please, Mrs Triffett," he said, his voice even and professional. "Please, take a seat."

The room was as stark and unwelcoming as I had imagined. A cold, metal table dominated the centre, flanked by two chairs that looked as unforgiving as the fluorescent light overhead. A large mirror stretched across one wall, and I didn't need years of watching crime dramas to recognise it as a two-way mirror. The thought of unseen eyes observing us sent a shiver crawling down my spine.

I lowered myself into the hard chair opposite a tape recorder perched precariously on the edge of the table. Crossing my left leg over the right, I leaned forward, resting my hands on the cold surface of the table. The chill of the metal was strangely grounding, a small physical tether to cling to amidst the emotional storm inside me.

Detective Jenkins took the seat opposite me, moving with the kind of practised efficiency that suggested this was just another routine for him, another case in a long line of stories he had heard. He slipped a small pad and pen from his jacket pocket, the pen poised with precision over the notepad. His movements were calm and deliberate, as though he was careful not to startle me further.

"Your full name, please?" he asked, his tone professional but not unkind.

"Jenny Alexandra Triffett," I replied, my voice surprisingly steady considering the weight pressing down on me. The formality of the question and my response felt surreal, almost absurd in the face of the trauma that had consumed my life in the past day.

"Thank you," he said, his pen moving swiftly as he wrote my name in bold, capital letters at the top of the page. His gaze shifted briefly to the upper-right corner of the notepad, where he wrote the date: Sunday, 29 July 2018. Seeing the date written so plainly, so formally, jolted me. Had it really only been a day since Nial disappeared? It felt like weeks, like months – as though time itself had been warped by the gravity of his absence.

I sat there nervously, waiting for him to ask the inevitable question—the reason I was here. My eyes flicked to his mouth as it moved awkwardly while he wrote, though no sound escaped. It was such a peculiar detail to focus on, but in that moment, every action, every movement felt magnified. It was as though my heightened state of anxiety had turned the room into a tableau where nothing escaped notice. Even the faint scratch of his pen on the notepad seemed unnaturally loud, underscoring the tension.

"My husband, Nial, is missing. He has been since yesterday morning," I said abruptly, my voice steady but layered with urgency. I leaned slightly forward as I spoke, my need to make him understand pressing. I couldn't wait for Jenkins to gently prod the story from me piece by piece. He had to know the gravity of the situation immediately.

Jenkins looked up from his notes, his sharp eyes meeting mine. "How do you know he has gone missing?" he asked, his tone straightforward, professional. It wasn't unkind, but the starkness of the question cut through me. He didn't offer the sympathy I craved, only the pragmatism of a man used to such conversations.

I tensed, feeling a swell of frustration. "Because I haven't seen him since yesterday morning," I replied, my words clipped. My grip tightened on the edge of the chair as if grounding myself there might help keep the emotion from spilling out. *Why did they keep questioning the obvious? Couldn't they see how wrong all of this was?*

Jenkins' posture shifted slightly, his interest sharpening. I noticed a glint in his eye, a spark of curiosity that hinted at something beneath his calm exterior. "But you've heard from him, yeah? That's what the receptionist was saying?" he pressed, his voice probing but neutral. He was referring, of course, to the text message. That damn message.

I felt my stomach twist. That single text had become the sticking point in every conversation about Nial's disappearance, as if it could erase the glaring wrongness of his absence. "I thought Linda was my friend," I said coldly, my gaze shifting to the two-way mirror. My tone was deliberate, my bitterness aimed not at Jenkins but at the betrayal I felt. I wanted to steer the conversation away from that cursed text, to focus on the broader picture of what was happening.

"Linda?" Jenkins repeated, a flicker of curiosity in his expression. His pen hovered over the notepad, ready to capture whatever connection I might reveal.

I turned back to him, irritation flaring briefly. "Linda. The receptionist," I clarified, my tone sharp. My frustration wasn't directed at him, but at the situation that demanded I explain the obvious. Couldn't they see how interconnected our lives were in a place like Hobart?

"So you know her, then?" Jenkins asked, though it wasn't really a question. There was a subtle undercurrent of interest, as if he were filing away this detail for later.

"Yes," I said, my tone softening slightly. "Apart from also being my sister-in-law, our families have known each other for years. We share great-grandmothers on my mother's side." The explanation tumbled out of me, and as I spoke, I realised how quintessentially Tasmanian that sounded. Everyone seemed connected by a web of shared history, no matter how thin the thread.

"You must be Tasmanian then," Jenkins said with a small chuckle, his tone warming as he leaned back slightly in his chair. The shift in his demeanour caught me off guard—a sudden departure from his earlier detachment.

I allowed myself a small smile, a brief flicker of levity breaking through the tension. "Yes. A bit obvious that, isn't it?" I replied, feeling the tiniest release of pressure in my chest. The brief moment of humour was a welcome reprieve, however fleeting. "Are you from here?" I asked, curious now about this man who seemed so removed from the familial knots and connections that bound so many of us in Hobart.

Jenkins' smile softened his features, a genuine expression that made him seem more approachable. "No," he said, shaking his head slightly. "I was born in South Australia, but my family moved to Queensland when I was a young boy. Somehow, I've ended up here."

I returned his smile, the warmth in his voice momentarily easing the weight on my shoulders. Despite the swirling fear and frustration in my heart, I felt a flicker of hope that this detective, an outsider to our tightly-knit Tasmanian web, might see something others had missed. As much as I resented being here, being forced to explain and justify my fears, I resolved to make the most of this interaction. If anyone could help me untangle the mystery of Nial's disappearance, perhaps it was Jenkins.

"Tell me about the last time you saw your husband," Jenkins prompted, his voice gentle but insistent, a reminder that this was no casual conversation. His tone carried the weight of necessity, urging me to recall every detail, no matter how small or seemingly insignificant.

I took a deep, steadying breath, trying to focus, to block out the swirl of emotions threatening to consume me. The memory of that morning with Nial was still vivid, but the more I replayed it, the more I worried about details slipping away, like sand through my fingers.

"Nial had just finished in the shower," I began, my voice low, tinged with both sorrow and regret. The image of him standing before the bathroom mirror was seared into my mind. "He was staring off into the mirror. He seemed... distracted, almost as if he were lost in thought." I hesitated, trying to put the feeling into words. "His eyes had this faraway look, you know? Like he was seeing something beyond his own reflection, something I couldn't see."

As I spoke, the memory became sharper, every detail coming back to me with painful clarity. "I rubbed his shoulder gently," I continued, my voice trembling slightly. "That always worked. It would calm him, help him relax. I could feel the tension in his muscles ease under my hand, just a little." The words hung in the air between us, a fragile thread connecting me to that moment, to the Nial I knew.

"For a second, he seemed to come back to himself. He smiled at me through the mirror, but..." I paused, the lump in my throat making it difficult to continue. "It didn't quite reach his eyes." The realisation hit me anew, and I fought against the tide of guilt rising within me. "I should have said something then. I should have asked what was wrong. But I didn't." My voice cracked slightly. "God, why didn't I?"

Detective Jenkins shifted in his chair, the faint sound of the metal legs scraping against the floor grounding me momentarily. His face remained calm, but I could sense his unease. My words, meant to paint a clear picture, might have felt uncomfortably intimate, revealing a side of marriage most people never show to strangers. I glanced down at the table, embarrassed by the rawness of my own emotions.

"And then his phone rang," I added quickly, returning to the sequence of events. The shift back to fact felt safer, a lifeline to cling to in the storm of emotion.

Jenkins leaned forward slightly, his pen poised above his notepad. "Do you know who he was speaking to?" he asked, his voice even but carrying the weight of his curiosity.

I rubbed my temple, trying to summon the memory, but it remained frustratingly incomplete. "No," I admitted, shaking my head slowly. "I had de-robed myself and gotten into the shower. The water was running, so I couldn't hear anything clearly." The memory felt disjointed, like trying to piece together a puzzle with missing edges.

I paused, doubt creeping into my voice as I spoke. *Or did the phone ring before I rubbed his shoulder?* I faltered, my thoughts tangling as I tried to sort through the sequence. The more I reached for certainty, the more it seemed to slip away. A wave of panic rose in my chest, cold and suffocating. *Is the memory already fading?* I wondered desperately. *Is Nial disappearing from my mind, just as he disappeared from our lives?*

Detective Jenkins leaned forward slightly, his pen hovering over his notepad as he prompted gently, "What happened after the phone call?"

Struggling to steady my thoughts, I answered as best as I could. "Well," I began, the words feeling fragile, as though they might crumble under scrutiny. "I was still in the shower when he poked his head in to say he was just going out to meet with a new client about a potential fencing job. And then... I assume he left."

"You assume?" Jenkins queried, his tone even but his eyes sharp, catching the hesitation in my voice.

"When I was done in the shower, he was not around," I clarified, my hands twisting together on the cool surface of the table. "His ute was also gone."

Jenkins nodded, jotting something down in his notebook before looking back up at me. "And the dog? Did you say before that your dog was also missing?"

"Yes," I confirmed, then quickly shook my head, realising the need to clarify. "Well, yes, Buffy is now missing. But she wasn't earlier in the morning. Sammy was playing with her after Nial had left." I paused, the memory of Sammy's carefree laughter, echoing through the house as he played with Buffy, flashing painfully through my mind. It felt impossibly distant, like a fragment of another life.

"Sammy. Your son?" Jenkins asked, his tone softening slightly, his pen momentarily still.

"Yes," I replied, my voice carrying the weight of my emotions. "He's three." The thought of Sammy missing his father hit me like a physical blow, threatening to unravel the composure I was desperately trying to maintain. "He misses his father so much already. He was so upset when Nial wasn't there to tuck him into bed and read him his bedtime story. They have a nightly routine," I explained, my voice cracking with unshed tears.

I could see it so vividly in my mind's eye – Nial sitting on the edge of Sammy's bed, the warm glow of the bedside lamp casting a comforting light over the room. Sammy tucked under his arm, his favourite teddy bear clutched tightly as they pored over the pages of a picture book together. Nial's deep voice animated, changing for each character, drawing giggles and squeals of delight from our son. The absence of that nightly ritual had left an unbearable void in our lives last night, a gaping wound in the rhythm of our family.

Detective Jenkins reached out, his hand resting briefly on mine, a gesture of reassurance. "It's okay, Jenny. We'll find Nial," he said firmly, his voice carrying a note of conviction that offered a glimmer of solace. There was a warmth in his eyes, a humanity that seemed rare in the cold, bureaucratic system I'd encountered so far.

"Why aren't all police officers as kind as you are," I said without thinking, my voice a mix of gratitude and exhaustion. The contrast between Jenkins' compassion and the clinical detachment I had faced earlier was stark, and my words carried the weight of that realisation.

Jenkins' brow furrowed slightly at my comment. "What do you mean? Have you already spoken to another officer?" he asked, his tone calm but laced with curiosity.

"Yes. Of course," I replied, the frustration from earlier bubbling back to the surface as I recalled my interactions at the front desk.

"Really? Please, do tell," he urged, leaning forward slightly.

"Well, naturally, after Buffy disappeared, which gave me quite the fright, I called the police to report her disappearance," I began, my voice carrying a mix of exasperation and lingering fear. I hesitated briefly before adding, "And Nial's." The words felt heavier than I'd anticipated, each syllable laced with the gravity of our situation.

"But they didn't seem too worried about Nial. Did they, Mrs. Triffett?" Jenkins asked, his voice careful but probing. There was something in his tone – a quiet understanding, perhaps – that made me feel seen, even in my vulnerability.

"No," I said with a huff, the frustration bubbling up again. "They didn't."

"And why was that?" he pressed, his gaze steady, his pen poised above the page.

I closed my eyes, taking a deep breath as I grappled with the weight of my response. The next words felt as though they could change everything, determining whether Jenkins would truly understand or dismiss me like the others.

"You can tell me the truth, Jenny. I won't judge you," Jenkins assured me, his voice gentle, his empathy evident.

"Judge me?!" I snapped, my frustration boiling over. "You're no different from the rest of them. I know what you're all thinking," I said, the words spilling out in a torrent of fear and anger. The moment they left my mouth, regret crashed over me. Jenkins had been nothing but kind, and I hated myself for lashing out at him.

But to my surprise, Jenkins didn't react with offence. Instead, his expression softened, and he leaned back slightly, giving me space. "They questioned his fidelity, didn't they?" he asked, his tone calm but direct.

"Yes," I admitted quietly, the word heavy with pain. The memory of the thinly veiled insinuations about Nial's possible infidelity from the officers last night stung anew. It wasn't just the idea of their doubt – it was the sheer impossibility of it. Nial wouldn't do this. He wouldn't betray me, betray us. But in the eyes of others, doubt seemed to overshadow truth.

Detective Jenkins leaned forward, his gaze steady but kind, and his tone gentle yet insistent. "And there was something else you told them, wasn't there, Jenny? Something that pressed them to conclude that you had no case for a missing persons report?".

The question cut through the fragile walls I'd built around my fears. I nodded slowly, the weight of the truth pressing down on me like an anvil. "Yes," I whispered, my voice barely audible as a tear traced a hot, wet line down my cheek. I felt cornered and helpless, the little hope I had left teetering on the edge of collapse.

Jenkins' tone softened further, coaxing without pressing. "What did you tell them?"

I drew in a shaky breath, the act of speaking feeling like a betrayal of my own instincts. My shoulders sagged under the heaviness of the admission I was about to make. Part of me wanted to hold back, to cling to the notion that not sharing this detail might somehow keep the case alive. But another part knew there was no sense in hiding the truth—not when it mattered so much.

"While the police were with me, I received a text message from Nial," I confessed, my eyes fluttering shut, unwilling to see Jenkins' reaction. "He said that he was still with the potential client and was going to be home late."

The room fell into a tense silence, heavy with the unspoken implications of my words.

"Fuck!" Jenkins' exclamation startled me, his reaction raw and immediate, breaking the strained quiet. My eyes snapped open, meeting his as he leaned back in his chair, the legs scraping loudly against the hard floor. The unexpected sound underscored the gravity of what I had just revealed, amplifying the fear knotting in my chest.

Another tear slipped down my cheek, the sting sharp against my skin. I knew exactly what that text message meant to the police. In their eyes, it was proof of life, a justification to classify Nial's disappearance as voluntary rather than concerning. Yet to me, it was anything but.

Desperate to make Jenkins see the truth, I pressed on, my voice trembling with conviction. "He told me not to wait up for him," I added, the words barely above a whisper. My heart clenched painfully as I said it. "He's never said that to me before. In all our years together—through late jobs, early mornings, everything—he's never once told me not to wait up. It's... it's not him, Detective. I *know* it's not him."

Jenkins' expression shifted subtly as he absorbed my words. He wasn't dismissive, as others had been. Instead, his eyes reflected a spark of interest, of engagement with the intricate web of details I was laying before him. It wasn't skepticism—it was analysis. That faint glimmer gave me hope.

After a long pause, Jenkins asked a question that felt entirely out of left field. "Do you know of a Luke Smith?"

The abrupt shift left me momentarily stunned. I blinked, processing his words. "No," I replied, confusion evident in my voice. "The name doesn't sound familiar. Should I know him?" The question hung in the air, tension coiling in the room.

Jenkins' face gave nothing away, his tone suddenly clipped. "No," he said, his answer curt and devoid of explanation. But something flickered in his eyes—something fleeting and inscrutable. Recognition? Concern? I couldn't be sure, and before I could press for clarification, the moment passed.

My heart pounded as I leaned forward, pleading with him, my voice thick with desperation. "Are you going to help me?" The question escaped before I could fully form it, raw and unfiltered. "Please, Detective Jenkins. I know how it looks. I know what the text message means in terms of official procedure. But I know my husband. I *know* something is wrong. Please... please help me find him."

For a long moment, Jenkins was silent, his dark eyes locked onto mine. I felt laid bare under his scrutiny, the weight of his stare pressing down on me. Yet, in that quiet moment, something shifted. He reached into his pocket, pulling out a business card.

Wordlessly, he slid it across the table towards me. I picked it up with trembling fingers, my eyes scanning the details printed neatly across the surface. **Senior Detective Karl Jenkins, Hobart Police Department, Major Crimes Unit.** The words sent a shiver down my spine. Major Crimes. Was this really happening?

"I'll open a case file," he said finally, his words a lifeline pulling me back from the edge. Relief coursed through me, a flood of gratitude so overwhelming I felt momentarily lightheaded. "I need you to contact me the moment you hear anything further from your husband. Anything at all," he instructed, his tone firm but kind.

"Of course," I promised, my voice trembling as I reached out, briefly touching his hand in a gesture of gratitude. "Whatever you need to do your job."

Jenkins offered me an awkward smile, a fleeting glimpse of the man behind the professional exterior. It was a small moment of connection, but one that gave me hope.

As he escorted me out of the room, I clutched the business card tightly in my hand, its edges digging into my palm. The physical weight of it was reassuring, a tangible reminder that someone was finally listening, finally taking me seriously. For the first time since Nial had disappeared, I felt the smallest flicker of hope. The search had officially begun.

Stepping back into the bustling reception area of the Hobart Police Station, the fluorescent lights bore down with an unforgiving glare, turning the room into a stark, clinical tableau. The chatter of voices, the occasional ringing of phones, and the low hum of the air conditioning felt louder, more intrusive, than when I had first entered. Shadows flickered at the edges of my vision, a disorienting reminder of the uncertainty that clung to me like a second skin. My heart pounded relentlessly, still echoing the tension of my conversation with Detective Jenkins, each beat underscoring the perilous uncertainty of my situation.

I cast a quick glance across the room and saw Linda at the reception desk, her attention focused on another visitor. Her head was bowed, her face partially obscured by a curtain of hair, but her demeanour was familiar in its precision—controlled, polite, detached. Her voice, though low, carried the faint cadence of someone deeply engaged in conversation.

The memory of her earlier dismissal lingered, the sting of her formal "Mrs Triffett" still fresh. Her refusal to help, her cold adherence to procedure, felt like a betrayal. Yet even in my anger, I couldn't entirely banish the twinge of doubt. Was she simply doing her job, caught between the rigidity of protocol and the personal ties that bound us? Or had she truly abandoned me, washing her hands of a family crisis she couldn't—or wouldn't—handle?

I shook my head, banishing the thought. This wasn't the time for second-guessing, for introspection that led nowhere. My mission was clear: find Nial, uncover the truth, no matter how deep I had to dig or how many walls I had to break through. Linda was just another obstacle, another face in the growing gallery of people who didn't seem to believe me, who didn't understand the depths of my certainty.

Without breaking my stride, I quickened my pace, refusing to let my gaze linger on her for another second. The sight of her was a reminder of everything I was fighting against—doubt, dismissal, and the suffocating bureaucracy that seemed determined to minimise my fears. I barely registered the curious glances from others in the lobby, the faint murmur of voices as they turned to watch me leave. *Let them look*, I thought, the resolve tightening in my chest like a clenched fist. *Let them see a woman on a mission. Let them see a mother, a wife, who wouldn't be silenced.*

The polished floor echoed with each step I took, the sound ricocheting through the sterile space like a drumbeat of determination. It was a small, defiant act, a way of marking my presence in a place that seemed designed to erode individuality, to reduce every person's pain to a case number or a report filed away in a drawer. I was more than that. Nial was more than that.

As the automatic doors slid open, the cold winter air hit me like a slap, sharp and bracing. I inhaled deeply, letting the chill burn through the fog of frustration and anger that clouded my mind. Outside, the world felt simultaneously vast and stifling, the streets teeming with people oblivious to my pain. Cars passed by, their engines rumbling like distant thunder, and the sky above was a steel-grey canopy that promised rain.

For a moment, I hesitated, my steps faltering as I reached the pavement. The enormity of what lay ahead loomed over me, a shadow that threatened to engulf me. But then I tightened my grip on the small business card Detective Jenkins had given me, the edges biting into my palm like a lifeline. I thought of Sammy, his bright eyes searching mine for reassurance, his small hands clutching his favourite teddy as he waited for his daddy to come home.

I straightened my shoulders, squaring them against the weight of the unknown. There was no room for doubt, no space for fear. I would find Nial. I had to. And no amount of indifference, no wall of bureaucracy, would stand in my way.

BROKEN

4338.210.3

The journey to my mother's house stretched interminably, each passing kilometre weighed down by the churning storm of emotions inside me. The familiar Hobart landscape rushed by in blurred monotony—winter-bare trees clawing at the pewter sky, their skeletal branches a stark reflection of my fractured state of mind. The unrelenting grey enveloped everything, seeping into the world as if it shared my grief, my uncertainty.

Inside the car, silence pressed down like a physical weight, broken only by the rhythmic hum of the engine and the soft hiss of tyres on the road. Occasionally, a sharp gust of wind would jolt the vehicle, its shuddering frame mimicking the tremors of anxiety coursing through me. I tightened my grip on the steering wheel, the worn leather cool beneath my white-knuckled fingers—a small, tangible connection to the normality that once was.

Every few moments, my gaze flicked to the phone lying on the passenger seat, its blank screen an unsettling void. The yearning for it to ring—to see Nial's name, to hear his voice—was almost unbearable. Yet, beneath that hope lurked a darker fear, one that whispered that any news might not bring relief but devastation.

The events of the morning replayed in relentless loops, a jumbled cacophony of emotions and unanswered questions. Linda's cold detachment haunted me, her once-familiar face a mask of indifference that stung like a betrayal. The dismissal of my fears by those who should have helped gnawed at me, their patronising tones painting me as nothing more than a hysterical wife. And then there was Detective Jenkins, with his sharp, probing eyes and unexpected willingness to listen. His measured words had planted a fragile seed of hope, but they'd also left me with questions—questions that twisted through my thoughts, refusing to let go.

Who was Luke Smith? The name Jenkins had mentioned lingered, unconnected yet feeling significant, like a piece of a puzzle whose edges didn't quite fit. The way the detective had said it, the subtle shift in his expression—it all hinted at something larger, something I wasn't privy to but couldn't ignore.

As the road wound its way towards the hills, a creeping unease settled over me. My fingers brushed the rearview mirror more often than they should have, my eyes scanning for shadows that weren't there. Was it paranoia? A by-product of days spent teetering on the edge of fear and despair? Or was it something more? Each car that followed for more than a minute felt like a potential threat, each passing ute or sedan a fleeting source of suspicion. When a red Commodore stayed behind me for a few turns, my heart thudded faster, only to settle when it veered off at a junction.

By the time my mother's house appeared on the horizon, I was raw, my nerves frayed to the edge of breaking. The sight of it—a charmingly haphazard Federation-style home—brought a pang of bittersweet emotion. Perched atop a gentle rise, its weatherboard exterior was painted a cheerful yellow that seemed to defy the gloom of the day. The wraparound veranda, cluttered with mismatched furniture and overflowing plants, spoke of a life lived on its own terms, steeped in chaotic beauty.

The garden, a riot of wildflowers even in the heart of winter, seemed untouched by time, its resilience a sharp contrast to my fractured sense of stability. As I pulled into the gravel driveway, I couldn't shake the feeling that I was stepping into another confrontation—one I wasn't ready for.

I sat there for a moment, the engine idling, the warmth of the car cocooning me against the cold reality awaiting beyond the windshield. My eyes drifted to the front window, where the curtain fluttered—a subtle movement that betrayed Rowena's watchful presence. I could almost feel her gaze, her curiosity mingled with concern as she waited for me to make my way inside.

The weight of the moment settled on me like a lead blanket. It wasn't just my mother waiting in that house; it was the embodiment of everything I was fighting to hold together—the questions, the worry, the agonising absence of Nial. How could the world carry on, unchanged, when mine had been upended?

Forcing a steadying breath, I turned the key and silenced the engine. The stillness that followed was deafening, broken only by the ticking of the cooling car. As I reached for the door handle, I caught my reflection in the rearview mirror. My eyes were tired, shadowed with worry; my face looked older, worn.

The sharp coolness of the air bit at my cheeks as I stepped out of the car, its crispness laden with the earthy scent of rain on the horizon. The faint aroma of wood smoke from a neighbour's chimney lingered in the air, stirring memories of childhood winters spent here.

I had barely made it up the porch steps when the front door swung open, revealing Rowena. She stood framed in the doorway, her expression a mix of worry and determination. Her eyes, so much like my own, scanned my face with a piercing intensity that only a mother could muster. I saw the recognition there—the dark circles under my eyes, the tautness in my jaw, the barely veiled anguish written in every line of my face.

"Oh, Jenny," she murmured, her voice thick with emotion, as she pulled me into an embrace. There was no hesitation, no need for words. Her arms encircled me, firm and unyielding, a bulwark against the storm of emotions threatening to consume me. I leaned into her, feeling the strength of her hold, the way she seemed to absorb some of my pain, if only for a moment. The familiar scent of her perfume—light, floral, and unchanging over the years—wrapped around me like a second layer of comfort. It brought with it a flood of memories: scraped knees soothed with whispered reassurances, bedtime stories read under soft lamplight, arguments over curfews resolved with reluctant hugs.

For a fleeting moment, I let myself feel safe, held in the arms of the woman who had always been my first line of defence against the world, even when I hadn't realised or appreciated it. But reality was quick to intrude, the weight of Nial's absence pressing against me like a physical force. I pulled back, blinking rapidly to ward off the tears threatening to spill.

"Come in, love," Rowena said, stepping aside and gesturing for me to enter. Her tone was gentle, but her eyes betrayed the sharp curiosity I knew so well. She was worried, yes, but she was also searching for answers, piecing together the unspoken truths I was carrying like a heavy burden.

Crossing the threshold, I was immediately enveloped by the familiar warmth of her home. The scent of lavender mingled with something sweet and freshly baked, a sensory snapshot of countless afternoons spent here. The house itself was as I remembered—slightly chaotic but deeply lived in, every corner filled with personality and the echoes of a life rich with memories.

Family photos lined the walls, a gallery of frozen moments chronicling decades of love, laughter, and growth. My gaze snagged on one in particular: a photograph from my wedding day. Nial and I stood at the centre, our families flanking us, all smiles and sunshine. My younger self looked radiant in white, my eyes fixed adoringly on Nial. He stood tall beside me, his dark hair tousled just enough to make him look effortlessly charming, his eyes crinkled with the intensity of his smile.

I remembered that moment as though it had happened yesterday—the way he'd squeezed my hand and whispered, "I love you," just before the camera snapped. That whisper had been a promise, a vow layered over the one we had just spoken aloud: to build a life together, to face everything as a team. My throat tightened as I stared at his frozen expression of joy. Where was he now? Who was he with? Was he even safe? The questions clawed at me, each one more unbearable than the last.

"Jenny? Are you alright, dear?" Rowena's voice, tinged with concern, pulled me from my thoughts. I turned to face her, instinctively plastering on a smile, ready to offer some meaningless reassurance. But the look in her eyes stopped me. There was no point in pretending, not with her. Rowena had always been able to see straight through me. From the fibs of my childhood to the guarded silences of my adult years, my mother had an unerring ability to read my heart like the pages of an open book.

I swallowed hard, the words I'd been preparing dissipating into the air. "I—" I started, then faltered, unsure how to continue.

The sound of Sammy's small feet pattering against the hardwood floor tugged at my heart before I even saw him. His joyful shout as he launched himself into my arms was a brief reprieve from the whirlwind of my thoughts, a moment of pure, unfiltered love. His tiny arms wrapped tightly around my neck, and I clung to him just as fiercely, as if holding him could anchor me to some semblance of stability.

His familiar scent filled my senses—a blend of baby shampoo, biscuits, and that indefinable sweetness that was uniquely Sammy. His curls brushed against my cheek, soft and wild, as he nestled against me. I could feel the steady rhythm of his heart, a reminder of everything that still grounded me despite the swirling storm of uncertainty.

For a few precious seconds, the world beyond Sammy's embrace ceased to exist. But as I eased him back to look at him properly, the joy in his eyes gave way to something more solemn. He studied me, his little brow furrowing as if trying to solve a puzzle far beyond his years. His blue eyes, a mirror image of Nial's, reflected both innocence and an unspoken understanding that not everything was as it should be.

"Mummy, where's Daddy?" The words fell softly from his lips, but their weight hit me like a thunderclap. His voice was laced with confusion, edged with a fear that no child his age should ever feel.

My chest tightened, and tears that I had been so determined to suppress broke free, carving hot trails down my cheeks. I cradled him closer, burying my face in his hair, desperately trying to shield him from the truth even as it suffocated me. How could I explain the unexplainable to him when I could barely grasp it myself?

"Daddy's... Daddy's not here right now, sweetheart," I managed, each word a struggle against the knot of emotion lodged in my throat. "But he loves you so much, Sammy. He misses you terribly, I'm sure." The reassurance in my voice was a lie I needed to believe as much as he did, even though the words felt hollow, echoing in the void left by Nial's absence.

Sammy pulled back slightly, his wide eyes brimming with tears that mirrored my own. His small voice wavered as he asked the question that tore at my heart. "But why did he go away? Doesn't he want to be with us anymore?"

I swallowed hard, the pain in his voice like a dagger twisting deep within me. There were no words to explain the inexplicable, no way to soothe his fears when I couldn't even quiet my own. My mouth opened, but no sound came out, the enormity of my helplessness silencing me.

And then Rowena was there. Her arms enveloped us both, pulling Sammy and me into the warmth of her embrace. She didn't hesitate or falter, her presence as steady and dependable as it had been all my life, regardless of whatever disagreements or differences we might have. Her strength wrapped around me like a lifeline, a reminder that, even in the darkest moments, I wasn't alone.

"Now, now," she murmured, her voice low and soothing, yet imbued with that firm authority only a grandmother could wield. "Let's not jump to conclusions. Your daddy loves you both very much, Sammy. Sometimes grown-ups have to go away for a little while, but that doesn't mean they don't love us or want to be with us."

I looked up, catching Rowena's eye over Sammy's head. Her words weren't a solution, but they were exactly what I needed in that moment—something gentle, something hopeful, something to steady the ship amidst the storm. I nodded at her, a silent thank you, as I stroked Sammy's curls, willing him to feel the truth of her words, even if I couldn't quite believe them myself.

"Why don't we all go into the kitchen?" Rowena suggested, her tone brightening slightly as she pulled back, guiding us down the familiar hallway. "I've just taken a batch of your favourite chocolate chip biscuits out of the oven, Sammy. And I think we could all use a nice cup of tea."

Sammy's sniffles began to subside, his face lighting up at the mention of biscuits. "Biscuits!" he exclaimed, his small voice brimming with enthusiasm as if the mere thought of chocolate chips could momentarily banish the worries clouding his young mind.

I managed a weak smile, grateful for Rowena's deft ability to redirect his focus. As she led us towards the heart of the house, the kitchen—always the centre of comfort and connection in Rowena's home—I found myself clinging to the hope that perhaps, somehow, the warmth of this space and the strength of my family could provide a balm for the ache of Nial's absence, if only for a little while.

As we gathered around the familiar kitchen table, its surface worn smooth by years of family life, I felt an odd mix of comfort and pain. The scratches and faded stains told stories of countless shared meals, laughter, and even the occasional heated argument. But today, the empty seat at the table seemed to overshadow everything else, a glaring reminder of Nial's absence.

Sammy, his biscuit already halfway to his mouth, swung his little legs back and forth under the table. The simple joy of chocolate chip biscuits was a balm to his young heart, even if only temporarily. Rowena moved about the kitchen with practised ease, the rhythmic clatter of cups and saucers a comforting soundtrack. The steam rising from the kettle swirled in the air, mingling with the warm, buttery aroma of freshly baked biscuits, creating a momentary illusion of normality.

"Now then," Rowena said as she placed a steaming mug of tea before me, the fragrant brew promising a brief respite. A small glass of milk found its way to Sammy, who beamed up at her. She sat down and fixed me with her steady gaze. "Why don't you tell me exactly what happened at the police station?"

The weight of her question brought me back to the stark reality of the day. I wrapped my hands around the mug, letting its warmth seep into my chilled fingers as I tried to gather my thoughts.

"They... they weren't very helpful at first," I began quietly, conscious of Sammy's presence. I glanced at him to make sure he was absorbed in his biscuit. For now, he seemed blissfully unaware of the undercurrent of tension between the adults. "Linda was there, at the front desk. She treated me like a stranger, Mum. Like I was just another hysterical wife overreacting."

Rowena's eyes flashed with indignation, her lips tightening into a thin line. "Linda? Your sister-in-law Linda? Well, I never! Just wait until the next family gathering. I'll give her a piece of my mind—"

"Rowena, please," I cut in, shaking my head. The last thing I needed was for mum to launch into one of her legendary tirades. "It's not important right now. The thing is, she refused to file a missing persons report. Because of the text message."

Rowena's brow furrowed, her fingers tightening slightly around her own cup. "The one from Nial saying he'd be home late?" she asked, her tone sceptical.

I nodded, frustration bubbling to the surface. "Yes. Linda said it counted as contact. That he wasn't really missing because of it. But you know Nial. He'd never just disappear like this. He wouldn't leave Sammy without saying goodbye. Something's wrong, I know it."

Rowena reached across the table, her warm hand covering mine. The simple gesture was enough to steady me, if only for a moment. "A mother's instinct is rarely wrong," she said softly, her eyes searching mine. "But if the police won't help, what are you going to do?"

I opened my mouth to tell her about Detective Jenkins when Sammy's voice broke through. "Mummy, can we call Daddy? I want to tell him about the big cat I saw in Grandma's garden."

The innocent request felt like a punch to the gut, sharp and unexpected. My breath caught, and I had to fight to keep my voice steady. "Oh, sweetheart," I began gently, forcing a smile. "I don't think we can call Daddy right now. His phone... it's not working properly." The lie burned in my throat, but how could I tell him the truth? That every attempt to reach Nial had been met with the cold finality of voicemail?

Sammy's face fell, his shoulders slumping as he set his biscuit down. The light in his eyes dimmed, replaced by a confusion and hurt no child should ever feel. Seeing his disappointment was almost too much to bear. How could Nial do this? How could he leave us—leave Sammy—without a word? The surge of anger that followed was sharp and all-encompassing, momentarily overtaking the fear.

I reached out, brushing a crumb from Sammy's cheek. "Daddy loves you so much, Sammy," I said, my voice thick with emotion. "He misses you terribly. And I promise, we'll find him. Okay?"

Sammy nodded slowly, his little hand reaching out to clasp mine. His trust in me, so absolute and unwavering, only deepened my resolve. I glanced at Rowena, whose expression mirrored my own mix of determination and heartbreak.

"Jenny," Rowena said softly, her voice cutting through the stillness of the kitchen. Her eyes, so like my own, met mine with an intensity that made me pause. They were filled with concern, but beneath it, there was something sharper – suspicion, perhaps, or an unspoken question. "What aren't you telling me?"

The weight of her gaze was almost too much. I sighed heavily, running a hand through my hair as I struggled to decide how much to reveal. The fragments of information I had were hardly comforting, and some of it felt too fragile to share. "There was one detective," I began cautiously, "Detective Jenkins. He seemed to believe me, at least more than the others did. He's opened a case file, but..." I hesitated, unsure if voicing my doubts would make them more real. "I don't know, Rowena. I feel like there's something he's not telling me. He asked about someone named Luke Smith, but I've never heard of him."

Rowena's reaction was immediate. Her eyebrows shot up, and she tilted her head slightly as if the name had struck a chord. "Luke Smith?" she repeated, her voice tinged with curiosity. "That name sounds familiar, but I can't quite place it." Her brow furrowed deeply, her expression shifting as she tried to tug a half-formed memory into focus.

A flicker of hope ignited in my chest. Could she know something? Could this lead, tenuous as it was, finally give me some direction? "You know him?" I asked urgently, leaning forward. "Rowena, this could be important. Think hard – where have you heard that name before?"

Rowena pursed her lips, her gaze growing distant as she delved into the depths of her memory. The kitchen seemed to grow quieter, the only sound the soft crunch of Sammy munching on his biscuits. "I'm not sure, dear," she admitted after a moment, her tone apologetic. "It's right on the edge of my memory, but I can't quite grasp it. Give me some time. It might come to me."

I nodded, trying to temper my disappointment. It was something, at least – a glimmer of hope in a sea of uncertainty. "Alright," I said, forcing a small smile. "Just... let me know if you remember anything, no matter how small it might seem."

Rowena reached out and squeezed my hand, her grip warm and steady. "Of course, Jenny."

As the warmth of the kitchen pressed around us, I couldn't shake the feeling that the name Luke Smith was more than just a random detail. It felt like a key, but what it might unlock was a mystery I wasn't sure I was ready to face. My mind churned with questions, the possibilities both thrilling and terrifying. Who was Luke Smith? And was he actually connected somehow to Nial's disappearance?

Sammy's cheerful voice broke through my racing thoughts. "Mummy, can we go look for the big cat again?" he asked, standing in the doorway with his hands on his hips, his face still smeared with chocolate. His wide grin and bright eyes were a reminder of the innocence I was desperate to protect.

I smiled despite myself, grateful for the brief distraction. "Of course, sweetheart," I said, ruffling his curly hair. "Why don't you go get your shoes on?"

As Sammy bounded away, Rowena leaned in closer, her voice dropping to a conspiratorial whisper. "Jenny," she began, her tone serious yet tender. "I know we've had our differences, but no matter what's going on with Nial – whatever trouble he might be in – you know I'm here for you and Sammy, right? No matter what."

Her words, so unexpected in their warmth and unconditional support, brought a fresh wave of emotion crashing over me. Tears stung my eyes as I nodded, swallowing hard against the lump in my throat. "I know," I whispered, my voice trembling. "Thank you."

The moment was interrupted by Sammy's triumphant shout. "I'm ready, Mummy!" he called, stomping back into the kitchen with his shoes on the wrong feet and a gleeful grin plastered across his face.

As we stepped out into the crisp Tasmanian afternoon, the chill air wrapped around me, invigorating yet sobering. The name Luke Smith echoed in my mind like a refrain, growing louder with each step I took. I didn't yet know how significant it was, how it would change everything, but I could feel its weight pressing against the fragile threads of our unravelling lives.

As the afternoon wore on, we settled into a peculiar routine, a strained performance of normality as fragile as a delicate porcelain vase perched on the edge of a shelf. The kitchen, once bathed in the inviting warmth of golden sunlight, grew dimmer with the encroaching shadows of late afternoon. Outside, the winter sky turned a brooding steel grey, its oppressive weight pressing down on the small world inside Rowena's home.

Sammy, always attuned to the emotions of those around him, seemed to absorb the tension hanging thick in the air. His usual boundless energy had faded into something brittle and uncertain, manifesting in repeated tugs at my sleeve and relentless questions that cut straight to the heart of my fears.

"When's Daddy coming home, Mummy?" he asked, his small voice trembling with uncertainty. It was a question that landed like a blow each time he asked it, exposing the widening cracks in the veneer of control I was desperately trying to maintain.

I knelt down to his level, cupping his round face in my hands. "Soon, sweetheart," I murmured, forcing my voice to remain steady. "He's just... working late." The lie rolled off my tongue for the hundredth time, each iteration heavier with guilt and self-loathing. I stroked his curls—so like Nial's—and held his gaze, willing him to believe me even as I doubted my own words.

Rowena, sensing my fraying nerves, stepped in with the practiced finesse of a matriarch well-versed in soothing troubled waters. She launched into a string of stories from her youth, anecdotes of defiance and mischief that drew Sammy's attention away from his questions, if only briefly.

"Did I ever tell you about the time I snuck into the town hall dressed as a man?" Rowena began, her tone playful and conspiratorial. Her eyes sparkled with a mischievous light, her storytelling an act of love and preservation.

Sammy perked up, his curiosity piqued. "No, Grandma! What happened?" he asked, leaning forward with wide eyes.

"Well," Rowena continued, her voice lowering as if to share a great secret, "it was 1968, and women weren't allowed in the public gallery during council meetings. Can you imagine that, Sammy?"

He shook his head vigorously, his little mouth forming an indignant "No!"

"So," Rowena said, pausing dramatically, "I borrowed your grandfather's best suit, padded myself out with some socks for a belly, and waltzed right in. Nobody suspected a thing!"

Sammy erupted into giggles, his laughter a sweet reprieve in the heavy atmosphere. "Did you get caught, Grandma?"

"Eventually," Rowena admitted, her grin widening. "But not before I managed to give the councillors a piece of my mind. They were so shocked, I think I actually made them forget their agenda for the evening."

As Sammy's laughter filled the room, I felt a wave of gratitude towards my mother. Her stories, though familiar to me, brought comfort and lightness to a space that had been overshadowed by worry. For a moment, I allowed myself to smile, but it was fleeting. Beneath the surface, my mind was a churning sea of anxiety and unspoken questions.

I stared out the window, drawn to the deepening twilight outside. The garden, usually a vibrant sanctuary even in winter, now seemed cloaked in menace. The gnarled branches of the old oak tree swayed in the rising wind, their movements casting jagged shadows across the lawn. Every rustle in the undergrowth made my heart jolt, my overactive imagination conjuring figures lurking just out of sight.

I needed to act. The waiting, the stillness—it was suffocating. My mind raced, searching for the next step, the next move that might bring me closer to answers. Detective Jenkins had opened a door, but it felt as though I stood on the threshold of something vast and unknowable, hesitant to step into the unknown.

As the dimming light painted the kitchen in sombre hues, shadows stretching across the floor like silent sentinels, I made my decision. I couldn't remain here, bound by inaction, while Nial's whereabouts—and his safety—remained a cruel mystery. The weight of uncertainty clawed at my resolve, but it was tempered by the clarity of purpose that came with deciding to act. Nial needed me, and sitting idly while others searched wasn't an option.

The resolve steadied me, as if forging a plan had allowed me to grasp something solid amidst the storm of doubt and fear. The terror of the unknown still lurked, whispering its dreadful possibilities at the edges of my mind, but it no longer controlled me.

"Rowena," I interrupted her mid-story—a tale about a stolen boat and an enraged fisherman that had Sammy wide-eyed with delight. My voice, quiet but firm, sliced through the cosy atmosphere. "I need to ask you a favour."

Rowena turned to me, her expression softening as she studied my face. She knew, of course. She always did. Her ability to read me, even through the years of distance and tension, felt uncanny in moments like this. "You want me to keep Sammy for a bit longer, don't you?" she said gently.

I nodded, relief washing over me at her perceptiveness. "Just for a day or two," I said, my words tumbling out in a rush. "I need to... I need to do something. I can't sit here waiting for the police to figure things out. I need to start looking for answers myself."

Rowena didn't hesitate. "Of course, dear," she said, her tone steady and resolute. Her gaze moved to Sammy, who was watching us with curiosity, his earlier unease momentarily replaced by interest. "Sammy and I will have a grand time, won't we, my little prince?"

Sammy brightened at this, his small body almost vibrating with renewed excitement. "Can we make more biscuits, Grandma?" he asked, his voice tinged with hope.

"As many as you like, sweetheart," Rowena replied with a warm smile, brushing a stray curl from his forehead. Then, turning back to me, her expression grew serious. Her eyes glimmered with concern. "Just promise me you'll be careful, Jenny. And keep me updated. I worry about you, you know."

Her words hit me squarely in the chest, stirring a mixture of gratitude and emotion. Despite the years of friction between us, the petty grievances and misunderstandings, the bond we shared as mother and daughter shone through in this moment.

"I will. I promise," I said, my voice thick with emotion. The words felt painfully insufficient to express my gratitude, but they were all I could manage.

As I gathered my belongings, I gave Sammy a long hug, holding him tightly as if the strength of my embrace could shield him from the shadows creeping into our lives. His small hands clung to me, his head resting against my shoulder. For a moment, I didn't want to let go, the thought of leaving him gnawing at my resolve.

I knelt to his level, looking into his eyes—Nial's eyes—and felt a renewed sense of determination rise within me.

"Mummy has to go away for a little bit," I told him, my voice calm and measured, though the effort of keeping it steady was immense. "But I'll be back soon, and maybe I'll bring Daddy with me. Okay?"

Sammy's brow furrowed in concentration as he processed my words, then he nodded solemnly. "Okay, Mummy. I'll be good for Grandma."

"I know you will, sweetheart," I said, pulling him close once more. How I longed to stay, to keep him safe and close. But I knew I couldn't.

Standing, I turned to Rowena, who placed a reassuring hand on my shoulder. "Go do what you need to do," she said simply, her voice steady, her strength a quiet balm.

Stepping out into the crisp evening air, the first stars beginning to punctuate the darkening sky, I felt the weight of my choice settle on me. It wasn't just for Nial—it was for Sammy, for our family. Whatever I found, whatever lay ahead, I would face it. And I wouldn't stop until I brought Nial home.

THE EMPTY HOUSE

4338.210.4

The key trembled in my hand as I turned it in the ignition, the familiar hum of the engine breaking through the oppressive silence that had wrapped itself around me since leaving my mother's house. As I pulled away from the kerb, the sight of Rowena's yellow house, glowing faintly in the gathering darkness, shrank in my rear-view mirror. It felt as though I was leaving the last fragile thread of safety behind.

The route back to our house was etched into muscle memory—a path I had driven countless times without a second thought. But tonight, the journey felt different, weighted with dread. Each turn of the wheel seemed laboured, as if the car itself understood the gravity of where I was going.

The empty backseat was a void, its silence more deafening than the quiet of any empty room. Normally, Sammy's chatter would fill the air—questions about everything from kangaroos to why the moon follows the car. His absence was a hollow ache, accentuated by the sight of his stuffed koala slumped against the corner of his car seat. Its once-fluffy ears were worn smooth by his small hands, a silent witness to a childhood that, for now, was missing its anchor. The sight of it made my throat tighten, but I blinked back the threatening tears. Not now, I told myself. Not here.

In a futile effort to drown out the silence, I flicked on the radio. Static crackled for a moment before the clipped tones of the news anchor broke through, his voice brisk and detached from the anguish that filled my world.

"...and in local news, health officials are urging residents to remain vigilant as the flu epidemic continues to grip Hobart. Hospitals report..."

The mundanity of it was unbearable. How could the world carry on with its banal reports and everyday concerns while mine had crumbled into pieces? My hand shot out to switch it off, the silence that followed feeling somehow louder, pressing against my ears with its weight. All that remained was the rhythmic thrum of the tyres on the road and the hollow cadence of my own breath.

As I turned onto our street, a chill rippled through me, prickling the back of my neck. The winter air, sharp and crisp, seemed to seep through the car's windows, despite the heater blowing tepidly. In the fading light, our neighbourhood no longer felt like the safe haven it once was. The houses, with their neat gardens and familiar fences, seemed to loom with a quiet menace. Shadows stretched across the pavements like dark tendrils, and the skeletal branches of bare trees clawed at the twilight sky.

When I pulled into the driveway, the sight of our house hit me like a punch to the gut. Its quiet facade, once inviting with its warm porch light and cheerfully painted door, now looked forlorn, its shutters like closed eyes averting their gaze from the pain within. This was the home we had built together, the place where every wall held a memory, where every corner bore the imprint of our lives. But now it stood as a hollow monument to Nial's absence.

I sat in the car, my hands still gripping the steering wheel, unable to make myself move. From here, in this liminal space, I could pretend. Pretend that everything was fine. Pretend that Nial was inside, standing at the stove with his sleeves rolled up, a wooden spoon in one hand and a dish towel over his shoulder, Sammy perched on the counter, listening raptly as his father spun some fantastical story.

Pretend that I would walk through that door and find our life, whole and intact, waiting for me.

But the weight of reality pressed down with an unrelenting force. I could feel it in my chest, squeezing, making it hard to breathe. Nial wasn't inside. The silence that awaited me on the other side of that door was different from the silence in the car. It would be oppressive, a vacuum of warmth and life that once filled the space.

I inhaled deeply, trying to summon the courage to step out of the car. The frosty evening air fogged the windshield slightly, blurring my view of the house. It seemed fitting somehow—my sanctuary, once so clear, now obscured by fear and uncertainty.

Taking another deep breath, I forced myself to step out of the car, the cold evening air biting at my skin. Each footfall on the gravel driveway seemed unnaturally loud, the crunching sound reverberating in the stillness. The wind swirled around me, carrying the scent of impending rain and something else – a faint metallic tang that I couldn't quite place. It sent an uneasy shiver down my spine, tightening the knot of tension already coiled in my stomach.

Reaching the front door, I hesitated, my hand hovering over the doorknob. The house loomed before me, no longer the welcoming refuge it had once been, but a silent witness to the turmoil of the past few days. As I steeled myself to enter, a flicker of movement at the edge of my vision made me freeze. My heart leapt into my throat, pounding furiously as I spun around, every muscle in my body bracing for something – I wasn't even sure what.

A neighbour's cat slinked lazily across the road, its dark form disappearing into the shadows. The rush of adrenaline left me trembling, and I let out a nervous laugh, brittle and strained. "Get a grip," I muttered to myself, forcing my hand onto the doorknob and turning it.

The door creaked open, and I stepped inside, the familiar space instantly unfamiliar in its emptiness. The stillness wrapped around me like a shroud, cold and unyielding. The rooms, once filled with the comforting hum of daily life, now felt desolate, each empty corner an accusation, each shadow a reminder of what was missing. The faint smell of lemon cleaner lingered in the air, a ghost of routine chores performed in a world that no longer existed.

In the hallway, the ticking of the clock – a wedding gift from Nial's parents – seemed impossibly loud. Each second was a tiny hammer against my heart, a constant reminder of time slipping away, of questions unanswered and fears unrelenting.

I moved through the house like an intruder, my steps hesitant and slow. The air was heavy, laden with the echoes of laughter and conversation that felt a lifetime away. In the kitchen, a cupboard door stood slightly ajar, and I nudged it closed with a gentle push. My eyes fell on the calendar pinned to the fridge, its cheerful floral design incongruous with the stark reality of the moment. The days were neatly marked with appointments, reminders, and plans – a roadmap of the life we'd built. But now, those plans felt like artefacts from another era, mocking in their optimism.

The urge to do something – anything – became overwhelming. The oppressive weight of the house, of Nial's absence, pressed down on me, suffocating in its intensity. I pulled out my phone, the device cool and impersonal in my trembling hands. I stared at the screen, my thumb hovering over the keypad. Who could I call? Who might have answers?

Against my better judgment, I dialled Nial's number again. The ringing filled the room, hollow and relentless, each unanswered tone a fresh stab of anguish. When his voicemail picked up, the sound of his voice – light, casual, full of warmth – was a cruel juxtaposition to the cold void that now defined my days.

"Hey, it's Nial. Sorry I missed your call. Leave a message and I'll get back to you as soon as I can. Cheers!"

The cheerful beep that followed was almost unbearable. My breath hitched, and I forced myself to speak, though my voice wavered with the weight of unshed tears.

"Nial," I began, the word coming out as a plea. "Please, if you're getting these messages, just… just let me know you're okay. Even if you don't want to come home, even if…" My voice cracked, and I swallowed hard, pushing through the ache in my throat. "Just let me know you're safe. Please."

I ended the call, the emptiness in the room rushing back in to fill the void left by his recorded voice. I dropped the phone onto the counter, its dull thud echoing in the quiet. For a moment, I stood there, paralysed by the enormity of my helplessness.

The house was too silent, too still. I needed to move, to escape the suffocating grip of my thoughts. My feet carried me to the sink, where I braced myself against the counter, staring out the window into the darkened garden. The shadows outside shifted and swayed with the wind, their movements almost hypnotic. For a moment, I imagined Nial stepping out from between the trees, his familiar figure illuminated by the faint light spilling from the window.

But the garden remained empty.

Almost without conscious thought, I found myself drifting into our bedroom, a space once filled with warmth and companionship, now a hollow testament to Nial's absence. The room, bathed in the dim glow of the bedside lamp, felt strangely alien despite its familiarity. It was here, surrounded by the fragments of our shared life, that I began to unravel a new layer of the mystery.

My gaze roamed the room, catching on small, mundane details that now seemed laden with significance. The nightstand on his side of the bed was bare, save for the lamp and a book he had been reading – a detective novel he'd been enjoying over cups of tea before bed. It was still there, untouched, the bookmark peeking out midway through, as though he intended to pick it up again. But the faintest sense of disquiet grew as my eyes landed on his closet, the door ajar.

The absence hit me like a physical blow. Clothes that had once hung in neat rows, a comforting part of his daily routine, were gone. Shirts I had ironed for him, jackets that carried the scent of his cologne – the same scent that lingered faintly in the air – were missing. And in the corner where his overnight bag was always tucked, there was now an empty, accusatory space.

The implications settled heavily in my chest, stealing my breath. A wave of nausea rose as my mind scrambled to make sense of it. My knees buckled, and I sank onto the bed, gripping the edge of the duvet. The fabric was soft under my fingertips, imbued with the faint scent of us, of better days. I clutched it tightly, as though it could tether me to the past and hold back the tidal wave of doubt crashing over me.

Had Nial chosen to leave us? The thought was unbearable, a jagged wound tearing through my heart. The man I knew, the man who had built a life with me and adored Sammy with all his heart – would he simply walk away without a word? My mind rebelled against the idea, yet the missing clothes and the empty space mocked me with their stark simplicity.

Desperation clawed at me, and I fumbled for my phone. Dialling his number again, I pressed the device to my ear with trembling hands, the cold surface grounding me as the line rang out. Once more, his voicemail greeted me with that cheerful, maddeningly normal tone.

"Hey, it's Nial. Sorry I missed your call. Leave a message, and I'll get back to you as soon as I can. Cheers!"

The beep that followed was like a slap. "Nial," I whispered, my voice barely audible. "Please, if you're hearing this, just… let me know you're okay. That's all I need. Just let me know." My words faltered as I ended the call, the oppressive silence rushing back to fill the void.

A jumble of contradictions churned in my mind. If Nial had chosen to leave, why sever all ties? Why disappear so completely, without a word of explanation or even a goodbye to Sammy? It didn't fit. It wasn't Nial. The man I knew wouldn't leave his son to wonder, wouldn't leave his family to drown in uncertainty. The thought of Sammy, with his wide blue eyes and innocent questions, brought fresh tears to my eyes. How could I explain this to him? How could I make sense of something I didn't understand myself?

I rose from the bed, pacing the room, the motion an outlet for the storm of emotions inside me. My eyes kept drifting to the empty hangers, the neatly stacked but depleted drawers, as if staring at the absence could will an answer into existence. The spaces seemed to mock my understanding, challenging everything I thought I knew about Nial.

But amidst the jumble in my mind, a small, stubborn voice pushed back. This wasn't like Nial. This wasn't the man who had held my hand through hours of labour, who had whispered his love for me as tears slid down his cheeks when Sammy was placed in his arms for the first time. This wasn't the man who left notes in my lunchbox, whose laughter still echoed in the corners of this house.

"This isn't Nial," I said aloud, the words a lifeline in the sea of doubt threatening to pull me under. "Something else is going on. It has to be."

That spark of hope, fragile but persistent, burned brighter. I couldn't let myself believe he had simply abandoned us. There was more to this – there had to be. The truth wasn't in the absence of his clothes or the silence of his phone. It was out there, hidden in shadows, waiting for me to find it.

I stopped pacing and stood still, letting the quiet settle around me. With trembling hands, I straightened the duvet on the bed, as though restoring some semblance of order to the disarray within me. Then, with a deep breath, I stepped back into the house that no longer felt like a home.

With renewed determination, I made my way to Nial's home office. If answers were to be found, surely they would be here, in this space where he had spent so many hours of his life. The room was neat—*too* neat. Every item was precisely where it belonged, the surfaces spotless. Nial had always been organised, but this felt different. It was as if he had carefully curated the space, wiping away any hint of disruption or spontaneity. It didn't feel like Nial. It felt... clinical.

I sat at his desk, my fingers tracing the smooth woodgrain of its surface. How many nights had I watched him work here, his brow furrowed in concentration, the glow of the computer screen casting soft shadows on his face? How many times had Sammy burst through the door, clutching a toy or a drawing, demanding his father's attention? These memories, so vivid, so steeped in love and warmth, felt like daggers now. I had to push them away, had to stay focused on the task at hand.

I began searching methodically, starting with the desk drawers. The top ones yielded nothing unusual—pens, paperclips, sticky notes, and an assortment of old receipts. I rifled through them quickly, my frustration growing with each empty find. But in the bottom drawer, hidden beneath a stack of dog-eared construction magazines, something caught my eye.

It was a small, leather-bound notebook, the cover worn smooth with use. My breath hitched as I pulled it out, a strange mix of anticipation and dread twisting in my stomach. I flipped it open, my hands trembling slightly. The pages were filled with Nial's familiar handwriting, the distinctive slant of his letters immediately recognisable. But as I scanned the entries, my heart began to race for an entirely different reason.

The contents were unlike anything I had ever seen Nial write. Strings of numbers filled many of the pages—some grouped together in patterns, others seemingly random. Scattered among them were names I didn't recognise: *Daniel Keller. Sara Lin. Eric Hunter.* And there, on one page, underlined twice, was a name that sent a shiver down my spine: *Luke Smith.*

My mind reeled. This was the name Detective Jenkins had asked about. It wasn't a coincidence. It couldn't be. I stared at it, my pulse hammering in my ears. What was Nial doing with Luke Smith's name in this notebook? Who were the other people listed? And what did the numbers mean?

Flipping further through the notebook, I found more cryptic entries. Notes jotted in shorthand, fragments of sentences that hinted at something far darker than I wanted to believe. "*Need to confirm location by Friday.*" "*Meeting pushed. Late arrival suspicious.*" "*Don't trust Keller.*"

My chest tightened as I read. This wasn't the Nial I knew. This was someone else entirely—a version of my husband I had never glimpsed, a man whose actions I couldn't begin to understand. My thoughts spun in wild, desperate circles. Was Nial in trouble? Was he running from something? Or worse, had he been involved in something dangerous, something that had finally caught up to him?

I flipped to the last few pages, my hands shaking. The handwriting grew more erratic, the notes shorter and more fragmented. *"It's done."* *"Smith knows."* *"They'll come soon."*

My breath caught in my throat. *They'll come soon?* Who were *they*? And what had Nial done? I clutched the notebook to my chest.

A sound from the living room shattered the fragile quiet of the house, leaving me frozen in the aftermath. The faint creak of a floorboard—it was deliberate, cautious. Someone was here, and they weren't supposed to be.

Fear clawed at me, paralysing my limbs for a long, suffocating moment. My mind raced with possibilities: a burglar? Or someone connected to Nial's disappearance? Whoever it was, they were moving through my house with purpose, the unsettling deliberation of someone who knew what they were looking for.

I shoved the notebook into my pocket, its weight against my hip an unsettling reminder of the potential answers—and dangers—it might hold. My hands trembled as I grabbed the paperweight from Nial's desk, the polished Tasmanian granite cold and reassuring in my grip. The absurdity of defending myself with a desk ornament didn't escape me, but it was all I had.

I edged toward the door, each step measured and cautious, trying to keep the element of surprise on my side. The house had fallen silent again, but the air felt charged, heavy with the presence of another. My heart pounded so hard it drowned out my breathing, every beat a desperate reminder of the fragility of this moment.

Then it came again—a faint sound, this time from the kitchen. Whoever it was had moved further into the house. Were they searching for something? Or waiting for me to come to them?

A part of me screamed to run, to flee into the night and call for help from somewhere far away. But another part, the part that refused to let fear rule me, urged confrontation. I wanted answers. No, I needed them. If this intruder was tied to Nial in any way, I couldn't let them escape.

Steeling myself, I crept into the hallway. The dim light spilling from a single lamp in the living room cast long, flickering shadows, exaggerating the dark voids of the house. My hand clenched the paperweight so tightly my fingers ached. My pulse thundered in my ears as I took another step forward, the floorboard beneath me betraying me with a loud creak.

The sound was like a starting pistol. From the kitchen, there came a rush of movement—rapid, purposeful footsteps heading toward the living room. My breath hitched as the realisation struck: they were trying to escape.

I bolted into the living room, adrenaline overriding caution. "Stop!" I shouted, my voice trembling but loud enough to echo off the walls. "Who are you? What have you done with Nial?"

The only answer was the sound of retreating footsteps. My eyes swept the room, catching sight of a figure darting back into the kitchen. Heart hammering, I surged forward, gripping the heavy paperweight tighter. I reached the kitchen just in time to see a shadow slipping through the opposite doorway, its movements quick and deliberate.

"Wait!" I yelled, my voice cracking with fear and frustration, but the intruder didn't stop. A moment later, the unmistakable sound of the back door opening and slamming shut echoed through the house.

I followed without hesitation, bursting through the backdoor. The cool night air struck my skin like a slap as I rushed onto the deck.

The yard was empty. My chest heaved as I scanned the darkness, desperate to spot the intruder, but they were gone. It was as if they had been swallowed by the shadows themselves.

And then I saw it: a small piece of paper on the top step. It hadn't been there earlier—I was certain. The wind teased its edges, threatening to carry it away, but I snatched it up with shaking hands.

The photograph felt old, its edges soft and worn. Under the yellow glow of the porch light, I saw two figures—a man and a woman, their faces turned slightly away from the camera. I squinted, trying to discern more detail, and my stomach lurched as recognition dawned. The man's build, the slope of his shoulders, the way he stood—it was Nial. There was no mistaking it.

The photograph felt like a punch to the gut. Why would someone have this? And why leave it behind? My mind raced with possibilities, none of them comforting. Was it dropped accidentally, or had it been planted for me to find? Was it a taunt, a breadcrumb in a twisted game meant to unravel me further?

I turned the photograph over, half-expecting to find a message, a clue, something to make sense of the chaos. But the back was blank, stark in its lack of explanation. The weight of its silence pressed down on me, thick and suffocating.

My thoughts spiralled, a torrent of questions and suspicions. Who was the woman in the photograph? Why was Nial with her? And, more chillingly, when was this taken?

A sharp gust of wind tore through the yard, carrying with it the smell of rain and the faint metallic tang I had noticed earlier. The photograph fluttered in my hand, and I clutched it tighter, as if it might slip through my fingers and take its secrets with it.

My knees buckled slightly as the storm of paranoia swept through me. What if Nial wasn't the victim I had thought he was? What if he wasn't running *from* something... but *to* something? The image of him with this unknown woman added a new layer of doubt, and a darker possibility began to take root: What if Nial had secrets, ones I had never been meant to uncover?

The cold night pressed in around me, the shadows seeming to shift and move as my mind raced. The photograph burned in my hand, a physical embodiment of the mysteries that had consumed my life. I couldn't make sense of it now, but I knew one thing for certain: whoever had been in my house wasn't a random intruder. They had come for a reason, and this photograph was part of it.

The edges of the photograph dug into my palm as I clutched it tighter. This wasn't over. Not by a long shot. If someone was trying to frighten me, to dissuade me from searching for Nial, they had made a grave miscalculation. The fear was there, yes, but it wasn't enough to stop me.

I stepped back inside, locking the door securely behind me, each click of the locks an attempt to reclaim a sense of safety. But the house was irrevocably altered. It no longer felt like a sanctuary. The warmth, the comfort of familiarity, was gone. In its place was a gnawing unease, an almost physical sense of violation that seemed to cling to the air.

Clutching my phone, I began a desperate round of calls, each one a lifeline cast into an ocean of uncertainty. My voice, strong at first, wavered as call after call ended in futility. No one had heard from Nial. Friends who had shared meals with us, colleagues who had laughed with him over coffee, acquaintances whose lives had briefly intertwined with ours—they were all as baffled and concerned as I was.

The supposed job Nial had mentioned before he left that morning—the reason for his departure—remained a void of unanswered questions. No one knew of any potential client or upcoming project. Each denial, each expression of helplessness, was another thread unravelling in the fabric of my reality.

The walls of the house seemed to press in with every passing minute, the silence around me amplifying the chaos in my mind. I could almost hear the echoes of Nial's laughter, see his smile lighting up the dimly lit kitchen. The familiar became oppressive, the memories taunting reminders of a life now fractured. My hope, once a flickering candle in the darkness, began to falter, replaced by the cold weight of despair.

As the last conversation ended and the finality of our situation settled in, the phone felt heavy in my hand, a tangible symbol of the distance that had opened up between Nial and the life we had shared. The silence of the house, once a comforting embrace at the end of a long day, now felt like a chasm widening with each passing moment, filled with the echoes of a life put on pause, waiting for a sign, a word, anything to fill the void left by Nial's disappearance.

The phone felt leaden in my hand as the last call ended, the emptiness of the line mirroring the void left by Nial's disappearance. I sank onto the sofa, the cushions swallowing me in a way that felt less like comfort and more like resignation. The events of the day bore down on me—the cold bureaucracy of the police station, the aching goodbye to Sammy, the haunting emptiness of Nial's closet, the chilling presence of the intruder. Each moment played back in relentless clarity, tightening the knot of fear and confusion in my chest.

Tears came at last, breaking through the dam I had built all day. They flowed freely, hot and silent, carving paths down my face. My body shook with the force of emotions I could no longer contain, and I let them come. There was no point in holding back anymore; the enormity of it all demanded release.

Through my tears, my gaze fell on the family portrait hanging across the room. It was taken on Bruny Island last summer, during a day of golden sunshine and carefree laughter. Nial, Sammy, and I stood before the towering lighthouse, our faces glowing with happiness, our arms wrapped around one another. The sight of it struck me like a blow. How had we come to this? Was that joy nothing more than a fragile veneer, hiding cracks that were now splitting wide open?

My hand tightened around the photograph I had found outside. I looked at it again, its edges crinkled and worn, its contents a stark contrast to the idyllic image on the wall. The woman's long, dark hair, the closeness between her and the man beside her—it all seemed damning. And the man... he looked so much like Nial. Too much. My mind screamed for answers even as it rebelled against the implications.

Could Nial have had another life, one I never knew? Was this a secret finally forcing its way into the light, or a cruel misunderstanding designed to twist the knife of his absence?

Lightning split the sky outside, filling the room with a momentary, blinding glare. The thunder came immediately after, a low growl that rattled the windows and vibrated through the floorboards. The storm had arrived, its fury echoing the tempest within me.

I sat in the flickering shadows, clutching the photograph and trembling, caught between the need to know and the fear of what I might uncover. The storm outside was a force of nature, but the storm inside me was far more dangerous.

4338.211

(30 July 2018)

WE GO ON

4338.211.1

The pre-dawn chill of a Hobart winter morning wrapped around me like a shroud as I stood on my mother's doorstep, my hand hovering just inches from the doorbell. The silence was almost oppressive, broken only by the sporadic sigh of the wind as it swept through the skeletal branches of the old oak in the yard. It was a tableau of greys and blues, the muted colours of an overcast sky painting a bleak promise of rain yet to come. The air was heavy with moisture, clinging to my skin and adding to the weight that already pressed on my chest.

I inhaled deeply, the damp air sharp and cold in my lungs, trying to summon the strength to face what lay beyond the door. Every fibre of my being ached with the events of the past days. Yet I had no choice but to push forward—for Sammy, if not for myself.

Before I could press the bell, the door opened abruptly, as if Rowena had been waiting for me. Her expression, etched with worry, softened as her eyes met mine. "Jenny," she murmured, her voice a mixture of relief and concern as she enveloped me in a warm embrace. Her arms around me, steady and sure, momentarily quelled the tremors of anxiety rippling through my body.

"You're here early, love," she said, pulling back slightly to study my face. There was no judgment in her tone, only a quiet understanding that threatened to unravel me.

I nodded, swallowing hard, afraid to speak lest my voice betray the storm inside. The scent of tea drifted from the house, rich and familiar, a cruel reminder of a routine that had been shattered. I stepped inside, Rowena's hand on my back a gentle reassurance.

"Come in," she said, guiding me through the threshold. "Sammy's still asleep. I was just about to start breakfast."

The warmth of the house enveloped me, a stark contrast to the bitter cold outside and the hollow ache in my chest.

In the kitchen, Rowena moved with practiced ease, the soft clink of the kettle against the stovetop and the quiet rustle of tea bags in their tin creating a fragile illusion of normality. I sank heavily into a chair at the table, my body aching as if the weight of the last few days had aged me decades in just hours.

"How did he sleep?" I asked, my voice barely more than a whisper. The words felt brittle, as though they might shatter under the strain of the emotions tangled up in them.

Rowena turned to me, her face softened by a mixture of understanding and concern. "He had a bit of trouble settling," she admitted gently, "kept asking for you and Nial. But once he drifted off, he slept soundly all through the night."

I nodded, relief and guilt surging through me in equal measure. The thought of Sammy finding a moment of peace in all this turmoil was a comfort, but it came with a sharp edge. I should have been the one to soothe him, to reassure him, not leave him in the care of someone else. Yet here I was, at my mother's table, grasping at straws and struggling to keep it together.

Rowena set a steaming mug of tea in front of me, the scent of Earl Grey curling up in wisps of steam, carrying with it a fleeting sense of comfort. "You know you're doing the right thing, don't you?" she asked, her voice firm but kind. She leaned against the counter, watching me with that knowing expression she always had, the one that cut through my walls with surgical precision. "Sammy's safe here, Jenny. You need time to... to figure things out."

I wrapped my hands around the mug, the ceramic almost scalding against my icy fingers. "I know," I murmured, though the words felt hollow, spoken more for her benefit than mine. "It's just..." My voice faltered, catching on the knot in my throat. "It feels wrong, being apart from him. Like I'm... like I'm failing him."

The admission cracked something in me, and I looked down at the tea, unwilling to meet her gaze. The weight of my inadequacies, real or imagined, bore down on me. Rowena crossed the small space between us and rested a hand on my shoulder. The warmth of her touch, her quiet solidarity, threatened to undo me completely.

When I finally looked up at her, the worry etched into her face struck me. The fine lines around her eyes seemed deeper, her mouth set in a tight line that spoke of a restless night and unspoken fears. In that moment, I realised the strain wasn't mine alone to carry. My mother, who had always seemed so steady and strong, was wearing the stress of this ordeal like a shroud. She shouldn't have to bear this burden, not now, not at this stage of her life. And yet, here she was, holding everything together for me when I couldn't.

"I have to go to work," I said suddenly, the words feeling wrong and necessary all at once. They tasted bitter, an almost physical reminder of the way life continued to demand normality despite the gaping hole where Nial should have been. "I can't afford to miss it. I can't... I can't lose my job on top of everything else."

The pragmatic part of me knew this was true. The world didn't stop for grief or fear. There were bills to pay, routines to uphold, a semblance of stability to maintain. But another part of me raged against the injustice of it, the absurdity of pretending everything was fine while my life crumbled around me.

Rowena nodded slowly, her understanding a balm I didn't deserve. "Of course, dear," she said, her voice steady and calm. "You do what you need to do. Sammy will be fine here with me."

Her confidence in her words, in herself, was something I clung to like a lifeline. But deep down, I wondered how much longer I could keep walking this tightrope, how much longer I could pretend to balance on the edge without falling into the abyss.

As if on cue, the soft patter of small feet against the wooden floor reached us, a sound both familiar and heart-wrenching. My pulse quickened, and my breath caught in my throat—a visceral, instinctive response to my son's presence. Sammy appeared in the doorway, his pyjamas slightly rumpled, and his hair an adorable mess from sleep. The sight of him, with his wide, curious eyes and tiny frame, brought a surge of emotions crashing over me. Love, fierce and unyielding, mixed with guilt and fear.

"Mummy?" he asked, his voice soft and uncertain. The simplicity of that one word, laden with so much trust and expectation, nearly undid me.

I was on my feet before I could think, sweeping him into my arms as if holding him close could shield him from the harsh realities that had invaded our lives. His warmth seeped into me, and I buried my face in his hair, breathing in the scent of him—soap, sleep, and that indefinable essence that was purely Sammy. My arms tightened around him, as though letting go might somehow make everything worse.

"Good morning, sweetheart," I managed, though my voice was thick with emotion. "Did you sleep well at Grandma's?"

Sammy nodded, his cheek brushing against my shoulder, before pulling back to look at me with those big, searching eyes. "When are we going home, Mummy? Where's Daddy?"

The questions landed like punches, each one driving the air from my lungs. How could I answer him? How could I explain that home didn't feel safe anymore, that his father—the man who read him bedtime stories, who tucked him in with a kiss—was gone without a word or a trace? The instinct to protect him collided with the cold reality that I couldn't shield him forever.

I forced a smile, though it felt brittle on my face. "We're going to stay with Grandma for a little while longer, love," I said, injecting as much cheer as I could muster into my tone. "It'll be like a holiday. Won't that be fun?"

Sammy's small brow furrowed, his innate perceptiveness cutting through my facade. "But what about Daddy? Is he on holiday too?" he asked, his voice tinged with confusion and a hint of betrayal.

I glanced at Rowena, my silent plea for help so stark that it practically shouted across the room. Her gaze met mine, and for a moment, I saw the understanding there—the unspoken acknowledgment of how fragile I felt, of how much I needed her to intervene.

"Who wants pancakes for breakfast?" she interjected smoothly, her voice light and inviting. "Sammy, why don't you help me mix the batter?"

It worked, at least for the moment. Sammy's face lit up at the prospect, and he scrambled onto a chair, momentarily distracted. As he reached for the spoon Rowena handed him, I turned away, closing my eyes and letting out a slow, measured breath. The reprieve was temporary, but it gave me the space to pull myself together.

The clock on the wall ticked loudly, reminding me that time was slipping away. I needed to leave soon if I was going to make it to work on time. The thought of stepping back into a classroom, of pretending everything was fine while my life was in shambles, felt impossible. Yet, it was a tether to normality I couldn't afford to let go of—not now, not with so much uncertainty looming over us.

I turned back toward the kitchen and froze. Sammy, giggling as Rowena showed him how to stir the pancake batter, was a vision of innocence and joy. The sight struck me with an unexpected pang of fear. The very normality of the scene felt fragile, as if it could shatter at any moment. My heart raced with the sudden, urgent need to protect him, to ensure that nothing—nothing—would harm him.

"Rowena," I said abruptly, my voice low and insistent. Rowena looked up, startled by my tone. The spoon in her hand paused mid-stir, and Sammy's laughter trailed off as he glanced between us.

"Go on, sweetheart," I said gently to him, forcing a reassuring smile. "Keep helping Grandma. I just need to talk to her for a minute." Sammy nodded, his attention already back on the batter.

Rowena stepped aside, setting the spoon down as she turned to me. "What is it, Jenny?" she asked quietly, her tone tinged with concern.

I hesitated, the weight of my fears threatening to choke me. When the words finally came, they tumbled out in a rush, raw and unfiltered. "I need you to promise me something," I said, my hands gripping the edge of the counter as if it were the only thing keeping me upright. "Don't leave the house with Sammy. Please."

Rowena's eyes widened, and I saw the flicker of doubt there. I knew how I sounded—paranoid, irrational—but I couldn't help it. The fear that had been building in me since Nial disappeared had sharpened into something visceral, something I couldn't ignore, especially after the blatant intrusion into our home last night. The very sanctity of our sanctuary felt as though it were almost irreparably violated. If someone had become so bold as to enter our home, what else might they be capable of? The thought sent a terrifying shudder down my spine.

"Jenny..." Rowena began, but I cut her off.

"Just promise me," I urged, the desperation in my voice cracking through the calm I'd been trying so hard to maintain. "I'm scared, Rowena. I'm scared Nial is planning to take him."

I chose not to tell Rowena my other fear, the one that gnawed at me relentlessly—that I still didn't believe Nial was capable of infidelity, but instead, something far worse had happened to him. To voice this thought aloud felt like inviting it into reality, giving it a power I wasn't ready to confront. So I kept it locked away, a shadowy spectre in the periphery of my mind, constantly whispering doubts and worst-case scenarios.

Rowena didn't press me further. Her sharp eyes lingered on me, searching, but she said nothing. Whether she believed my fears or thought them the product of stress, I couldn't tell. But she didn't question me, and for that, I was deeply grateful. Her unspoken support was a balm to the raw edges of my nerves, a silent affirmation that I wasn't entirely alone in this fight. It wasn't an answer to my fears, but it was enough to buoy me, however briefly, in the storm.

"Alright, love," she said finally, her voice as calm and steady as the hand she placed on mine. The warmth of her palm seeped into my cold skin, grounding me in a way I hadn't realised I needed. "We'll stay in today. I'll tell Sammy we're having a special day at home."

The relief hit me like a wave, leaving me momentarily lightheaded. My shoulders sagged, tension easing just slightly as her promise settled over me. "Thank you," I whispered, blinking back tears that threatened to spill. It wasn't just gratitude for her words but for everything—for her willingness to anchor me when I felt untethered, for creating a safe haven for Sammy, for stepping into a role I hadn't realised I needed so badly.

Rowena gave my hand a final squeeze, her smile faint but reassuring. "We'll be fine, Jenny. You focus on what you need to do. Sammy and I will make it a day to remember."

Her words carried a quiet determination that I tried to cling to as I prepared to leave. I gathered my things with slow, deliberate movements, steeling myself for the day ahead. But as I slung my bag over my shoulder, I couldn't shake the overwhelming sense that I was teetering on the edge of a precipice, the ground beneath me crumbling bit by bit. The life Nial and I had built together, the future we'd planned, seemed to be slipping further out of reach, replaced by an abyss of questions and uncertainties. And yet, I had no choice but to keep moving forward, to keep searching for answers even as the unknown loomed ahead.

Crossing the kitchen, I pulled Sammy into a tight embrace. His small arms wrapped around my neck, his warmth a fleeting comfort against the cold reality pressing down on me. "Be good for Grandma," I murmured, brushing his hair back and pressing a kiss to his forehead. "I'll be back before you know it."

Sammy leaned back slightly, his big, solemn eyes studying my face with the perceptiveness only children seem to possess. "Okay, Mummy," he said, his voice soft but steady. Then, with a sincerity that shattered my already fragile composure, he added, "Will you bring Daddy home?"

I swallowed hard, fighting to keep my emotions in check, even as my throat tightened and my chest ached with the pressure of unshed tears. I cupped his face gently, marvelling at how much he resembled Nial—the same sharp features, the same trusting gaze. "I'm going to try my very best, sweetheart," I said, my voice barely above a whisper. The words felt both like a promise and a plea, a hope I clung to even as doubt gnawed at the edges of my resolve.

Sammy nodded, his small hands patting my cheeks reassuringly, as if he could sense the storm roiling inside me and wanted to soothe it. I kissed him again, then forced myself to turn away before the emotions overwhelmed me entirely.

Rowena was waiting by the door, Sammy now perched on her hip. They looked so normal, so safe, framed by the warm glow of the house. It was a picture of stability, of love and familiarity, and it only made the contrast with my reality more jarring. I stepped out into the morning, the air biting at my skin with the sharp chill of winter, and glanced back one last time.

Rowena raised her hand in a small wave, her expression steady but shadowed with worry. Sammy waved too, his little hand flapping enthusiastically despite the solemnity in his eyes. I waved back, forcing a smile that felt brittle, a mask to hide the turmoil beneath.

As the door closed behind me, sealing them safely inside, I sent up a silent prayer that they would remain untouched by whatever darkness was encroaching on our lives. For their sake, and for mine, I needed answers. And I needed them soon.

AN EARNEST PERFORMANCE

4338.211.2

The morning sun, muted and ineffective, cast a pale glow over St. Michael's Collegiate School as I approached its towering brick facade. Normally, the sight of the historic building, nestled against rolling hills, would evoke a sense of pride, even comfort. Today, it felt foreboding, a fortress that I had to breach, armed only with a brittle facade of normality. The air was crisp, carrying the faint scent of damp earth and eucalyptus, but it did little to clear the fog clouding my thoughts.

Students milled about the grounds, their laughter and chatter creating a symphony of youthful energy. The stark contrast to the turmoil roiling within me was almost unbearable. How could their world be so bright and uncomplicated when mine had been plunged into shadow? My heart ached with the weight of unanswered questions about Nial. Where was he? Why hadn't he called? What secrets had he taken with him when he disappeared?

Turning off the engine, I gripped the steering wheel tightly. My knuckles were bone-white, the pressure my only anchor against the chaos in my mind. This place, these walls—once a refuge of creativity and inspiration—now felt like an alien landscape. It was no longer a sanctuary but a stage, one where I was expected to perform the role of "Mrs Triffett, drama teacher," a role I wasn't sure I could inhabit today.

Glancing in the rearview mirror, I barely recognised the woman staring back at me. Her eyes were hollow, encased by dark circles that no amount of concealer could hide. Her lips were pressed into a hard line, her pallor betraying sleepless nights and unanswered prayers. I took a deep breath, attempting to summon some semblance of composure. Not for me, but for them—for the students, the staff, anyone who might look at me too closely. My job was to inspire and lead, not to crumble.

Fumbling in my bag, I retrieved a tube of lipstick. The vivid red shade I applied felt out of place against my ashen complexion, yet it was the armour I needed. It was a small, defiant act, a splash of colour against the grey wash of my reality. This was my war paint, a shield to deflect the questions and pitying glances that I knew would come. One last steadying breath, and I opened the car door, stepping out into the biting winter air.

The school grounds bustled with activity. Students hurried to classes, their footsteps crunching against the frosty paths. The distant peal of the bell broke the stillness, signalling the beginning of the day. Normally, these sights and sounds would comfort me, reminding me of routine and purpose. Today, they felt hollow. I moved through the gates like a ghost, the familiar vibrancy of the campus blurred by the glass wall of my disconnection. The world continued to turn, oblivious to my private grief, to the mystery and fear that had consumed.

As I approached my classroom, my pace slowed. The door loomed before me, an entryway not to sanctuary, but to an arena. I opened it with hands that trembled slightly, stepping into the room that had always been a haven of creativity. The familiar scent of greasepaint and worn scripts hung in the air, but it no longer comforted me. Instead, it felt oppressive, a reminder of all the roles I had played and the one I now needed to embody—the strong, reliable teacher who could carry on despite the cracks spreading beneath the surface.

The walls were adorned with posters from past productions, each one a snapshot of moments brimming with joy and camaraderie. Those frozen smiles now seemed to mock me, their cheerfulness a stark contrast to the emptiness I felt. Scripts were stacked in the back cupboards, their pages offering neatly structured stories with clear resolutions. How I longed for my life to mirror their tidy narratives, for an end to this relentless uncertainty.

In the corner of the room, a rack of costumes stood untouched, their vibrant colours and intricate textures a jarring reminder of the theatrical magic I was supposed to conjure here. Each garment was a tool for transformation, a means for students to step into someone else's skin, to live another life for a while. But I couldn't summon the energy to draw on that magic for myself. My own costume of normality —hastily stitched together with red lipstick and a forced smile—felt heavy and ill-fitting, threatening to unravel with every passing moment.

I moved to my desk, sinking into the chair with a sigh. The worn wood beneath my fingers was solid, grounding me briefly. The first students would arrive soon, and with them, the need to put on my performance. The script was simple: a confident teacher ready to inspire. But inside, I felt like an understudy who had been thrust onto the stage without warning, the lines unfamiliar, the stakes impossibly high.

As the first students began to trickle into the classroom, their chatter and laughter filled the air. I summoned a smile, though it felt brittle, as if a single wrong move might shatter it entirely. "Good morning, everyone," I said, the words forced but steady. My voice sounded unfamiliar to my ears, a performance I hadn't rehearsed but was compelled to deliver nonetheless.

The students, blissfully unaware of my inner turmoil, settled into their seats, their expressions bright with anticipation for the morning's lesson. Among them, Serena stood out. Always the first to arrive, always eager. Her dark, perceptive eyes lingered on me a moment longer than the others, and I caught a flicker of something in her gaze—concern, curiosity, or perhaps suspicion. It was subtle, but in my heightened state, I noticed it.

"Good morning, Mrs Triffett," she said, her tone warm yet tinged with hesitation. "Are you alright? You look... tired."

The question struck me like a blow, the panic rising swiftly. Was my carefully constructed facade already cracking? Could they see through it so easily? My mind raced, and I forced the corners of my mouth upwards, willing the smile to appear genuine. "I'm fine, Serena," I replied breezily, waving a hand as though to brush away her concern. "Just stayed up too late marking papers. You know how it is. Nothing a strong coffee won't fix."

Serena tilted her head slightly, her gaze lingering. For a moment, it felt as though she might press further, but instead, she simply nodded, her expression neutral. Yet the intensity of her stare unsettled me. Could she sense the fractures beneath my polished exterior, or was it simply my own paranoia casting shadows where none existed?

The class filled quickly, and the day's activities began to blur into one another, my actions mechanical as I moved through the routine of teaching. Today, we worked on *The Importance of Being Earnest*, and I found myself struck by the irony of the play's themes. Wilde's sharp wit dissecting the absurdity of maintaining appearances seemed almost cruelly relevant. How fitting that I was performing my own act of social theatre, clinging desperately to propriety while my life unravelled.

"Excellent work, Serena," I heard myself say, the words flowing on autopilot as she finished her monologue. Her delivery was flawless, every line imbued with the natural charisma that made her stand out among her peers. "Remember, timing is everything in comedy. Let's try it again, but this time, really savour the pauses. Allow the audience to anticipate the punchline."

As Serena nodded and launched into the scene again, my thoughts began to drift. Timing. Anticipation. Was Nial somewhere, savouring the pauses between actions? Was he waiting for something—someone? Or was he... I stopped the thought before it could spiral further, forcing myself back into the present.

Serena's performance was brilliant, her delivery polished to a degree that belied her years. She moved with confidence, her voice clear and engaging. When she delivered Gwendolen's line—*"I am glad to say that I have never seen a spade. It is obvious that our social spheres have been widely different."*—her tone brimmed with wry disdain, and the class erupted into laughter.

The sound jolted me, momentarily pulling me out of my haze. I found myself smiling, not just at Serena's talent but at the pure, unfiltered joy of the moment. The classroom buzzed with energy, the students' excitement infectious, if only for a fleeting second.

Yet, even as the laughter subsided, I caught Serena watching me again. Her small smile was enigmatic, and her dark eyes seemed to hold secrets of their own. Was it admiration in her gaze? Or something else, something harder to name? The thought unnerved me, but I quickly pushed it aside. She was a student, after all, a teenager seeking approval like any other.

As the rehearsal continued, the stark contrast between the lively classroom and the darkness in my heart became impossible to ignore. Here, life thrived—students debated their lines, experimented with delivery, and formed fleeting alliances over shared scripts. Meanwhile, I stood in the centre of it all, my heart weighed down by a suffocating dread. It was like being a shadow in a room full of light, present but never truly part of the brightness.

The play's themes of deception and appearances gnawed at me as the class wore on. In this room, I was not Jenny Triffett, the woman teetering on the edge of despair. I was Mrs Triffett, the drama teacher, a role that required poise and energy. The performance was exhausting, but it was also necessary. To break character now would be to let the fear win. And I couldn't afford that—not yet.

During a brief lull in the rehearsal, I found myself drawn to the window. My eyes fixed on the distant hills, their undulating forms shrouded by the low-hanging mist of an overcast winter day. Somewhere out there, Nial was... what? In trouble? Hiding? The possibilities spun through my mind. The static of worry filled my thoughts so completely that I didn't hear the approach of footsteps until Serena's voice jolted me back to reality.

"Mrs Triffett?" she said, her tone cautious yet warm. Her presence beside me startled me, and I turned to face her, the abruptness of the motion betraying the tension I felt.

"Serena," I managed, plastering on a smile that felt more like a grimace. "Is everything alright?"

Her dark eyes searched mine, her expression tinged with an uncharacteristic seriousness. "Are you sure *you're* alright? You seem... different today."

The question hit me harder than I expected. I forced a chuckle, waving her concern away with a too-casual flick of my hand. "I'm fine, Serena. Just a bit tired, as I said."

Serena didn't look convinced. Her gaze lingered on me, her brows knitting together in a way that made her seem older than her seventeen years. "Sometimes," she said, her voice measured, "it helps to talk to someone. Even someone unexpected."

Her words, spoken with an earnestness that belied her age, left me momentarily speechless. For a fleeting moment, I considered it—spilling everything. Telling her about Nial's disappearance, about Sammy's confusion and my own spiralling fears. But what would that achieve? She was a child, a talented and precocious one, but still a child. This burden wasn't hers to bear.

"That's very thoughtful of you, Serena," I said finally, my voice carefully composed. "But I promise, I'm fine. Now, why don't we see how you're coming along with the rest of Gwendolen's lines?"

A flicker of something—frustration, perhaps?—crossed her face, but it vanished just as quickly. She nodded, her professional poise snapping back into place. "Of course, Mrs Triffett."

As Serena began her monologue again, her delivery sharp and polished, I couldn't help but marvel at the absurdity of it all. Here I was, teaching Wilde's satire on deception and identity, while my own life was unravelling into a bewildering mystery. The irony felt almost cruel, a cosmic joke at my expense.

The bell rang, its sharp, discordant sound slicing through the room like a razor. Students scrambled to gather their belongings, their chatter fading into the hallway as they dispersed for lunch. Scripts lay abandoned on desks, and the classroom, once alive with the energy of rehearsal, fell into silence.

The stillness pressed down on me, heavy and suffocating. I sank into my chair, my head dropping into my hands. The veneer of composure I had so carefully maintained all morning cracked under the weight of my despair. My phone, its screen as blank as the void in my chest, sat accusingly on the desk. No messages. No calls. No answers.

A soft knock on the door pulled me out of my spiral. I quickly wiped at my eyes, straightened my posture, and tried to summon what remained of my professional demeanour. "Come in," I called, my voice steadier than I expected.

The door creaked open, revealing Serena once more, hovering uncertainly on the threshold, her expression a mix of hesitation and determination. "Mrs Triffett," she began, her voice soft, "I forgot my script. I wanted to practise over lunch, but… are you sure you're okay?"

For a moment, the air seemed to grow thicker, the space between us charged with an unspoken tension. I forced another smile, though my cheeks ached from the effort. "I'm fine, Serena. Just a little under the weather. Your script's on the front desk. Don't forget—Act Two is our focus tomorrow."

Serena moved towards her script but lingered, her gaze heavy on me. "Mrs Triffett," she said again, her tone shifting to one of quiet insistence. "I hope you know you can trust me. If there's anything you need… anything at all… I'm here."

Her sincerity was disarming, and for a moment, I felt the dam within me begin to crack. I wanted to tell her everything, to unload the weight of my fear and confusion onto someone willing to listen. But I couldn't. She was my student, not my confidante.

"That's very sweet of you, Serena," I replied, keeping my voice light. "But I'll be alright. Go enjoy your lunch break—and practise those lines!"

She nodded, though her movements were slow, reluctant. As she turned to leave, I caught a flicker of something in her eyes—disappointment, perhaps, or frustration. It was gone in an instant, replaced by her usual warmth. "Of course, Mrs Triffett. I'll see you tomorrow."

As the door clicked shut behind her, the silence in the classroom seemed heavier, pressing in on me from all sides. A wave of guilt surged through me, sharp and unrelenting. These students looked up to me, trusted me to guide them, to be a stable presence in their lives. And yet here I was, lying through my teeth, pretending that my carefully constructed facade of normality wasn't cracking under the weight of my private turmoil.

But what choice did I have? They were teenagers, caught up in their own dramas and dreams. How could I burden them with mine? Still, as I sat there in the empty room, surrounded by the familiar echoes of my day-to-day life, I couldn't shake an unsettling thought.

Serena. Her insistence on helping me, the intensity of her gaze, the way her concern felt almost… rehearsed. It lingered in my mind like a thorn just beneath the surface of the skin. I had been so quick to dismiss it as nothing more than youthful empathy, but now, in the stillness, doubts began to creep in. Her presence, usually so vibrant and effortless, had felt slightly off, as though she were reading from a script written in a language only she understood.

I scolded myself for the thought. *She's just a student,* I reminded myself. A talented, kindhearted young woman with a gift for acting. My paranoia, fuelled by sleepless nights and unanswered questions, was making me see shadows where there were none. *Isn't it?*

I exhaled sharply, dragging my hands over my face in an effort to clear the fog of suspicion clouding my thoughts. *Focus.* That's what I needed to do. For Sammy, for my students, for myself. Whatever had happened to Nial, whatever dark truths lay hidden in the folds of our life together, they would come to light eventually. They had to.

Until then, I had to keep moving forward. The show must go on, as they say. Even if the stage beneath me felt like it might give way at any moment.

But just as I began to turn back to the pile of papers scattered across my desk, a detail caught my eye, stopping me cold. Serena's script. The one she had returned to retrieve during lunch. The one I had specifically pointed out to her.

It was still there, untouched, exactly where I'd told her it would be.

A chill ran down my spine, slow and deliberate, settling into the pit of my stomach like a stone. It was such a small thing, so easily explained away. Perhaps she'd simply forgotten it, distracted by my insistence that I was fine. And yet, as I stared at that abandoned script, a sense of wrongness began to grow, unbidden and undeniable.

I tried to push it away, to brush it off as nothing more than an overactive imagination. *Coincidence. It's just a coincidence.* But the thoughts wouldn't leave me alone, circling like vultures. What if it wasn't? What if Serena's concern wasn't as innocent as it seemed?

I clenched my fists, annoyed with myself for even entertaining the idea. Serena was just a teenager. A student. A talented actress, yes, but still a child in so many ways. She couldn't possibly have anything to do with this tangled web of lies and disappearances.

Could she?

The thought clung to me like a shadow, refusing to let go.

The afternoon dragged on, each minute stretching into an eternity. I moved through the motions of teaching like a marionette, my body performing while my mind churned with unanswered questions and worst-case scenarios. The classroom, once a sanctuary of creativity and expression, now felt oppressive, the vibrant posters and props mocking my efforts to maintain a facade of normality.

The walls seemed to close in around me, the air thick and stifling with the weight of unspoken tension. I stumbled over lines I had recited flawlessly countless times before, my voice faltering mid-sentence. The students exchanged uncertain glances, their whispers a barely perceptible hum that pricked at my nerves like static. I forced myself to keep going, ignoring the gnawing sense that they could see through me, that they knew something was wrong.

When the final bell rang, slicing through the heavy atmosphere, I felt a strange mixture of relief and dread. Relief that the day was over, that I could finally drop the act. Dread at the prospect of returning to an empty house, to another night filled with silence and the gnawing ache of uncertainty. The bustling noise of students packing up, chattering about their after-school plans, grated on my raw nerves. Their laughter, their carefree energy, felt like an affront, a cruel reminder of a normality that had been ripped away from me.

I was gathering my things, mechanically shoving papers and books into my bag, when a knock at the door startled me. I looked up to see Rufus, the English teacher from next door, lingering in the doorway. His familiar face, framed by a slightly unruly mop of greying hair, was etched with concern.

"Jenny?" he said softly, stepping inside. "Do you have a moment?"

I nodded, gesturing for him to come in, though my heart was already pounding inexplicably. Rufus was someone I liked—a kind, thoughtful colleague who shared my passion for literature and theatre—but we weren't close. His unexpected appearance in my classroom now, with that particular look in his eyes, felt like an intrusion into the delicate balance I was trying to maintain.

He moved closer, his steps slow, almost hesitant, as if sensing the fragility of the moment. His eyes searched mine, and I felt exposed under his scrutiny, as if the carefully constructed mask I had worn all day was slipping. "Jenny," he began again, his voice low, steady. "You seem... not quite yourself today. Is everything alright?"

For a heartbeat, I considered brushing him off, offering another empty reassurance: *I'm fine. Just tired.* The words formed automatically, like a script I'd rehearsed a hundred times. But something about Rufus' tone, his genuine concern, caught me off guard. The dam I had been holding together all day with sheer willpower cracked, and a torrent of emotion surged forward.

"I..." My voice broke, and I looked away, my hands tightening around the strap of my bag. The urge to retreat, to hide, was overwhelming, but so was the need to unburden myself, if only for a moment. "I'm sorry," I managed, my voice barely audible. "It's... it's been a tough few days."

Rufus pulled a chair from one of the desks and sat down, his movements deliberate and unthreatening. "It's okay," he said gently. "You don't have to apologise. We all have rough patches. But if there's something you need to talk about, I'm here to listen."

His words, so earnest and unassuming, felt like a lifeline I wasn't sure I could trust. My vision blurred again, tears pressing hotly behind my eyes, but I held them back. "It's Nial," I said, the weight of his name making my voice tremble. "He's... he's missing. He left two days ago, and I haven't heard from him since."

The words felt heavier than ever, hanging in the air like a storm cloud. Saying it aloud, to someone else, made it feel more solid, less like a terrible dream I could wake from. "He left to meet a client von Saturday morning," I continued, my voice cracking slightly, "and... he hasn't come back. No one's heard from him. I don't know what to do, Rufus. I don't know what to think."

Rufus' eyes widened as he rose from his chair, his brow knitting in shock. His hand came to rest on my shoulder, the gesture both steadying and unnerving. "Oh, Jenny," he murmured, his voice full of sympathy. "I had no idea. Have you gone to the police?"

I nodded quickly, frustration and despair bubbling to the surface. "They won't do anything. They say it hasn't been long enough, and that the text message I received proves he's fine." My words came out in a rush, the unfairness of it still fresh and raw. "But I know something's wrong, Rufus. I *know* it. I can feel it in my bones."

As I spoke, I studied Rufus' reaction. His expression was sympathetic, his concern seemingly genuine. But there was something else there, wasn't there? A flicker of... curiosity? Or was it calculation? The flicker passed so quickly I couldn't be sure, but the moment lingered in my mind, unsettling in its subtlety. Was I letting my fear warp my perception, or was my unease justified?

Rufus squeezed my shoulder again, his touch lingering just a heartbeat longer than I expected. "What can I do?" he asked softly, his tone steady but tinged with urgency. "How can I help?"

His offer, so unexpected and earnest, brought fresh tears to my eyes, but it also sent a ripple of unease through me. Rufus and I were colleagues, friendly acquaintances at best. His eagerness to involve himself struck me as both kind and slightly... odd. Why was he so willing to step into the fray for someone he barely knew?

"I don't know," I admitted, the vulnerability in my voice almost painful to hear. "I don't know what anyone can do. I feel... lost. But I have to keep it together. For Sammy, if nothing else."

As I spoke, I could feel the carefully constructed walls I'd spent the day reinforcing beginning to crumble. My fears, my uncertainties, my desperate need for answers—all of it spilled out in halting words. Rufus listened, nodding at the right moments, his expression a careful blend of shock and compassion. And yet, there was something in his eyes—a gleam of intensity that made me wonder if I'd been wise to let my guard down.

"Jenny," he said gently once I finished. "You don't have to face this alone. We're all here for you—the whole staff. Let us help, even if it's just covering your classes so you can take some time off. Or keeping an ear out for any news about Nial."

His words were a balm to my battered spirit, a small but significant reminder that I wasn't completely alone in this. For the first time since Nial's disappearance, I felt a flicker of hope—not that he would suddenly walk through the door, but that maybe I could find a way to weather the storm.

But then reality slammed into me like a cold wave. Letting others in meant inviting speculation, rumours, and questions I wasn't ready to answer. My instinct to keep my personal life separate from work had always been a source of pride, but now it felt like a matter of survival. I couldn't afford to lose control of the narrative—not here, not now.

"Thank you, Rufus," I said at last, forcing a small, tight smile. "I appreciate that more than you know. But... I think I need to handle this on my own for now. I'm not ready for everyone to know. Not yet."

Rufus hesitated, just for a moment, and in that pause, I thought I caught a flicker of something in his expression—disappointment? Annoyance? It vanished as quickly as it appeared, replaced by his usual kind smile. "Of course,

Jenny," he said smoothly, his voice warm again. "I understand. Just remember, my offer stands. Anything you need, anytime."

As Rufus turned and left, a wave of unease rippled through me. My chest tightened, a sudden irrational fear gripping me. Had I said too much? Could I trust him to keep this to himself? My stomach churned with doubt, the weight of uncertainty pressing heavily on my shoulders.

Rushing after him, "Rufus," I called out, my voice breaking slightly. The sound echoed faintly in the now-empty corridor beyond the door. He reappeared in the doorway, his expression calm but tinged with curiosity. "Please," I continued, hating the desperation in my tone, "please don't tell anyone about this. Not yet. Not until I know more about what's really going on."

He hesitated, his dark eyes meeting mine with an intensity that was impossible to decipher. Finally, he nodded, offering a faint, reassuring smile. "Your secret's safe with me, Jenny," he said softly, the words measured, deliberate. "I promise."

I managed a small nod of thanks, though the knot in my stomach didn't ease as he turned and walked away. When the door closed behind him, the faint sound of his footsteps fading down the hallway, I sank heavily into my chair. My body felt like lead, every limb weighed down by the events of the day.

What had I done? Confiding in Rufus felt like a gamble I hadn't fully considered. Had I made the right choice, or had I just complicated things further? My mind churned with possibilities, replaying every moment of our interaction. Had his reaction been genuine concern, or was there something else lurking beneath the surface?

I rubbed my temples, my fingers pressing into the tension building there. The more I thought about it, the more I began to question everything. His promise had sounded sincere, but something about his lingering gaze, the way his voice had dipped slightly as he spoke, set my nerves on edge. Was I imagining it? Was my paranoia painting shadows over an otherwise innocent exchange? Or was there something I wasn't seeing?

The classroom, so familiar and comforting on any other day, now felt foreign. The silence was deafening, the emptiness oppressive. The long shadows cast by the fading winter light seemed to stretch unnaturally, clawing across the room like dark spectres. I shivered, unable to shake the feeling of being watched, even though I knew I was alone.

My gaze drifted to the script for *The Importance of Being Earnest* lying on my desk, its pages slightly ruffled from the day's rehearsal. The irony of it struck me like a cruel joke—a play built around deception, false identities, and hidden truths, mirroring the tangled web my life had become. The line between fiction and reality felt thinner than ever, and I couldn't help but wonder: Who in my life was truly earnest? Who could I trust?

I shook my head sharply, forcing the thoughts away. I couldn't afford to spiral, not now. There were too many unanswered questions, too many unknowns. Rufus had no connection to Nial, no reason to betray my trust. Didn't he?

I gathered my things, shoving papers and personal items into my bag with more force than necessary. My eyes darted around the room one last time, landing briefly on the darkened corners where the shadows pooled. The sense of unease lingered, heavy and suffocating, but I had to push through it.

Stepping out of the classroom and closing the door behind me, I forced myself to breathe deeply. The corridor was empty, the muffled sound of distant conversations from the staffroom the only sign of life. The air was cold against my flushed skin as I moved towards the exit, my steps quick and purposeful.

But the questions wouldn't leave me. Trust was a fragile thing, and mine had been shaken to its core. I wasn't just questioning Rufus now—I was questioning everything and everyone.

4338.212

(31 July 2018)

A DIGITAL BEACON OF HOPE

4338.212.1

Another day had crawled by, heavy with unanswered questions and unrelenting worry. Nial's absence had become a shadow that loomed over every moment, suffocating and inescapable. Each forced smile, every hollow reassurance to colleagues and students alike, had chipped away at the fragile facade I was barely holding together. And now, as the late afternoon sun poured into the empty drama classroom, I stood alone, the weight of it all threatening to crush me.

The golden light filtering through the tall windows cast long, eerie shadows across the floor, illuminating the dust motes that floated aimlessly in the still air. I turned away from the windows, wiping a stray tear with the back of my hand, the fragile mask I had worn all day slipping dangerously close to shattering. My mind was a maelstrom of fear and doubt. The unsettling conversation with Rufus still echoed in my thoughts, leaving behind a residue of unease I couldn't scrub away.

A movement in the doorway caught my attention, and I froze. Three figures stood there, lingering in the threshold as if unsure whether to step forward or retreat. Ruth, Emma, and Serena—three of my brightest and most empathetic students—hovered like hesitant ghosts. Their presence was unexpected, and for a fleeting moment, I felt exposed, caught in a moment of vulnerability I had worked so hard to hide.

My heart clenched as I realised how much they might have seen. The tear-streaked face, the trembling hands—it wasn't the image of the composed drama teacher they had come to know. I inhaled deeply, summoning what was left of my crumbling resolve, and straightened my shoulders. I had to reclaim my role, even if only for their sake.

"Girls," I began, my voice hoarse from the emotions I'd been suppressing all day. "Is there something I can help you with?"

As they stepped further into the room, their presence seemed to shift the energy, the awkwardness of their approach giving way to a quiet determination. Ruth, Emma, and Serena had always been natural leaders in the drama club. Now, they were a united front, their concern radiating from them like a palpable warmth.

Ruth, the tallest of the three, with her fiery red hair and freckles that seemed to multiply under the warm light, spoke first. "Mrs Triffett," she said, her voice unusually gentle. Emma and Serena stood on either side of her, their expressions mirrors of quiet empathy. It was a reminder of what I cherished most about teaching—the surprising depth and kindness my students so often displayed.

"We couldn't help but notice," Emma added, her usual effervescence tempered by the seriousness of the moment, "that you've seemed... not yourself these past couple of days."

I opened my mouth to deflect, to offer some platitude that might shift the conversation away from me, but the words caught in my throat. How could I possibly explain? How could I lay bare the despair in my heart, the fear gnawing at my edges, without shattering completely?

Serena, usually the quietest of the trio, stepped forward then, her dark eyes brimming with an intensity that seemed to pierce through the veneer I was so desperately trying to maintain. "Mrs Triffett," she said softly, "we're worried about you. Is there anything we can do to help?"

Her question, so direct and yet so full of genuine concern, caught me off guard. For a moment, I was transported back to yesterday's conversation with Rufus. The same offer of help, the same show of support. But this felt different somehow. These were my students, young women I had watched grow and mature over the years. Their concern felt pure, untainted by the doubts and suspicions that had clouded my interaction with Rufus.

"I... I don't know what to say," I managed, my voice thick with emotion. I found myself torn between the instinct to protect them from my troubles and a desperate need for support, for understanding.

Serena did something then that broke through my last defences: she hugged me. It was a simple gesture, but in that moment, it was everything. A reassurance that I wasn't alone, that these remarkable young women were here for me, just as I had always strived to be there for them. Her embrace was warm and comforting, reminding me of Sammy's hugs, and for a moment, I allowed myself to be held, to be comforted.

As Serena stepped back, her quiet voice steady and sure, she offered a suggestion that would change the course of my search for Nial. "We overheard you talking to Mr Chalmers yesterday," she admitted, her eyes meeting mine with unwavering conviction. "About Mr Triffett being missing. We think you should start a Facebook campaign to find him. We can help."

Their offer, so earnest and sincere, caught me off guard. Here were my students, ready to stand by me, to take on a piece of my burden as their own. It was a testament to their character, to the unexpected ways in which we can find light in the darkest of times.

"A Facebook campaign?" I echoed, the idea taking root in my mind. It was so simple, yet it held so much potential. In this digital age, information could spread like wildfire. If Nial was out there, if anyone had seen him or knew anything about his whereabouts, this could be the key to finding him.

Emma nodded eagerly, her enthusiasm infectious. "We can create a page, share photos of Mr Triffett, ask people to keep an eye out for him. It could reach thousands of people in no time."

"And we can organise search parties," Ruth chimed in, her practical nature shining through. "Get volunteers to comb different areas of Hobart. Someone must have seen something."

As I looked into their faces, I saw not just the compassionate leaders of the drama club, but a glimmer of hope, a beacon guiding me through the storm. The despair that had been my constant companion since Nial's disappearance began to recede, replaced by a cautious optimism.

But even as hope bloomed in my chest, a tendril of fear curled around my heart. What if this drew unwanted attention? What if whoever was responsible for Nial's disappearance saw the campaign? What if it put Nial – or worse, Sammy – in danger?

"I appreciate your offer, girls, I really do," I said, my voice wavering slightly. "But I'm not sure if that's the best course of action. The police are already involved, and I wouldn't want to interfere with their investigation."

Serena's eyes narrowed slightly, a flicker of something – disappointment? frustration? – passing across her face. "But Mrs Triffett," she pressed, her voice taking on an intensity that surprised me, "the police aren't doing enough. You said so yourself yesterday. We can't just sit back and do nothing."

I felt a chill run down my spine at her words. Had I really said that out loud yesterday? I thought back to my conversation with Rufus, trying to remember exactly what I'd said. How much had these girls overheard?

"Serena's right," Emma chimed in, her usual cheerfulness tinged with a determination I'd never seen before. "We want to help, Mrs Triffett. Please, let us do this for you. For Mr Triffett."

I looked at each of them in turn, feeling a mix of gratitude and unease. Their desire to help was touching, but I couldn't shake the feeling that I was standing on the edge of a cliff. If I agreed to this, there would be no going back. The whole of Hobart would know about Nial's disappearance. The carefully guarded privacy of our family would be shattered.

And yet... what choice did I have? The police seemed to have little interest at all. My own attempts to find answers had led nowhere. Maybe this was the push we needed to break the case wide open.

"Alright," I said finally, the word feeling heavy on my tongue. "We can try the Facebook campaign. But we need to be careful about how we do this. We can't just rush into it."

The girls' faces lit up with excitement and relief. They began talking all at once, their voices overlapping as they threw out ideas and suggestions. But my eyes were drawn to Serena. While Ruth and Emma chattered animatedly, Serena remained quiet, a small smile playing at the corners of her mouth. There was something in her eyes, a gleam of... satisfaction? It was gone in an instant, replaced by her usual calm demeanour, but it left me feeling unsettled.

The heavy doors of the school library creaked softly as we pushed them open, the sound echoing in the hushed interior like a whisper of warning. As we stepped inside, the familiar scent of old books and polished wood enveloped us, a comforting embrace that momentarily dulled the edge of my anxiety. The library had always been a sanctuary for me, a place of quiet contemplation and literary escape. But today, it was to become the launching pad for a mission that felt both monumental and terrifyingly personal.

Ruth, Emma, Serena, and I made our way through the maze of bookshelves, our footsteps muffled by the thick carpet. The late afternoon sun slanted through the high windows, casting long shadows and bathing the room in a warm, golden glow. It felt surreal, this pocket of normality in a world that had tilted off its axis. The contrast between the peaceful, scholarly atmosphere and the turmoil roiling inside me was almost painful.

We found an empty computer station tucked away in a quiet corner, far from the prying eyes of other lingering students. As we settled into our seats, the weight of our task descended upon us like a physical presence. This wasn't just another school project or drama club activity. This was a desperate attempt to find a missing person - my husband, my Nial. The reality of what we were about to do hit me anew, sending a shiver down my spine despite the warmth of the room.

I logged into the computer with trembling fingers, acutely aware of the girls' eyes on me. They had seen me vulnerable earlier, had witnessed the cracks in my carefully constructed facade. Now, they were here, ready to help piece me back together, to channel my fear and desperation into action. Their presence was both a comfort and a source of anxiety - I was grateful for their help, but ashamed of my weakness, my need for support from my own students.

"Okay," I said, my voice barely above a whisper, mindful of the library's quiet atmosphere. "Where do we start?"

Emma leaned in, her dark eyes intense with focus. "We need a strong opening," she said, her voice low but filled with determination. "Something that will grab people's attention and make them want to help."

I nodded, grateful for her clear-headed approach. My own thoughts felt muddled, clouded by fear and lack of sleep. The past few days had been a blur of worry and unanswered questions, each hour blending into the next in a haze of anxiety. "You're right," I agreed, trying to inject some confidence into my voice. "But how do we convey the urgency without sounding... alarmist?"

Ruth, ever practical, pulled out a notebook. The soft scratch of her pen against paper was oddly soothing, a tangible reminder that we were taking action, doing something. "Let's start with the facts," she suggested, her freckled face serious. "When was Mr. Triffett last seen? What was he wearing? Any distinguishing features people should look out for?"

As Ruth spoke, I felt a lump form in my throat. How could I reduce Nial, my vibrant, complex husband, to a list of physical characteristics? How could I compress our life together, our love, our family, into a few sentences designed to catch a stranger's eye? The thought made me feel sick, as if I was somehow betraying the depth of our relationship, the richness of our shared life.

Serena must have sensed my distress. She placed a gentle hand on my arm, her touch grounding me in the present. "Mrs. Triffett," she said softly, her voice barely audible above the hushed murmur of the library. "Why don't you tell us about Mr. Triffett? Not just what he looks like, but who he is. It might help us find the right words."

I took a deep breath, closing my eyes for a moment. When I opened them, I found myself looking directly at Nial's face - or rather, a photograph of him on my phone's lock screen. It was a candid shot from our last family picnic, his eyes crinkled with laughter, Sammy on his shoulders reaching for the sky. The sight of it sent a pang through my heart, a mixture of love and longing so intense it was almost physical.

"This," I said, holding up the phone, my voice thick with emotion. "This is Nial."

The girls leaned in, studying the image. I watched their faces, seeing the impact of the photo reflected in their eyes. This wasn't just a missing person to them anymore - this was a real man, a father, a husband.

"It's perfect," Emma breathed, her eyes wide. "We should use this photo in the post. It shows who he really is, not just what he looks like."

I nodded, a lump forming in my throat. "He's... he's not just my husband," I began, my voice barely above a whisper. The words seemed to catch in my throat, each one a struggle to voice. "He's Sammy's world. He's the kind of father who never misses a bedtime story, who makes up silly songs about brushing teeth and eating vegetables."

As I spoke, Ruth's pen flew across her notebook, capturing the essence of my words. Emma nodded encouragingly, while Serena's eyes shone with unshed tears.

"He's a builder," I continued, the words coming easier now, as if a dam had broken inside me. "He loves working with his hands, creating things. But he's also a dreamer. He's always coming up with these grand plans - a treehouse for Sammy, a greenhouse for my herbs, a sailboat to explore the Tasman Sea."

I paused, a memory surfacing. The image was so vivid, so real, that for a moment I could almost believe Nial was there with us. "The morning he disappeared, he was talking about a new job. Something about a potential client who needed urgent work done. But he never said who it was or where he was going."

The girls exchanged glances at this, and I could see the gears turning in their minds. "That's important information," Ruth said, underlining something in her notes. Her voice was steady, but I could see the concern in her eyes. "We should definitely include that in the post."

For the next hour, we worked tirelessly, crafting and refining our message. The library around us faded into the background, the soft rustling of pages and muted conversations becoming white noise as we focused on our task. Emma's way with words transformed my rambling recollections into a compelling narrative. Ruth's practical mind ensured we included all the necessary details - Nial's physical description, the clothes he was last seen wearing, the make and model of his ute.

Serena, quiet but observant, suggested we include a call to action. "We should ask people to share the post," she said, her dark eyes intense. "And maybe set up an email address where people can send tips or information."

As our post took shape on the screen before us, I felt a mix of hope and trepidation. Would this work? Would someone out there have the key to unlocking the mystery of Nial's disappearance? Or were we just shouting into the void, our plea for help lost in the endless sea of information that was the internet?

Finally, after what felt like hours of tweaking and refining, we had our final draft. The once-bustling room had quieted, most students having left for the day. In the hushed atmosphere, my voice seemed unnaturally loud as I read our post aloud:

"MISSING: Nial Triffett, 32 years old, last seen Saturday morning 28 July 2018 in Hobart. Nial is a loving husband and father, a skilled builder with a passion for his craft. He left for an urgent job with a former client and hasn't been seen or heard from since. Nial is 6'1", with brown hair and blue eyes. He was last seen wearing a red flannel shirt, jeans, and work boots, driving a white 2015 Toyota Hilux ute.

If you have any information about Nial's whereabouts, or if you saw him or his vehicle after Saturday morning, please contact the Hobart Police or email findnialtriffett@gmail.com. Every piece of information, no matter how small, could be crucial.

Nial, if you're out there and able to see this, please come home. Sammy and I miss you terribly. Whatever's happened, we can face it together. We love you."

As I finished reading, I looked up to see tears in the girls' eyes. Emma reached out and squeezed my hand, her touch warm and comforting. "It's perfect, Mrs. Triffett," she said softly, her voice thick with emotion. "If anyone knows anything, this will reach them."

With trembling fingers, I uploaded the photo of Nial - my smiling, carefree husband, so full of life and love. As I positioned it above our carefully crafted message, I felt a surge of emotion so strong it nearly overwhelmed me. This digital representation of Nial, this plea for help, felt like the most important thing I had ever created.

"Are we ready?" I asked, my cursor hovering over the 'Post' button. The question seemed to hang in the air, loaded with all the fear and hope and uncertainty of the past few days.

The girls nodded, their faces a mixture of determination and apprehension. We all understood the gravity of this moment. Once I clicked that button, our private worry would become public knowledge. We would be inviting the world into our tragedy, opening ourselves up to sympathy, speculation, and scrutiny. There would be no going back.

I took a deep breath, steeling myself for whatever might come next. The library around us seemed to hold its breath, the usual background noise fading away until all I could hear was the pounding of my own heart. "Here goes," I whispered, and clicked 'Post'.

For a moment, nothing happened. The library around us continued its quiet hum of activity - pages turning, keyboards clacking softly, the occasional muffled cough. But to me, it felt as if the world had stopped turning, holding its breath along with us as our message began its journey across the digital landscape.

I looked at the girls - Ruth, Emma, and Serena - their young faces etched with concern and determination. They had become more than just my students today. They were my allies, my support system, my beacon of hope in the darkness that had engulfed my life. Their willingness to help, to shoulder this burden with me, was both touching and slightly unsettling. I found myself wondering what motivated them, what made them so eager to involve themselves in this adult drama.

"Thank you," I said, my voice thick with emotion. The words felt inadequate to express the depth of my gratitude, but they were all I had. "I couldn't have done this without you."

They smiled back at me, a united front of compassion and resolve. "We're not giving up, Mrs. Triffett," Emma said firmly, her young face set with a determination that seemed beyond her years. "We'll find Mr. Triffett. Whatever it takes."

As we gathered our things to leave the library, I cast one last look at the now darkened computer screen. Our post was out there, Nial's smiling face staring back, our plea for help now visible to the world. It felt like a lifeline, a thread of hope stretching out into the unknown. But it also felt like an invasion, a public airing of our private grief. I found myself wondering what Nial would think of all this, if he could see it. Would he approve of our methods, or would he be horrified at the exposure?

DRAWER

4338.212.2

The early evening light had long faded, leaving our bedroom cloaked in a dim, heavy gloom. The once-familiar space felt alien now, haunted by Nial's absence and my spiralling thoughts. Mechanically, I sorted through the laundry, folding clothes and matching socks with a kind of robotic precision, desperate for even a shred of normality. The mundane routine offered a flimsy distraction, a momentary respite from the storm of emotions that had consumed me since his disappearance.

As I picked up a stack of freshly laundered underwear and moved to put them away, I pulled open my drawer. The faint scent of lavender fabric softener rose to greet me, a fragrance that had once symbolised the simple comforts of home. But the comforting association was abruptly drowned out by a pang of unease. Something was wrong.

Nestled among the neatly folded garments was an intruder —something unfamiliar, something foreign in this most private of spaces. My fingers froze mid-motion as my eyes locked onto the object. "What on earth..." The words slipped from my mouth in a whisper.

With trembling hands, I reached in and pulled out the garment. A pair of lacy panties dangled before me, dark pink and provocatively designed. They were completely unlike anything I owned. My breath caught in my throat as I stared at the delicate fabric, my mind racing to make sense of their presence.

At first, I clung to the hope that this was a misplaced romantic gesture, a playful gift from Nial. It wouldn't have been out of character for him to surprise me with something daring and intimate. But as I turned the garment over in my hands, doubt began to creep in. If it was a gift, why would it be tucked away in my drawer, hidden among the mundane folds of everyday life? And why hadn't I noticed them before now?

The fabric felt cold and damp against my skin, a chilling detail that stopped me short. I flipped the garment inside out, and my heart sank as I noticed a faint dark spot on the lining. Not fully dry. The implications of that dampness sent my thoughts into a spiral of suspicion and dread. A memory surfaced—of Nial's playful indulgences with intimate gifts in the past, moments that had once brought laughter and intimacy to our relationship. But this felt... different. Wrong.

I hesitated, my fingers clutching the lace as if it might yield some hidden truth. There was a sickening part of me that needed to confirm what my rational mind was already screaming. Reluctantly, I lifted the panties closer to my nose, inhaling sharply.

The scent that reached me was not what I had hoped for. It wasn't Nial's distinctive musk, that familiar marker of shared intimacy. Instead, it was something else entirely. A scent disturbingly familiar in its own right, but one that didn't belong here. My stomach churned as I tried to place it, a feeling of disorientation settling over me like a cold fog.

"Oh God," I muttered, the realisation hitting me like a physical blow. "Vaginal discharge." The words tasted bitter in my mouth, almost making me gag as the full implication sank in. These weren't a gift. They weren't even Nial's misguided attempt at roleplaying. These were another woman's soiled undergarments, left carelessly - or perhaps deliberately - in my drawer.

Blood boiling, I stormed out of the bedroom, clutching the offending item as if it might combust in my hands. My feet pounded down the stairs, each heavy step a physical outlet for the tempest of emotions surging inside me. The house, silent but for the echo of my movements, seemed to hold its breath, as if anticipating the explosion to come.

Reaching the kitchen, I didn't hesitate. Without Nial here to provide an explanation—not that any excuse could possibly justify this—I flung the panties into the bin with a force that belied their weight. The soft thud as they hit the bottom of the otherwise empty container felt deafening in the stillness, a damning punctuation to this surreal moment. It was as if the house itself was absorbing my outrage, amplifying it in the absence of anyone else to witness it.

I stood frozen, staring at the bin as if it might offer me answers. My chest heaved with the effort of containing the whirlwind inside me—confusion, betrayal, disbelief, all clamouring for dominance. How had it come to this? When had our life together—a life I had believed was built on love, trust, and shared dreams—devolved into this grotesque farce?

The need to act, to do something, anything, to rid myself of the lingering taint of what I had just held overwhelmed me. I stumbled to the bathroom, my steps unsteady, my pulse pounding in my ears. Reaching the vanity, I flipped on the light with more force than necessary. The harsh fluorescent bulb flickered briefly before settling into a steady, unforgiving glare, illuminating every hollow in my cheeks, every line etched by sleepless nights.

I didn't wait for the water to warm. Shoving my hands under the icy stream, I gasped at the shock but welcomed it, needing the cold bite to tether me to the here and now. Grabbing the soap, I pumped an excessive amount into my palms, the sharp frangipani scent filling the small room like an invasive presence. I scrubbed with a frantic intensity, as though I could erase not only the physical contact with the underwear but also the knowledge of their existence, the implications they carried.

Words spilled from my lips, a raw stream of confusion and fury that mirrored the violent motion of my hands. "What the hell is Nial up to?" I demanded, my voice trembling with emotion. My eyes locked onto my reflection in the mirror, and for a moment, I didn't recognise the woman staring back. Wild-eyed and hollow-cheeked, she was a stranger—someone consumed by rage and hurt, someone on the edge of unravelling.

The questions continued, growing louder, harsher, echoing off the cold tiles. "And how in God's name did those panties get into my drawer?" The disbelief in my voice twisted into a feral growl, my rage spiralling beyond my control. Each unanswered question was like a slap, the silence that followed a mocking retort.

My voice cracked as I hurled my next accusation, tears threatening to spill. "There'll be hell to pay if he's had some… some woman in our bed!" The words felt like acid on my tongue, each syllable laced with the raw pain of betrayal. The thought of Nial entwined with another woman, in the sanctuary of our home, our bed, twisted the knife deeper into my heart.

My reflection blurred as tears finally broke free, streaming down my face in hot, stinging rivulets. I clenched the edge of the sink, my knuckles white, as I let the sobs wrack my body. Rage and despair mixed into a toxic cocktail, their sharp edges slicing through me with each shallow breath.

Just as I was about to unleash another torrent of profanity, my phone chimed with a new message. The sudden, jarring sound pierced through the fog of rage and despair, startling me enough to cause another muttered curse as I fumbled to turn off the tap. Water splashed messily against the sink as I grabbed the hand towel, drying my hands with frantic, almost aggressive motions that left damp streaks on the fabric.

Pulling my phone from my pocket, I stared at the screen. An unknown number glowed in the dim light of the bathroom. Ordinarily, I might have dismissed it—another scam, another wrong number. But nothing about today, or the past few days, was ordinary. A chill ran through me as I noticed the preview of the message. The first few words urged me to read further, a sense of foreboding curling in the pit of my stomach.

With a deep, steadying breath, I tapped the notification. My heart was pounding so loudly it felt like a drumbeat in my ears. The words sharpened into focus, each one hitting me like a blow:

Hi Mrs Triffett. This is Serena. From drama class. Pretty sure I just saw your husband getting into his ute with another woman. They looked to be pretty friendly. Just thought I'd let you know.

For a moment, my body refused to move. The phone, cold and impersonal in my hand, seemed to vibrate with the weight of the message. My grip loosened, and the device slipped from my numb fingers, clattering against the porcelain sink.

I stared down at the phone where it lay, the screen still glowing with Serena's damning words. Nial, alive. Nial, with another woman. The implications hit me like a freight train. He wasn't missing. He wasn't in danger. He had abandoned me—*us*—and had the audacity to carry on as if none of it mattered.

The scream that rose from my chest was unlike anything I'd ever heard from myself before—raw, primal, filled with a rage so intense it felt like it might tear me apart from the inside. It ricocheted off the bathroom tiles, filling the small space with a sound that felt both foreign and deeply familiar.

I gripped the edges of the sink, my knuckles white, the cool porcelain grounding me in the midst of my spiralling thoughts. Everything I thought I knew—about Nial, about us—shattered like fragile glass. Our marriage, our home, our carefully built life together—it was all crumbling into dust before my eyes.

Questions clawed at the edges of my mind, each one sharper than the last. How long had this betrayal been going on? Who was she, this woman Serena had seen? Was she the owner of those panties I'd found? The thought twisted like a knife in my gut, a sickening confirmation of my worst fears.

I forced myself to meet my own gaze in the mirror. The reflection that stared back at me was unrecognisable. My eyes, usually so calm and steady, were wild with fury and pain. My face was flushed, streaked with angry tears. My hair hung in dishevelled strands around my face, a perfect match for the chaos roiling inside me.

This wasn't the Jenny Triffett I knew. This wasn't the devoted wife and loving mother, the dedicated teacher who found solace in guiding young actors through tales of heartbreak and triumph. This was a woman stripped of pretence, laid bare by betrayal and consumed by questions that had no easy answers.

The phone, now silent but still glowing faintly, seemed to mock me with its stillness. Serena's message lingered on the screen like a wound that wouldn't close. I wanted to throw it, to hurl it against the wall and shatter it into pieces. But instead, I forced myself to pick it up, to hold the device steady in trembling hands.

In that moment, something deep inside me shifted. The fear and worry that had gnawed at me since Nial's disappearance hardened into something unyielding, something colder and sharper. It wasn't just a need for answers anymore; it was fury. Determination. A burning resolve to expose the truth, no matter how ugly, and to hold him accountable for the chaos he had wrought.

I straightened up, squaring my shoulders and lifting my chin. If Nial thought he could walk away from us, leaving Sammy and me in the wreckage of a life he had abandoned, he was gravely mistaken. If he believed he could start anew, carrying on as though we didn't exist, while leaving me to untangle the lies, he was about to learn just how wrong he was.

I would find him. I would confront him. And I would make him pay for every tear I had shed, for every sleepless night spent in torment, and for the gnawing uncertainty that had consumed me. This wasn't just about Nial anymore. It was about reclaiming my life, my dignity, and my family.

With renewed resolve, I quickly typed out a reply, my fingers flying over the keypad.

Thank you, Serena. Please let me know if you saw where they went or any details about the woman. Anything at all could help.

I paused, my thumb hovering over the send button, considering my next move. The police? Detective Jenkins had seemed understanding, but would this change anything? Nial being spotted alive didn't necessarily mean he was safe—or innocent. Would they write this off as a domestic issue now, dismissing my concerns entirely?

No, I thought, clenching my jaw as I sent the reply to Serena. This wasn't a matter for the police, not now. This was personal. This was about uncovering the truth and confronting the betrayal that had turned my world upside down. I couldn't wait for someone else to piece it together. I had to take control.

Scrolling through my contacts, I landed on a name that stirred a mix of nostalgia and hesitation: **Jack Reilly**. We'd been close at university before life had taken us in different directions—he into private investigation, me into teaching. We hadn't spoken in years, but if anyone could help me find Nial and uncover what he was hiding, it was Jack.

The decision felt right, like the first solid step I had taken since Nial's disappearance. Without giving myself time to overthink, I pressed the call button. The dial tone buzzed in my ear, each ring heightening the strange calm that had settled over me. The stillness before the storm.

On the third ring, a familiar gruff voice answered. "Reilly Investigations. How can I help you?"

The sound of his voice brought a rush of memories—late-night study sessions, his dry humour, the easy camaraderie we'd shared. But there was no time for nostalgia. I steeled myself, taking a deep breath before speaking.

"Jack? It's Jenny. Jenny Triffett. I need your help."

A pause. "Jenny? Bloody hell, it's been ages. What's going on?"

As I began to explain, the words poured out in a rush. I told him about Nial's disappearance, the cryptic text message, the panties, Serena's sighting. With every detail, the weight of my burden seemed to shift, shared, if only slightly, by someone who might actually be able to help.

Jack listened without interrupting, his occasional hum of acknowledgment the only indication he was still on the line. When I finished, there was a beat of silence before he spoke, his voice measured and firm.

"Alright, Jenny. I'll take the case. But I need everything—addresses, phone numbers, names, and anything else you've got. You're holding something back. I can hear it."

Caught off guard by his perceptiveness, I hesitated. How much should I tell him? How much could I trust him? But as I glanced at my reflection in the mirror, I knew there was no room for half-measures. If I wanted answers, I had to commit.

"I'll send you everything," I said finally, my voice steady with newfound determination. "Just... help me find him, Jack. Whatever it takes."

"I will," he said, his tone leaving no room for doubt. "We'll get to the bottom of this."

As I ended the call, I caught sight of myself in the mirror. The woman staring back was still dishevelled, still marked by exhaustion. But there was something new in her eyes—a steely resolve, a glint of defiance. Nial might have underestimated me. He might have thought he could slip away, leaving me to pick up the pieces.

But he was wrong.

The game had changed, and I wasn't playing by his rules anymore. Whatever secrets he was hiding, whatever lies had tainted our life together, I would uncover them. One way or another, I would bring him—and the truth—into the light.

4338.213

(1 August 2018)

CALLS FOR ANSWERS

4338.213.1

The silence in our house was deafening, a force that seemed to amplify every creak, every whisper of the winter wind against the windows. Five days. It had been five days since Nial's disappearance, and the emptiness he left behind filled every corner like a fog, clinging to the walls, the furniture, my very skin. The bitter Hobart winter had seeped into the house, chilling it in a way that no heater could remedy. Without Nial's warmth, it felt more like a mausoleum than a home.

I paced the living room, the plush carpet muffling the soft thuds of my stockinged feet. It was a futile attempt to distract myself, to keep my mind from circling the same haunting questions. What had happened to Nial? Where was he? Why had he been seen with another woman? Every thought led to another dead end, another wall of uncertainty that I couldn't scale.

The mantelpiece clock ticked steadily, each sound a taunt, a reminder of time slipping through my fingers. Five days. Every moment that passed without word from Nial was another moment stolen, another chance for the trail to go cold. My gaze flickered to the clock, then to my phone, which lay on the coffee table like an inert talisman. I'd spoken to Jack Reilly yesterday, and while his involvement gave me a small measure of comfort, I knew that it wasn't enough.

I needed to take every avenue available, and that meant calling Detective Jenkins. Perhaps I'd been too hasty in assuming the police couldn't—or wouldn't—help. After all, if

Jenkins had asked about Luke Smith, there was a chance he knew more than he was letting on. I couldn't afford to let my suspicions about anyone, even him, cloud my judgement. If the police had any piece of this puzzle, I had to get it.

I picked up the phone, my fingers trembling as I dialled his number. Each ring seemed to stretch into eternity, the sound pounding in my ears, echoing the frantic thud of my heart. Ring. Thud-thud. Ring. Thud-thud. I closed my eyes, willing myself to stay calm, to focus on the task at hand.

Finally, there was a click, followed by his voice: "Detective Karl Jenkins," he said, his tone clipped and professional.

I drew in a sharp breath, the cool air searing my lungs as I tried to steady myself. "Detective," I began, my voice low and strained, betraying the effort it took to maintain control. "It's Jenny Triffett."

There was a pause on the other end of the line, heavy with recognition and the weight of all that hadn't been said. I could picture him, leaning back in his chair, his expression guarded as he prepared for whatever this call would bring. His silence stretched just long enough to make my stomach knot before he responded.

"Mrs Triffett," he said, his tone softening slightly. "What can I do for you?"

The formality of his address felt like a slap, a reminder of the impersonal distance that lay between us. We weren't strangers discussing a bureaucratic matter. This man held the answers to the most important question of my life. I didn't want polite detachment; I wanted urgency. I wanted action.

"I need an update on the investigation into my husband," I said, the words coming out like a demand, cutting through the air with a force that surprised even me.

Jenkins hesitated for a fraction of a second—long enough to stoke the flames of my frustration. "Have you not heard anything further from him?" he asked, his tone measured, cautious. "No calls? No text messages?"

"Nothing!" I snapped, the dam holding back my composure starting to crack. Did he think I would be calling if I had heard from Nial? "Absolutely nothing," I added, softer this time, the reality of those words sinking in anew. My voice faltered, and I felt the beginnings of a sob rise unbidden in my throat.

"We're still investigating several new leads," Jenkins said, his voice taking on a soothing quality that only served to heighten my anxiety. What wasn't he telling me? There was something in his tone, a hesitation that made my skin prickle with unease.

"Leads?" I pressed, the single word laced with desperation. "What kind of leads? What are you finding?"

"We're still working on it," he said vaguely, a masterclass in non-answers. "I assure you, Jenny, we're doing everything we can."

The use of my first name, though meant to sound reassuring, only fuelled my frustration. I didn't want reassurances; I wanted clarity, transparency—something to hold onto in this endless spiral of uncertainty. "You don't understand," I said, my voice breaking as tears welled up, hot and insistent. A sob slipped out, raw and unrestrained. "Please, Karl," I pleaded, dropping the formalities entirely. "Just tell me something, anything. I need to know what's happening."

There was a pause, longer this time, and the sound of shuffling papers came through the line. In the background, I could hear the distant bustle of the station: phones ringing, muffled voices, the faint rustle of activity. It was a cruel contrast to the stillness of my own world, which had ground to a halt five days ago.

"Are you still there, Detective?" I asked, panic edging into my voice. I gripped the phone tighter, my free hand balling into a fist as if bracing for whatever he might say next.

"Ah, yeah," but his tone had shifted—distracted, preoccupied. More sounds followed: the scratch of a pen, the hurried exchange of whispers. He was paying attention to something else. Something urgent.

"Look, Jenny, I'm really sorry," he said at last, his voice tinged with regret. "I'll call you back in a couple of hours."

Before I could protest, before I could demand more, the line went dead.

I stared at the phone in disbelief, the silence that followed mocking me. How dare he dismiss me like that? How dare he prioritise whatever was happening on his end over the agony of my unanswered questions? I wanted to scream, to throw the phone across the room, to do something, anything to release the rage and helplessness that threatened to take hold.

I sank onto the sofa, my legs no longer willing to support me. The familiar surroundings of the living room suddenly felt vague, the once-welcoming space now oppressive and cold.

Photos of happier times stared down from the walls, silent witnesses to the life we had built together. Nial and I on our wedding day, beaming with joy; Sammy's unsteady first steps, his chubby hands reaching for us; family holidays filled with laughter and love, frozen in moments of perfection. Each image was a dagger to my heart, twisting with every glance, a cruel reminder of everything I stood to lose.

My eyes landed on a picture taken last Christmas. Nial stood behind me, his arms encircling my waist, both of us laughing at some forgotten joke. The lights of Hobart's waterfront sparkled behind us, a backdrop of twinkling promise. I remembered the evening with painful clarity – the warm summer air, the glow of the festivities, the solid comfort of Nial's embrace. In that moment, it had felt like nothing could touch us, like our love was an unshakable foundation.

And now, here I was, barely six months later, holding onto that memory like a lifeline as my world crumbled around me. Where was Nial now? Was he cold, scared, thinking of me and Sammy, desperate to come home? Or was he somewhere far away, his thoughts already detached from the life we'd built together?

The questions spiralled, looping endlessly in my mind, each one darker and more harrowing than the last. Jenkins' abrupt end to our call only added to my unease, the sharp edge of his dismissal cutting deep. What had he seen? What could have been so urgent that he would hang up on me in the middle of my plea for answers?

Had they found Nial? The thought sent an icy shiver down my spine. Was he hurt? Or... The word lodged in my throat, too horrific to give voice to. Was he... gone?

The image of Nial lying somewhere cold and alone, his life extinguished, made my stomach churn. I pressed my fists into my thighs, willing the thought away, but it clung stubbornly to the edges of my mind. Or perhaps the truth was even more sinister. What if Jenkins had uncovered something—something that would forever shatter the image of the man I thought I knew?

No. I couldn't accept that. Nial was a good man. He was a devoted father, a loving husband. Whatever had happened to him, it wasn't by choice. It couldn't be. Could it?

The deep chime of the mantelpiece clock cut through my thoughts, its resonant tones reverberating through the silent room. I jumped, my heart hammering in my chest as though it were trying to escape. The sound was startling in its normality, a jarring reminder that time was still marching on, indifferent to my turmoil.

Two hours, Jenkins had said. Two hours until he called me back.

But could I trust him to keep his word? The doubt gnawed at me, its teeth sharp and relentless. Jenkins was the only link I had to Nial's disappearance. But he was also a man consumed by the demands of his job, by whatever had pulled him away from our conversation. Could I trust him to prioritise Nial over everything else?

Could I really trust anyone anymore?

The day was fading into evening, the last rays of sunlight casting long, eerie shadows across our living room. I sat in Nial's favourite armchair, my fingers absently tracing the frayed edges of the worn fabric, each thread a tether to memories I wasn't ready to let go. The room, once a sanctuary of laughter, warmth, and shared moments, now felt like a mausoleum of memories. Every familiar object—Sammy's scattered toys, the blanket Nial and I had shared on countless movie nights—was a painful reminder of his absence, their presence mocking me with their normality.

Hours had passed since my frustrating call with Detective Jenkins, and, as I had feared, his promise to call back had been empty. The silence from him was deafening, a betrayal that only fuelled my growing mistrust. What had been so urgent that he couldn't spare even a minute to ease my fears? What had he uncovered that he felt I couldn't handle? My mind conjured dark possibilities.

The house groaned and creaked, the sounds of its settling amplified in the oppressive quiet that had become my constant companion. Outside, the wind whistled through the skeletal branches of the old trees lining our yard, their mournful tune perfectly matching my mood. Winter in Hobart had always carried a certain chill, but this year, it seeped deeper, into the very marrow of my bones. It was a cold I couldn't escape, no matter how many blankets I wrapped around myself or how close I huddled to the heater.

I had spent the late afternoon pacing, making fruitless phone calls to Nial's colleagues, even dredging up old acquaintances I hadn't spoken to in years. Each call was a dead end, another brick in the wall of despair that surrounded me. It was as if Nial had evaporated, leaving nothing behind but a void in the shape of him. A husband. A father. A man I thought I knew better than anyone. Now, I wasn't so sure.

The encroaching shadows deepened as the last light outside faded, but I didn't bother to turn on the lamps. Darkness felt like the only honest company I could keep. It cloaked the room in a heavy stillness, a perfect reflection of the emptiness gnawing at me from the inside. I leaned back in the armchair, closing my eyes and letting the gloom envelop me. For a brief moment, I surrendered to the stillness, allowing it to swallow me whole.

Then, the shrill ring of the phone shattered the quiet, piercing through the cocoon of shadows like a knife. My eyes snapped open, my heart leaping into my throat.

I lunged for the mobile, my movements frantic and clumsy in the dim light. My knee struck the side table, sending the lamp wobbling precariously. I caught it just in time with my free hand, steadying it as I pressed the phone to my ear. My breath came in short, uneven bursts as I struggled to compose myself.

"Hello?" I said, my voice trembling, thick with anticipation and dread. The single word carried the weight of every desperate hope, every unspoken fear. Was it Nial? Jenkins?

Another well-meaning but useless friend offering hollow reassurances?

The silence on the other end stretched for a heartbeat too long, filling my chest with icy dread. I gripped the phone tighter, my knuckles whitening as I willed the caller to speak, to be the answer I so desperately needed.

The voice on the other end was unfamiliar, a woman's, tinged with the same undercurrent of anxiety that had become my constant companion. "Is this Jenny Triffett?" she asked, her tone tentative yet urgent.

"Yes, speaking," I replied, my mind instantly racing. Who was this woman, and how had she gotten my number? A flicker of hope ignited in my chest, quickly tempered by the cold hand of caution. In the fractured world I now inhabited, every unexpected call, every unknown voice, carried the potential for both salvation and devastation.

"My name is Sharon Pafistis," the woman continued, her words tumbling out in a rush, as if she feared I might hang up before she could explain. "I—I found your number through the Facebook post about your husband."

My breath caught. The Facebook post. Of course. In the chaos of the past few days, I had almost forgotten about the online campaign we'd launched. How many people had seen it? How far had Nial's face travelled across the digital landscape? I pictured his smiling image—his eyes crinkling at the corners, the soft tilt of his head—being shared and reshared, scattered like breadcrumbs across the internet, each click a potential lead, a fragile thread of hope pulling me closer to him.

"My husband has also gone missing," Sharon added, her voice breaking slightly on the last word.

The statement hit me like a physical blow, sharp and unexpected. Another missing husband? The coincidence was too stark to ignore, and yet my mind struggled to process it.

Was this a cruel hoax? A trap? Or was it possible, in this vast and indifferent world, that I had stumbled upon someone who truly understood the hell I was living through?

"I'm so sorry to hear that, Sharon," I said softly, my own troubles momentarily receding in the face of her confession. My words felt woefully inadequate, a pale reflection of the empathy I wanted to convey. "When did he disappear? Have you contacted the police?"

As Sharon began to recount her story, I sank deeper into Nial's armchair, my free hand gripping the worn fabric of the armrest so tightly that the pressure made my knuckles ache. Her tale was uncannily similar to my own—a loving husband vanishing without a trace, leaving behind an empty space where answers should have been. The void her words painted was a mirror of my own.

"It was three days ago," Sharon said, her voice unsteady, each syllable trembling like a fragile leaf in the wind. "Adrian left for work in the morning, just like he always does. He kissed me goodbye... And he never came home. His phone goes straight to voicemail, his car's gone. It's like he just... vanished into thin air."

The parallels sent a shiver down my spine. The eerie symmetry of our experiences was chilling, as if some invisible thread connected our lives. And yet, amidst the discomfort, I felt the faint glimmer of something else—a connection, a fragile but welcome sense that I wasn't navigating this nightmare alone.

"Have the police been any help?" I asked, though I already knew the likely answer. My own exasperating interactions with Detective Jenkins echoed in my mind, particularly his abrupt dismissal earlier. The sting of it was still fresh, a wound I couldn't stop prodding.

Sharon let out a bitter laugh, the sound sharp and brittle. "They think he just... walked out," she said, the disbelief in her voice mirroring my own feelings. "That he decided to abandon me and our kids, our whole life, without so much as a note. As if that's something Adrian would ever do."

I nodded instinctively, though she couldn't see me. "I know exactly what you mean," I replied, the words heavy with shared understanding. "They said the same about Nial. That he probably just... left. But that's not who he is. It's not who your husband is either. They don't seem to understand that, do they?"

"No, they don't," Sharon agreed, her voice cracking slightly, the weight of her emotions spilling into her words. "And it makes you feel so... helpless. Like you're screaming into a void, and no one's listening."

For a moment, neither of us spoke. The silence crackled between us, heavy with the unspoken truths we both carried. Despite the distance, despite being strangers, I felt an odd sense of solidarity. Here was someone who truly understood —the fear, the frustration, the maddening sense of being unheard.

"Jenny," Sharon said hesitantly, breaking the silence. Her tone was cautious, as though she wasn't sure how her next words would be received. "I know this might sound odd, but... do you think we could meet? In person? I just—talking to you helps. It makes me feel like I'm not losing my mind."

Her suggestion caught me off guard, but the idea took root quickly. The prospect of meeting her face-to-face, of sharing our fears and piecing together our parallel stories, was as frightening as it was compelling. I had felt so isolated since Nial's disappearance, as though I were trapped in a soundproof box, shouting for help that never came. Sharon's offer of connection was like a hand reaching through the glass.

"Yes," I said, almost before the thought had fully formed. "Yes, I think that's a good idea."

"Could we meet at the school?" Sharon asked, her voice lighter now, tinged with cautious hope. "St Michael's Collegiate, right? I looked it up online. It seems... safe. Public."

"That works," I agreed. The familiar environment of the school felt like neutral ground, a place where the unknown might feel less threatening.

We quickly finalised the details, arranging to meet the following afternoon. As I hung up the phone, I stood motionless in the middle of the room, the device still warm in my hand. The weight of the conversation lingered in the air, a tangible reminder that this bewildering saga had just shifted in a new and unexpected direction.

Sharon's story wasn't just a parallel to mine—it was an entry point, a potential key to understanding whatever dark forces had upended our lives. I wasn't sure what we would uncover, or whether I was ready for the answers we might find. But for the first time in days, I felt something I hadn't dared to hope for: a glimmer of purpose, and the faintest thread of hope.

I moved to the window, pulling back the curtain to gaze out at the darkening street. The faint hum of Hobart's winter evening settled over the neighbourhood, the streetlights flickering to life one by one, their amber glow pushing back against the encroaching night. Pools of light marked the pavement like scattered breadcrumbs, guiding familiar feet homeward. Across the street, Mrs Carmichael wrestled with her shopping bags, her slight frame bent under their weight. Moments later, her husband appeared, trotting down the driveway to relieve her of the burden. The easy rhythm of their movements, the unspoken partnership of their everyday lives, was both beautiful and excruciating to witness.

The pang in my chest was sharp and immediate. Somewhere out there, Nial was... what? In danger? On the run? Each possibility felt more unbearable than the last. My thoughts strayed to Sharon, a woman who, even now, might be staring out of her own window, battling the same storm of confusion and dread. Her husband, Adrian, had vanished just as mysteriously as Nial. The parallels between our lives were too uncanny to ignore. What if this wasn't mere coincidence? What if the disappearances were somehow connected? The question coiled in my mind like a snake, its presence both ominous and impossible to ignore.

Tomorrow's meeting with Sharon loomed large in my thoughts, a glimmer of light in the shadowy landscape of uncertainty. Would her story mirror mine in ways I hadn't yet imagined? Would sharing our experiences bring clarity, or would it only deepen the labyrinth we were both lost in? What kind of woman was Sharon? Desperate like me? Determined? Or perhaps barely holding herself together? I tried to imagine her face, her voice, but all I could conjure was my own reflection: tired eyes, furrowed brow, and the ever-present lines of worry that had become etched into my features.

Turning away from the window, my gaze landed on a photograph resting on the mantelpiece. It was from a holiday, one of our best. The three of us—Nial, Sammy, and me—were huddled together, sun-kissed and smiling against the backdrop of a dazzling Tasmanian beach. My finger traced the contours of Nial's face in the photo, his laughter captured forever in the crinkle of his eyes, the slight tilt of his head. He looked so happy, so certain, so... present. It was hard to reconcile the man in the photograph with the ghost he'd become in my life.

"Where are you?" I whispered, the words barely audible in the quiet room. They hovered in the air like a plea, a fragile thing that dissolved into silence. The absence of a response felt heavier than ever, pressing down on my chest like a physical weight. My mind churned with unanswerable questions. Had there been signs I'd overlooked? Unspoken words, fleeting gestures, subtle clues that should have hinted at the upheaval to come? The sheer uncertainty of it all gnawed at me, a relentless ache that I couldn't escape.

With a sigh, I replaced the photo and turned to switch on the lamp. A warm glow filled the room, softening the edges of the dark and lending a faint comfort to the otherwise oppressive atmosphere. The light illuminated the familiar clutter of our living room, where the ordinary details of our life together felt charged with a new significance, reminders of everything I was fighting to hold onto.

For a moment, I allowed myself a flicker of cautious optimism. Tomorrow, I would meet Sharon Pafistis. Together, perhaps, we could begin to make sense of this nightmare. Two strangers united by shared grief and a burning need for answers. Maybe, just maybe, we could start to untangle the twisted threads of our husbands' fates.

Hope was a fragile thing, but tonight, it was enough to keep me upright.

4338.214

(2 August 2018)

A SHARED ORDEAL

4338.214.1

The shrill ring of the lunch bell echoed through the corridors of St Michael's Collegiate, signalling a brief respite from the day's lessons. My Year 10 drama students filtered out of the classroom, their laughter and chatter dissipating into the growing hum of the bustling school. I remained rooted behind my desk, my heart pounding with a rhythm far too fast for the stillness of the room. The impending meeting with Sharon Pafistis weighed heavily on my mind, a fragile buoy in the sea of uncertainty I'd been floating in since Nial's disappearance.

I glanced at the clock mounted above the whiteboard, its hands crawling with a deliberate, almost mocking pace. Ten minutes. Ten minutes to collect myself, to organise my thoughts, to brace for a conversation that might finally cast a sliver of light on the darkness surrounding Nial's absence. Or one that might deepen it further.

Seeking distraction, I turned to the disarray of my desk, organising the cluttered surface with methodical precision. I straightened a stack of Shakespeare anthologies, pausing as my fingers brushed against a battered copy of *Hamlet*. The sight of it sent a jolt through me, bittersweet and sharp. Inside the cover, Nial's handwriting remained as vivid as the day he had penned it:

"*To my Ophelia—may our love story have a happier ending.*"

The memory hit like a punch to the stomach, a rush of warmth and pain entwined. My fingers lingered on the inscription, but the sentiment, once a cherished memento of our bond, now felt like an open wound. I closed the book and set it aside, inhaling deeply to steady myself.

As I moved around the room, my gaze fell on the *Wall of Fame*, a collage of students' accomplishments—paintings, essays, poems—that I had curated over the years. A recent addition caught my attention, its bright border drawing my eye. It was a poem about family, penned in Sarah Pafistis' delicate handwriting. The surname landed with a dull thud in my chest. *Pafistis*. Sharon's surname.

My breath hitched as realisation bloomed. Could Sarah be Sharon's daughter? How had I not made the connection sooner? Sarah had always been a quiet presence in class—a diligent and thoughtful student, though never one who demanded attention. She had been here all along, weaving her own existence quietly into the fabric of my classroom, while her family faced a tragedy so eerily similar to my own. If they were indeed mother and daughter, the strangeness of our meeting would deepen. Our shared grief had brought us together, transcending the boundaries of a typical parent-teacher relationship and plunging us into uncharted territory.

I stepped closer to the wall, my eyes scanning Sarah's poem.

"*Family, our anchor in the storm,*
A constant in life's changing form.
Through thick and thin, they'll always be,
The heart of our security."

The words twisted something deep inside me. They carried a poignant simplicity, an almost painful sincerity. *An anchor in the storm.* My throat tightened as I read the line again. Where was my anchor now? Where was the stability, the security, that Nial had once promised? Each word of Sarah's poem felt like a blade, cutting through the fragile defences I had constructed to keep my emotions in check.

I blinked hard, refusing to let tears fall. This wasn't the time for self-pity. The clock continued its inexorable march forward, and in just a few minutes, Sharon Pafistis would walk through that door. I had to be ready—not only to hear her story but to weave it into my own, to search for the threads that connected our lives in this shared nightmare.

The wind howled faintly outside, rattling the windowpanes, and the room seemed to grow colder. *Focus, Jenny.* I squared my shoulders, drawing strength from somewhere deep within.

A gentle knock at the door pulled me from my thoughts. Turning, I saw a tall, slender woman standing hesitantly in the doorway, her figure silhouetted by the bright corridor light behind her. Even at a distance, the toll of the past few days was etched plainly on her face – dark circles framed her wary eyes, her shoulders bore the weight of exhaustion, and there was a haunted air about her that mirrored my own reflection all too well.

"Jenny?" she asked, her voice tremulous, balancing on the edge of hope and uncertainty.

I nodded, managing a strained smile that felt more like an apology than a greeting. "Sharon. Thank you for coming. Please, come in."

As Sharon stepped into the classroom, I studied her more closely. She wore a charcoal grey suit that hinted at her professional life, her dark hair neatly pulled back into a bun. At first glance, her appearance suggested poise, even control, but as she drew closer, the cracks in her composure became apparent. A slight tremor betrayed her tightly clasped hands, and the red rims of her eyes spoke of sleepless nights and tears hastily wiped away.

"I hope I'm not interrupting anything," Sharon said, glancing around the quiet, empty classroom.

I shook my head, gesturing towards the vacant chairs. "Not at all. It's lunch hour. I was thinking we could talk in the teacher's lounge if that's alright with you. It's more comfortable there, and..." I faltered, unsure of how to articulate my unease.

Sharon's lips pressed into a thin line, and she nodded, as if reading my hesitation perfectly. "And there will be other people around," she said, finishing my thought. Her voice was low, but there was a certainty to it. "I was thinking the same thing. It feels... safer, doesn't it? To have this conversation somewhere public?"

I exhaled, a subtle wave of relief washing over me. "Exactly. I know it might seem paranoid, but after everything that's happened..."

"We can't be too careful," Sharon agreed, her tone sombre. "Not until we understand what we're really dealing with."

Her words carried a weight that settled uncomfortably between us as we made our way out of the classroom and towards the teacher's lounge. As we walked, I noticed how Sharon's eyes swept the school, taking in every detail – the artwork lining the walls, the rows of lockers, the occasional echoes of laughter and chatter spilling from classrooms where students enjoyed their lunch. It was the normality of the environment that seemed to hold her attention, as if it were an unfamiliar concept, a stark contrast to the turmoil that had overrun both our lives.

"It's a lovely school," Sharon commented as we neared the lounge. There was a faint wistfulness in her voice, a longing for stability. "Sarah speaks very highly of it. And of you, especially. She was so excited when she found out she'd be in your drama class this year."

The mention of Sarah caused my chest to tighten, the innocence of her excitement a sharp counterpoint to the darkness we were now facing. "She's a wonderful student," I said sincerely, grasping for a thread of positivity. "Her poem... it's on our Wall of Fame, actually. The one about family."

Sharon's steps faltered. I glanced at her, seeing her composure waver. "Oh," she murmured, her voice catching. "I... I haven't read it. Adrian usually... he was always the one who..." Her words trailed off, lost in the weight of an unfinished thought.

Without thinking, I reached out and placed a hand on her arm. The contact was brief but gentle, a small offering of solace. "I'm so sorry, Sharon," I said quietly. "I didn't mean to..."

She shook her head, drawing in a steadying breath as she squared her shoulders. "No, it's alright," she said firmly, though the fragility in her tone was unmistakable. "We can't avoid these reminders, can we? They're everywhere."

Her words resonated deeply. *They're everywhere.* The echoes of lives once whole, now fragmented. The small, seemingly innocuous moments that opened wounds you thought might begin to heal. We continued towards the lounge in a shared silence, heavy with unspoken fears and the faintest flickers of hope.

As we stepped into the teacher's lounge, the hum of conversation dipped momentarily, a ripple of awareness passing through the room. Heads turned in our direction, some openly curious, others more discreet in their glances. I caught snippets of whispered exchanges, the faint murmur of my name mingled with speculation. The social media campaign had ensured that my personal life was no longer entirely my own, and though I appreciated the concern, the attention made my skin crawl.

I guided Sharon towards a small table tucked into the corner, a spot that offered a semblance of privacy while keeping us within view of the rest of the room. It felt safer that way, the presence of others a buffer against the dark undercurrents of our conversation. As we settled into our chairs, I felt the weight of the room's collective gaze, though most pretended to focus on their sandwiches or grading.

From across the room, Mike Doherty, the PE teacher, caught my eye. He gave me a brief, understanding nod, his usually boisterous demeanour subdued. The gesture, simple yet meaningful, was a reminder that amidst the whispers and curiosity, there were those who genuinely cared. I returned the nod, a flicker of gratitude breaking through the storm cloud of my thoughts.

Sharon leaned in slightly, her voice low but urgent. "Jenny, I can't tell you how much it means that you agreed to meet with me. When I saw your post about Nial on Facebook… I couldn't believe it. The similarities to Adrian's disappearance… it can't be a coincidence, can it?"

I shook my head, the doubts and fears that had haunted me coalescing into grim certainty. "I don't think so. The timing, the circumstances… it's too much to be random chance." My voice was calm, but my knuckles whitened as I gripped the edge of the table. "Sharon, please. Tell me everything about what happened with Adrian. Every detail could matter."

She took a steadying breath, her hands clasped tightly together on the table, fingers twisting as if trying to wring sense from the unknown. "It was Tuesday morning. Adrian left for work just like he always does – same time, same routine. He kissed me goodbye, told the girls he'd be home for dinner. But he never came back. His phone goes straight to voicemail. His car is gone. It's like he just… vanished."

Her words hit me with a sickening familiarity, each one aligning too perfectly with my own nightmare. The steady chatter of the lounge faded into background noise as my focus narrowed entirely to Sharon, her voice trembling as she laid bare the agony of her husband's disappearance.

"The police," she continued, her tone sharp with bitterness, "they think he just walked out. That he... he chose this." Her voice cracked, and she closed her eyes briefly, gathering herself. "As if Adrian would ever abandon us. Twenty years of marriage, Jenny. Two kids. And they think he'd just... leave. Just like that."

I nodded, the weight of my own frustrations surfacing as her words mirrored my experience. "It's the same with Nial. They don't understand. They don't see what we see."

"Exactly!" Sharon's voice rose slightly, before she caught herself, glancing at a pair of nearby teachers who turned in our direction. She lowered her tone, leaning closer. "They see statistics, patterns. They don't see the man who never missed a single one of Brooke's piano recitals, who stayed up all night to finish Sarah's science project when she fell ill."

I reached across the table, resting my hand on hers. "I know. They don't see the man who surprised me with breakfast in bed every anniversary. The man who spent three weekends building Sammy a playhouse, complete with a tiny white fence, because he wanted it to be perfect."

For a long moment, we sat in silence, our shared pain a tangible presence between us. Around us, the room carried on as if nothing had changed – mugs clinked, papers rustled, muted laughter punctuated quiet conversations.

Finally, Sharon broke the silence, her voice subdued but resolute. "Jenny, I don't think this is just bad luck. Two men, same city, same circumstances... it can't be random. There's something more here. There has to be."

I nodded, a slow, deliberate motion that felt like a promise. "We'll find out," I said quietly, my own voice firm with resolve.

When it was my turn, the story of Nial's disappearance spilled from me in a torrent, each word laden with the fear and confusion I had been carrying. I recounted every detail –

the morning that began with a kiss goodbye and descended into a waking nightmare, the frantic phone calls to his colleagues, the hours spent pacing the house with my phone in hand, and the gut-wrenching realisation that our dog, Buffy, had vanished too. As I spoke, Sharon's expression shifted, her eyes widening with each new revelation, her features tightening as the weight of our shared reality settled over her.

"The worst part," I said, my voice faltering as I reached the darkest corners of my fears, "is not knowing. Is he in danger? Did he leave voluntarily? Is he... is he even alive?" The final word caught in my throat, heavy and bitter, the enormity of the possibility too terrible to fully voice.

Sharon reached out, her hand grasping mine. The warmth of her touch was comforting. "I know," she said softly, her voice carrying the weight of her own anguish. "I ask myself the same questions every day. Every time the phone rings, every knock at the door... I think, 'This is it. This is the moment I'll know.' But it never is."

The raw honesty in her words hit me like a punch to the chest, the stark reality of our situations binding us together in a way nothing else could. For the first time in days, I felt a flicker of connection, a sense that I wasn't entirely alone in this dark and twisted ordeal.

As we talked, a disquieting pattern began to emerge, threading Nial's and Adrian's disappearances together with eerie precision. The timing, the secrecy, the peculiar behaviour in the days leading up to their absences – it all pointed to something larger, something unseen but undeniably present.

"Jenny," Sharon said, leaning closer, her voice dropping to an urgent whisper. "Have you considered that this might be... bigger than just our husbands? That there might be a reason they both disappeared?"

A shiver ran down my spine at her words. The idea had haunted my thoughts in the sleepless hours of the night, a nebulous fear that refused to take shape. But hearing it spoken aloud, seeing the same dread reflected in Sharon's eyes, made it suddenly, terrifyingly real.

"What are you saying?" I asked, my voice barely audible, though deep down I already knew.

"Is there any chance Nial and Adrian knew each other?" Sharon asked, her eyes searching mine for answers. "Could there be a closer connection we're missing?"

I furrowed my brow, racking my brain for any mention Nial might have made of Adrian. His work was often solitary, focused on his small fencing business. "I don't know," I said slowly. "Nial runs his own fencing business. It's a small operation, just him and a couple of workers. He mostly deals with private clients."

Sharon's lips pressed into a thin line, disappointment flickering in her expression. "Adrian manages a large construction firm. I suppose it's possible they crossed paths on a job site, but…"

"But it seems unlikely," I finished for her, though the small size of Hobart made me wonder. "Still, we can't rule anything out. Maybe they met socially? At a networking event or through mutual friends?"

Sharon shook her head, her frustration mirrored in the tight set of her jaw. "I can't remember Adrian ever mentioning a Nial. And I'm sure I'd remember if he'd talked about someone in fencing. He was always lamenting how hard it was to find good contractors."

Her next words sent a fresh wave of unease rippling through me. "I've been doing some digging," Sharon admitted, lowering her voice. "Adrian was working on a big project before he disappeared. Something he couldn't talk about. I think... I think he might have uncovered something. Something dangerous."

My heart sank as her words unlocked a memory I'd been suppressing – the way Nial had left the house that final morning, his expression tense and guarded, his voice clipped when I asked about his plans for the day. "Nial was acting strange too," I said, my voice barely more than a whisper. "He'd come home late, distracted. He kept saying it was just work stress, but I knew it was more than that. I could feel it."

"What kind of project was Adrian working on?" I asked, leaning closer. "Did he tell you anything about it?."

Sharon hesitated, her gaze darting around the room before returning to mine. "He never told me much. But I overheard him on the phone once. He was arguing with someone, saying something about 'irregularities' and how 'we can't let this continue.' When I asked him about it later, he brushed it off, said it was just a difficult client."

The words sent a chill racing down my spine. Nial had received mysterious phone calls too, late at night when he thought I was asleep. I remembered the tension in his voice, the cryptic snippets of conversation that I'd chalked up to work stress at the time.

Sharon glanced around nervously, her voice dropping to a whisper as she continued. "Before Adrian disappeared, he mentioned someone named Luke Smith. I overheard the name during one of his phone calls. I didn't catch any other details, but it sounded urgent."

She hesitated, then added, "When I spoke to the detectives—Sarah Lahey and Karl Jenkins—I told them I was pretty sure Adrian was going to meet this Luke Smith the morning he vanished. You should have seen Karl's reaction. He couldn't hide it. The moment I said the name, I saw the recognition in his face. Concern, too, like he knew exactly who Luke was. He tried to cover it, but I could tell."

A chill ran down my spine at her words. "Detective Jenkins mentioned Luke's name to me as well," I said, my voice low. "When I first spoke to him about Nial's disappearance, he asked if the name Luke Smith meant anything to me. At the time, it didn't. But now..." I trailed off, the pieces beginning to click into place.

"Now it feels like too much of a coincidence," Sharon finished for me, her expression grim. "If both our husbands were connected to this Luke Smith somehow, then he's more than just a missing piece. He could be the key to the whole puzzle."

I nodded, my mind racing. The urgency in Sharon's voice mirrored the pounding of my own heart. Luke Smith wasn't just a name. He was a link, the thread tying Nial and Adrian together—and perhaps the person who could unravel the mystery surrounding their disappearances.

"Sharon," I said, my voice trembling as I spoke, "I think whatever Adrian uncovered... Nial was involved in it too."

As we continued to share our stories, the parallels became impossible to ignore. Both our husbands had been uncharacteristically secretive in the days leading up to their disappearances. Both had hinted—however subtly—at something significant, something dangerous. And both had vanished within days of each other, leaving behind lives now tangled in uncertainty and fear.

The realisation that our experiences were entwined, that our stories were fragments of a larger, more intricate puzzle, settled over me like a heavy cloak. It was comforting in one sense: Sharon was living proof that I wasn't alone, that someone else understood the depths of my fear and the relentless need for answers. But it was terrifying too, the undeniable connection hinting at forces beyond our comprehension, forces that might be watching even now.

Sharon and I sat in silence, each lost in our own thoughts. What had Nial and Adrian uncovered? Who—or what—had taken them from us? Were we prepared to face the answers, no matter how devastating they might be? The questions spiralled in my mind, a web of possibilities that threatened to ensnare me.

"What do we do now?" I finally asked, breaking the silence. My voice sounded somewhat small, but there was a steel beneath it, a determination that surprised even me.

Sharon's gaze locked onto mine, her expression a mirror of my own resolve. The fire in her eyes was unmistakable, a kindred flame that reignited something in me. When she spoke, her voice was steady, almost defiant, each word heavy with intent.

"We demand the police give us answers," she said, her tone as firm as steel. "They've dismissed us, patronised us, and ignored the evidence staring them in the face. No more. If they won't listen, we'll make them."

Her words landed like a spark in a room full of dry tinder. Something within me shifted—a resolve hardened, a sense of purpose that had been elusive until now. I nodded, slow and deliberate, the motion more a declaration than a response.

"You're right," I said, my voice growing stronger. "If they won't take us seriously, we'll force them to. They can't ignore us forever."

Sharon straightened in her seat, her shoulders squared and her expression resolute. A determined glint sparked in her eyes. "I'm going to call the police," she declared, her tone steady but underscored with a simmering tension. "Right now. We need answers, and I'm tired of waiting."

I watched as she retrieved her mobile phone from her bag, her movements deliberate yet rigid with tightly contained frustration. The room seemed to constrict around us, the walls creeping closer as the stakes of this moment settled over me like a suffocating fog. Each passing second sharpened the air with a taut, electrified anticipation.

The first ring of the call sounded like a hammer strike in the silence. Then another. And another. Each chime mirrored the thrum of my pulse, a frantic beat I couldn't steady. My eyes darted across the lounge, catching fleeting glances from colleagues engaged in casual conversations, blissfully unaware of the storm brewing at our corner table. They couldn't possibly understand the magnitude of what was happening. How could they?

"Hello," Sharon began, her voice crisp, brimming with control despite the tremor that quivered beneath it. "This is Sharon Pafistis. I'm calling for an update on my husband Adrian's case... and on Nial Triffett's as well."

She threw a quick glance my way, her lips pressed into a tight line, as if to say, *We're in this together.* I nodded silently, my throat too dry to offer any verbal encouragement. As Sharon listened to the response on the other end, her features shifted—her brow furrowing, her lips thinning further. The tension radiating from her was palpable, matching the growing knot of dread in my stomach.

I leaned forward, straining to catch any snippets of the conversation. The voice on the other end was muffled, the words indistinct, but Sharon's reaction spoke volumes. Her fingers gripped the phone so tightly her knuckles turned white. I didn't need to hear the words to know that we were being stonewalled.

"They keep saying it's an ongoing investigation," Sharon muttered under her breath, cupping the phone slightly as if to shield her frustration from the caller. "That they're following leads. But it's all vague. They're not telling me anything useful."

The mounting irritation in her voice felt like a mirror of my own emotions. My nails dug into my palms as I clenched my fists tightly, trying to steady the surge of helpless anger threatening to bubble over.

Then a chilling thought crossed my mind, one I had been too afraid to voice until now. The words slipped from my mouth like venom, low and urgent. "Ask them..." My voice wavered, my throat tight. "Ask them if they've found any bodies."

Sharon's eyes flickered with shock, and for a moment, I regretted the suggestion. But then, understanding replaced the hesitation in her gaze. She nodded grimly and relayed the question, her voice hard and unwavering despite the implication.

The pause that followed felt endless, each second stretching into an eternity as the air in the room grew heavy and oppressive. My breath hitched, my heart pounding so loudly it drowned out the muffled sounds of my surroundings. Every tick of the wall clock seemed to mock me, a cruel reminder of the time slipping away, of the ever-deepening void where answers should have been.

Finally, Sharon's expression shifted, though the response she received offered no clarity, only more deflection. "*No bodies recovered at this time.*" The words, relayed in an indifferent monotone, landed like a sledgehammer, cracking the fragile veneer of my composure.

I felt the dam within me break. A torrent of emotions surged forward—grief, fear, anger—all colliding in a chaotic storm that I couldn't contain. My chest heaved as ragged breaths fought their way in and out, the weight of despair pressing down on me with suffocating force.

Images flashed in my mind like cruel spectres—Nial's warm smile, the twinkle in his eye when he teased Sammy about being the fastest runner in their games, the quiet strength in his embrace when the world seemed too much to bear. The thought that these moments might now be confined to the past, that the man who had been my anchor, my partner, was lost to me forever, was a reality too unbearable to confront.

Sharon's hand found mine, her grip firm but grounding. "Breathe, Jenny," she said softly, her own voice trembling. "We're not giving up. Do you hear me? We're not giving up."

I nodded mechanically, though the hollow ache inside me felt insurmountable. The words were a lifeline I wanted to believe in, even as the shadows of doubt and despair coiled tighter around my heart.

With a deep sigh, Sharon ended the call, her expression grim, yet marked with a flicker of determination. She turned her full attention to me, and I could feel the edges of my carefully constructed resolve beginning to fray. The weight of the past days—the sleepless nights, the relentless worry, the unanswered questions—crashed over me like a breaking wave. It was too much.

Tears spilled down my cheeks, unchecked, as the fear I had tried so hard to suppress erupted in a torrent. "I can't do this," I sobbed, the words coming out in jagged gasps. "What if he's... what if they're..." My voice broke, the sentence hanging in the air, unfinished. I couldn't say it. I couldn't breathe life into the possibility of Nial being gone forever.

The teacher's lounge blurred around me, a distorted haze of muted colours and faint sounds. Panic clawed at my chest, a suffocating force that made the world feel smaller, darker, more menacing.

Sharon didn't hesitate. She moved closer, her arm wrapping securely around my shoulders, a gesture both firm and tender. Her warmth cut through the cold spiral of my despair, her presence like a lifeline tethering me to reality. In that moment, she wasn't just a fellow traveller through this nightmare—she was my anchor.

"We don't know anything for certain," she said, her voice low, steady, and insistent. "And until we do, we have to believe they're alive. Do you hear me, Jenny? We *have* to keep fighting."

I nodded, the motion small and hesitant, a fragile thread of hope woven through the tangle of my fear. Sharon's words planted a seed, though the soil of my mind felt too barren to nurture it. Still, her conviction was undeniable, and for a fleeting moment, I clung to it like a child to a comforting story.

The rawness of my breakdown, the sheer vulnerability of it, left me drained. Yet, as the flood of emotions began to recede, it also brought a painful clarity: there was no room for surrender. The stakes were too high, the questions too urgent, and the absence of answers too unbearable. For Nial, for Sammy, for myself—and now, for Sharon and Adrian—I had to keep moving forward.

The bitter sting of being stonewalled by the police lingered in my chest like a sharp splinter, a constant reminder of the barriers we faced. Sharon, however, refused to let it deter her. With a purposeful glint in her eye, she pulled out her phone again.

"I'll try calling the detective directly," she said, her tone resolute. Her words gave me a sliver of hope. Detective Jenkins had been one of the few in authority who seemed to care, to actually *listen*. If anyone could offer us even the smallest of leads, it was him.

I held my breath as she dialled, the sound of each ring slicing through the tense silence in the lounge like a blade. Around us, the murmurs of casual conversations and the occasional scrape of chairs felt like a distant hum, utterly disconnected from the charged reality of our situation. The room seemed to hold its breath with me.

But instead of Karl's voice, there was only his voicemail—a cold, impersonal message that extinguished the small ember of hope we had stoked.

Sharon's shoulders slumped, her composure cracking just slightly as disappointment carved itself into her expression. She pulled the phone away from her ear, staring at the screen as though willing it to change. "Voicemail," she muttered, her voice laced with frustration.

The fog of despair thickened around us, but Sharon's resolve didn't waver. Her grip on the phone tightened, her jaw set with renewed determination. "If he won't answer, then we keep calling," she said, her words as firm as steel. "We don't stop, Jenny. Not until we get what we need."

Her unwavering persistence rekindled something in me—a flicker of defiance against the darkness threatening to consume us. I wiped my tear-streaked face, straightening in my seat.

"We won't stop," I echoed, the words quiet but charged with intent.

Sharon's eyes lit with a sudden spark of inspiration. "I've got an idea," she said, her voice carrying an edge of renewed determination. "I need to go home for something. I'll call you again shortly."

Her cryptic declaration piqued my curiosity, a flicker of hope amidst the gloom that had settled over our efforts. As she rose, her movements brisk and purposeful, I couldn't help but feel a mix of anticipation and unease. What could she have at home that might help us?

"What are you planning?" I asked, my voice raw and uneven from the storm of emotions I'd barely contained. I wiped at my tear-streaked cheeks, desperate to compose myself, to match Sharon's sudden energy.

Sharon paused at the door of the lounge, her hand resting on the handle as she turned to face me. "Something that might just get us the answers we need," she said, a flicker of a smile tugging at her lips. Her tone was a mixture of reassurance and intrigue. "Trust me, Jenny. We're not beaten yet."

Before I could ask her to elaborate, Sharon was gone, leaving her enigmatic promise hanging in the air like a lifeline tossed into a stormy sea.

I stood there for a moment, the expanse of the room closing in around me, amplifying the roar of my restless thoughts. Questions swirled like a tempest: What was Sharon planning? Could her idea really help us? And what if it didn't? What if this too ended in another dead end, another avenue that led only to more questions and no answers?

Needing to expel the restless energy thrumming through my veins, ignoring the sideways glances of my colleagues, I began to pace the length of the teacher's lounge. My eyes darted over the room, taking in the familiar surroundings that now felt strangely foreign. The motivational posters on the walls—once sources of light-hearted encouragement—now seemed to mock my despair.

"Perseverance is the key to success," one proclaimed in bold, cheerful lettering. I scoffed under my breath. If only it were that simple.

My gaze landed on the staff noticeboard, its colourful jumble of announcements and memos an odd contrast to the heavy weight of my reality. Among the schedules and reminders, a flyer caught my eye: "**Community Meeting: Addressing Recent Break-Ins in the Area.**"

The bitter irony was impossible to ignore. While Sharon and I wrestled with the sinister complexities of our husbands' disappearances, the rest of Hobart continued on with its mundane problems, blissfully unaware of the nightmare that had overtaken our lives.

My thoughts shifted to Sammy—my sweet, innocent boy whose biggest concerns should have been scraped knees and learning his spelling words, not the absence of his father. How much longer could I protect him from the dark truth that loomed over us? The thought of sitting him down, of trying to explain why his dad hadn't come home, twisted a knot of dread in my stomach. It was a conversation I prayed I'd never have to have.

Blinking back tears, I forced myself to refocus. I had to stay in the present, to direct my energy toward finding Nial. Sitting here, waiting for the police or someone else to solve this for me, was no longer an option.

If this were a play, what would the protagonist do next? The thought drifted in unbidden, a testament to my ingrained drama teacher's mindset. A protagonist wouldn't sit idly by, waiting for the plot to resolve itself. She'd take the stage, drive the story forward with action and determination.

The idea sparked something deep within me—a sense of agency I hadn't felt in days. Why had we put so much faith in others, in the police, in Karl, when they had offered little more than platitudes and evasions? We had waited long enough. It was time to take control of the narrative.

But how? Where would we even begin?

THE WAITING GAME

4338.214.2

The moment I stepped through the front door, the silence hit me like a physical blow, the kind that leaves you reeling and grasping for air. The house, once a haven of warmth and family life, now felt like a mausoleum of memories, each room a monument to Nial's absence. The scents of home still lingered—faint traces of his aftershave, the subtle lavender from the potpourri I'd arranged in the hallway days before he vanished. But instead of comforting me, these familiar fragrances felt like cruel reminders of a life that had been abruptly derailed.

Unbidden, my feet carried me to our bedroom, the very heart of what our shared life had been. The room seemed to hold its breath, expectant and oppressive, as though it too mourned the loss. Nial's cologne stood on the dresser, its bottle still bearing the faint smudges of his fingerprints. His slippers, perfectly aligned by the bed as always, sat waiting for feet that might never return. Each object seemed to mock me with its stillness, a silent testament to the sudden, jagged edges of our interrupted existence.

The steady glow of the bedside clock cut through the quiet. Time marched on, indifferent to my turmoil, counting the hours of his absence with cold precision. The promise of Sharon's mysterious plan was the only thread tethering me to hope, its fragility matched only by the uncertainty of what it might reveal.

I moved aimlessly around the room, my stockinged feet muffled by the thick carpet. The late winter light filtered through the curtains, throwing warped shadows across the walls. Everything about the room felt altered, as if the air itself carried the weight of secrets. My gaze snagged on the wardrobe, its door slightly ajar, and a sense of unease coiled low in my stomach.

I crossed the room with measured steps, my fingers brushing against the smooth wood as I eased the door fully open. The wardrobe, once brimming with both our clothes, now looked barren. Nial's side was almost empty, save for a few hangers and a handful of shirts that hung limply, their absence far louder than their presence. My hand moved almost of its own accord, grazing the sleeve of his favourite blue Oxford shirt. The fabric was cool, and for a fleeting second, I could almost convince myself it still carried his warmth, his scent.

But the moment shattered as reality reasserted itself, sharp and unyielding. My mind returned to the red lace panties I'd found in my drawer, the ones that weren't mine. That discovery had been like a gut punch, a revelation that knocked the wind from me. Yet, as I stared at the barren wardrobe, the thought of Nial abandoning us for another woman felt false. It didn't fit. It was a dissonant note in a song I had known too well.

Years of teaching drama had trained me to detect falsehoods, to recognise when a performance didn't ring true. The clues—the panties, the photograph, the sparse wardrobe —felt too staged, too deliberate. It wasn't the organic chaos of a man walking away from his life; it was something more sinister, more calculated. The pieces were there to tell a story, but it wasn't one I believed.

The chilling alternative began to crystallise. Someone had been in our house. Someone had placed those panties in my drawer, left the photograph, and ensured the wardrobe told a specific tale. Someone had orchestrated these events to drive a wedge of doubt into my mind. But who? And why?

I thought of Sharon, of her eerily similar story, of her husband vanishing under equally strange circumstances. It couldn't be a coincidence.

The realisation sent a shiver down my spine, icy and relentless. Every creak of the house, every faint sound from outside, took on a menacing edge. We weren't just grieving Nial's absence—we were being manipulated, played in a twisted game I didn't understand.

Every creak of the house, every distant car engine, sent my heart racing. Was it Sharon? Had she found something? The anticipation was a living thing, coiling in my stomach, making it impossible to stand still.

I turned toward the window, drawn by a need to connect to the world outside, however falsely reassuring it might be. The street looked deceptively normal, bathed in the pale glow of late afternoon. A child pedalled a bicycle past our house, their laughter drifting faintly through the glass. An elderly couple walked hand in hand, their small dog trotting obediently beside them.

The ordinariness of it all felt surreal. How could life outside continue so serenely while my own had been turned inside out? How could this street—our street, with its neatly trimmed hedges and rows of weatherboard houses—be the backdrop to such a sinister reality?

I pressed my forehead against the cool glass, staring out at the world that seemed to mock my pain with its tranquillity. Somewhere out there, someone held the answers I so desperately needed. And somewhere, Nial existed—alive or dead, in safety or peril. The thought twisted my insides, spurring me toward action even as the mounting dread threatened to overwhelm me.

Whoever had done this—whoever had invaded our lives and planted these seeds of torment—thought they were in control. They believed they could manipulate me into submission, into despair. But they were wrong. A new determination gripped me, cold and fierce. I would find Nial. I would uncover the truth. And I would confront whoever had done this to my family.

Because if this was a game, it was one I was no longer content to be a pawn in.

In an effort to distract myself from the relentless churn of my thoughts, I pulled out my mobile and dialled Rowena's number. The ache in my chest momentarily eased at the thought of hearing Sammy's voice. He was my anchor, the one unbroken thread in the fraying fabric of my world.

The phone barely rang before Rowena picked up, her voice warm and steady. "Jenny," she greeted, her tone imbued with the unspoken understanding only she could offer. "Sammy's here, playing with his trains. Would you like to speak with him?"

"Yes, please," I said quickly, the weight of longing in my words. I sank onto the bed, clutching Nial's pillow to my chest. Its fading scent—a mixture of his shampoo and that ineffable quality that was just *him*—wrapped around me like a ghost of his presence, offering both comfort and a pang of fresh sorrow.

Moments later, Sammy's bright, excited voice burst through the line. "Mummy!" he exclaimed, his joy a piercing contrast to the gloom that had settled over my days. That single word, filled with pure, innocent delight, brought instant tears to my eyes.

"Hello, my darling," I said, my voice soft and shaky. "Are you having fun with Grandma?"

"Yes! My red train saved the blue train today, Mummy! It was stuck in the tunnel, but the red train is super brave!" His words tumbled out in an excited rush.

I closed my eyes, letting the sound of his chatter paint a vivid picture in my mind. I could see him sitting cross-legged on the floor, his blonde curls bouncing as he animatedly described his imaginary adventures, his little hands gesturing as if to physically pull me into his world. For a moment, I allowed myself to linger in this vision, pretending that everything was as it should be.

"That sounds like an amazing rescue, sweetheart," I replied, a smile finding its way to my lips despite the heaviness in my heart. "The red train must be very brave."

"It is, Mummy! Just like Daddy!" Sammy's declaration, so earnest and unguarded, sent a jolt of pain straight through my chest. "Daddy always says we have to help people when they're stuck."

I swallowed hard, fighting to keep my voice steady. "He's right, sweetheart. Daddy is very wise."

But the brightness in his tone dimmed, replaced by a softer, more hesitant voice that broke me further. "Mummy, when is Daddy coming home? I miss him."

The question hung in the air, its innocence clashing with the unbearable weight of my own uncertainty. My breath caught, the knot in my chest tightening as I struggled to find the right words. How could I answer when I didn't know the truth myself? How could I protect him from the reality that terrified me?

"Soon, darling," I said finally, the lie cutting through me like a blade. "I'll come and get you tomorrow, and we'll wait for Daddy at home. Would you like that?"

"Yes, Mummy," he replied, his small voice trusting and full of love. "I love you."

"I love you too, my sweet boy. More than anything," I whispered, my voice breaking as fresh tears rolled down my cheeks. Hanging up, I pressed the phone to my lips, as if the device itself could somehow bring me closer to him.

The silence that followed was suffocating, the house once again swallowing me whole with its oppressive stillness. I wandered from room to room, each space a snapshot of the life we had shared before everything unravelled.

And then, finally, the phone rang, slicing through the suffocating quiet with the urgency of a siren. My heart leapt into my throat as I lunged for it, my hand trembling as I snatched it up. The caller ID displayed Sharon's name, and a rush of anticipation surged through me.

"I know where we can find Luke Smith," she said, skipping any preamble, her voice crackling with excitement and determination.

Her words electrified me, sending a jolt of adrenaline racing through my veins. Luke Smith—the elusive name Sharon had mentioned before, someone she suspected might hold the key to the tangled web surrounding our husbands' disappearances. This was it. This was the lead we had been desperate for.

"How?" I managed, my voice taut with a mix of hope and trepidation. "Where is he?"

"I'll explain everything when I see you," Sharon replied quickly, her tone edged with tension. "But Jenny, we need to move fast. If I'm right about this, we might not be the only ones looking for him."

Her warning sent a chill down my spine, my pulse pounding in my ears. What had Sharon discovered? What danger were we walking into? The weight of her urgency settled heavily on my chest, and I knew we were about to cross a line—into what, I wasn't sure.

"Come and get me," I said, the words firm despite the fear curling in my stomach. This was not a journey I could make alone, nor did I want to. In Sharon, I had found more than just a kindred spirit; I had found an ally, a partner in this relentless quest for truth. "We'll go together."

Sharon hesitated, the pause between us filled with the gravity of what we were about to undertake. "Are you sure?" she asked softly, her voice laced with concern. "Jenny, this could be dangerous. We don't know what we're walking into."

I thought of Nial, of Sammy, of the life that had been ripped away from us like a thread unravelled from a cherished tapestry. I thought of the notebook I had found in Nial's office, its cryptic notes a maddening riddle I hadn't yet solved. "I'm sure," I said, my voice steadier than I felt. "Whatever this is, whatever we're facing, we face it together."

"Alright," Sharon said, her tone shifting to one of resolve. "I'll be there soon. Be ready to leave as soon as I arrive."

As the call ended, I stared at the screen for a moment before texting Sharon my address, the message feeling far more significant than its simplicity implied. This was it. The next step in a journey neither of us had ever wanted to take.

The house felt eerily quiet as I moved through it, gathering what I thought we might need. A torch, some cash, a first aid kit—it all felt surreal, like I was preparing for some strange, improvised mission rather than a potentially dangerous confrontation. I slipped Nial's notebook into my bag, its contents still a mystery even to me. For now, I wasn't ready to share it with Sharon. Not yet.

As I moved to the hallway, my eyes landed on the framed photo that sat on the table—a candid shot of Nial and me from our last anniversary. We were at a vineyard, bathed in golden light, his arms wrapped securely around me. Both of us were laughing, our faces alight with the simple joy of being together.

I picked it up, my fingers brushing against the glass, as if I could reach through it and touch the man I loved. My gaze lingered on his face, memorising every detail: the warm brown of his eyes, the dimple in his cheek when he smiled, the way his head tilted slightly when he looked at me. My chest ached with the intensity of my longing, the deep, unrelenting need to bring him back home.

"I'm coming for you," I whispered, my voice steady despite the whirlwind of emotions within. My reflection in the glass stared back, determined and resolute, a glimpse of the woman I had been before Nial's disappearance—a fighter, unyielding in her quest of life.

"Just hold on," I added softly, a promise to the man I loved and to myself.

ACCOMPLICE

4338.214.3

"Shit! Where the heck are you, Sharon?" The words escaped in a harsh whisper, barely audible even to myself as I peered through the narrow gap in the blinds. The quiet street stretched out before me, bathed in the dim, fading light of early evening. My gaze darted from one shadow to the next, scanning for any sign of movement, my heart pounding with a mix of anxiety and anticipation.

It had been nearly an hour—far longer than the fifteen minutes Sharon had said it would take her to get here. Each passing minute wound the knot in my stomach tighter, the tension creeping up my spine like icy fingers. The unanswered message on my phone taunted me from the coffee table, its silent glow a cruel reminder of my growing fear. *Has something happened to her?* The question looped in my mind, relentless and unforgiving, feeding the gnawing sense of unease.

A sudden, sharp honk jolted me, the sound cutting through the oppressive quiet like a knife. My breath hitched as I rushed back to the window, pulling the blinds aside to see a silver car idling in the driveway. Relief surged through me, tempered by the lingering edge of anxiety. *Finally. Sharon.*

I hurried to the kitchen, my movements brisk and deliberate. My keys, cold and metallic in my grasp, felt heavier than they should, as if they carried the weight of what was to come. The coat rack proved its usual uncooperative self, my jacket snagged on one of the hooks. I tugged it free with more force than necessary, the motion nearly toppling the entire stand.

Outside, the cold air bit at my cheeks, sharp and unforgiving. I pulled my jacket closer, my breath puffing out in soft clouds that dissipated into the approaching dusk. The faint smell of wet leaves and distant woodsmoke hung in the air, a reminder of the encroaching winter.

The car honked again, the second blare more insistent. My steps quickened, boots crunching on the gravel as I descended the driveway. A faint unease lingered despite the relief of seeing her; Sharon's urgency was palpable, almost tangible, and it set my nerves on edge.

"Everything okay?" I asked as I slid into the passenger seat, closing the door firmly behind me. The weight of the door thudding shut reverberated through the stillness, louder than I expected. Sharon didn't answer immediately, her hands gripping the steering wheel with white-knuckled intensity.

"Yeah," she replied, her voice clipped and tight. Her eyes flicked to the rearview mirror, scanning the street behind us with a quick, darting motion. The movement wasn't lost on me, nor was the tension that seemed to radiate off her in waves.

"You're late," I said gently, hoping to probe without pressing too hard. "I was starting to worry."

Sharon exhaled sharply, her lips pressed into a thin line. "I got held up," she admitted after a moment, her voice low. She didn't elaborate, her attention split between the road ahead and the mirrors. "We need to move."

The weight in her words silenced any follow-up questions I might have asked. I sat back, fastening my seatbelt with a decisive click, my heart pounding against my ribs. The sense of urgency in Sharon's demeanour was contagious, sparking a fresh wave of adrenaline. Whatever was about to unfold, it was clear we were stepping into something far more complicated—and dangerous—than either of us had anticipated.

For the first five minutes of our journey, silence enveloped us, a tangible presence that seemed to press down on the confined space of the car, thickening the air until it felt almost suffocating. The only sounds were the steady hum of the engine and the faint whisper of tyres on asphalt, a rhythm as steady as my racing heartbeat. The weight of unspoken fears hung between us, an invisible barrier neither of us seemed willing—or perhaps able—to breach.

In a bid to ease the oppressive tension, I reached over and lowered the window a few inches. The rush of cold air stung my face, a brisk distraction that momentarily cut through the unease lodged in my chest. It was grounding, the chill offering a strange sort of comfort, even as it set goosebumps rippling along my arms.

As the landscape blurred past in the deepening dusk, the world outside the car seemed to dissolve into shadowy shapes, indistinct and fleeting. My attention, however, remained fixed on Sharon. Her knuckles were a stark white against the dark leather of the steering wheel, her grip so tight it seemed as though she was anchoring herself to it. Yet, it wasn't her hands that unnerved me—it was her eyes. They flitted to the rearview mirror with a rhythm that was too deliberate, too frequent. Each darting glance betrayed a tension that seemed to radiate from her in waves.

The movement was quick and precise, but it carried an air of urgency, almost of dread. It wasn't idle caution; it was the behaviour of someone who expected to see something—or someone—lurking just out of sight. A shiver prickled at the back of my neck, crawling over my skin like an invisible thread. The possibility that we might not be alone, that someone might be watching us even now, tightened my chest with a cold, creeping dread. Was Sharon afraid of being followed? Did she have reason to believe we were in danger?

I studied her profile, her jaw set, her gaze sharp. The tension in her posture, the way she seemed to keep one ear tuned to the sounds of the road—it all suggested a readiness for something, though I couldn't yet fathom what. The silence between us pressed down like a weight, thick with unspoken fears and questions I wasn't sure I wanted answered.

It struck me then how little I truly understood about what we were walking into. Sharon had a plan; of that, I was certain. But the details of it, the risks she must have weighed before setting this into motion, remained a mystery to me. And yet, I was here, seated beside her, plunging headfirst into an unknown that suddenly felt more immediate, more perilous, than ever before. The gravity of our situation hit me with startling clarity: we were two women, bound by shared loss, venturing into the dark with nothing but our determination and a tenuous lead to guide us.

Despite the cold air seeping through the slightly lowered window, a bead of sweat slid down my temple, tickling as it moved, a physical manifestation of the adrenaline coursing through me. My pulse thrummed in my ears, its rhythm out of sync with the steady hum of the engine. Every nerve in my body felt primed, as though the tension radiating from Sharon had ignited a matching flame within me.

Whatever lay ahead, whatever danger Sharon might be bracing herself for, I was part of it now. There was no turning back, no opportunity to retrace my steps to the safety of ignorance. The road ahead seemed to stretch endlessly, a tangible representation of the uncertainty we faced.

I took a deep, deliberate breath, the cool air filling my lungs and momentarily steadying the chaotic rush of my thoughts. With each exhale, I focused on the reason we were here—the men we loved, the answers we desperately sought, the truths that had been stolen from us. The silent pact between us, formed in the crucible of our shared grief, was an unspoken promise that we wouldn't stop until we uncovered the reality behind their disappearances.

"How did you know how to find Luke?" The question burned within me, refusing to be silenced by the hum of the engine or the rhythmic thrum of the tyres on the road. Each kilometre that ticked by only magnified my need for answers. The silence between us had become a tangible presence, heavy and suffocating, and I knew I couldn't let it stretch any longer. Turning towards Sharon, I sought her gaze, hoping to untangle the thread that had led us here, down this dark and uncertain path.

Sharon's response wasn't immediate. Her eyes were fixed on the rearview mirror, her attention split between the road ahead and some invisible threat she seemed to anticipate behind us. Her lips pressed into a thin line, and for a moment, I wondered if she had heard me at all. Then, she exhaled deeply, the sound heavy and resigned, filling the car like the prelude to a confession.

"I found his details in Adrian's bookwork," she said finally, her voice low and edged with tension. "Adrian did some work for Luke a few years ago."

"What kind of work?" The question tumbled from me without hesitation, my need to understand pressing against the already fragile boundary of my composure.

Sharon's shoulders lifted in a small shrug, the gesture carrying the weight of ambiguity. "Looks like it was just a building inspection for a property Luke was buying."

"The same property we're going to now?" My voice was barely above a whisper, the implications settling over me like a shadow, dark and suffocating.

"Yeah."

I leaned back in my seat, my fingers tightening on the hem of my jacket. The air in the car felt colder, the shadows outside deepening as the sun slipped lower. My mind raced, circling around questions I couldn't yet bring myself to voice. What the hell are we doing? The thought echoed in my head, insistent and dissonant. What do we think we'll actually achieve by talking to Luke?

Doubt surged forward, crashing over my fragile resolve like a wave. The conviction that had driven me to climb into Sharon's car now felt tenuous, flimsy against the enormity of what lay ahead. If he had harmed our husbands, would he really tell us anything? The thought of confronting a man who might have destroyed our lives sent a shudder through me, and my breath caught in my throat.

And worse, whispered a darker voice within, what if he tries to hurt us too?

The icy realisation settled in my chest like a block of stone, pressing against my ribs and making it difficult to breathe. My hand moved instinctively to my stomach, my fingers rubbing in slow, circular motions in a futile attempt to soothe the nauseous fear churning within.

Beside me, Sharon remained focused on the road, her grip on the steering wheel firm, her jaw set in a way that suggested she wasn't giving in to the same tide of uncertainty that threatened to sweep me away.

As we veered off the Brooker Highway, the car began its ascent up Berriedale Road, winding through an area that tugged at the edges of my memory. I had been here before, years ago, visiting a friend who lived near the roundabout at the top of the hill. The vague familiarity offered a fleeting distraction from the gnawing anxiety that had settled like a stone in my stomach. But as we continued, a new realisation crept in, casting a shadow over the tenuous comfort of recognising the landscape.

Sharon was navigating the twists and turns with an ease that bordered on instinctive, her hands steady on the wheel as she guided the car through the neighbourhood without hesitation. There was no map, no GPS, no glances at a phone for directions. It was clear that she knew exactly where she was going. The observation unsettled me, stirring a quiet storm of questions. How did she know this route so well? How much did Sharon know that she hadn't shared?

"You live in the area?" The question slipped out before I could consider its implications. My voice sounded strained, as though the words themselves carried the weight of the doubts I hadn't dared voice until now.

"No," Sharon answered curtly, her grip tightening on the steering wheel. The single syllable hung in the air, stark and unyielding, inviting no elaboration. Her response only deepened the knot in my stomach, the lack of explanation fuelling a suspicion I couldn't shake.

"Pull over," I heard myself say. The words came out sharper than I'd intended, but they carried an urgency I couldn't ignore. My hands curled into fists in my lap, an effort to still their trembling as a cold sweat dampened the back of my neck.

"What?" Sharon's confusion was evident in her voice, her focus breaking from the road for a fraction of a second to glance at me. Her brows furrowed, the slight crease on her otherwise expressionless face betraying her surprise.

"Pull over," I repeated, this time firmer. My request was more than a need for a pause; it was a demand for clarity in a situation growing murkier with every passing kilometre.

Sharon hesitated, her fingers tightening on the wheel as if grounding herself against the command. She cast another quick glance at me, her expression difficult to read. Her sharply defined brows, stark against the foundation smoothing her complexion, barely twitched, but her lips pressed into a thin line.

"We're almost there," she said finally, her tone calm but edged with finality. The dismissal in her words sent a shiver of unease through me, an unspoken refusal that felt both calculated and disconcerting.

I swallowed hard, the motion catching painfully in my dry throat. My request had been more than just a plea for a break—it was a test, a quiet challenge to the unspoken rules of this fragile alliance. It was a demand for transparency, an invitation for Sharon to dispel the fog of secrecy that seemed to envelop us. Her reluctance to heed my call, to provide even a moment's reassurance, felt like a breach in the fragile trust we had built.

The silence between us stretched taut, the only sound the steady hum of the engine and the rhythmic crunch of tyres on asphalt. My thoughts spiralled, a cacophony of doubts and fears that clawed at the edges of my resolve. Where were we going? What did Sharon know that she wasn't sharing? And, most chillingly, was I walking into something far more dangerous than I had anticipated?.

I turned my gaze to the road ahead, the looming shadows of the hillside swallowing us in their embrace as dusk deepened around us. Whatever lay ahead, one truth pressed itself relentlessly against my mind: I was no longer entirely certain I could trust the person sitting beside me.

A few hundred metres past the roundabout, Sharon signalled and guided the car into a small parking space across the road. The tyres crunched against the gravel as she manoeuvred us to the end of the lot and then turned the car to face the road again, coming to an abrupt stop that sent a ripple of unease through me. My heart pounded in my chest, anticipation and dread mingling in a heady rush. Was this the place we were meant to find, or had Sharon finally listened to my earlier plea to pull over?

"That's the house," Sharon said, her voice cutting through my spiralling thoughts with an unsettling calm. She nodded toward the row of backyards lining the road, her gaze fixed on one property in particular.

"Which one?" I asked, my words barely more than a whisper, as I leaned towards her, my eyes following her line of sight.

"The two-storey one on the corner," she clarified, pointing directly at it with a steady hand.

I squinted through the windshield at the house she indicated. It was ordinary at first glance, a modest brick home with large windows facing both the road and the empty corner block beside it. A weathered, wood-paling fence encircled the property, standing slightly askew in places as though leaning away from the burden of its years. There was nothing overtly menacing about the house, yet the sight of it sent a chill crawling over my skin.

"How do you know that?" The question slipped out before I could stop myself, the mixture of curiosity and suspicion sharp in my tone. A cold prickle of unease danced along my spine. Sharon's familiarity with the property felt... off, as though she had skipped several steps in a logical chain that I wasn't privy to.

Her silence was as unsettling as her earlier certainty. The windows of the car began to fog, a visible testament to the tension that seemed to fill every molecule of air around us. My breath quickened, matching the pounding of my heart, and I couldn't help but glance back at the house, its mundane exterior now looming with an ominous air.

Her knowledge, her certainty about the location, made the hairs on the back of my neck stand on end. It was one thing to follow a lead, quite another to realise the person sitting beside you might be harbouring deeper connections to the very mystery you were trying to unravel.

"I came by earlier," Sharon said finally, her voice low, almost reluctant, as though weighing the cost of her admission. The words sliced through the silence like a scalpel, exposing a truth I hadn't expected.

"You came here without me?" The accusation in my voice was unrestrained, the betrayal I felt bubbling to the surface.

"Nobody was home," she replied evenly, her eyes trained on the house as though expecting someone to appear in the windows. The flatness of her response stoked my frustration, its simplicity grating against the growing complexity of my doubts.

I rubbed my temples with the tips of my fingers, trying to process her revelation. "Why?" I demanded, my voice sharp with bewilderment. "Why would you come here before now? And why wouldn't you tell me?"

Her response didn't come immediately. Instead, she unlatched her door and stepped out into the cold without so much as a glance in my direction. The sudden rush of icy air filled the car, amplifying the chill already crawling through my veins.

"Sharon!" I called, my voice tinged with exasperation, but she didn't turn back. She stood next to the car, brushing her hair away from her face as the wind played with the loose strands.

"Are you coming?" she asked at last, her tone clipped and her expression inscrutable. Her words carried an unspoken message: whatever explanations I wanted, they would have to wait. For now, we had work to do.

I stared after her, torn between indignation and the unshakable pull of our shared purpose. She had kept secrets, yes, but she was also the one who had driven us here, who had uncovered the thread that might lead us to answers. My desire for clarity warred with my need to keep moving forward, to take another step closer to understanding what had happened to Nial.

Closing my eyes, I drew in a slow, deliberate breath, holding it for a moment before exhaling through my nose. I repeated the action twice more, each breath an attempt to tether myself to the resolve I'd fought so hard to maintain. The doubts, the anger, the fear—they were still there, but I pushed them aside, steeling myself for the unknown.

When I opened my eyes, my course was set. With a determined pull on the handle, I stepped out of the car, the wind biting at my cheeks and pushing against me as if to dissuade me from what lay ahead. But nothing could stop me now—not the cold, not the unanswered questions, and not my unease with Sharon.

The descent into dusk seemed to accelerate with each step we took across the grassy expanse towards the house, the dimming light stretching shadows that twisted and warped like ghostly fingers reaching for us. The small, square front porch loomed ahead, bordered by several overgrown flax plants swaying gently in the evening breeze, their rustling a quiet, dissonant accompaniment to our tense approach. The house seemed to crouch in the twilight, as if guarding its secrets.

"It's very quiet," I whispered, my voice barely audible as though speaking louder might disturb the uneasy stillness. The empty driveway, devoid of any sign of life, added to the sense that we were stepping into a place detached from the ordinary, a place where the usual rules no longer applied.

A storm churned within me, a dizzying rush of nerves and adrenaline that made my limbs feel both too heavy and too light. The air itself seemed charged, pressing against my skin like an electric current. I stole a glance at Sharon, searching for reassurance, only to find her crouched in front of the door, her actions stopping me in my tracks.

"Sharon! What are you doing?" The words left my mouth in a sharp hiss, disbelief and alarm sharpening the edges of my voice. My stomach twisted as I realised what was happening. Sharon was bent over the lock, a set of thin tools in her hands, her movements quick and precise. The shock of her intent—of us bypassing the boundary of legality entirely—hit me like a physical blow.

"Getting answers," she replied evenly, her voice steady but cold, her focus unbroken. There was no hesitation in her movements, no room for doubt in her tone. It was as though she had crossed this moral threshold long before we reached this house, the decision made in some dark, private place.

"Shit," I murmured under my breath, my hand reaching for the porch railing as though it might steady me in the face of this rapidly spiralling situation. A flurry of emotions collided within me—fear, disbelief, and a sickening thrill of anticipation. Part of me wanted to bolt, to put as much distance as possible between myself and this criminal act. But a deeper, darker part of me, fuelled by desperation and the relentless ache of Nial's absence, urged me to stay. To see this through.

The soft click of the lock giving way sent a jolt through me, the sound sharp and final, like the snap of a trap closing. My breath caught in my throat as Sharon slowly straightened, casting me a glance over her shoulder. Her expression was a mixture of grim determination and cautious expectancy, as if daring me to back out now. The tension carved into her features mirrored my own turmoil, and for a fleeting moment, I felt a reluctant kinship in our shared desperation.

Without waiting for a response, she turned the handle and pushed the door open.

"Wait!" I blurted out, stepping forward to grasp Sharon's arm. My fingers closed around her sleeve, the action driven more by instinct than conscious thought. The chill of her jacket against my palm was grounding, but it did little to quell the rapid beating of my heart.

Sharon turned to face me, her eyes narrowing slightly, their intensity cutting through the dim light. Her patience, or lack thereof, was clear, but so was the unyielding determination that had carried her to this point.

"Do you really think..." I began, but the words faltered, my question dissolving under the weight of my uncertainty. What was I even asking? Did I want reassurance, or permission to turn and run? But the thought of leaving now, of letting this chance slip through our fingers, was unbearable. My voice steadied as I tried again. "Are you sure there's nobody home?"

For a moment, Sharon studied me, her gaze unreadable. Then she gave a slight shrug, her calm demeanour unnervingly at odds with the gravity of our situation. "Nobody alive," she murmured, her voice so quiet it seemed to dissolve into the air around us.

Her words sent an icy spike of dread down my spine, the implication heavy and suffocating. My hand fell away from her arm as the weight of what might await us inside took hold. The house, which had seemed ominously quiet before, now loomed like a mausoleum, each shadowed window a hollow eye staring back at me. Sharon stepped forward, crossing the threshold with a steadiness I envied but couldn't yet emulate.

I hesitated, my gaze darting to the yawning emptiness beyond the open door. The house felt alive with possibility, each corner and crevice a potential harbinger of answers—or horrors. Drawing a shuddering breath, I pushed the fear aside, reminding myself why I was here, why I couldn't walk away.

With one last glance at the quiet street behind us, I stepped forward, following Sharon into the unknown.

THE CREATURE

4338.214.4

As we stood just inside the door, the oppressive stillness of the house engulfed us like a smothering cloak. The air was thick, heavy with an indefinable tension that pressed against my skin and sent a shiver coursing down my spine. The dim light filtering in through the curtained windows did little to dispel the shadows, which pooled and stretched across the floor like malevolent entities waiting to strike. The enormity of what we were doing—trespassing into a stranger's home based on fragile threads of hope and intuition—descended on me like a weight, making my every breath feel laboured.

A swell of nausea clawed its way up my throat, sharp and acidic, as my mind conjured scenes of unthinkable horror hidden behind these walls. The thought of what we might find—evidence of violence, remnants of a struggle, or something far worse—churned my stomach and made my pulse race. I closed my eyes briefly, swallowing hard to suppress the wave of bile threatening to rise. This house, with its air of abandonment and latent menace, felt like a stage set for tragedy, its secrets crouched just out of sight.

I cast a wary glance at Sharon, her figure framed against the darkened interior. She moved with a purposeful silence, her every step an act of defiance against the encroaching fear. Yet, even as she pressed forward, I couldn't ignore the unease prickling at the back of my mind. What *did* Sharon really know? The thought gnawed at me, relentless and unsettling. Her admission that she'd been here earlier without me opened a chasm of doubt, raising questions I wasn't sure I wanted the answers to. Was she keeping something from me, or was her focus simply narrower, more driven? Either way, her secrets cast a long shadow over our fragile alliance.

"Be careful," I murmured, the words slipping from my lips almost unconsciously as we moved through the living room. Each step felt like trespassing, as if the house itself resented our presence. The hallway ahead promised answers but also harboured the potential for revelations I wasn't sure I was prepared to face. "We don't know what we might find in here."

"I know," Sharon replied, her voice steady but low, each syllable infused with a determination that bordered on desperation. "But if there's any sign our husbands were here, I want to find it." Her words hit me like a hammer, forcing me to confront the grim reality of our mission. This wasn't just about answers; it was about clawing back some measure of control in a situation that had stolen everything from us.

Sharon came to an abrupt halt in the doorway, causing me to stumble into her. Her body was taut, her hand gripping the doorframe as though bracing for an impact only she could anticipate. "What is it?" I whispered, the unease coiling tighter around my chest as I waited for her to speak.

She tilted her head slightly, her posture alert. "Do you smell that?" she asked, her voice tinged with both curiosity and dread.

I hesitated, letting the silence stretch as I focused on my senses. It didn't take long for the odour to hit me, sharp and putrid, turning my stomach with its vile potency. "It smells like… rotten meat," I confirmed, my words faltering as the realisation settled in. My gaze followed Sharon's to a door at the far end of the room, its shadowed edges framing the source of the stench.

For a moment, neither of us moved, the foul smell and the door ahead forming a grim tableau of foreboding. Then

Sharon stepped forward, her jaw set, her strides purposeful. Her single-minded resolve was a jarring contrast to the dread rooting me to the spot. My heart thudded loudly in my ears, drowning out the creaks of the floor beneath her feet.

I stood frozen, watching her approach the door as if drawn by some magnetic force. It took a monumental effort to unstick my feet from the floor and follow, my steps hesitant and faltering. My every nerve screamed at me to turn back, to flee the house and its unsettling odour. But the thought of Nial, of the truth buried somewhere in this mystery, propelled me forward, even as fear threatened to consume me.

By the time I reached Sharon's side, she was already gripping the edge of the sliding door, her fingers curling tightly around its surface. Her knuckles were pale, her grip firm, but she hesitated, her gaze flicking to mine. The look in her eyes wasn't one of fear but of grim anticipation, as though she were steeling herself for whatever horrors might lie on the other side. I tried to mirror her resolve, swallowing the lump of anxiety lodged in my throat.

"Ready?" Sharon asked, her voice low but unwavering.

I nodded, though my trembling hands betrayed the thin veneer of bravery I tried to project. "Do it," I whispered, the word barely audible over the pounding of my heart.

With a deliberate motion, Sharon slid the door to the side. The rollers groaned against the track, the sound cutting through the stillness like a blade. As the gap widened, the shadows inside seemed to reach out, and the source of the stench hit us full force, making my eyes water and my stomach churn.

The door opening revealed a small landing at the top of a narrow staircase, the space completely enclosed by walls on both sides, making the descent feel claustrophobic. The journey down the carpeted stairs stretched endlessly, each step groaning under our weight, adding an unsettling soundtrack to our cautious movements. The faint, failing rays of the winter sun struggled to penetrate the stairwell's shadows, casting distorted patterns that seemed to ripple along the walls with every flicker of light.

At the bottom of the staircase, we came to a closed door. Sharon approached it with deliberate care, her movements slow and calculated, as though the very air around us demanded reverence. Just as her hand hovered near the edge of the white wooden door, she froze. Her head turned sharply in my direction, her eyes wide and alert. Lifting a finger to her lips, she signalled for silence, her expression taut with a mix of urgency and caution.

"Do you hear that?" she whispered, the words barely more than a breath.

Time seemed to stand still, the air around us charged with anticipation and fear. My ears strained to catch any sound that might explain Sharon's sudden caution, the beating of my own heart thunderously loud in the silence. The realisation that we might not be alone, that the answers we sought could be just beyond the door, was both exhilarating and terrifying.

My pulse quickened as I strained to listen, every nerve in my body on edge. The oppressive stillness of the house amplified every tiny sound—the faint creak of settling wood, the distant murmur of a breeze against the windows, and then, there it was. A faint rustle, barely perceptible, as if something stirred on the other side of the door. My heart pounded in my chest, each beat a reminder of how deeply we'd ventured into the unknown.

The gravity of our situation was suddenly undeniable. The search for answers about Nial and Adrian had led us here, to this door, to this moment. The air between Sharon and me was electric, charged with the shared understanding that whatever lay beyond this threshold could irrevocably alter the course of our lives.

Sharon's hand finally closed around the handle, her grip firm yet hesitant. The soft rattle of the knob as she tested it broke the heavy silence, the sound echoing faintly in the confined space. Then it came—low, guttural, and unmistakably alive. The growl reverberated through the door, a sound so raw and primal that my entire body tensed, instinctively recoiling from the threat it promised.

A cold sweat broke out along my spine, and I felt the fine hairs on the back of my neck rise in unison with the tightening in my chest. My voice, barely a whisper, found its way to Sharon's ear. "We should go," I murmured, the words trembling with the weight of fear and a desperate plea for retreat.

Sharon's face tightened, her brow furrowing as she met my gaze. "It's probably just a frightened dog," she whispered, her tone calm but unconvincing. Her attempt at rationality did little to dispel the dread pooling in my stomach. Her hand twisted the handle slowly, the deliberate movement betraying her own unease.

The growl came again, louder this time, vibrating through the door like a warning. My stomach churned, the acidic tang of bile rising in the back of my throat. Every instinct in me screamed to turn back, to flee this house and the oppressive darkness it contained. Yet something deeper—a stubborn need for answers, for understanding—rooted me to the spot, forcing me to confront the unknown that loomed just beyond the thin barrier of the door.

With a final, reluctant click, the door opened, revealing a sight so grotesque that it rooted us to the spot, paralysing terror seizing our every muscle. The room was a tableau of unspeakable horror. A black creature, its form unnervingly similar to a panther but cloaked in unnatural shadows, crouched over the lifeless body of a man. Its dark, sinewy frame was hunched low, its face buried deep in the man's abdomen. The grisly sight of blood pooling beneath the victim, staining the concrete floor, was enough to wrench the air from my lungs. For a moment, time seemed to stop, suspended in the stark, horrifying reality of what lay before us.

Then, as if sensing our intrusion, the creature lifted its head. The motion was unhurried, deliberate, a predator acknowledging new prey. Blood glistened across its sleek, furred face, dripping from its jaw in slow, viscous rivulets. Entrails hung grotesquely from its razor-sharp teeth, and its eyes—dark and empty, glaring with a malevolent intelligence—locked onto ours. The nausea that surged through me was instant and overwhelming, a primal response to a terror so visceral it felt as though it might physically crush me.

Nearby, another figure came into focus—a second man, slumped against the wall. His ashen face held an unsettling stillness, his eyes closed as if in repose, but the brutal reality of his condition was betrayed by the blood seeping from his mouth and the jagged gash that cleaved across his abdomen. The cruel tableau was a testament to the savagery that had unfolded here, the violence still palpable in the air.

The creature's growl broke the oppressive silence, a deep, guttural sound that reverberated through the room and shook me to my core. It was a sound of warning, of dominance, and it carried with it the unspoken promise of death. The spell that had paralysed me shattered, and a scream erupted from my throat, raw and unrestrained, filling the enclosed space with its piercing intensity.

Before I could comprehend what was happening, Sharon's hand struck my face. The slap was hard, sharp, the sting radiating through my jaw. It wasn't anger that drove her action but sheer, desperate instinct—a need to silence me before the creature turned its full attention on us.

The growl deepened, rumbling like thunder in the confined space, and suddenly, impossibly, the second man moved. His eyes snapped open, wild with fear and pain, and he fixed them on us. His mouth worked soundlessly for a moment before he managed to form a single word, silently yet urgently mouthed: **"Run."**

The unspoken command hit me like a jolt of electricity, galvanising me into action. But Sharon was already moving, her voice cutting through the horror in a panicked shriek. "Run!" she yelled, her tone raw and jagged with terror. She shoved me hard, propelling me towards the stairs, her frantic urgency overriding any semblance of composure.

My legs, trembling with fear and adrenaline, faltered beneath me. On the second step, I stumbled, my foot catching awkwardly on the edge. The impact was brutal, my knees slamming into the unforgiving surface, pain exploding through my body. Before I could recover, Sharon collided with me, her momentum driving her forward. Her knee struck the back of my thigh with enough force to send me sprawling to the side, and she tumbled down beside me, her cry of frustration mingling with the sharp slap of flesh against wood.

"Shit!" she hissed, scrambling to untangle herself. Her hands clawed at the banister, trying to pull herself upright, but my clumsiness had turned our escape into a chaotic scramble.

Behind us, the room was eerily quiet, the silence more terrifying than any sound. My mind screamed at me to move, to get up, to flee, but my limbs felt like lead, my movements sluggish and uncoordinated. The terror that gripped me was paralysing, a suffocating force that left me gasping for air.

The creature was still there, I knew it, watching us, savouring our fear. And we were completely at its mercy.

Then, with a sharp and deafening bang, the door slammed shut behind us, its finality echoing through the confined space and driving an icy spike of panic through my chest. The sound jolted me from my paralysis, sending an involuntary shudder through my body. Twisting awkwardly, pain flared in my back as I managed to look over my shoulder. The sight that met my eyes sent a fresh surge of terror coursing through me.

The man at the bottom of the stairs, his bloodied face twisted in agony and desperation, fixed his wild eyes on us. His expression was a grotesque mask, equal parts pleading and rage. "Get the fuck out of here!" he bellowed, his voice raw and urgent, slicing through the suffocating tension like a blade.

His words were the lifeline we needed, shocking me into action. The stark reality of our situation—the relentless danger that surrounded us—crystallised in that moment. We were trapped in a house with a creature capable of unspeakable violence, and the only path to survival was escape.

Adrenaline flooded my system like a tidal wave, fuelling a speed I didn't know I possessed. I scrambled up the stairs, my legs pumping in a desperate rhythm, pain and fear eclipsed by the sheer instinct to survive. Sharon was just behind me, her breath coming in sharp, panicked gasps that mirrored my own. The terror forged an unspoken bond between us, a shared resolve that drove us towards safety with reckless urgency.

As we reached the top landing, a fleeting glance back revealed the man still hunched over at the bottom of the stairs, his figure bathed in the dim, sickly light from the moon that shone through the window beside us. His face was a mask of anguish, but his voice rose again, commanding and desperate. "Go!" he shouted, the word ricocheting up the stairwell, reigniting the urgency in my chest.

Sharon's hand clamped around my arm, her grip unyielding as she pulled me forward, propelling us across the living room. Our movements were frantic, disjointed, and bordering on chaotic, each step driven by the singular focus of reaching the front door. My heart thundered in my chest, each beat a drumbeat of panic as we sprinted towards what felt like salvation.

Ahead of me, Sharon surged forward, her desperation lending her a speed that I struggled to match. Her grip on my arm slipped away, her focus narrowing to a razor-sharp point as she reached the door and threw it open. She didn't hesitate, didn't look back, her sole aim to escape the nightmare that had engulfed us.

"The door!" I shouted, my voice hoarse and strained. It was a plea for her to wait, to ensure we left no barrier open to whatever was inside. But Sharon didn't stop. She didn't even glance back. Her figure disappeared into the night as I skidded to a halt at the threshold, my shaking hands fumbling to slam the door shut behind me.

The cold evening air hit me like a slap, sharp and bracing, my breath forming frantic clouds in the darkness. "Sharon, wait up!" I yelled, panic rising in my chest as I turned and bolted after her. The grass was damp beneath my feet, its slickness threatening to unbalance me as I sprinted towards the car.

Sharon flung herself into the driver's seat. The door slammed shut with a finality that mirrored my own desperate gesture moments before, and the roar of the ignition ripped through the quiet night. The sight of the car shuddering to life, the taillights glowing like embers, sent a fresh wave of dread through me.

Terror twisted in my gut as I pushed my legs harder, every fibre of my being screaming at me to move faster. The thought of being left behind in that house of horrors, alone with the creature, was a fear that eclipsed everything else. It was primal, a survival instinct clawing its way to the surface.

"Don't you dare leave me!" I screamed, my voice cracking under the weight of desperation as I closed the gap to the car.

In the distance, the shrill wail of police sirens rose above the quiet hum of the evening, their eerie cadence slicing through the night like a blade. The sound, both a harbinger of help and a reminder of danger, spurred me to action, my legs pumping harder as if fleeing from the echoes themselves. A visceral instinct to survive propelled me forward, and within seconds, I was in the passenger seat, slamming the door shut with such force the entire car shuddered. The jarring thud reverberated through the confined space, a grim punctuation to the chaos we'd left behind.

For a heartbeat—or perhaps an eternity—Sharon and I sat frozen, our breathing ragged, our wide-eyed stares locked in a shared moment of paralytic fear. Neither of us spoke; the silence was alive, a suffocating entity in the small cabin of the car. Our faces, pale and streaked with sweat, reflected back at us faintly in the windshield, ghostly apparitions of the terror we carried with us.

The rising crescendo of the sirens drew closer, snapping us from our stupor. "Drive!" I barked, my voice hoarse, raw, and filled with urgency. The single word, so forceful and primal, cut through Sharon's inertia like a whip crack. Without hesitation, her foot slammed onto the accelerator, sending the car hurtling forward. The rear tires spun briefly against the gravel, kicking up a cloud of dust that lingered in the air like a ghostly veil, marking our hurried escape.

As we sped down the dark road, the flashing blue and red lights of several police cars blazed past us, heading in the direction of Luke's house. Their sirens screeched like mournful wails, and for a fleeting moment, I felt a twinge of relief. They weren't coming after us. They had bigger horrors to contend with. Still, the sight of those vehicles, vanishing into the night, left my stomach knotted with dread. Whatever lay behind us now belonged to them—and I couldn't decide whether to feel grateful or horrified.

I collapsed into the passenger seat, my body going slack as the adrenaline that had sustained me finally ebbed away. My muscles felt like jelly, weak and trembling with exhaustion, while my chest heaved in an effort to calm the erratic rhythm of my breathing. Outside, the blurred streetlights streaked past like spectral sentinels, their faint, repetitive glow stark against the darkness that swallowed everything else. The world beyond the car was surreal, a dreamscape of moving light and shadows that clashed with the turmoil churning within me.

Tears pricked at the corners of my eyes, their presence a testament to the emotional weight I could no longer hold back. I clenched my hands tightly together, forcing them into a semblance of control as they shook uncontrollably in my lap. The tremors were involuntary, a physical manifestation of the fear and horror still coursing through my body.

The silence between Sharon and me was heavy, oppressive, yet necessary. It wrapped around us like a thick fog, offering temporary respite from the need to confront what had just happened. Words felt impossible, each unspoken thought swirling in the void between us. But even in that silence, the images of what we had seen replayed relentlessly in my mind—a grotesque film reel I couldn't stop, couldn't unsee. The room, the smell, the creature, and the man's desperate eyes as he screamed at us to run.

❖

"Get out."

Sharon's words sliced through the tension in the car with the precision of a scalpel, sharp and chilling. The weight of her tone made the temperature in the cabin seem to drop several degrees, the chill seeping into my bones. As the car rolled to a stop outside my house, her directive hung in the air like a judgment passed, final and inescapable.

"Keep your mouth shut. We were never there," she added, her voice steady but strained, each word laced with a controlled desperation. Yet, beneath the hardened exterior, a faint tremor betrayed the fear gnawing at her resolve.

I sat frozen, paralysed by the abruptness of her command, my mind still caught in the unravelling trauma of the evening. The enormity of what we'd witnessed refused to release me, its grip on my thoughts relentless and suffocating. I turned to Sharon, my expression blank, my mouth opening slightly as though to form a protest, a question, anything—but no words came.

"Get the fuck out!" she screamed, the sharp escalation of her voice snapping me out of my stupor. The raw desperation in her tone was like a slap across the face, jolting me into movement. I noticed her hands gripping the steering wheel, trembling violently, their whitened knuckles a stark contrast against the worn leather. She was barely holding it together, her composure a fragile mask threatening to shatter at any moment.

It felt as though she'd fired a bullet directly into my chest, the impact of her words physical, visceral. My body moved automatically, clumsy and disjointed, fumbling with the door handle as though I'd forgotten how to perform even the simplest of tasks. My legs felt like lead as I stumbled out of the car, nearly tripping over the kerb in my haste to comply.

I barely managed to stand upright before Sharon leaned across the passenger seat and slammed the door shut with such force that the sound reverberated down the otherwise silent street. The thud echoed in my ears, a punctuation mark to the fractured connection between us.

For a moment, I stood there, rooted in place under the harsh glare of the streetlight. Its cold, artificial glow illuminated my stillness, turning me into a solitary figure on the deserted street. I watched, helpless and dumbfounded, as Sharon's car screeched away, her reckless departure mirroring the chaotic energy that now coursed through my veins.

The roar of her engine faded into the distance, leaving me alone with the hum of the streetlight and the whispers of the night. My body trembled, my heart pounding against my ribcage like a drumbeat of despair. I wrapped my arms around myself, suddenly aware of the cold seeping into my skin, though whether it came from the air or the icy aftermath of Sharon's departure, I couldn't tell.

I turned towards the house, my feet moving mechanically. Each step felt heavy with the weight of what had transpired, as I walked towards the door and into the fragile sanctuary of home.

EXPOSED

4338.214.5

My head spun, a chaotic whirlpool of dread and confusion, as I fumbled with the front door. My fingers, numb and trembling, slipped over the cold metal of the lock, the simple act of turning the key suddenly an insurmountable task. When the door finally swung open, I stumbled inside, the familiar hallway yawning before me like a distorted funhouse, the shadows stretching and twisting into grotesque forms.

I clung to the walls, their cold, unyielding surface my only anchor in a sea of turmoil. Each step forward felt like trudging through quicksand, the weight of my fear dragging me down. The house, once a sanctuary, now felt foreign and menacing, every creak of the floorboards and rustle of the wind outside amplified into a deafening roar in my mind.

At the base of the stairs, I stopped, gasping for air as though I'd run a marathon. My chest heaved under the vice grip of fear, the memory of blood and black fur flashing in my mind like a macabre strobe light. Each vivid image punched through my defences, leaving me reeling and breathless.

The stairs loomed above me, an impossible ascent. Summoning what little strength I had left, I forced myself to take the first step, then the second, each one a Herculean effort. By the time I reached the third, my legs felt like jelly, and my vision swam with the effort. "One more," I whispered to myself, a mantra of desperation.

As I reached the fifth step, my foot slipped, and the world tilted dangerously. My body slammed into the wall, the impact jolting through me with a searing pain that radiated up my spine. The sharp sting forced a guttural cry from my lips, but I had no strength left to do more than slump against the wall.

A rancid burn clawed its way up my throat, the bile a cruel reminder of my body's rebellion against the night's horrors. Gagging, I clutched at my neck as though I could somehow expel the sensation, but it was futile. The first wave of vomit came violently, a hot, acidic eruption that splattered onto the stairs in front of me.

The smell—acrid and sour—clung to me like a shroud, curling around my senses and making me gag again. My shirt was soaked, the fabric plastered to my skin with the remnants of my humiliation. My body convulsed with each retch, a betrayal of my attempts to maintain control.

When the spasms finally subsided, leaving me weak and trembling, I wiped my face with the back of my hand. The sticky residue was a grim reminder of how far I'd fallen, both physically and emotionally. A wave of disgust surged through me as I felt the bile-soaked fabric against my skin. With a surge of revulsion, I yanked the shirt off, its clammy embrace replaced by the icy bite of the air against my bare skin. I flung it down the stairs, watching it tumble away as if I could cast off the terror and shame along with it.

"You have to keep moving," I whispered, my voice hoarse and trembling. The command was a fragile lifeline, a desperate attempt to push myself forward. Each step up was a war against my own failing strength, my limbs leaden and uncooperative. The distance to the top of the stairs, no more than a few feet, felt like miles.

When I finally reached the landing, I collapsed onto it, my body shaking with exhaustion. The air burned in my lungs, each breath a painful reminder of the events I had endured. I pressed my forehead against the cool surface of the floor, letting its solidity ground me for a moment.

But even as I lay there, my mind refused to quiet. The horror of the night, the blood, the growl, the man's desperate plea—it all clawed at me, demanding to be acknowledged. I closed my eyes tightly, as if I could will the images away, but they were etched too deeply, branded onto my soul.

Somewhere deep within me, the flicker of resolve burned on. I had survived the house. I had made it back. But survival was not enough. I needed answers. I needed Nial. With a shaky inhale, I pushed myself up, my limbs protesting with every movement.

Dragging myself into the bedroom, the sanctuary I sought felt warped, its comforting familiarity twisted into something unrecognisable and unsettling. The bed, the wardrobe, the little trinkets that once held the warmth of routine now seemed stark and accusatory, as if they bore silent witness to the wreckage of my composure. My body betrayed me, trembling uncontrollably, a tremor coursing through my veins like an unrelenting current, eroding the fragile dam of self-control I had been clinging to.

My mind raced ahead, untethered, thoughts colliding and fracturing into chaotic shards that offered neither solace nor clarity. A desperate attempt to anchor myself—to still the frantic, pounding drumbeat of fear within—yielded nothing. Each breath I took seemed shallow and inadequate, as though the very air had become insubstantial, slipping through my lungs in cruel defiance.

With a frantic need to escape the weight pressing down on me, I began tearing at the clothes still clinging to my body. Each discarded garment felt like shedding a layer of dread, yet beneath the fabric, the clammy grip of fear remained. The chill of the room prickled my exposed skin, a sharp contrast to the feverish chaos swirling inside me.

I stumbled into the en suite, the glass door of the shower clicking shut behind me with a sound that felt too loud, too final. The moment the water began to cascade over me, warm and soothing, I let out a shuddering breath that I hadn't realised I'd been holding. The water wrapped around me, a small mercy against the raw edges of my turmoil, rinsing away the grime, the sweat, the sour remnants of my stomach's revolt. Yet, as it ran in rivulets down my body, it became painfully clear that no stream, however pure, could cleanse the deeper stains left by the night's horrors.

I slid to my knees, the hard tiles of the shower floor meeting me with a cold, unyielding certainty that reverberated up my bones. My arms curled instinctively around my torso, as if the act could hold together the fracturing pieces of myself. It was there, in the solitude of the water's embrace, that the tears finally came.

They spilled freely, mingling with the spray, indistinguishable to the eye but heavier in their purpose. Each sob that escaped me was raw and unrestrained, a torrent that matched the water pouring down from above. "I'm sorry," I whispered, the words choked and fragmented, carried on the breath of my despair. "So sorry, Nial."

His name was an anchor and a torment, a tether to a love that felt increasingly fragile in the face of the unknown. My voice cracked, dissolving into silence as I imagined him—his face, his voice, his presence that was so glaringly absent. My husband is missing. The words surfaced in my mind, stark and unvarnished, a truth that refused to be suppressed. Each repetition hammered the thought deeper into my consciousness, the reality of his absence sharpening with every beat of my heart.

The uncertainty was an insidious predator, its claws digging into the edges of my resolve. Was he safe? Was he hurt? Was he... gone? The questions swirled like a maelstrom, each possibility a blade that carved deeper into the raw ache of my heart. I gasped for air as the enormity of it all pressed down on me—the helplessness, the unyielding void where certainty should have been.

I thought of Sammy, his innocence a fragile thing I had promised to protect. How could I shield him from the storm when I was drowning in it myself? The weight of my failure felt suffocating, the guilt mingling with the grief and fear that churned within me.

The warm water continued, the passage of time marked only by the strengthening heat against my skin. Still, I remained where I was, my head bowed, the water drumming a relentless rhythm against my back. My sobs had quieted to a steady stream of tears, the pain no less profound but the storm within momentarily stilled.

I closed my eyes, clinging to the memory of Nial's voice, his laugh, the way his arms had always felt like home. "I'll find you," I whispered, the vow trembling on my lips like a fragile flame against the gale of my despair. "Whatever it takes, I'll find you."

Faint footsteps entering the bathroom snapped my head up, a sudden jolt of alertness piercing through the fog of my despair. "Nial?" I dared to voice the hope, a fragile whisper carrying the weight of my longing and fear. It was a question, a plea, a prayer all rolled into one, sent out into the void with the last flicker of hope I harboured in my heart.

My eyes widened in terror as the reality before me unfolded, a stark contradiction to the reunion I had envisioned in my mind. My mouth moved to speak, an instinctive reaction to call out, to question, to demand explanations, but no words would form. My voice, like my hope, had deserted me, leaving me in a silent scream of confusion and dread.

Paralysed, I watched in bewilderment as the silky bathrobe slunk from Serena's body and fell to the bathroom floor with a soft whisper, a sound incongruously gentle in the maelstrom of my emotions. The fabric pooled at her feet, a discarded shell that seemed to mark the boundary between normality and the surreal scenario unfolding before me.

Wild shaking wracked my entire body, an uncontrollable tremor that echoed the chaos swirling within. It was as if the cold tiles beneath me had seeped into my bones, filling me with a chill that no warmth could dispel. The glass door squeaked open, a sound now eternally etched into the soundtrack of my nightmare, as Serena stepped into the shower. The intrusion of her presence into this last bastion of solitude shattered the fragile veneer of composure I had clung to.

Sinking to the floor beside me, Serena wrapped her arms around me. Her touch, meant to comfort, felt torturous and intrusive, a physical manifestation of the surreal turn my life had taken. "Everything will be okay," Serena whispered in my ear, her words a stark contrast to the maelstrom of panic and fear that raged within me. They were words meant to soothe, to reassure, but they landed like stones in the pit of my stomach, their assurance hollow in the face of my terror.

Sheer panic gripped me at the unfolding scene, a visceral reaction that seized my heart and squeezed until I thought it might burst. My throat was dry, a barren landscape where not even a whisper of comfort could take root. My heart thumped in my chest, a frenetic drumbeat that underscored my fear, each beat a reminder of the precarious thread by which my sanity hung. My head pounded, a relentless pressure that mirrored my tumultuous thoughts, a cacophony of fear, confusion, and disbelief that swirled in a dark dance.

My vision blurred as I gasped for the air that refused to oblige, each breath a battle in itself, fought in the shadow of the overwhelming presence that now shared this most intimate of spaces. The world seemed to contract to the point of suffocation, the walls of the shower a transparent barrier that nonetheless felt as impenetrable as steel, trapping me within this nightmare from which there was no awakening.

EXPELLED

4338.214.6

"Get out!" The scream tore from my throat, raw and primal, as I lurched away from Serena's touch. My hands scrambled against the slick shower wall, seeking purchase, seeking escape from this nightmare that had materialised in my most vulnerable moment. Water cascaded around us, steam rising like a spectre in the harsh bathroom light.

Grabbing the nearest towel, I flung it at her face while snatching another to wrap around myself. My movements were frantic, uncoordinated, driven by pure instinct and terror. "How dare you!" My voice cracked, hysteria rising like bile in my throat. "How bloody dare you!"

Serena caught the towel with an unsettling grace, holding it almost contemplatively against her chest. Her dark hair clung to her shoulders in wet rivulets, making her look younger, more vulnerable - and somehow more terrifying for it.

"You're upset," she said softly, that same gentle tone she used in class when reading Shakespeare's sonnets. "I understand. It's been a difficult night."

"Difficult?" I barked out a laugh that bordered on hysterical. "You're in my house. In my bathroom. You're my student, for God's sake!" The absurdity of having to state these obvious facts made my head spin. "How did you get in here?"

Her smile was serene, almost indulgent. "I've had a key for months. Ever since that day you let me borrow your drama texts." She wrapped the towel around herself with deliberate slowness. "You really should be more careful with your belongings, Mrs. Triffett. Jenny. My Jenny."

The use of my first name sent a shiver down my spine. "Don't," I warned, backing towards the bathroom door. "Don't you dare call me that."

"But it's your name," she insisted, taking a step forward. "The name Nial calls you. Called you." The slight emphasis on the past tense made my blood run cold.

"What have you done?" The question escaped me in a whisper. "What do you know about Nial?"

"He wasn't good for you," Serena said, her voice taking on an edge I'd never heard before. "He didn't understand you like I do. The way you light up when discussing theatre, how your hands move when you're explaining stage direction." She took another step closer. "How you sing lullabies to Sammy when he has nightmares."

My heart stopped. "You've been watching us? In our home?"

"Watching over you," she corrected, as if the distinction was crucial. "Protecting you. Sammy's night terrors started getting worse, did you notice? Around the same time Nial began staying late at work, making all those secret phone calls."

The implications of her words hit me like a physical blow. Six months. Sammy's increasing anxiety, his reluctance to sleep alone, the way he'd wake screaming about shadows in his room... "You've been in my son's room?"

"Our son," Serena said with that same gentle smile. "He likes it when I sing to him. The same songs you use, but he says I do the voices better."

The room tilted dangerously. I grabbed the doorframe to steady myself, bile rising in my throat. "You're sick," I managed to choke out. "You need help."

Her expression darkened. "I'm not sick. I'm the only one who truly sees you, who understands what you need." She moved closer, water dripping from her hair onto the tile floor. "Did you think I wouldn't notice the way you looked at me in class? How you always chose my scenes to workshop, always found time for extra rehearsals?"

"I was doing my job!" The words exploded from me. "You were a talented student who needed guidance. Nothing more!"

"Lies," she hissed, her mask of serenity cracking. "You're lying to yourself, just like you lied about being happy with Nial. But I fixed that. I made it so we could be together."

Horror crawled up my spine. "What did you do to my husband?"

"What I had to." Her voice was almost childlike now. "He was in the way. But now we can be a proper family. You, me, Sammy..." She reached out to touch my face. "I've taken care of everything."

Something in me snapped. With strength born of terror and maternal rage, I shoved her away. Her feet slipped on the wet tile, and she went down hard, her head cracking against the edge of the bathtub. The sound was sickeningly solid.

For a moment, neither of us moved. Serena lay sprawled on the floor, a thin line of blood trickling from her hairline. Her eyes, when they met mine, were wide with hurt and confusion.

"You're just like him," she whispered, touching her fingers to the blood. "You're hurting me, just like he did when he caught me in Sammy's room."

The implications of her words sent fresh horror coursing through me. "Get out," I commanded, my voice shaking. "Get the fuck out of my house right now, or I swear to God..."

She rose slowly, clutching her towel around her. "You'll understand eventually," she said, that eerie serenity returning to her face despite the blood staining her temple. "When you're ready to accept what we mean to each other. What we could be."

"If you've hurt Nial..." The threat died in my throat as she smiled - that same sweet, disturbing smile she'd given me in class just yesterday.

"I'll come back when you're feeling more reasonable," she said, gathering her clothes. "Give Sammy a kiss for me. He'll be asking where his 'night-time friend' has gone."

The scream that built in my chest never made it past my lips. I could only watch, paralysed, as she dressed and walked away, her footsteps echoing through my house as if she owned it. The sound of the front door closing was both a relief and a new kind of terror.

She had a key. She'd been watching us, entering our home, touching my child. And somewhere out there, my husband...

My legs gave way, and I slid down the bathroom wall, the cool tile grounding me in this new reality. The shower was still running, steam filling the room like fog, but I barely noticed. My mind was racing, connecting dots I should have seen months ago.

Serena's obsession hadn't just destroyed my life - it might have destroyed Nial's too. And now she was out there, watching, waiting, while somewhere in the darkness, a black creature crouched over its prey, and Sharon's warning echoed in my head: "Keep your mouth shut. We were never there."

I hugged my knees to my chest, shivering despite the steam. The night pressed in around me, full of monsters both human and otherwise. And I had no idea which ones had taken my husband.

4338.215

(3 August 2018)

NO CONTACT

4338.215.1

Morning seeped into my bedroom like a thief, unwelcome and intrusive. The pale winter sunlight crept through the gaps in the curtains, casting long, accusatory beams across the room. It illuminated everything—my crumpled sheets, the glass of untouched water on the bedside table, the phone lying silent and inert. There had been no sleep for me; every time I dared to close my eyes, Serena's image sprang to life in my mind. I saw her standing in my bathroom, water cascading down her body, that eerie smile twisting her face as she spoke of us being a family. The memory clung to me, sharp and inescapable.

The phone screen remained dark, a silent reminder of the isolation that had settled around me. Sharon had not called, offered no explanations for the nightmare we'd faced at Luke's house. No answers about the creature we'd seen, about the bloodied man who had urged us to flee. The lack of communication only fed my unease, the unanswered questions growing heavier with each passing minute.

Pulling myself from the bed was like climbing out of quicksand. My limbs felt weighted, my body protesting every movement. The house, bathed in weak daylight, felt exposed, as though its walls offered no protection from the horrors lurking just beyond them. Paranoia gripped me with icy fingers. Every shadow seemed to shift ominously, every corner held the possibility of an intruder's presence. I wandered through the house like a restless spectre, checking locks, testing windows, yanking curtains shut against imagined eyes watching from the outside.

Calling in sick to work was both a relief and a burden. The idea of facing Serena across a classroom was unbearable, the thought of her calculating gaze and her unsettling smile more than I could endure. But staying home also meant surrendering to the fear she had planted deep within me.

The school secretary answered on the second ring, her tone sympathetic but detached, a professional veneer that didn't waver. "Of course, Mrs. Triffett. I'll let your classes know. Will you be able to email through some work for the students?"

"Yes, yes, of course," I replied hastily, though the very thought of Serena sitting in my drama class, free to plot her next move unobserved, made my stomach churn. I couldn't let her hold power over my life, even remotely. "I'll send it through shortly."

I spent the next hour creating assignments—busy work designed to keep the students occupied but Serena especially distracted. My fingers trembled as I typed her name into the list. The memory of those same hands pushing her away the night before, of the sickening thud as she hit the bathtub, made me pause, bile rising in my throat.

The morning dragged on, each moment an ordeal of waiting and uncertainty. Every noise set my heart racing—a car door slamming outside, the creak of the house settling, the whisper of the wind through the trees. My mind leapt to Serena with every sound, imagining her return, her knocking on my door with that same unnerving smile. Or perhaps Sharon, finally breaking her silence. Or, worse still, something else entirely, something darker and inexplicable.

I drifted from room to room, unable to settle, my thoughts circling endlessly. I checked the locks again, my fingers grazing the cool metal, finding no reassurance in their firm resistance. Somewhere deep inside, I knew this routine of vigilance was futile. The threat didn't feel external anymore—it was within, a shadow in my mind, a darkness I couldn't escape.

The phone's shrill ring startled me, and the sight of Dr Carmichael's name flashing on the screen sent a ripple of unease through my chest. After last night's revelations and the twisted shadow Serena had cast over my family, even the thought of discussing Sammy's condition felt heavier, fraught with implications I couldn't yet fully grasp.

"Mrs. Triffett," Dr Carmichael greeted, his professional tone carrying a warmth that felt almost incongruous given the tension gripping me. "I hope I haven't caught you at a bad time?"

I had just reversed out of my driveway, the well-worn route to Rowena's house unfolding ahead of me. "No, not at all," I lied, setting the phone to speaker mode and trying to keep my voice steady. "What can I do for you?"

"I've been speaking with Dr Petrov regarding Sammy's case," he said, his words precise, measured. "She's very interested in the patterns you've described - his behavioural changes and the physical symptoms, particularly the bruising."

The mention of the bruises made my stomach twist. Serena's voice echoed in my mind, sickly sweet and laced with menace: *"He likes it when I sing to him. The same songs you use, but he says I do the voices better."* My knuckles whitened around the steering wheel as a new wave of nausea surged through me. Had she been responsible for those marks on my son? Had the night terrors and mysterious bruises been her doing all along, part of some cruel, calculated game?

"Mrs. Triffett? Are you still with me?"

"Yes, sorry," I said quickly, trying to push Serena's sinister smile from my mind and focus on the conversation. "You were saying about Dr Petrov?"

"She's available to see Sammy next Tuesday," Dr Carmichael continued. "She's particularly interested in the connection between his sleep disturbances and the physical manifestations you've noted. The patterns you described are... unusual."

Unusual. The word landed heavily, its clinical detachment stark against the emotional storm brewing inside me. I turned onto Rowena's street, the familiar rose garden outside her house coming into view, though it offered little solace today.

"Dr Carmichael," I began hesitantly, my words slow as I tried to untangle the thoughts racing through my mind. "What if... what if there's a simpler explanation for Sammy's symptoms? Something more... mundane?"

There was a pause, a beat of silence that carried the weight of his consideration. "What kind of explanation did you have in mind?"

How could I even begin to explain? That my student—an unbalanced teenager with a chilling obsession—had been breaking into my home at night? That she'd claimed to know my child intimately, her words taunting me with the possibility that she was the source of his suffering? That I'd found her in my bathroom, her presence a grotesque intrusion into the sanctuary of my family's life?

"I just..." I faltered, the words catching in my throat as I pulled up outside Rowena's house. "I'm wondering if we're looking for complicated answers when the simple one is staring us in the face."

"Mrs. Triffett—Jenny," he said, his tone softening. "I understand your reluctance. But Sammy's symptoms aren't simple. The language he uses, the patterns in his behaviour, the physical evidence—they're complex and warrant a thorough investigation. If there's anything you haven't shared, something that might help us understand..."

The front door of Rowena's house creaked open, and Sammy stepped out, clutching his beloved stuffed dinosaur. The sight of him—the wide grin lighting up his small face, the way his curls caught the sunlight—tugged at my heart. For a moment, all the fear, the confusion, the darkness fell away, replaced by an overwhelming surge of love and protectiveness.

"Mummy!" Sammy's voice carried across the garden, pure and joyful. He broke into a run, his dinosaur trailing behind him, its battered tail dragging along the path. My chest ached as I watched him, a small figure so full of light in the midst of the storm that had engulfed us.

"I need to go," I said hurriedly into the phone, my attention fixed on Sammy as he drew closer. "Can I think about the appointment? Call you back?"

"Of course," Dr Carmichael replied. His voice held a note of concern that made my stomach twist. "But please, Jenny, don't wait too long. Whatever's happening with Sammy, he needs help. Professional help."

I ended the call just as Sammy reached the car, his hands pressing eagerly against the window. His smile radiated the unbridled joy of a child, untainted by the horrors that had encroached on our lives. I opened the door, and he launched himself into my arms, wrapping his little hands tightly around my neck.

"Hi, sweetheart," I murmured, my voice thick with emotion as I held him close. My mind raced with questions, my heart heavy with fear. How much of his suffering had been caused by Serena's sinister presence? And how much was part of something deeper, something darker—something I still couldn't fully understand?

"I missed you, Mummy," he mumbled into my neck, his small arms tightening around me in a way that was both comforting and heart-wrenching. "Did you catch all the bad dreams?"

The question, so innocent and yet so freighted with an undertone I couldn't quite place, made my throat tighten. I swallowed hard, trying to keep my voice steady. "What bad dreams, sweetheart?"

He pulled back, his eyes locking onto mine with an intensity that seemed far beyond his years. They were serious now, wide and filled with a gravity that no child should carry. "The ones that make the shadows dance," he said, his voice hushed, as though he feared the shadows might overhear. "The night-time friend says they're getting stronger."

Ice flooded my veins, chilling me to the core. "The night-time friend?" I forced myself to sound calm, my tone measured. "Can you tell me about them?"

For a moment, I thought he might. His brow furrowed, as though he were searching for the right words, but then his attention shifted. His gaze followed a single leaf tumbling past the window, its edges catching the pale winter sunlight as it swirled in the breeze. The moment was gone, leaving me clutching at the air, desperate for answers that remained out of reach.

Rowena appeared in the doorway, her expression creased with the kind of concern that only she could convey. "Jenny, love, you look exhausted. Come in for a cuppa before you go?"

I hesitated, torn between the instinct to retreat and the longing for her warmth and understanding. "I should really get Sammy home..."

"Ten minutes," she said firmly, already turning back towards the house. "You look like you could use it."

Inside, the comforting scent of fresh-baked scones and Earl Grey tea wrapped around me like an aromatic embrace. Sammy made a beeline for his toy corner in the living room, chattering happily to his beloved dinosaur as he set about arranging his little world.

"Now then," Rowena said, setting a steaming mug in front of me, her eyes soft but probing. "What's really going on? And don't tell me it's nothing—I know that look."

I stared into the tea, the swirling patterns of milk hypnotic, drawing me into their eddies. How could I possibly explain? The unspeakable horror at Luke's house, Sharon's erratic behaviour, Serena's disturbing intrusion into our lives? And the constant, gnawing fear about Nial's absence—a shadow that loomed over everything.

"I'm just worried about Sammy," I said finally, the partial truth bitter on my tongue. It was the easiest place to start, even though it barely scratched the surface. "His appointment with Dr Carmichael last week..."

"Ah," Rowena said with a nod, her expression softening. "The night terrors are getting worse, then?"

I glanced over at Sammy, ensuring he was absorbed in his play before lowering my voice. "He talks about shadows, Rowena. About stars falling and gateways opening. And now this... 'night-time friend'..."

"Children his age often have imaginary friends," Rowena offered, her tone gentle but unsure. "Especially when they're going through difficult times. With Nial missing..."

"It's more than that," I interrupted, the words tumbling out before I could stop them. My voice dropped further, barely above a whisper. "The bruises, the strange patterns he makes with his toys, the way he speaks sometimes—like he's not himself anymore."

Rowena reached across the table, her hand warm and steady on mine. "Have you considered that maybe he's acting out because of Nial's disappearance? Children process trauma differently than adults."

I wanted to laugh at the simplicity of her suggestion, even as I yearned for it to be true. If only she knew about Serena's nocturnal visits, about the horrifying creature we'd seen at Luke's house, about the web of secrets tightening around us all like a noose.

"The specialist Dr Carmichael wants us to see," I said instead, deflecting slightly, "she's flying in next week. But I'm not sure... I don't know if..."

"Jenny," Rowena said, her voice gentle but firm, "if there's a chance this doctor can help Sammy, you have to take it. Whatever's causing these changes in him, he needs help."

I nodded, but the words I didn't say hung heavy in the air. If the full truth about Serena and everything else came out, my life would be destroyed. Even though I was the victim, even though I'd done nothing wrong, the fallout would be catastrophic.

"Mummy, look!" Sammy's voice shattered my thoughts. He had arranged his toys in a circle, the dinosaur standing proudly in the centre. The pattern was unmistakable—the same one I'd found in his room countless times before.

"That's lovely, darling," I managed, but the strain in my voice was evident. Was this his own creation, or had Serena taught him to make these patterns during her secret visits?

"The stars want to dance," Sammy said, his voice shifting into that unsettling, older cadence that had unnerved Dr Carmichael. "But the shadows keep getting in the way."

Rowena's gaze darted from Sammy to me, her fear plain now. She opened her mouth to speak, but no words came. Whatever was happening to Sammy—whether it was Serena's doing or something far darker—it was getting worse.

My phone buzzed in my pocket, a sharp vibration that jolted me out of my thoughts. For a fleeting moment, hope surged—Sharon? But as I glanced at the screen, my stomach sank. An unknown number. Still, I answered, the faint ember of anticipation refusing to be extinguished.

"Hello?" I said, moving away from the table to shield the conversation from Mum's curious gaze. My voice echoed faintly in the stillness of the hallway.

Silence. Not the ordinary kind, but the oppressive, intentional sort that made my pulse quicken. "Hello?" I repeated, the word sounding smaller, more fragile.

Then, faintly, I heard it. Breathing. Slow, deliberate, and measured, as if the caller wanted me to know they were there, listening, without saying a word. A chill slithered down my spine, prickling every nerve in its wake.

"Who is this?" My voice dropped to a low, sharp whisper, tinged with the rising edge of fear.

The line went dead. The abruptness of the disconnection made me flinch, my hand gripping the phone so tightly my knuckles whitened. I stared at the screen, as though willing the number to reveal something—anything—about the person on the other end.

"Wrong number?" Rowena's voice cut through my mounting unease as I returned to the table, her expression curious but tinged with concern.

"Something like that," I muttered, sliding the phone back into my pocket with forced nonchalance. But inside, the knot of dread coiled tighter, the sense of being watched swelling until it was almost suffocating.

"We should go," I said abruptly. "Sammy, sweetheart, time to head home."

"But Mummy," Sammy protested, looking up from his carefully arranged circle of toys. His eyes—so bright, so innocent—were earnest. "The pattern isn't finished yet."

"We can finish it at home," I said, injecting my voice with a cheerfulness I didn't feel. There was no way I would let him complete whatever ritualistic arrangement he was creating. "Say goodbye to Grandma."

As we left, Rowena hugged Sammy tightly, her eyes lingering on me for a moment too long. Her unspoken worry hung heavy in the air. I offered a strained smile, promising, "I'll call you later."

The drive home felt endless, the air in the car thick with my unease despite Sammy's carefree chatter from the backseat. He recounted his time with Grandma in vivid detail, his words a bright counterpoint to the storm in my mind. I couldn't shake the feeling that we weren't alone—that unseen eyes followed our every move.

At every red light, my eyes darted to the rear-view mirror, scanning the cars behind us for anything out of the ordinary. The silver flash of Sharon's car? The lurking face of Serena? Neither appeared, but the certainty of being observed refused to leave me. Every corner I turned felt like a test, every unfamiliar car a potential threat.

By the time we pulled into the driveway, my nerves were frayed to the breaking point, every sound amplified, every shadow suspicious. I glanced at Sammy through the rear-view mirror as he unbuckled his seatbelt, his innocent smile a painful reminder of what I had to protect.

As we entered the house, the comforting creak of the front door felt hollow, unable to dispel the creeping dread that clung to me like a second skin. Someone was watching. Waiting. Planning.

And I still had no idea who I could trust.

4338.216

(4 August 2018)

ARRIVALS

4338.216.1

The knock on my front door was sharp, authoritative. Three precise raps reverberated through the silent house, each one landing like a blow to my already fraught nerves. I froze, coffee cup halfway to my lips, my heart leaping into a frantic rhythm. After Serena's invasion, after the horrors of that house, every unexpected sound was a harbinger of dread.

Another series of knocks followed, harder this time, demanding attention.

My hands shook as I lowered the cup, coffee sloshing over the rim and pooling on the table. I wiped it absently with my sleeve, my focus locked on the door. The solid wooden barrier revealed nothing of who stood behind it, no hints of their intentions. Was it Sharon, finally breaking her silence? The police with news about Nial? Or... something far worse?

"Mrs. Triffett?" A man's voice cut through the tension, firm yet unfamiliar. "My name is Luke Smith. I need to speak with you about your husband."

The name sent a bolt of ice through my veins, freezing me in place. Luke Smith. The man tied to that house. The man tied to that *thing*. The air seemed to solidify around me, each breath a struggle. How had he found me?

"I saw your Facebook post," he continued, his tone steady but urgent. "About Nial and your Dalmatian, Buffy. I know where they are."

The words slammed into me, scattering my thoughts like leaves in a storm. Buffy. My dog. The connection to Nial was as undeniable as it was impossible to ignore. I edged closer to the door, my hand instinctively pressing against its cool, unyielding surface.

"How do I know you're telling the truth?" My voice was thin, fragile against the thickness of the moment.

"Check your Facebook page," he replied, his tone calm and measured. "I'm holding up my phone right now. You can open your own device and verify who I am."

My trembling fingers fumbled for my mobile. I unlocked it with a swipe and navigated to Facebook, my heart pounding louder with each second. There it was: my post. Nial's smiling face stared back at me, a bittersweet beacon of hope. Among the notifications, a new message from Luke Smith. Sent minutes ago.

The reality of it hit me like a physical blow. He was here. The man who might hold the answers to my husband's disappearance was standing on the other side of my door.

"Sammy?" The word came out involuntarily, driven by an instinctive need to protect. "Darling, are you still reading?"

Silence.

A cold dread seeped into my chest, its icy fingers squeezing my lungs. "Sammy?" My voice rose, edged with panic. I stepped away from the door, leaving it unanswered, and moved down the hallway. He'd been in his room, nestled among his picture books when I'd last checked. That had only been minutes ago.

"Sweetheart, answer Mummy!" My voice wavered, echoing hollowly in the stillness.

Nothing. No giggle, no soft rustle of pages, no eager call in return.

My pace quickened, my breath coming in shallow gasps. "Sammy!" I reached his bedroom, the door standing wide open. Afternoon sunlight spilled across the floor, illuminating a tableau of emptiness. His books were scattered on the bed, their pages crinkled as if disturbed in haste. The small space was conspicuously void of the child who should have been there.

"No, no, no..." The words spilled from my lips, an unconscious chant, as I darted across the room. I dropped to my knees, peering under the bed. Empty. The wardrobe next. I flung the doors wide, half-expecting his small form to leap out in a game of hide-and-seek. Nothing but hanging clothes swayed mockingly in response.

Behind the curtains? Empty.

"*SAMMY!*" The name tore from my throat, raw and anguished, a desperate plea that echoed through the house.

"Your son is safe, Mrs Triffett." Luke's voice carried up the hallway, cutting through my rising panic with an unnerving calm. The sound seemed to slither closer, the distance between us vanishing faster than my ability to comprehend what was happening.

I turned sharply, stepping into the doorway, and there he stood—the man I assumed to be Luke Smith. He was tall and broad-shouldered, his shaved head glinting faintly in the dim light. But it wasn't his appearance that froze me—it was the sheer impossibility of it. The front door was still closed behind him, the lock I had just checked securely in place.

"How did you..." My voice faltered as the room seemed to shrink around me.

"He's with the babysitter," Luke interrupted smoothly, as if that answered everything. His casual tone struck me like a blow, as though we were discussing something mundane.

The world tilted on its axis. "*Babysitter?*" My voice cracked, the word tumbling out in disbelief.

"A teenage girl," he elaborated, his nonchalance chilling in its detachment. "She said she was from your school. Very concerned about him, she was. Said she needed to take him somewhere safe."

Time seemed to stop as his words sank in, each one a fresh stab of cold dread. All the terror, confusion, and anger about how this strange man had entered my home evaporated, replaced by a single horrifying realisation: *Serena*. Serena had my son. The same Serena who'd crept into our lives, who had invaded our home, who had claimed Sammy as her own.

"No…" The denial tore from my throat, raw and primal, as the weight of what he was saying hit me like a freight train.

Without thinking, I grabbed Luke's shirt, my fingers twisting into the fabric with a strength I didn't know I possessed. "Where are they?" I demanded, my voice trembling with fear and fury. "What has she done with my son?"

Luke didn't flinch under my grip. If anything, he seemed almost resigned, his eyes steady on mine. "They're safe in Clivilius," he said, his tone maddeningly calm, as though the words carried any meaning whatsoever.

"Clivilius?" The word tasted foreign on my tongue, absurd against the backdrop of the spiralling nightmare. "Stop talking in riddles! *Where is my son?*"

"I can show you," he said, his voice lowering into something almost conspiratorial. "But first, you need to understand—everything you think you know about reality is about to change."

His words hit like a hammer, shattering what little composure I had left. "You're working with her, aren't you?" My voice cracked as fresh terror bloomed in my chest. "Serena sent you!"

"No," Luke said firmly, shaking his head. "I found them in the backyard." His gaze softened slightly, a flicker of something almost like understanding passing across his face. "I can take you to them, through the portal, but we have to move quickly."

I stared at him, my chest heaving with shallow, ragged breaths. Desperate hope and paralysing fear warred within me. My mind screamed for logic, for clarity, but nothing about this made sense. A *portal? Clivilius?* These were words ripped from a fever dream, yet they were spoken with conviction.

Had I finally snapped? Was this the breaking point, the culmination of everything—Nial's disappearance, Serena's obsession, the horrors we'd seen at Luke's house? Had my own mind betrayed me, constructing an elaborate fantasy to shield me from the truth?

Luke's hand hovered near mine, his expression unwavering. "Please, Jenny. I can take you to him. But you have to trust me."

Trust him? The thought twisted through my mind like barbed wire. This was the man standing in my hallway, tied irrevocably to the vortex of every nightmare that had consumed my life.

"You're not leaving this doorway until you tell me exactly what's happening to my family," I said, my voice steely, surprising even myself with its edge.

Luke's expression softened slightly, though the urgency in his eyes never wavered. "Your husband is in a different place. A place called Clivilius. Sammy and the babysitter are with him now."

The words struck like a thunderclap, absurd in their enormity. I searched his eyes for any hint of deceit, desperation sharpening my focus. But all I found was an unyielding urgency, and beneath that, something deeper—a knowledge of things that should have been impossible.

"If you're lying to me…" The threat slipped out, jagged and unfinished, but heavy with intent.

"Every second we wait puts them further beyond reach," Luke said softly, his tone almost pleading. "Will you trust me enough to save your family?"

Trust. That word again. It cut through me like a dull blade, dragging with it the bitter memories of betrayal. Trust had died the morning Nial vanished. It had been buried when Serena invaded my home, clawing her way into our lives. It had rotted in the cold, stinking darkness of that ghastly room with the creature we'd seen.

But out there, my young son was with a disturbed teenager who had declared herself his mother. Somewhere beyond that, Nial waited. Or so Luke claimed.

I grabbed my phone, my hand trembling as I unlocked the screen. "I'm calling the police," I said, my voice quivering with a mix of anger and fear. Whatever bizarre game Luke was playing, whatever fantastical claims he was making, I needed real help—help grounded in reality.

"Jenny." Luke's voice, firm and commanding, cut through the turbulence of my thoughts. It wasn't a shout, but it held the power to arrest my movement. "Look."

In his palm, Luke held a small rectangular device, sleek and unassuming, not unlike a USB stick. Before I could question him, he pressed a button on its surface.

A sudden burst of light shot from the device, a brilliant, pulsating orb that streaked across the hallway and collided with the opposite wall. My breath hitched as the light erupted, spreading like ripples on water, until the wall was no longer a wall but a swirling vortex of impossible colours. The hallway was bathed in a kaleidoscope of hues, the portal's edges pulsing rhythmically, casting fluid shadows that danced across the floor and ceiling. It radiated a hum—not a sound, but a vibration that seemed to resonate in my bones, in my very soul.

The phone slipped from my nerveless fingers, clattering to the floor as my legs threatened to give way beneath me.

"What..." My voice faltered, lost amidst the hypnotic spectacle before me. My mind screamed at me to reject it, to deny its existence. But the evidence was undeniable, shimmering in defiance of all logic.

"This is how Nial disappeared," Luke said quietly, his gaze fixed on the swirling vortex. "This is where Serena has taken Sammy. Through there"—he gestured at the portal, his voice steady yet sombre—"is Clivilius."

"This isn't real," I whispered, backing away until my shoulders collided with the wall behind me. My breathing came in short, ragged gasps as I shook my head, the words falling from my lips like a desperate mantra. "This can't be real."

Luke took a step closer, his figure silhouetted against the glowing maelstrom of the portal. "Your son is waiting," he said, his tone gentle but insistent. "Your husband too. But we must hurry."

The pull of his words was magnetic, a call to action that warred against every ounce of doubt and terror within me. Reality fractured around me, the familiar world slipping further away with each passing second. Yet, through the fog of fear, one thought cut through with crystalline clarity: Sammy was out there. Nial was out there. And somehow, impossibly, this was my only chance to find them.

As if to solidify Luke's words and my spiralling thoughts, the portal flickered, its edges wavering like heat distortion rising from sunbaked tarmac. My breath caught as I took an involuntary step forward, drawn by the hypnotic, mesmerising dance of colours that seemed to ripple and pulse in time with my hammering heart.

Jenny. The whisper wasn't a sound—it bypassed my ears entirely, blooming instead inside my mind. *Your family needs you.*

The voice was unlike anything I had ever experienced—neither male nor female, neither old nor young. It simply existed, natural and seamless as my own thoughts, yet unmistakably not my own. Another step forward.

They're waiting, Jenny. Just beyond the colours. Sammy misses his mother.

"No," I said aloud, my voice trembling as I tried to shake free from the portal's insidious pull. The word felt thin, frail against the vibrant hum of the vortex. "This isn't possible."

All things are possible in Clivilius, the voice purred, its tone gentle but commanding, urging me closer. *Come and see.*

The swirling colours deepened, shifting from dazzling brilliance to richer, darker hues, as though the portal itself was reaching out to me, coaxing, tempting. My instincts screamed at me to turn away, to run, to call the police, to do anything but take another step toward this impossible threshold. Yet the thought of Sammy—his bright eyes, his small hand gripping his stuffed dinosaur—anchored me in place. He was *through there*. And Nial...

They're waiting, the voice insisted, intimate and familiar. *Just a few steps more.*

"How do I know this isn't a trap?" I asked Luke, my voice barely audible, trembling under the weight of my fear. "How do I know Sammy's really... there?"

"You don't," Luke replied, his voice calm but firm, his gaze steady. "But ask yourself this—what choice do you have?"

His words landed like a blow, cutting through the fog of my doubt with brutal clarity. He was right. If there was even the faintest chance that Sammy and Nial were on the other side of that kaleidoscopic doorway, how could I not take it?

The portal flickered again, its edges shrinking ever so slightly, the contraction almost imperceptible yet laced with urgency.

"We need to go. *Now,*" Luke urged, his voice sharpening. The intensity in his eyes matched the quickening rhythm of the portal's pulse.

Now, Jenny, the voice echoed in my mind, a resonant, compelling whisper. *Before it's too late, and you lose your precious Sammy and Nial forever.*

I took another tentative step forward. The swirling colours seemed to respond, their shimmering tendrils reaching out like ethereal fingers, dancing just beyond my reach. The air thrummed with an energy that vibrated against my skin, sharp and electric, raising goosebumps along my arms.

"Will it..." My throat tightened, the words almost choking me. "Will it hurt?"

Luke's expression softened, just for a moment. "Like stepping through a waterfall," he said gently. "Close your eyes if you're afraid."

But I couldn't close my eyes. I couldn't look away from the vortex, its hypnotic swirl promising salvation and dread in equal measure. One more step brought me to its very edge, so close the light seemed to bleed into my skin, illuminating me in its impossible glow.

Choose, Jenny Triffett, the voice whispered, its tone lilting, urgent. *Choose now.*

The weight of that choice bore down on me, crushing, suffocating. Drawing a deep breath, I steeled myself against the tide of fear surging through me. With one final glance at Luke—his face impassive yet expectant—I stepped forward into the light.

The world dissolved instantly, swallowed by a maelstrom of pure, radiant colour. A sensation of falling gripped me, a weightless, endless descent through an infinity of swirling brilliance. Time stretched and collapsed, every second an eternity, every moment no more than a fleeting heartbeat.

Then, as suddenly as it had begun, it stopped, and the same voice echoed in my mind:

Welcome to Clivilius, Jenny Triffett.

Solidity returned beneath my feet. Warmth enveloped my skin, the air dry and tinged with an unfamiliar, earthy scent. My heart raced as I squinted against the brightness that greeted me. Above, a sky stretched impossibly wide, a shade of blue so vivid it seemed almost unreal. All around, ochre dunes rolled out like a vast, sunlit ocean, their crests rippling in the soft breeze.

I turned slowly, the surreal beauty of the scene filling me with equal parts wonder and disorientation. And then I saw him.

Not twenty paces away, his figure standing tall against the endless expanse, was Nial.

BABYSITTER

4338.216.2

"Nial." His name escaped my lips in a breathless whisper, and for a moment, the world stood still.

He looked the same—exactly the same as the day he disappeared. The same worn work clothes, the same tired but kind eyes. It was as though no time had passed at all. Relief and disbelief warred within me, their push and pull threatening to overwhelm as I stumbled towards him.

"Jenny." His voice broke the spell, cracking through my frozen state like a lightning strike. He rushed forward, his arms outstretched.

I hurled myself into his embrace, gripping him tightly, half afraid he would vanish if I let go. The feel of him—solid and warm—sent a wave of emotion crashing over me. Tears sprang to my eyes, the torrent of relief almost too much to bear. But even as I clung to him, a darker current surged beneath the surface. The initial flood of joy began to ebb, and with it, reality came roaring back.

"Where's Sammy?" I pulled back sharply, my hands clutching at his shirt, desperation sharpening my voice. "Where is he, Nial?"

He hesitated, his gaze darting over his shoulder as though searching for something—or someone. "He's safe," he said carefully, his tone maddeningly measured, as if speaking to someone fragile. "He's with the babysitter."

The babysitter. The words dropped into me like lead, spreading cold through my veins. My grip on his shirt tightened, my knuckles whitening. "The babysitter?" My voice rose, trembling on the edge of hysteria. "You mean Serena? Nial, no. She's dangerous. She's been stalking us! She broke into our house. She thinks she's his mother!"

"What are you talking about?" His expression shifted, relief giving way to alarm. "Jenny, calm down—"

"Don't tell me to calm down!" I shoved him back, my heart hammering against my ribs. The fear was molten now, spilling out in uncontrollable waves. "Where is he? Where is my son?"

He raised his hands, palms outward, a gesture of peace that only fuelled my anger. "Over there," he said, nodding towards a small cluster of people gathered a short distance away. "He's fine, Jenny. I promise."

I didn't wait for more. The words barely registered before I took off, the adrenaline coursing through me making my legs feel both weightless and leaden. My breath came in ragged gasps, the sound of my heartbeat roaring in my ears as my eyes locked onto the figure I dreaded most.

Serena stood in the midst of the group, her hand resting on Sammy's shoulder in a gesture that sent bile rising in my throat. She looked so normal—her school uniform immaculate, her hair pulled back into its usual ponytail. The very picture of a conscientious teenager. But I knew the truth. I'd seen her true face, heard her obsession dripping from her honeyed words.

"Sammy!" I screamed, the cry tearing from me with primal force, reverberating across the barren landscape.

"Mummy!" His little face lit up, pure joy transforming his features. He wriggled free from Serena's grasp and ran towards me, his arms outstretched.

I fell to my knees, catching him as he collided into me. I wrapped him in a fierce embrace, holding him so tightly I could feel the steady thrum of his heartbeat against my chest.

Tears streamed down my face, a mixture of relief and terror tangling in the moment.

"Are you okay?" I whispered, my voice breaking as I pulled back just enough to scan him for injuries. My hands ran over his arms, his face, desperate to find proof that he was unharmed. "Did she hurt you?"

He shook his head, his small brows knitting together in confusion. "No, Mummy," he said earnestly. "She's been looking after me."

Looking after him. The words churned my stomach, a sickening twist that made my legs feel weak. I looked up, and there she was, just a few steps away. Serena stood with a calmness that felt entirely out of place, her posture unthreatening, her expression serene. Her lips curved into a soft, reassuring smile—a smile that sent an icy shiver crawling down my spine.

"Mrs. Triffett," Serena said warmly, as though this were a casual meeting at the school gates. "I'm so glad you made it. Sammy's been asking for you."

"You," I hissed, pulling Sammy closer, the protective instinct roaring within me. My arms encircled him like a shield, a barrier against the horror standing before me. "You stay away from him!"

"Jenny," Nial's voice came from somewhere behind me, laced with concern, but I didn't turn. My focus was locked on Serena, on her maddeningly composed face, her unflinching gaze.

"You broke into our house," I snarled, my voice trembling with rage as I rose to my feet. I pulled Sammy behind me, my body acting as a wall between him and the danger I knew she posed. "You watched us sleep. You took my son!"

"Mrs. Triffett, please." Serena's tone was gentle, patronisingly so, her words carrying the smooth cadence of someone soothing a tantrum. "You're clearly upset. But Sammy's safe now. That's what matters."

"Safe?" The laugh that escaped me was bitter, hollow. "You're insane. Do you hear me? You're absolutely insane!"

"Jenny, stop." Nial stepped into my line of sight, his hands raised as though he could physically push the escalating tension away. His presence was a barrier I neither wanted nor needed. "You're frightening Sammy."

"She's been grooming him, Nial!" I shouted, my voice cracking under the weight of my desperation. "The bruises? The patterns? The nightmares? It was her! It's always been her. She's been manipulating him this whole time!"

Murmurs rippled through the gathered crowd, a low hum that buzzed at the edge of my awareness. The weight of their stares pressed down on me, their whispered words an unwelcome intrusion. But I didn't care. Let them watch. Let them judge. My son's safety was all that mattered.

"Jenny." Luke's voice cut through the noise with razor precision. He stepped forward, his expression calm but his eyes hard, scrutinising. "You need to listen."

"Not you too!" I turned on him, the boiling frustration spilling over. "I'm taking Sammy, and we're leaving. Now."

"You can't," Luke said simply.

The words hit me like a slap. I froze, every muscle in my body tightening. "What do you mean, I can't?"

"The portal only works one way," he said, his tone flat, his gaze unwavering. "Once you're here, there's no going back."

"You're lying," I whispered, shaking my head as the room—or the barren plain—seemed to tilt around me. "It's a lie."

"It's the truth," Luke said. His voice held no malice, only resignation. "I'm sorry, Jenny."

The weight of his words slammed into me with the force of a tidal wave. My knees buckled, and I clutched Sammy as though holding him could anchor me to a world that no longer felt real. The sky above seemed to darken, the vivid colours dimming as though reflecting the rising despair in my chest.

"We're stuck here?" My voice was barely a whisper now, rasping against the sudden dryness in my throat. "Forever?"

"Not stuck…" Serena interjected, her words maddeningly light, though a flicker of uncertainty flared in her eyes, making her tone falter ever so slightly.

I turned to Nial, desperate for clarity, for hope, for any sign that this nightmare could be undone. "You believe this?" My voice broke as the question escaped. "You're okay with this?"

His face was pained, a flicker of guilt clouding his features. But when he spoke, his voice was steady, final. "It's not about being okay," he said quietly. "It's about accepting reality. And right now, our reality is here."

"No," I whispered, my voice trembling as my knees threatened to buckle again.

As the weight of Nial's words bore down on me, Serena stepped closer. Her smile faltered, just for a moment, and when she spoke, her voice carried an uncharacteristic wobble. "Mrs. Triffett," she began softly, "I don't really understand what's happening either. But Sammy is safe, and we need to keep him that way."

Her hand moved toward Sammy, brushing gently against his hair with a practised familiarity that made my stomach churn. Sammy didn't flinch, didn't pull away. Instead, he leaned into her touch, his small body relaxing as if it were the most natural thing in the world. The sight twisted the knife in my chest, the pain sharp and immediate.

"Stay away from him!" I shouted, the words tearing from my throat with raw, desperate force. My voice cracked under the strain, but I didn't care. "You don't get to touch him! You don't get to act like you're his mother!"

Serena's eyes widened, and for the first time, she looked genuinely rattled. "I'm not trying to—" she began, her voice trembling. But before she could finish, the sound of footsteps interrupted her.

"Enough." The voice was firm, commanding, and cut through the tension like a blade. A woman stepped forward from the crowd, her presence immediately commanding attention. Her brown, slightly greying hair was pulled back into a severe bun, and her sharp eyes flicked between me, Nial, and Serena with practised precision. She radiated authority, her calm steadiness a stark contrast to the danger swirling around me.

"Everyone needs to take a breath," she said, her tone measured but unyielding. "We're all newcomers here, and panic won't help anyone."

"Greta," Nial said, his voice tinged with relief. "Thank God you're here."

Greta nodded briefly in acknowledgment, but her attention remained fixed on Luke, her brow furrowing in clear disapproval. "You should have explained things better, Luke," she said sharply. "Dropping people into this situation without preparation—" She stopped herself, shaking her head with a sigh. Then, turning to me, her expression softened. "You're Jenny, yes?"

I nodded, struggling to find my voice past the lump in my throat.

"And this is your son, Sammy?" she asked, her tone calm, almost gentle.

"Yes," I croaked, clutching Sammy as though my grip could keep him from slipping away again.

Greta stepped closer, her movements deliberate, careful, like someone trying to calm a frightened animal. "Jenny, I know this is overwhelming," she said. "But you're safe here. Sammy's safe. Whatever happened before—whatever brought you here—doesn't matter right now. What matters is finding a way forward."

"Safe?" The word came out as a bitter laugh. "How can you say that when she—" I gestured wildly at Serena, my voice rising again—"has been stalking us for months, breaking into our house, manipulating my son!"

Serena flinched, the calm mask she'd been wearing cracking under the force of my accusation. "I wasn't— I didn't mean to hurt anyone," she stammered, her voice small and faltering. She turned to Greta, her eyes wide with something that almost looked like genuine confusion. "I thought I was helping. I thought I was just Sammy's babysitter."

Greta's sharp gaze pinned Serena in place, her expression unreadable. "It seems you've caused quite the misunderstanding, young lady," she said, her tone cool but edged with a quiet authority. "But this isn't the time to unpack that. Right now, we need to focus on ensuring Sammy's wellbeing—and yours, Jenny."

I shook my head, the enormity of the situation pressing down on me like a crushing weight. "We don't belong here," I whispered, my voice cracking under the strain. "We need to go back. We need to—"

"You can't go back," Greta said, her voice firm, cutting through my rising hysteria. "I'm sorry, Jenny, but the portal doesn't work that way. None of us can return to where we came from."

The finality of her words struck like a hammer blow. My knees buckled, and Nial caught me before I could collapse. "This isn't real," I whispered, my voice trembling. "This can't be real."

"It's real," Greta said, her voice steady and unyielding. "And I know it's hard to accept, but you're not alone in this. We'll help you adjust."

Adjust. The word echoed in my mind, hollow and meaningless, as if it had no place in the world I'd known. How could I ever adjust to this? To being trapped in this strange, desolate place with no escape? To being stuck here with Serena, her presence a constant shadow over my family's fragile existence?

"Mummy," Sammy's small voice broke through the storm of my thoughts. "I'm hungry."

The simplicity of his request was jarring, cutting through the suffocating weight of fear that had settled over me. For a moment, the normality of it seemed absurd, like a child asking for a bedtime story in the middle of a battlefield.

Greta smiled softly, her voice soothing. "Let's get you all some food," she suggested. "A warm meal can do wonders."

I looked down at Sammy, his wide, trusting eyes fixed on me. Then my gaze flicked to Nial, his face lined with a weariness that mirrored my own. Finally, I looked at Serena. She stood a little apart, her expression subdued, almost uncertain. The fiery determination to fight drained out of me, replaced by a bone-deep exhaustion. For now, I would follow. For Sammy's sake.

As we began the trek toward the settlement, Sammy's small hand slipped into mine, his fingers warm and solid, a comforting anchor against the creeping chill of dread in my chest. Nial walked just ahead, his shoulders hunched slightly as the loose sand shifted under his boots. Beside him, Luke moved with quiet purpose, his confidence unsettling in a way I couldn't quite articulate.

Greta stayed by my side, her steady presence a faint reassurance, though her occasional sidelong glances revealed her concern. She didn't say much, her focus seemingly on ensuring I kept moving, but her silence spoke volumes. She was watching me, assessing, weighing.

Trailing slightly behind us was Serena. Her expression was unreadable, her calm composure unnerving. Her eyes followed Sammy's every movement, her focus so intense it made my skin crawl. Every so often, I glanced back, catching her gaze just long enough for her to avert her eyes. Her silence was worse than any words she could have spoken, a void that gnawed at my already fraying nerves.

"How much farther?" I asked Greta, my voice sharper than I intended. I needed something tangible, something concrete in this surreal nightmare.

"Not far," Greta replied evenly. "Just over that rise. You'll see the settlement."

Serena's voice broke the tense quiet, soft but startling in its suddenness. "A settlement," she murmured, as though testing the word. It wasn't a question but a thought spoken aloud, her tone more curious than anything else.

The flatness of her words sent a chill skittering down my spine. She didn't sound triumphant, as I might have expected. Instead, there was something... detached about her tone, as though she were trying to make sense of it all herself.

"You don't even know what this place is, do you?" I demanded, stopping abruptly and spinning to face her.

Serena met my gaze, her lips curving into a small, infuriatingly calm smile. "Do you?"

Her question hit harder than it should have, not because of its audacity but because she was right. I didn't know. None of this made any sense. And yet, seeing her standing there, so composed, so maddeningly normal, made my blood boil.

"Why did you bring him here?" I hissed, my voice low but seething with venom. "What was your plan? To play happy families? To steal him away completely?"

Serena tilted her head slightly, her brow furrowing as though considering my words. "I didn't bring him here, Mrs.

Triffett," she said evenly, her tone free of malice or mockery. "Luke did."

At the mention of his name, Luke glanced back briefly but didn't break stride. His pace remained as steady and deliberate as ever, his silence speaking volumes.

"That's not—" I started, but Greta's calm voice cut across mine.

"Jenny, let's keep moving," she urged, her tone gentle but firm. "We can talk when we get to the settlement."

Serena fell silent again, her attention drifting back to Sammy. He, blissfully unaware of the undercurrents between us, hummed softly to himself, swinging my hand as we walked. The sound was so innocent, so pure, that it struck something deep within me. A raw ache, a primal need to shield him from everything—especially her.

I glanced at Serena, my gaze narrowing as she moved ahead. Her steps were calm, measured, each one deliberate. As she passed Sammy, her hand brushed his shoulder, light and fleeting, like a whisper against the air. The casualness of the gesture—the sheer audacity of it—made my skin crawl.

"Welcome home," she murmured, her voice pitched just for me. She didn't turn or pause, her words hanging in the air like a spectre. "We're going to be so happy here... Forever."

I froze, the sound of her voice reverberating in my skull. There was no mistaking the satisfaction in her tone, no denying the quiet triumph it carried. The chill that crept down my spine was colder than any winter's wind.

Ahead of us, the sparse settlement loomed, its simple structures standing silent and unassuming under the afternoon sun. It should have looked peaceful, inviting even, like a new beginning. But all I could see was a cage—a place where Serena's shadow would stretch over every moment, where her obsession would linger like a sickness we couldn't escape.

My feet refused to move. For a moment, the world seemed to narrow, the settlement's boundaries closing in, its quietness suffused with a sinister stillness. I could feel the weight of her presence pressing against me, suffocating, inescapable.

"Jenny." Greta's voice broke through the fog. She stepped closer, her hand resting lightly on my shoulder. The touch was steadying, an anchor against the storm raging in my mind. "I know it's not much right now, but you're safe here," she said gently, her tone firm enough to demand belief. "You're not alone."

Her words, meant to comfort, fell like stones into the churning waters of my thoughts. Because the truth was, I *was* alone. No one else seemed to see Serena for what she truly was. No one else felt the suffocating weight of her presence, the quiet menace lurking beneath her calm exterior.

And in this strange new world, with its unfamiliar sky and endless dunes, I had no idea how to protect my son from her.

No idea how to escape her.

TO BE CONTINUED...

Printed and bound by CPI Group (UK) Ltd, Croydon, CR0 4YY
17/01/2025
01822102-0003